Tormented

Out of the Box, Book 5

Robert J. Crane

Tormented
Out of the Box #5
Robert J. Crane
Copyright © 2015 Midian Press
All Rights Reserved.

1st Edition

To Mamaw—I'll miss you.

Prologue

It wasn't the six-hour flight delay, or even the nine hours on the plane that did it; it was standing in the U.S. Customs line for over an hour and dealing with the accompanying bullshit that made Benjamin Cunningham finally explode.

Benjamin was tired; his neck hurt. He'd been in the airport in Amsterdam for the better part of a day before the flight. He habitually showed up three hours early for any international flight, and since he'd flown into Amsterdam late the night before, he'd wanted to be absolutely certain he didn't miss the plane home to Minneapolis. So he'd woken up early, after three hours of sleep, thrown on a suit that had been neatly folded in the bottom of his luggage since the first day of his two-week trip, and gotten in a cab, eyelids fluttering and desperate for sleep.

When he'd gotten the notice that his flight had been canceled, he'd stifled the panic. Benjamin didn't travel much, so it was a first for him. But this happened to travelers, right? Right. Still, it had been a gut punch, and he couldn't control the helpless feeling that washed over him while he stood in the airport line for re-booking. His palms sweated, but he waited quietly for his turn without a word of complaint.

After over nine hours of waiting listlessly in the Amsterdam airport, he'd gotten on the flight to Minneapolis, tired and exhausted. He was situated in the middle seat on the right side of the plane, grateful just to be there. The people on either side took the armrests. Benjamin wasn't particularly tall, wasn't wide, and certainly wasn't a confrontational man, so he crossed his arms in front of him and prepared to endure a ten-hour flight situated in exactly that way. It would be all right, though. He'd be home before he knew it.

The plane hadn't even pushed back from the gate when he heard the first yelping bark of a dog behind him. He sniffed reflexively, already regretful, but it was too late. His eyes started burning from the pet dander minutes later, and by the time he'd been in the air for an hour he was crying involuntarily, tears rolling down his cheeks from the allergens. He sneezed six times in thirty seconds and had trouble opening his eyes again afterward. His nasal passages itched and ran.

The man sitting on the aisle had an enormous laptop out, tapping away like he was Beethoven and the keyboard was his own musical outlet. It looked like an older model, and the cord was plugged into the charger built into the seat, with a pair of noise-canceling headphones plugged into the side. Benjamin only needed one look to know that it would disturb the man immensely to have to unplug the headphones, unplug the laptop, fold it up, put up his tray table—he could envision the scornful look, the anger, the rolling of eyes, the snort of derision.

Benjamin wiped his nose on his sleeve eight times a minute for the first four hours of the flight until the person by the window asked to get out. She got the snort of derision, the scornful look, and the man with the laptop gave him just the same when he got out at the same time. It was like a stab right to Benjamin's heart, but by this point his sleeve was saturated and his voice was like a low croak.

When he got back to his seat, the man on the aisle took no time at all in setting back up again. Fortunately Benjamin had taken extra tissues from the plane's toilet and packed them into the breast pocket of his jacket, enough to last him

2

the entire rest of the flight. He settled back, closed his eyes, rolled up a tissue for each nostril and prepared to try to sleep his way through what was shaping up to be abject misery.

Then the yelping began in earnest.

They were small noises at first, the sounds of a dog unhappy with its confinement. They were coming from beneath his seat. Benjamin felt his emotions shift through the realm of pity first. How could the owner confine the dog in such a way, after all? It was stuck below his seat in something like a backpack or a purse, confined in the tiny space beneath him. He turned and tried to look through the seat, finally catching sight of a teenage girl with a sleep mask on, head tilted blissfully to the side. He turned back, fidgeting. She was sleeping through every bark.

The barking got more insistent and urgent as the flight wore on. Benjamin didn't even try to close his eyes; they were streaming far too much for that in any event. His sleeves were soaked from his tears, he was sneezing madly in regular bursts every ten minutes, prompting ugly looks from the man with the laptop, who could hear him even through the noise-canceling headphones. "I have pet allergies," he croaked in apology through his scratchy throat. The man with the laptop gave him a scorching expression, shook his head, and went back to typing.

Benjamin sat there in stiff-necked misery, listening to the miserable barks and yelps, wiping his eyes and nose and checking his watch every five minutes for the remaining hours until the flight finally, mercifully landed. His eyes were so red and swollen he could barely even see.

The rush to get off the plane was madness, but he tried to be patient. When he stepped out into the aisle to retrieve his carry-on from the overhead bin, the woman who had been in the window seat next to him the entire time pushed in front of him and yanked her bag out of the bin before he could even bring his down. Her bag hit him on squarely the head, and Benjamin saw a flash of light. Excruciating pain ran like hard wires dragged over his scalp, and he staggered back, stung, his already watering eyes springing to life with new tears. His head was burning, the allergens causing some sort of feverish reaction.

"Come on!" someone said and shoved him roughly from behind. When he opened his eyes, the woman was gone, her back receding down the aisle in front of him. "We're waiting, here!" said the same harsh voice. He turned around to see the girl with the dog in her purse, glaring at him. To add insult to injury, the dog yelped at him, making him jump nervously.

Benjamin retrieved his bag and hoisted the strap across his shoulder, hurrying to get out of the way. He could hear the mutters and curses of people behind him, raw, angry words hitting him right in the heart with every shot. He hurried, trying not to hold anyone else up as he got onto the jetway and headed into customs.

He turned on his phone as he passed the customs sign. It synced with the local network, and the time changed before his eyes, sending a bolt of fear right to his stomach.

12:59 p.m. He was supposed to have been at work five hours earlier.

"No phones or electronics allowed in the customs area, sir," an older, grey-haired woman in an official-looking vest said to him. She had the face of a librarian telling him to be silent.

"I just need to—" he started.

"No phones," the woman said again, more sternly. Benjamin wilted and pushed his phone into his pocket meekly. It could wait. He was already ridiculously late anyway, and there was nothing for it. He took a deep breath, eyes still watering, throat still scratching, and looked at the countless helpful notices posted in the area that warned him about importing fruits as he waited.

And waited.

And waited some more.

He threaded through a slow-moving line designated for

U.S. citizens. He lost count of how many snake-loops he went through, keeping between the rope lines that were strung to herd the passengers, before he finally reached another customs person who was barking orders. He'd heard her earlier but couldn't quite tell until he was on the last turn what she was doing. There was an open area ahead between the threaded black belt-lines that cordoned off each segment of the line. This one fed into a series of stations like the electronic check-in kiosks they expected people to use when getting their tickets. Benjamin always avoided them because he could never quite seem to get them to work properly.

Here he had no choice. The employee at the head of the line was another matronly woman barking orders. "You, go there, you, there," she pointed each time. She wore a dulled look, as though she'd been doing this for entirely too long. His eyes were still watering, though they were better. The dog in the purse was a good ten people behind him in the line, and the distance had helped his allergies.

"You, right there," the lady called, gesturing to a kiosk, and Benjamin stepped up. He did as he was told and went to the appropriate kiosk, following the on-screen instructions as prompted. It had a scanner that asked for his passport, and he fumbled with it for five minutes before getting it to scan properly.

"You, there," the line lady called, and he noticed the kiosk to his left was vacant. He had a momentary flash of panic, knowing he was not nearly done, and then he felt a strong thump to his shoulder as someone struck him while passing.

"God, do you have to take up the whole aisle?" The voice was sharp and bereft of even a drop of kindness. Benjamin turned and looked, eyes watering again, but he already knew what he'd see. It was the girl with the dog bag hanging off her arm. She couldn't have been more than fifteen and had an expression on her face stereotypical of a surly teen. He blinked at the bag before realizing it was empty. He felt something rubbing his pant leg. He looked down and sure enough, there was the little pooch. "Come on," the girl said and yanked the animal away on its leash so hard, he blanched in pain on the dog's behalf. It moved about six inches with a yelp as she slid into place at her kiosk, standing bored while an older man—her father, Benjamin presumed—scanned his passport and hers in about ten seconds.

Benjamin turned back and saw that the kiosk was prompting him to look into a camera mounted up top. It took him almost a minute to discern this through his watery eyes. His sleeve had almost been dry, too, before she'd brought the dog back into his proximity …

He looked into the camera as best he could, then back down at the screen, which prompted him to look at the camera. He blinked, and more watery tears rushed down his face. He sneezed, then again, and again, and then seven more times in a row.

As he opened his eyes again, he felt a tug and heard a growl. Teeth sunk into his shin and he yelped. The little dog had gotten a bite of him, and he pulled away from it as quickly as he could.

Laughter fell on his ears, and Benjamin felt the rush of hot shame on his cheeks. The girl was laughing at him as she tried to pull the dog back, half-heartedly. He could barely see her, doubled over with laughter, leash trailing out of her hand. He couldn't even hear her at this point, but she gradually retreated from his sight, pulling the dog with her. Someone else appeared at the kiosk a moment later, a man in a suit, and Benjamin blinked back tears that were no longer just from the allergies, and tried to focus on the camera again.

"Excuse me, sir?" The voice was harsh, loud, impatient. He turned to look at yet another woman in an official navy vest. He couldn't read her name badge, couldn't see it through his watering eyes. "Do you need assistance?" She stood inches away from him, looking him right in the eyes.

He wanted to look away in shame, but couldn't.

"I can't ... I can't read it, and it won't take my picture," Benjamin said, wiping futilely at his eyes again.

"You have to hold still and look right at it." She pointed at a dark circle. "At the camera, right there."

"All right." Benjamin held still as long as he could, tears dripping off his face, and then he brought up the back of his hand and wiped his eyes.

"You can't move like that," the woman said, clearly annoyed. "You have to hold still and look at the camera."

"I'm sorry," Benjamin said, genuinely contrite, "my allergies—"

"Look at the camera and hold it—hold it—*HOLD IT!*" she yelled at him, and he quailed, eyes dripping hot liquid down his cheeks. He wanted to fold double, to jab his fingers in his sockets and scratch at the itching, offending bits, but he held there, the sound of her disapproval hot in his ears. His eyes burned, his skin burned, his embarrassment shot through him coupled with the first strains of something else, something hotter. "Got it. Finally," she sneered.

"I'm sorry," he said, and meant every word of it.

She handed him a piece of paper that the kiosk had spit out and pointed toward another line. Benjamin grabbed his suitcase and walked toward it, weaving and weary, eyes dripping, nose doing the same, his head fuzzy beyond belief, feet dragging. He headed toward the place the woman had pointed him and saw people forming the line, leaving a large gap between two groups of them, two families. He thought it a little strange but rubbed at his eyes, grateful for some distance from the dog, hoping for a miracle, hoping that he would be able to stop crying.

The line moved like no one running it had any care. In ten minutes Benjamin moved five feet. He couldn't see more than blurry shapes, couldn't smell much of anything through his still-running nose. The man in front of him moved again, walking wide around the small patch of space the families in front of him had left open, and Benjamin thought nothing of it, he just followed the man so as not to jam up the line. Just because the people in front of him were being rude by leaving all that space didn't mean he had to, after all.

He heard the squish, but it didn't register to him what he'd stepped in until he heard the laughter and caught the faintest whiff of—

Of
the dog
the damned dog

"You stepped in dog poo," the woman two in front of him said, more than a little amused. He couldn't see her face, it was a blur through the tears, but he recognized the voice. He'd heard her speak on the plane when asking the flight attendant for a vegetarian meal. It was the woman next to him, the one who'd bombed his head with a suitcase and not even apologized.

"Hahahahaha!" he heard from ahead. The girl, the one with the dog. Laughing that he'd soiled his shoes. Laughing—

that
HER dog
had soiled his
HIS
shoes

"Ugh, that's disgusting." The man directly in front of him turned back. His features were all washed out, like someone had smeared Vaseline over Benjamin's eyes. "Heh." He chuckled—

and Benjamin
saw
the color red
vivid as an apple
dark like
blood

and it covered his vision.

The laughter swirled around his head. They were laughing at him—

at ME

all of them

at ME

and he'd been so nice

SO DAMNED NICE

and taken their bullshit

why?

"Why?" It came out whispered, low, out of his scratchy and hurting throat.

"You asked for it, man," the guy in front of him said. "You stepped right in it—"

asked for

it?

for IT?

for meanness

rudeness

unkindness

allergies

tears

pain

delays

an utter lack of care and concern and acknowledgment for his own

HIS OWN HIS OWN

humanity?

"I … didn't …" he gasped out. He felt so hot. So-

Hot

Feverish

Benjamin let out a hard, scratching breath that stroked his vocal chords like pins dragged roughly across sensitive skin. He smelled smoke. Smelled—

Fire

orange like a sunrise

smoke

black like a thundercloud at midnight

and then

Benjamin Cunningham did something he'd never done before.

He exploded into a fireball that burned through the belt-lines that hemmed him in—

shattered the windows that held him back

vaporized the people—AND YOUR LITTLE DOG, TOO, DAMMIT—around him

—and laid the U.S Customs area in the Minneapolis/St. Paul airport to utter waste.

His hands smoking, fingers still burning with fire, Benjamin Cunningham walked numbly and nakedly toward the nearest sign that said EMERGENCY EXIT, past the baggage claim in the customs area. He picked up his suitcase as he passed, causally, as though he hadn't just crossed the burning wreckage of the customs checkpoint naked. Fire alarms screamed in his ears, smoke as black as coal filled the air.

But his eyes were dry.

His throat was clear.

And he left a trail of scorched, black ground behind him as he walked, suitcase rolling behind him, feeling strangely free, to collect his car from the parking garage.

1.

Sienna

I could smell autumn in the air as the wind off Lake Superior hit me full in the face. I was riding at the front of a ferryboat, embracing the September weather and staring out over the sparkling waters. The sound of the boat's engines rumbled quietly in the background, and I could see the paradise of Bayscape Island ahead, waiting for me, a peaceful respite in the middle of a world of roaring chaos.

Peace? Me? Haha, right?

But it was peace I was seeking, on an island off the shores of the Northwoods of Wisconsin. I took a breath of fresh air that was not in reality much different from the air I breathed every day on the campus of my agency, southwest of Minneapolis. But it felt a world different, like it had been imported from somewhere across the planet just for me, chilled in a freezer and puffed whole into my lungs.

"Hell of a view, huh?" There was a guy next to me at the railing. I glanced over at him; he was a bigger guy, probably in his fifties, greying all around the temples but only salt and pepper up top.

"It's not bad," I conceded. Call me paranoid, but I'm immediately suspicious of anyone who talks to me these days. Sign of the times.

"You can't beat it for peaceful," he said, staring into the

11

bright blue skies above. He was dressed in jeans and a polo-style shirt. Reminded me a little of my brother like that. "Nice place to get away from the rat race."

"Mmm," I said, noncommittal. Why did people insist on approaching me? Wasn't it blazingly obvious by now what a bad idea that was?

"You're her, aren't you?" he asked, finally turning his head to look at me.

"If you think I'm Taylor Swift, then the answer is no."

He laughed. "No, I don't think you're Taylor Swift."

"Good, because my singing voice? Not so impressive," I said. "Also, I haven't yet mined my personal romantic tragedies for lyrical gold." Though there was certainly some fertile ground to work with in that area.

The guy laughed again, a lilting, genuine laugh that drifted over me. "That's a good one. No, I meant you're Sienna Nealon."

I blinked, the wind off the water blowing straight into my eyes. "I'm Sienna Nealon," I agreed.

"Everybody's got to get away some time, huh? Even you famous types."

I didn't look at him. "We 'famous' people are mostly like the rest of you. Also, I might have gone with 'notorious' in my case."

"Mostly, huh?" he asked, with a trace of humor. "Put your pants on one leg at a time and all that?"

"Well, no," I said. "I sort of lift off the ground into the air and drift down into my pants like a falling leaf. But other than that, I'm just like you normals. Except I can explode into flames on command. And heal wounds in seconds flat. And—"

He chuckled again. "Is snark one of your powers? Because it's ... strong with you."

"That's one of my more human attributes," I said and glanced at him. "One of the few, I'm told."

"It's a good one," he said, nodding. "My kids are like that, always got a good, dry remark about whatever we're doing. It's a nice trait to have on hand. Keeps things from getting too serious."

"Glad someone thinks so," I said.

"I'm Jake," he said, drifting toward me and offering a hand. "Jake Terrance."

I took his hand gently, for just a moment, giving it a quick pump before letting it loose. He didn't push the connection. "Nice to meet you, Jake. Your family with you today?"

"Kids are all grown up now, but my wife's already on Bayscape," he said, gesturing to the swelling, tree-covered island in the distance. It was getting closer all the time. "Her name's Sarah. We liked it up here so much she took a job as the local nurse. I just did a quick run to the mainland for supplies."

"You live here year-round?"

"All the time now," he said, nodding his head. His features were sharp, his smile warm. "It's paradise. Like heaven on earth."

"Really?" I asked. "I heard in the winters the temperature gets down to—"

He gave me a coy smile. "It's very cold, yes."

I shook my head. "I can barely tolerate Minneapolis. Can't imagine what you deal with."

He shrugged, still smiling. "Ferry shuts down when the ice gets out on the lake, and there's only a few hundred permanent residents, so … it's basically like being a shut-in for the winter. Kind of nice for a social outcast like my wife. I'd be lying if I said the solitude didn't get to me every now and again."

I cast my eyes forward again, staring at the island ahead. I had two weeks to spend here, two glorious weeks of no work, no stress, nothing to do to fill my time but that which I brought in my bag—which was a tablet filled with movies and an e-reader filled with books. "Solitude might be nice. Is it crowded right now?"

He nodded toward the trees in the distance. "Autumn's creeping in earlier than expected this year, so the leaves are turning quicker than people thought they would. Place is pretty desolate now, but it'll get busy this weekend. Even busier next weekend, even though the leaves will be mostly fallen by then." He cocked his head at me, a little curious. "There are quieter places you could see the leaves. Hell, wait a few weeks and you'll see them down in Minneapolis. Why come up here now?"

I opened my mouth to draw breath and answer, but found I couldn't find a way to easily explain it. "I … just needed to get away for a while."

"Mmhmm," he said, nodding like he knew. "You've got one of those jobs that demands all, I suppose."

"Something like that." I pulled my arms close around me as the chill of the wind felt somehow more powerful, more penetrating. My job certainly wasn't demanding much of me at the moment. Quite the opposite, in fact.

He slapped the rail with one hand and stood upright; I could tell he was looking for a polite exit. "I suspect you'll find what you're looking for here."

"I could use some solitude," I said, looking off into the distance again.

"Well, there are the places on the island you could go where you won't run into another human being—if that's what you want. But during the summer we've got all the bars and restaurants and small-town charm you could hope for if you change your mind. Nice to meet you, Sienna," he said and started to pull away. "I hope you have a peaceful stay."

"Thank you," I said, struggling to remember his name, "Jake." He wandered off toward the back of the ferry, where the cars were parked. I watched him go out of the corner of my eye, and as soon as I was alone, I turned back to the front to stare out at the glistening lake. "I hope so, too."

2.

Reed

The Minneapolis-St. Paul airport had a burned smell that hung in the air like a particularly heinous oven accident, the kind that always seemed to follow my sister's cooking attempts.

I'm sorry. That was crass. Tasteless. Way too soon.

There was still smoke billowing out of the terminal when we got there, what seemed like a hundred fire engines parked out front. Flight operations had been shut down, and the FBI had taken forever to call us for some reason. Like handling crazy meta stuff wasn't our specialty.

My fancy shoes were tight on my toes as we made our way toward the international flights area from the baggage claim, our guide hustling along in front of us under a cloud of annoyance. I don't know why he was annoyed; I always thought Agent Li's beef was with my sister, not with me, but since he'd greeted me and my partner pretty gruffly at the terminal loop, I had started to assume that he was just this kind of person. I guess I hadn't really thought about it before when we worked together.

"Man, the tension in here is almost as thick as the smoke," Augustus Coleman said from beside me. He looked a little uncomfortable dressed up in a suit. I was damned sure uncomfortable in mine, but going to a scene like this, we had to project a certain standard. I had my hair back in a ponytail and everything. It sucked. "What is up with you two? Failed romance?"

"With him?" I pointed at Li. "Dear God, no, he's not my type. I always thought he hated Sienna for killing his college roommate, but now I'm starting to think he's just got a bug up his ass."

Agent Li stopped and wheeled slowly around to face us. He looked cold as ice, like someone had chiseled him right out of a block of the stuff and set him out for display as a sculpture to be judged on lifelike realism. I gave him a five out of ten. Not human looking enough. "I'm trying to get to the business at hand. Did you want to stop in the middle of this terrorist attack and have a conversation about how much we must have missed each other since we last worked together? Should we pause for a beer?" He pointed at the Summit Brewery down the terminal, tables knocked over during the evacuation still lying on the ground. "Reminisce about the old times when we were trying to survive a war against overwhelming odds?"

"Hey, man," I said, "I'm totally down with your standoffish and straight-to-business nature. My partner, though, he's new to government service. He hasn't seen the inter-agency pissing matches yet."

Li just gave me another cold look. "I'm not in a pissing contest with you. This case is all yours. It's very clearly in your jurisdiction, and I wish you luck with it and all your justice-bringing endeavors."

"Dude," I said, turning to Augustus for comic effect, "did you know we're supposed to be engaging in 'justice-bringing endeavors'? That feels like a memo I missed."

"Man, I'm missing a class for this," Augustus said, suddenly impatient. "And it's been a few years since I last took an American government course, so I feel like missing lectures could cost me when it comes to my grades. Can we get on with it?"

"You're in a freshman survey course," I said. "It's five hundred people in a crowded auditorium. Find the cutest studious-looking girl in the room, put on the charm, and ask if you can see her notes. It's a great opportunity. Also, try and remember that we work for the executive branch. Should make things easier on the first test."

"I already got a girlfriend," Augustus said, clouds darkening above his eyes. "Can we move on now? Feel like I'm in an episode of *Law and Order: Special Metas Unit*." He tried to adjust his suit; he still looked uncomfortable.

I looked at Li and shrugged. "It's not good to see you again, Li. Let's catch up never. Lead on."

Li just shook his head and went back to walking down the terminal. Augustus and I followed in our own silence.

As we drew closer to the place where the incident occurred, the smell got thicker, heavier. It invaded my nose and filled my mouth with a charred taste. I held an arm up over my nose and watched Augustus do the same. Li didn't, but metas have a far more developed sense of smell than humans do.

"This way," Li said, leading us right into a hallway into the customs area. There were luggage carousels side-by-side, more suitcases than I could count practically falling off them. Ahead, past a checkpoint, the air turned even smokier. There were glass offices placed just this side of the checkpoints, clearly designed to allow for surveillance of the luggage carousels and the customs lines through windows.

The windows were shattered. Glass glittered on the floor all around the far end of the conveyors, and Li led us gingerly through to the office on the left. I could see a scorched crater beyond, in the place where the customs line had been. I paused as Li brushed into the office through a shattered glass door and stared into the space beyond. I'd been through here more times than I could count on the way to various destinations. It was never a pleasant return trip. The lines were always absurdly long and they were always undermanned. They'd recently modernized by adding some sort of computer check-in system, but they hadn't taken out any of the other customs-check steps, so the result was even longer lines, an apparent exercise in stupidity.

"What are you thinking?" Augustus asked me quietly.

"Of all the gin joints in all the towns in all the world," I said, "she had to walk into mine."

Augustus looked at me warily. "Quoting *Casablanca* in this context makes no sense, unless this exploding person was an old girlfriend of yours." He straightened up and bristled. "Also, if you tell me to 'Play it, Sam,' we're going to have words."

"I did have an ex who was somewhat explosive," I said. "But I was talking more in terms of ... why this airport? Of all the ones in all the world? Or even the U.S.? Is that just a wild coincidence? Minneapolis isn't exactly the best target— or the biggest."

"You think this dude's trying to get our attention?" Augustus asked.

"Not ours," I said. "We're nobodies."

"Pffft," Augustus said. "Speak for yourself. I'm somebody."

"We're not as well-known as another person who works with us, that's my point."

"Or as hated," Li called from inside the office. I glanced over to see him staring at me, unimpressed. "You gonna just sit out there all day and have a conversation? Because I can wait right here, I guess. I don't have anything else going on in my life or job that's of any import, really."

"Cool," I said. "Because we might be a few minutes." I then made a point of ignoring him.

"You think this dude blew up the Minneapolis customs line because he wanted to get your sister's attention?" Augustus asked, giving me what I liked to call his *You must be shitting me* look. "There's got to be an easier way."

"Than killing a whole bunch of people?" I asked.

"Doubtful. That's practically the only way to get her attention. Be better at her shtick than her."

He blanched. "That's cold."

"But it's true," I said, shrugging my way into the booth with Li. "Truth hurts."

"Hey, lies hurt, too," Augustus said. "And if you don't believe me, go call some biker's momma a whore and see what happens."

"We have footage of the incident," Li said, ignoring our discussion. I could tell he was annoyed. Augustus could tell he was annoyed. Anyone in earshot could tell he was annoyed. They could probably feel his annoyance down in the bathroom stalls in the airport mall. "At least up until the security cameras were destroyed." Li stood next to a monitor. The picture on the screen was frozen, but at the touch of a button it moved forward. "Suspect enters the frame here," he pointed to a shorter guy wearing a suit. I couldn't see much in the way of detail on his face, but he was at the very, very back of a long line when he entered the frame. "We have some footage of him deplaning, too, and he's staggering around like he's drunk."

"Flew first class?" I asked.

Li shook his head. "Coach all the way from Amsterdam. He only ended up on this flight at the last minute; his earlier scheduled one was canceled and he was rebooked. We've got people on the ground in Amsterdam gathering information on his stay right now, but it's the middle of the night there. It's slowing things down."

Credit to Li; he was a pro. Annoying and armed with a personality that I wouldn't choose over hugging a cactus whilst naked, but a pro all the way. "What's his name?" I asked.

"Benjamin Cunningham," Li said, picking up his clipboard. "Age 27. Lives in Roseville, Minnesota, which is presumably why this is the gin joint he chose to explode in." Li stiffened. "Though ... based on the footage, I'm not sure he *chose* it."

I stared at Benjamin Cunningham as he made his way through the line. Li had the recording on fast forward, and the comically quick motion of people milling about in an extremely slow line was the only hint that it was moving at abnormal speed. Because that line? It was molasses on the shores of Lake Superior in January: not going anywhere fast.

When Cunningham reached the electronic kiosks, we finally got somewhere. He started to rub his eyes heavily, like he couldn't see. An employee came over to help him, and they looked like they were squabbling. "What's that all about?" I asked.

"I can only give you the bad lip-read version," Augustus said.

"Microphones?" I asked Li. He shook his head.

Cunningham finally rejoined the line, looking like he was staggering side to side. If he wasn't drunk, he had something else terribly wrong with him.

"Hey, did that dog take a dump in the line?" Augustus asked, pointing to a gap in the people ahead of Cunningham.

"Unconscionable," Li said, shaking his head. He looked genuinely offended.

The three of us watched as Benjamin Cunningham staggered right into the dog pile, realized what he'd done, exchanged words with the people around him, now almost doubled over and pawing at his eyes.

Then he burst into flames. They covered his skin, draping him in orange fire from head to toe. There was a flash, and less than a second later, the screen went straight to fuzz.

"Looks like a Gavrikov," I said.

"That man had a bad day," Augustus said.

I looked at him with pure WTF-ery. "*He* had a bad day? How about all those people he scorched into nonexistence?"

"He didn't even look like he could see straight," Augustus said. "Unless you think he stepped on that dog poo intentionally?"

"No one steps in dog poop intentionally," Li said.

"Coprophiliacs," I muttered.

Li froze. "Well, then he wouldn't have been angry enough about it to explode, would he?"

"You assume it was linked to anger," I said. "It might not have been."

Li looked like he was about to pull a Cunningham and blow up on me. "You know damned well that Gavrikov-types typically manifest when presented with strong, uncontrollable emotion."

I blinked. "I ... actually did not know that. How did you?"

Li let out a sigh of exasperation. "Because I did the damned required reading back when I had *your* job."

"Now there's required reading?" Augustus asked. "I got enough coursework to deal with as it is. Did you know they try and weed you out in freshman and sophomore years just so they can keep the graduation ratio down? They don't give you a tuition refund, though, do they? I'm starting to smell a scam."

"You mean you picked over FBI files that you didn't bother to give the rest of us access to?" I asked Li.

"You had access," Li said evenly. "You just never went looking."

"Well," I said, bowing my head, "I defer to your experience as the number one person on the scene in the area of Gavrikov-types. You think this guy is one, and he triggered due to anger?"

"I do," Li said. "And also, I think I shouldn't be the damned expert on-site when it comes to Gavrikov-type metas, not when you've got someone on your staff who actually has the original Gavrikov in her head." He looked straight through me. "Where is she?"

"Unavailable," I said, suddenly a little uncomfortable.

Li smiled snottily. "Unavailable. Of course. She would take a vacation right now."

"Vacation?" Augustus asked. "Is that the polite, government way to say it? Because I heard 'suspension.'"

Li's smiled vanished. "She's suspended? What did she do now?" His eyes dulled. "Oh. That."

"Yeah, that," I said. "But honestly, does it matter?" I stared at the static-laden screen as my stomach dropped. "She's not here. She can't be here. Not for two weeks, so ..." I smiled, swallowing back all those fears I had about being in over my head and channeled it into a spiteful swipe instead. "Buck up, Buttercup. The pros are on the case."

3.

Cassidy

Cassidy Ellis watched the exploding footage on a loop, over and over again. She'd hacked the Minneapolis airport security system in about thirty seconds—yawn—and was already through the FBI firewall via a backdoor she'd installed months ago. She had three displays going at the moment in her sensory deprivation tank, and more thoughts in her head than could be controlled at any given time.

Benjamin Cunningham, age 27, of Roseville, Minnesota. No signs of being a meta at any prior point in his history. Did that mean he hadn't manifested yet? Or had he just kept it under wraps? It was possible, though unlikely given the reams of anecdotal evidence Cassidy had read on meta manifestation.

Or it could have been Edward Cavanagh's breakthrough, the one that unleashed meta powers. Cassidy hadn't been able to get her hands on the formula, though she'd tried. The Atlanta P.D. had locked down Cavanagh's testing site pretty quickly after the incident, boxing up the computers and shipping them off to a black site she hadn't been able to track them to. That was unusual, but not totally unexpected. She'd read the internet's version of tea leaves and knew that someone pretty powerful had played around with that data, deleting it off at the source. It took a lot to completely destroy a digital trail, and if Cassidy couldn't dig it out—

The rapping at the side of her tank threw her out of her blur of thoughts. That was Cassidy's gift—and her curse; she could think faster than anyone else. Her meta gift was cognition. The problem with it, of course, was that it overwhelmed, overloaded her in some cases, and she couldn't fully use it unless she eliminated the distractions of her other senses. Lying here in the warm salt water of the tank, listening to no sound but her own breathing, allowed her to get her thoughts out uninterrupted.

The thumping against the side came again, and she recognized who among her companions was knocking just by the tempo. Quick, impatient, repetitive, almost unhinged. Just like the person doing it.

Anselmo Serafini.

Cassidy turned her face to the side and burbled into the water, let her lips make a sputtering sound and the salty liquid get a few drops between them before blowing them out. It was a rich, echoing noise in the privacy of the tank, interrupted by another fevered thumping from Anselmo. Patience was not the man's strong suit.

Then again, very few things were.

Cassidy gingerly moved the specially-made waterproof screens and keyboards out of their positions and let the darkness envelope her. She took another breath, a slow one, steeling herself, and then fished her stiff, rubberized dressing gown out of the water where she always left it while floating in the tank, slipping into it with practiced ease. She fumbled with grasping fingers for her inhaler and took a hit. It was almost unheard of, as near as she could tell, for a meta to have asthma. Still, she had it, though she was fortunate in that it didn't affect her life much.

Cassidy closed her eyes and unlocked the tank. There was a keypad on the outside with a combination code that Eric could use to unlock it if need be, but Eric was gone at the moment, out of town. He left a lot lately, trying to spend as little time in Omaha as possible while they were bunkered here at the Clary house. He'd seemed willing to stay at first, and he certainly hadn't lost faith in her plans, but just dealing with the people they were living with on a daily basis was a challenge of its own sort, one that made Cassidy thankful that she could spend almost all her time locked away in here.

She didn't even get to push open the top herself; Anselmo seized it and pulled the tank open, bathing her in bright light from outside. She kept the screens in the tank at low levels, and the blinding light of the world outside streaming in was enough to force her to close her eyes.

"Get out here," Anselmo said, his voice as scratchy as ever. She'd heard the interrogation tapes of him before Sienna Nealon had burned his skin beyond its ability to heal; he sounded much different now.

"Give me a minute," Cassidy said, opening her eyes slowly to squint. The light was so bright.

"I said now, girl."

"Anselmo," a voice from behind him said, "be a gentleman and give her a moment, would you, please?"

Cassidy didn't need to open her eyes to recognize the speaker. The voice was thick and husky, the voice of woman who'd lived a hell of a life. It had taken some searching to find her, but she'd been quite the find once Cassidy had located her. Her name was Claudette Clary, but everyone just called her "Ma."

Ma's words landed on Anselmo like a perfectly aimed sedation dart. Before, Anselmo's heart had been hammering so loud that Cassidy could hear it. Ma's gently phrased request hit the Italian in just the right place, his ego, softening him up. Anselmo thought of himself as a gentleman first, a manly sort of man who, while always in charge, had manners. It didn't quite match up with Cassidy's vision of him, but she knew it was how he defined himself. Ma Clary wasn't exactly book smart, but she could read a person like Cassidy could read binary.

25

"But of course," Anselmo said with a magnanimous nod, taking a few steps back from the tank. Cassidy slowly sat up, leaning against the metal backing, letting the water slosh as she did so. The tank needed to be drained anyway, so she started the automated sequence for cleaning and refilling it. She'd need someone else to add salt later, which was a task of its own. She had a design to automate it for the most part, but she lacked the fabrication facilities here to carry it beyond the design phase.

For now, though, she had other things to worry about. "What seems to be the problem, Anselmo?" She looked over at him, finally, her eyes open enough to admit light—and a full image of the scarred man in front of her.

Anselmo Serafini had been handsome once, a bronzed sculpture of a human being impeccably dressed in every photo Cassidy had ever seen of him, his dark, wavy hair sculpted with gel. Now he had no hair, and his once-smooth complexion was nothing but scar lines, a hideous cross-hatching of swirls and redness, unnatural bumps dotting the surface. "Have you seen what is happening on television?" Anselmo asked, voice low and raspy.

Cassidy did a little rasp of her own inadvertently, a small gulp as she waited for the inhaler to work. "You talking about the airport thing? I've seen it. Why?"

Anselmo's eyes were dark, devious. Cassidy didn't like the man, didn't like anything about him. She'd read about what he'd done, the original complaints in Italy that had been all but ignored by the local police. She'd idly followed the trail of bribery, seen how much work Anselmo had done to buy himself out of trouble. He was probably the single biggest piece of pond scum she'd ever personally met, and every day that Eric was gone, she rued the fact that he'd brought Anselmo here on a whim. She was supposed to do the planning for them, and Anselmo ...

Well, the man was just too unreliable to make plans around.

"This … man … this Benjamin Cunningham … could be of aid to us," Anselmo said, raising his hands to gesture with. Her eyes followed his exposed forearm with a fascination bordering on horror. Nasty red swirls grew redder as he talked, as he moved. "Imagine someone capable of destroying—"

"We don't need him," Cassidy said, cutting him off. She'd been pursuing the information on Cunningham as more of an intellectual exercise, something fun to do while she waited for other plans to bear fruit, other wheels in motion to finish their spin.

"You are telling me that you cannot find something creative and fun to do with an exploding man?" Anselmo asked, cold menace in his voice. He didn't like to be interrupted, but it especially seemed to annoy him when a woman did it. Needless to say, Cassidy did it as often as she could.

"What'd you have in mind?" Ma Clary asked, reminding the Italian that she was there. Cassidy could see in the surprised way that he turned his head that he'd already forgotten about her. He forgot about any woman that didn't catch his eye, which suited Cassidy just fine. She ran a hand down her gown, wiping the excess water off her thin arms and into the draining tank.

"If I could get to him before they do," Anselmo said, now speaking to both of them, "I could persuade him to join us. They will hunt him, attempt to put him into confinement, or simply kill him for being too dangerous—"

"He's not just a danger to them—" Cassidy started.

"That seems like a good idea you've got there, Anselmo," Ma said, talking right over her. Ma's broad face was staring right at Anselmo, deep in thought. "Could always use a few more hands around here, after all."

"Exactly," Anselmo said, pointing a finger at her and smiling, his burned and cracked lips peeling back to expose perfect teeth and blackened gums. Cassidy suppressed a

ROBERT J. CRANE

shudder. "I realize that part of our revenge is already well in motion, but ... we are not all done yet, no? Reed Treston still requires dealing with. He will be in the thick of this ... manhunt." Anselmo's face went darker. His facial expressions had been blunted by the burns. He was scowling, that much was obvious, but anything more subtle was beyond him.

"Well, you ought to get out there and start tracking this fire-man down, then," Ma said, nodding her head slowly.

Anselmo raised what was once his eyebrow up slightly. "Me?"

"With Denise, Eric and Junior off on their own tasks right now," Ma said, "that just leaves you, me and Cassidy." She nodded at Cassidy, caught her eye, and Cassidy saw something there that prompted her to keep quiet about her feelings on this. "We can't send her; she can't leave her tank."

"Ah, yes," Anselmo said, nodding sagely, "she possesses a great weakness. Perhaps the time has come for the bird to leave the nest—"

"Anselmo," Ma said, chiding, "you wouldn't send a sickly girl to do a man's job, would you?" Cassidy blinked. Anselmo was a prideful sort of prick, but surely he wasn't *that*—

"Of course not," Anselmo said, shaking his head furiously. "And this is a man's job. This burning fellow must be talked to, man-to-man, so an understanding can be reached." Cassidy kept her lips zipped, even though practically every word that fell out of Anselmo's mouth offended her in some way. "I will leave immediately."

"You can take the car out in the shed," Ma said, nodding toward the back of the house. "It ain't got air conditioning, but you won't need that this time of year." She turned her head to Cassidy. "You mind getting him some directions to Minnesota?"

Cassidy stared at her for a quarter second, which was practically an eternity for her, pondering all the while. "Sure—"

"I do not require directions," Anselmo said, like some beautiful example pulled right out of a book of common stereotypes. "I can find my way."

Ma was a hell of a tough read some times, but there was no mistaking the amusement buried under a layer of apparent sincerity. "Of course you can. Spare keys are on the ring by the door. Burner cell phone on the counter, so you can keep in touch." She nodded toward the front of the house. "You need anything else? Cash for the road?"

"I have money," Anselmo said, and he started to back up toward the kitchen. Cassidy felt like she was watching the retreat of a wounded animal and couldn't take her eyes off of him. "I will go and find this man, this Benjamin Cunningham, and bring him into our fold. But first, I will take my revenge on Reed Treston." Anselmo took a breath, loud, satisfying, and smiled his hideous smile. "If there are no objections?"

"We have a plan—" Cassidy started.

"Oh, you go right ahead, darlin'," Ma said. She had a dish towel in her hand that was still damp. Cassidy could sense the wetness of it from across the room, could smell the scent of mildew within it, overwhelming her delicate senses. "He wronged you more than the rest of us, anyway. We'll get our revenge on the girl here in the next few days, you go ahead and take care of the brother, and then maybe we'll meet up in the middle on taking care of that gall-damned agency of theirs."

"Yes," Anselmo said, "there are good days ahead." He nodded, like what he was saying made any kind of sense at all. "I will be back before you know it," he said, "a victorious *man*," and then disappeared through into the kitchen. Cassidy heard him take the cell phone from the counter and the keys from the ring near the front door, and then listened to the screen door slam shut as he left. She sat in silence with Ma Clary, both listening until they heard a car start out back, roughly, on the third try. It ran for a couple minutes and then drove off, receding into the distance. Cassidy waited a minute more before she felt comfortable speaking.

"Are you out of your mind?" Cassidy asked, focusing wholly on Ma Clary. "You just sent that idiot—that maniac—out there on a mission to recover the exploding man?" She shut her eyes tight, shaking her head. "How does that—in any way—get us closer to our goals?"

"I don't really care whether this Reed Treston lives or dies," Ma said casually, sauntering over to her. "We've got the missile locked on target with Sienna, and that's all that matters to me; that she dies suffering and screaming."

Cassidy flushed. "But what about what *I* want? Don't get me wrong, I'm going to derive some serious satisfaction out of Sienna Nealon's painful death, especially after what she did to Eric—" Sometimes Cassidy watched the YouTube video of that bitch manhandling her man, "—but there are other things in mind here. All we need is meathead wandering around out there, screwing things up for the rest of us—"

Ma Clary took the last few slow, measured steps over to Cassidy's tank and dabbed at it with her damp towel. Cassidy blanched at the smell as she ran it along the wet, spotted edge of the tank opening. "Darlin', let me tell you something about Anselmo Serafini that you already know … he's a dog." She pursed her lips and dabbed at the tank again.

Cassidy waited for more, but Ma seemed to lose herself in mopping up the water on the edge of the tank. "… And?"

Ma took a long, lazy breath and let it out without a care in the world. "When my boy Clyde first had his babies, I had a dog. Old thing, contentious little bastard. Just a mutt with a bad attitude. But I liked him all right, see, so I kept him around. He'd drive off the damned stray cats, and that was useful, so he earned his keep.

"But one day," Ma said brightly, looking at Cassidy again, "that old dog took a snap at little Denise. She couldn't have been more than four at the time, and the dog just …" She clapped her hands together, dragging the rag along and spattering Cassidy with some of the moldy, stinky water. "Just took a snap at her. Didn't even get a tooth on her, but that was enough, you see?

"I dragged that dog out back," Ma said, eyes far off, like she was remembering it all right now. Her lip curled at the side. "Right out to the wood pile. I grabbed that axe up from where Clyde had been splitting wood, and I—"

She clapped her hands together again, and this time water from the rag hit Cassidy right in the face. It was foul, the stench of it, and she fought the urge to gag. "Wha ... why?"

"Because don't nobody mess with my family," Ma said, her brown eyes alive, mouth flat as if she'd just told a story about a loaf of bread she'd once baked. "Anselmo? He's a dog. Nothing but. Sooner or later, like any dog that's got it in his mind to do something, he's gonna snap at someone he shouldn't. I've already seen him eyeing you and Denise, and I don't care for it." Ma shrugged expansively. "If he drags back this fire-man, well, good for him. It'll get him out of the house for a spell, maybe allow him to express some of that tension he keeps throwing our way."

Ma put a hand on Cassidy's shoulder, strong, knotted, leathery fingers squeezing her bare skin. It was sensory overload, too much sensation by half. "And if he get hisself killed? Well ..." She clapped her hands together again, but this time the rag had already lost most of its liquid. "I ain't going to shed any tears about it. Are you?" And Ma Clary smiled, a deeply unsettling look that showed off her teeth, which looked to Cassidy a hell of a lot sharper and more predatory than any dog she could imagine.

4.

Sienna

I cut my hand on a piece of exposed metal on the ferry's railing, and it hurt. I didn't even see it coming, just a rough section of the rail that I was running my hand along idly as I made my way back to my rental car. It did a number on my palm, too, opening a six-inch gash that started bleeding immediately, made all the worse by my failure to pull my hand away in time. Dumb, dumb, dumb.

As far as pain went, it was minor, but I started dripping right away. Bright scarlet drops came running down my forearm in a stream, falling off my elbow in crimson raindrops. "Son of a …" I muttered.

"Whoa," Jake Terrance's voice came from behind me. I looked back to see him there, eyebrows elevated, staring at my injury. "You gonna heal that?"

I paused, staring at him, and chewed my lower lip. "I … uhm … kinda … can't … at the moment."

Jake maintained that eye-raised look. "… Can't? Admittedly I don't know much about you or your, uh, powers … but don't they work on command?"

I felt a pained expression spring onto my face that I couldn't quite control. "Most of the time, yes. But … I'm on vacation, and my powers are tied to some … uhm … metahumans that I … uh—"

"Absorbed, right?" Jake asked. He ran a hand through his grey hair, and I caught a whiff of concern that seemed genuine. "During the war? You took in some villains?"

"Mostly villains, yeah," I said, clenching my wounded hand tight to try and stop the blood drip. "Anyway, they, uhm …" I rolled my eyes. "They've kind of been arguing the last couple weeks. So I decided to shut them up for a little while … uh, chemically." I flushed.

"You drugged … yourself?" He looked amused and perplexed all at once. He was amuseplexed. Permused. Something. "Drugged them?"

"Sort of," I said. "I used to use this chemical called chloridamide to suppress them temporarily, and I take a shot every now and again if I need to quiet them." I glanced at my rental car. "I took a big dose before I drove up." I swept a hand over myself. "Hence the driving, not flying." Flying was generally more soothing, but it wasn't ideal for carrying a suitcase. Besides, the drive had been kind of leisurely and scenic and peaceful and stuff. Which I … needed. Or something. I'm still trying to convince myself.

"So … you're not going to heal lickety-split?" He nodded at my hand.

"Without Wolfe it'll take a few hours," I said, trying to figure out where I could mop up the blood. I'd usually just wipe it on my clothes because … well, when you've ruined as many wardrobes as I have, you don't get attached to your outerwear.

"Come on," he said, after a moment of chewing it over, "my wife's clinic is on the main street. I'll take you to Sarah and she'll get you patched up."

I stole a look at my rental car. The horn on the ferry blew once, loudly, as we approached the dock, the sense of movement through the water slowing. I was tempted to blow him off, say I'd just deal with it myself, grab some paper towels from the local store and just be on about the business of locking myself away so I could start my solitude, but …

There was something really warm and inviting about his manner, about the way he asked, about his ... genuine concern ... that took me off guard. I don't get genuine concern that much anymore. In fact, I was on a starvation diet of it lately—that, and the milk of human kindness, and what I got mostly came from Ariadne or Augustus Coleman, whenever he was actually around. Guy went home a lot. Which I couldn't blame him for, because I'd go home a lot, too—if I had one with family in it instead of an empty house in south Minneapolis.

"Okay," I said, nodding. "Let me get my car."

"Smart thinking," Jake said with a smile. "I'm parked right in front of you, so just follow me off?" The horn sounded above us again.

"Sure thing," I said and headed for my rental car. It was a silver sedan, sporty but not as cool as my brother's new car. I usually went everywhere in government sedans since I didn't own my own vehicle, but for this trip, I'd planned ahead. I got inside, shifted in my seat, and closed the door behind me. I looked around, fumbling in the arm rest before finding a packet of tissues that someone had left behind. Hallelujah. I wrapped one around my wounded hand, then another, clenching them tight against my palm.

It took a few minutes for the ferry to dock, but they passed quickly. It felt like I closed my eyes for a second, and the next thing I knew the rumble of car engines filled my ears. Jake's car flashed its brake lights. He had a big SUV, the kind that was probably required for navigating the snow banks of Bayscape Island during the winter. Daylight flared ahead of us as the ramp came down, and Jake was the first to drive off the boat. I followed behind him, and my eyes gradually adjusted, painting the scene before me in lush color as I reached the bottom of the ramp.

It was a small town straight out of a Norman Rockwell calendar. Or maybe *Jaws*. Lake Superior's waters lapped at the docks to my right, and an enormous American flag flew over a town hall at the end of the quaint main street. The street was lined with both trees and stores, the trees already turning beautiful shades of deep red and burnished gold, while the stores were trafficked with a few customers wandering here and there, dodging windswept leaves that had already started to fall. I smelled hot apple cider and realized there was a drink stand just by the end of the dock, steam piping out in little white puffs. I didn't even know apple cider needed to be heated or wafted or whatever they were doing, but it was a marvelous marketing strategy because I instantly wanted a cup.

Jake's SUV lurched forward as it came off the ramp onto the road, and he eased forward, waiting for me to catch up. I wasn't the most practiced driver and my reflexes tended to be dangerously fast, so I took my time cresting the small separation between the ferry ramp and the road. The car groaned a little as I rolled onto shore, and then I gunned the engine to cut the distance between Jake's car and mine to ten feet or so. I followed him at a crawl for all of a block and a half before he whipped into a parking space right there on the main street.

I took like ten minutes trying to parallel park my car before giving up and taking my next right. There were pull-in spaces there, which were a little more suited to my talents. I know when I'm beat, okay?

The sun was still shining when I met Jake on the sidewalk outside the building. The sign said "Clinic." It was a two-story red brick building that blended perfectly with the quaint main street. There was a bar next door, a grocery store a little down the way, and a host of other touristy places in between. I took another breath of that fresh air and felt a world away from where I'd started my day.

"Right through here," Jake said, leading me into the clinic. I stepped through the glass door that he held open for me, listened to the ring of a bell above my head, and saw a dark-haired woman in a white lab coat step out from a door

35

in the back.

"Hey, honey," Jake said. The woman was a little taller than me with hair that fell below her shoulders. At the sight of me, her expression went ... pinched. "Brought you another stray."

"Really?" she asked and didn't sound amused. She walked toward the front desk with measured steps and spun a clipboard around to face me. "You look unmistakably familiar."

"Need me to sign in?" I gestured to the clipboard with my bleeding hand, and flipped my palm up so she could see the red-stained tissues.

Her frown deepened. "Maybe later. Can you—"

"Not today," I said, shaking my head. "Don't have my powers at the moment."

"Uh," she said, looking up at me, "I was going to ask you if you could follow me. Doesn't really require much in the way of power, just using your legs for locomotion. Basic stuff."

"Oh," I said, a little embarrassed. "Yes, I can do that."

"Good," she said without a trace of levity. "Follow me."

"See you later, babe," Jake called, seemingly anchored to his spot by the door. "Nice to meet you, Sienna."

I glanced back at him. "You too, Jake. Thanks for ... well ... everything."

He smiled, again. "See you around. Unless you're too busy hiding out." With a wave he headed back through the door, and I turned to see his wife waiting for me, arms folded. Her whole manner said she was no-nonsense. I didn't have to work hard to guess who was the party person in their relationship.

I stepped into a treatment room, and Sarah closed the door behind me. She stepped around me nimbly, opening a blue-grey cupboard that looked like it had been there since the nineties, at least in its current form and color. She pulled out a plastic tray and nodded toward the exam bed behind me. "Have a seat."

"Thanks, nurse, uh ... Terrance?"

"It's Nelson, actually," Sarah said, still buried in the cupboard.

"Oh, uh, sorry," I said. "My bad. You know what they say about assuming."

"No," she said, coming out of the cupboard with bandages and sewing ... stuff. "What do they say about it?"

I tried to find a way to spin the old saying uniquely. "That you shouldn't," I said, giving up. It's my vacation, I'm allowed to give up if I want to.

"Sound advice," she said, putting one of those sets of magnifying glasses on her head and spinning her stool up so she could sit level with me. She put her tray on a rolling table and raised the top of it so her implements were in easy reach. "How long is it going to take you to heal from this cut?"

"It'll be gone by tomorrow," I said. "Bleeding should stop in a couple more minutes."

She glanced at her tray of supplies. "I'm just going to bandage it, then. No need to waste your time and mine with sutures."

"Good call," I agreed. I wasn't that keen on feeling a needle moving its way in and out of my skin anyway. She picked up a bottle of alcohol and started soaking a piece of gauze with it. "Get much business here?"

"Lots in the summer, yes," Sarah said, looking down at her work and not up at me. "Not much in the winter, though."

"Cool," I said. An uncomfortable silence settled over us. It persisted for five minutes.

Finally, Sarah looked up at me. "You don't mind sitting in utter silence?"

"Nope," I said, shrugging without moving the hand she was working on—with two sets of rubber gloves, I realized a bit belatedly.

"Hm," she said, "most people complain. Or try to make

small talk."

"Complain?" I asked. "About what? That you don't make small talk while you're focused on stitching up their boo-boos?"

"Bedside manner is the most common complaint," she said, focusing on what she was doing again, which, now, was applying some medical tape.

"You're a beautiful summer's day compared to my last doctor," I said. "You know how people tell horror stories about losing their doctor to an insurance change? In my case, it would be a 'happily ever after,' even if my new one was named Kevorkian."

"The co-pay on that next visit would be killer," Sarah said dryly.

"But you wouldn't feel a thing afterward," I said, continuing our little riff.

She didn't laugh, but I saw one corner of her mouth curl in amusement. "Not bad." She looked up, shifting the magnifying lenses up so she could look at me. "You're all set. I taped the bandages in such a way that you'll be able to just tear them right across the center here," she ran a finger across my covered palm, "tomorrow, when you're done healing."

I lifted my hand and flexed it experimentally. "Thanks, uh—" I caught myself before calling her 'Doc,' which is what I habitually said to Dr. Perugini, my present torturer—I mean, practitioner.

"You're welcome," Sarah said, and she said it slyly enough that I could tell she was thinking something snide. It's exactly how I sounded when I was holding back something snarky. "And just so you know, Jake is going to be waiting outside for you."

"Huh, what?"

"He's waiting outside," she said. "Right now. Guarantee it. It's not a stalker thing, he just wants to help you." She surveyed me with appraising eyes. "Where are you staying?"

"Cabin," I said. "Out of town a little ways."

"Better than the main street hotel," Sarah said, starting to clean up the mess of bloodstained gauze on the tray. "At least, if you're the type of person who likes to have a moment of peace."

"Just what I'm looking for," I said. "Moments of peace, as many as I can gather unto me." I almost sounded sincere.

Her eyes settled on me. "You really think you'll find it?" There was a piercing quality in her look, a soul-deep gaze that made it feel like a challenge, a harsh, discordant quality to her voice that was the equivalent of pushing me back a step.

"Excuse me?" I asked, trying not to leap to any conclusions.

"I said I think you'll find it out there," she said, inclining her head toward the wall, a vague indication of the direction the woods lay, I guess.

"I don't think that's what you ..." I let my voice trail off. Maybe she just misspoke. What was the point of pursuing it? She had her head tilted at me quizzically, no hint of guile. People misspeak all the time. Like that time I meant to call my boss, Andrew Phillips, a knucklehead but slipped up and called him an ignorant jagoff prick instead. "Guess I should let you get back to ... whatever you were doing before I got here."

"Just shutting down for the day," Sarah said with a forced smile.

"It's like ... noon," I said.

She shrugged. "If no one shows up before eleven, it's going to be a slow day. Island is quiet, so if you can refrain from cutting yourself, I'll probably be ready to leave at two. All the residents have my number, and we don't have much in the way of tourists at the moment."

"Thanks for your help," I said, not offering her my hand.

She smiled tightly and nodded her head. "Don't forget, Jake's waiting in ambush. Don't show weakness."

I cocked an eyebrow at her. "What happens if I show weakness?"

"He'll tour you around the whole island, regaling you with history you probably don't give a damn about," she said, dropping the bloody gauze in the waste basket. I watched it fall, the crimson catching my eye. "It'll get in the way of your hunt for inner peace. Take care." She made a motion toward the door. "I'd hate to see you have to come back here on your vacation." She said it in an ambiguous enough way that she could have meant she didn't want to see me because she didn't like me or because she didn't want to see me injured. I wondered if the people around me spent as much time decoding my sarcasm as I was spending on hers and decided that no, I was much more straightforward when people annoyed me. Wasn't I?

I walked out of the exam room and passed through the lobby, exiting onto the sidewalk to find the sky covered in clouds. It wasn't dim grey or anything; more like bright white, the sun making its presence known with a healthy glow from behind one patch. Still, it wasn't exactly blue skies.

"Hey," Jake said, right on command. He was standing to the side, against the wall, arms folded. "Sarah take care of you?"

"Yes," I said, taking a couple steps toward him. "Though I can't decide if she was happier to see me or to be rid of me."

Jake shrugged. "That's Sarah. She's … prickly."

"But warms up once you get to know her?"

He grinned. "Not really, no. But I love her anyway." He came off the wall. "Need a tour of the town?"

I regarded him with amusement. "How long will it take?"

"About two seconds," he said, and with one sweeping gesture encompassed the main street. "Here's the town … and this concludes our tour."

"Wow," I said, "that was really thorough."

"Sadly, it was," he said. "There's not much to it. If you want, though, I can give you my contact information so that in case you have any questions, or need help with anything, or just want to get together to have a drink or dinner with

Sarah and myself, you can. Wouldn't want you to feel completely isolated while you're here—unless that's what you want." He held up his hands and smiled. "No pressure. Whatever you want."

"Uh, sure," I said, not really sure how to turn him down. I pulled out my phone and unlocked it. "What's your number?"

He sidled over beside me and blinked when he saw my contact list. "You, uh … only have like five people in there. And one of them is your carrier's customer service number."

I jerked my phone away, like I could make him unsee what he'd just commented on. "It's new," I said, covering quickly. And so it was … two years ago.

"Right," he said and gently took the phone out of my hands. I watched him nimbly program in his contact info. He was done in a fraction of the time it would have taken me. "Like I said, up to you. If you enjoy the peace and quiet and I don't ever hear from you, I will not take any offense to it. But if you get lonely, call me up, and Sarah and I can have dinner with you. You know, if you want to hear another human voice."

"Thanks for the offer," I said. "I'll let you know."

"Then this is where I leave you," he said, bowing slightly. His smile just seemed so … genuine. "I hope you have a wonderful day, Sienna."

"I hope so, too," I said as he walked away. I turned and started to head for my car, but a peal of thunder far above stopped me. I looked up; the sky had grown a deeper grey, the cloud covering the sun suddenly dark. I felt a droplet splash on my forehead, then another. Little taps from cold fingers as the sky started to drizzle.

"Well, damn," I said as the cool autumn rain started to fall. For a brief moment, I stood there, hoping this wasn't a sign of things to come before I spied the restaurant next door and broke into a run, figuring I'd weather the adverse weather while I fed myself.

5.

Reed

I listened to the phone ringing through the car's speakers as I drove up interstate 35E in St. Paul. The low roar of my Dodge Challenger's engine was sweet music to my ears. A hell of a lot sweeter than the phone ringing, anyway.

"This is Phillips," came the answer at the other end of the phone as the ringing ceased with a click.

"Hey, boss," I said, glancing over at Augustus in the passenger seat. He was nodding his head along with music I couldn't hear, staring out the window. The speed limit here was an extremely lame 45, the only place in the entire federal interstate system where it was that low. There was a story behind it, but it was extremely predictable and dealt with local residents who didn't want an interstate in their back yard. "Got a report for you."

"I read the preliminary from the FBI," Phillips said. He was a relatively straight-to-business guy. "What else do you have?"

"Just the basics on the suspect, Benjamin Cunningham—"

"Already got it," Phillips said. "What's your next step?"

"Visiting the suspect's home," I said, moving quickly ahead to adapt to our conversation. Sienna had serious problems getting along with Phillips; I found him pretty easy to understand, easy to deal with, too. He wasn't unreasonable, he just had a mission to get accomplished and a limited tolerance for anything that got in the way. I suspected the reason he and Sienna were always at loggerheads is that they were way, way too similar to work together without bumping skulls. "Word is he lives with his mother. We're halfway to Roseville now."

"Good," Phillips said. "Keep me apprised of any changes. The FBI issued a BOLO to local law enforcement. Cunningham took his own car out of the garage at the airport."

"That could be dangerous," I said. "A local cop pulling over this guy? Don't you think that'll end in fire?"

"They're not supposed to pull him over," Phillips said. "They're instructed to contact us if they run across him, to keep their eyes open."

"Any chance you've got Rocha doing his 'all cameras' bit on this?" I asked.

"Rocha's at Fort Meade for the week," Phillips said matter-of-factly. "I've put in a request with the NSA, haven't heard back yet. Harper has a bird in the air. If the cops catch Cunningham's car, we'll have eyes on it in minutes. Harper's also got an eye on heat blooms, so if he decides to blow up again, we'll see it."

"Slick," I said. It was good thinking, really. "I'll let you know if we get anything from the mother."

"Keep your eyes open," Phillips said, "it's possible, though unlikely, that this Cunningham will head home at some point."

"I've got some of our new agents at his work and on the way to stake out the house," I said with a little pride. Phillips wasn't the only one that could anticipate and plan ahead. "We're going to start digging into this guy; figure out who he is and what he wants."

"Let me know what you find," Phillips said. And then he hung up. Like I said, he's a straightforward guy.

"Man," Augustus said, "y'all had a real mutual masturbation

circle going on there for a minute. Thought I was going to have to step out of the car and give you some privacy."

"Let me tell you something that you probably haven't picked up from hanging out with Sienna," I said, a little tightly, "you get no points in this world by being a dick to your boss." Sienna had proven that, once again, this very week.

"Hey," Augustus said, shaking his head, "that's not exactly something I didn't already know. I made supervisor in my factory because I knew the value of being the kind of employee the boss wants on his team. But this is different. You got something else going on here, like you're running to him as much as you're running away from her."

"If you'd been standing next to her for more than a couple months," I said, smirking, "you'd want to put some distance between you, too. It's not a healthy place to be for very long."

"This *job* ain't healthy," Augustus said. "Seems to me cozying up to the strongest meta in the world, knowing she's got your back, might be a smarter thing to do than kiss up to some dude in an office that's more worried about what's going on up the chain than down it."

"You've got it all wrong," I said, shaking my head. "You're seeing Phillips through her eyes, and she's never been able to look at him with a clear head because she's still burning that he 'took her job.' There are rules for a reason, and Phillips understands that."

"I know you two don't exactly see eye to eye," Augustus said, "but—"

"Hard to see eye-to-eye with someone who's being willfully blind," I said, cutting him off. "Who just goes out there and does whatever she feels like on any given mission instead of trying to do the job the way it was meant to be done."

"'The way it was meant to be done'?" Augustus said. I've seen supermarket turkey sliced thicker than his thinly-veiled

44

disbelief. "Before she came along, no one was doing this job at all, at least not for the government."

"This is a complicated conversation," I said, shaking my head. "There's a lot that goes into this, a lot of factors—"

"Maybe because I'm the new guy, it seems pretty simple to me," Augustus said. "Bad guy does something bad, we stop him and put him in jail. If he resists being stopped, we have to kill him in order to protect the people and ourselves. Don't get me wrong, I don't like that part either, but—"

"What if it didn't have to be that way?" I asked. "What if we're making it too easy to skip to the killing part?"

Augustus blew air through his lips. "*Pffft*. Nothing easy about it that I've seen, but I guess you've been on the job longer."

"Things should be different," I said confidently. "Like this Benjamin Cunningham. Looking at that footage, you know he didn't do this on purpose, right?"

Augustus hedged. "Maybe. Maybe not. I didn't have a camera inside his head."

"I don't think he intended to do it," I said. "I think he's scared. I think he got overwhelmed by his emotions, got too angry, blew his stack in a very literal way. Now we could approach this in the way Sienna would, which is, you know, a hundred miles an hour straight at him—"

"Straight at the dude who's already exploded and killed fifty people today," Augustus said. "Gee, why ever would we want to do that? It's almost as if we'd be trying to *stop him*."

"That's not the only way to do it, though. What if we took a gentler approach? Tried to talk him down, get him to surrender?"

Augustus frowned. "You think your sister doesn't talk people down when she thinks she can?"

"I think she backs them to the edge a lot of the time, then pushes them right off," I said. "Or corners them and expects them to do something other than come out swinging. She leaves a trail of bodies behind her everywhere she goes, and even when she doesn't kill, she does things like that leave PR time bombs all over the internet to make her—and us—look worse."

"So, in this instance," Augustus said, "you want to try to talk this man down." He gave me a nod. "Fair enough. What's your backup plan?"

It was my turn to blink at him. "I don't think it'll come to that, but Gavrikov-types are susceptible to bullets, provided they're not burning too hot. Or you could snuff him out with a ton of dirt."

"That's a lot of dirt," Augustus said. "I mean, I'm not in chemistry or thermodynamics or whatever class yet, but I'm thinking that'll be a whole construction site worth of earth to put out his fire if he goes. Not sure I'm that fast or that strong."

"We'll figure it out," I said confidently, "but I don't think it'll come to that. This man is scared. He killed fifty people in the blink of an eye, but he's a normal enough guy. He's probably scared, and the guilt's setting in. We just need to make him see reason." I steered us down the side street indicated on my GPS. "Let's go talk to his mom, see if she can steer us in the right direction for that." I pulled up to the curb and put the car in park.

"If you say so," Augustus said. I could tell he was skeptical.

"Listen," I said, "things are going to be different with me in charge, okay?"

"Oh, I'm seeing that," he said.

"No PR bombs this week," I said, opening the door and stepping out as I buttoned up my suit.

"I'm rooting for no bombs of any kind," Augustus said as he stepped out opposite me.

I thought about coming up with some quippy reply, but this was serious, and I was in charge, and he needed to see that I wasn't scared. "Let's go," I said simply, and we started up the walk toward Benjamin Cunningham's house, trying to figure out what made an exploding man tick.

6.

Sienna

I ducked into a place that had "Shorty's Restaurant and Bar" written on its overhanging sign in what looked like Comic Sans. I thought about avoiding it on that basis alone, but I was way too hungry to pass it up, and there wasn't a lot of selection here on Main Street, Bayscape Island. I hadn't eaten since before I'd left for the drive, and that had been hours and hours ago. When I stepped inside I found myself in a reasonably well-lit area, windows to the street casting clouded daylight over a darker room. Aged wood paneling gave the whole place an old-timey effect. There was a ramp that led up, with a wooden divider that kept me from seeing any of the rest of the place.

I took a stroll up the ramp and came out in a room that looked like it might have been dragged out of the Old West if not for the modern stuff like a soda fountain behind the bar. Also, I suppose the shiny metal bar stools capped with red vinyl upholstery wouldn't have fit in very well in Deadwood.

There was a man behind the bar in a very classic bartender getup: white shirt, black vest, black pants and a mustache, with a towel thrown over his shoulder. He was young, wore a smile that lit him up all the way to the eyes, and he was alone in the room.

"Hey howdy hey," he said, and to his credit, he said it in a way that didn't make me want to smack him for it. "Welcome to Shorty's. Sit down anywhere you'd like."

"Okay." I wandered from the top of the ramp over to the bar and situated myself on a stool gingerly, like I was expecting it to dump me off on the ground or something. I wasn't, actually; it just felt weird to be sitting alone in a bar with this guy. Not that I feared he'd try anything—I was more than confident I could wreck his entire life if he did—it just felt … weird. "Are you … Shorty?"

He laughed, and it was a nice sound. "No. I'm Brent. Shorty's is just a name. Like McDonald's."

I frowned. "Which was named for the McDonald brothers."

Brent cast his eyes upward, like he was searching for an answer before his gaze flitted back to me. "I thought Ray Kroc founded McDonald's?"

"He just franchised the hell out of it and—" I shook my head. "Never mind. There's no Shorty, and you're Brent. Got it. I'm Sienna, and I'm hungry. Can you help?"

"This isn't going to sound like much of a boast," Brent said with a grin, "but we've got the best food on Bayscape."

I thought about the little town that Jake had shown me with one sweep of a hand and tried to find a way to sugarcoat my reply. "But does that mean it's any good?" Probably needed more sugar on that.

Brent feigned an injured look. "It's decent," he said. "We're not an authentic French eatery or your mother's home cooking, but we're pretty good." He paused. "By which I mean I'm pretty good, since I'll be doing the cooking if you order something."

"My mother's home cooking all came straight out of a box," I said, pausing once I said it. "And coincidentally, so did I. What do you have that's … uh, palatable?"

He skated right past whatever oddness I'd packed into that statement and slid a plastic menu in front of me. "Today's special is a turkey sandwich with avocado.

Personally, I'm not sure what all the fuss is about avocado, but they're putting it on everything these days, so we're just following along out here. I'm trying to pioneer an avocado spaghetti, but so far it's resulted in three visits to Sarah over at the clinic."

"Did she induce vomiting to try and cure it?" I asked, looking down at the menu. "Because based on my limited interaction with her, that feels like something she'd do."

"Nice," Brent said, leaning over on the bar with both elbows. "That what happened to your hand?"

I held up the bandaged palm. "This old thing? Nah. I had a lightsaber duel with someone, and they almost Skywalkered me."

Brent kept a straight face. "Was it your dad?"

"Nah," I said, "unlike Vader, my father actually is dead." Long, long ago, before I even had a chance to meet him. "I pointed at one of the menu items. "This burger ..."

"Yes?"

"How is it?" I asked. "In your clearly impartial opinion of your own cooking?"

"Pretty good," Brent said, nodding his head. "And cheap, too, so you won't feel like I lifted your wallet afterward."

I felt a frown crease my eyebrows. That felt like a slightly odd thing to say. "Uhmmm ... I guess I'll take that."

"Comes with fries," he said, scooping up my menu, "and avocado, obviously."

"Obviously."

"Since we skipped right to food, I should probably ask you if you want anything to drink. Beer? Pop?" He lowered his voice. "The dreaded ice water?"

"Why is the ice water 'dreaded'?"

"It snows like half the year here," he said. "Once the white stuff clears out, I don't really care to even see a cube of it until November rolls around."

"You a year-round resident?" I asked.

"I'm even better than that," he said. "I'm a born and

49

raised resident."

"Uh huh," I said, not looking away. "Did Sarah deliver you?"

"Hah," he said. "A little before her time. What did you want to drink?"

I thought about it for a minute. I was on vacation, after all, and a quick glance back through the window suggested to me that the rain wasn't going to let up soon. "Got anything boozy and sweet? The sweet part needs to trump the boozy."

He thought about it for a minute. "I might have something along those lines. Give me a few minutes?"

"Sure, I'll just sit here and watch the rain come down," I said, half-serious.

"That's the spirit, you enjoy your little slice of the local weather." He headed through a set of saloon-style swinging doors to his left, and I found myself alone in an empty bar.

I stared around the room at the nondescript décor choices, the faded old town newspapers that didn't really register because the events were so prosaic; I mean, I couldn't drum up much interest in a town festival that ended in with a tractor pull. Maybe it was because I figured I could win a tractor pull myself.

I felt the call of nature and looked around, finding a dark hallway just to the right of the bar. I hesitated, wondering if I should ask Brent before going, then remembered that I don't really ask people for permission to do anything, especially not to go to the bathroom. I walked down the narrow hall and found the ladies' room, the floorboards issuing creaking warnings all the while that made me wonder if maybe I should have gone with the turkey sandwich and had him hold the avocado.

I pushed through into a dimly lit bathroom and locked the door. I did my business and washed my hands as best I could, avoiding soaking the bandage. I wondered if the lack of healing was worth the additional pain, and after a moment's consideration, I figured maybe it was. I stared at myself in the mirror, saw the dark circles under my eyes from years of stress, of hell, of the last few days of crap that had come cascading to a lovely finish, and I sighed. I ran the water over my uninjured hand and then wiped it across my face. "Two weeks," I muttered, staring down at the white porcelain sink.

I saw a spread of crimson on my hand and realized the bandage was soaking through again. I started to curse, then shook my head. Give it a night and this wouldn't matter. Being a plain old meta again was an adjustment, even though it was only for a few hours, probably.

I splashed my face lightly with water again, then brushed my hair back, letting it tangle a little as I did so. I stared at myself in the mirror, the glossy, black-painted bathroom walls a stunning contrast with my pale skin. The light over the sink flickered, then snapped off for a full second.

When it came back on, the face in the mirror wasn't mine.

Where my pale, make-up free face had been a moment earlier was a dark shadow, a featureless blur. It looked like someone had smudged black oil over the mirror, blotting me out, replacing me with something … else.

The sound of the humming fluorescent light filled my ears, and then, ever-so-quietly, I heard a voice, deep, sounding like it was somewhere in the distance.

"*You shouldn't be here,*" it said, as I stared at the faceless darkness in the mirror.

Then the light over the sink flickered again, and when I blinked, my face was back. I looked around the bathroom, searching for some sign of something awry, of a power cord leading to the mirror, of anything to explain that strangely freaky display.

I found nothing.

I took a deep breath, then another, then a third. The light was at a steady thrum now, no hint of power interruption or weirdness. The mirror was clear, my face visible in perfect clarity, down to the small beads of water that I'd left on my face from the splashing.

"Maybe I'm imagining things," I said and gave the bathroom another once over. There was nothing amiss here, nothing to hint that what I'd seen was anything other than a daydream or a delusion based on stress. Because I certainly had that.

Just the same, I took care when I came out the door. The hall was quiet, still no hint of anyone else in the bar. With a last look at the mirror, I left, walking back to the bar like someone was going to attack me at any moment.

Because let's face it, it's me. Someone was bound to try.

7.

Reed

Benjamin Cunningham's house was a simple one story built over a sunken garage. It was the sort of thing you see a lot in Minnesota, but not much in other parts of the country, especially the ones closer to sea level, because it essentially left the house with a garage that emptied right into the basement. The front door to the house was on the upper level, and Augustus and I walked up the steps leading up the small hill from the driveway to ring the bell. The air smelled of fall breeze, with a lovely crispness that was a little early for the season.

When the door opened, we were greeted by a woman that I put in her mid-fifties. She wore a concerned look, probably wondering why two guys in suits were at her front door. "Yes?" she asked.

"Ma'am, I'm Reed Treston of the, uh … Metahuman Policing and—"

"I know who you are," she said, staring out at me from behind a screen door. "Why are you here?"

My reputation preceded me. It often does; people seem to know my face from all the splash exposure I get with Sienna, but they get me mixed up with other people. Someone even asked if I was Scott Baio once. I wasn't impressed.

"We're here to talk about the incident at the airport this

morning, ma'am," Augustus said, leaping right in. "I'm Augustus Coleman, by the way." He shot me a pointed look for not introducing him, I presume.

"Oh, God," she said and pushed open the screen door. "Benjamin." Her face fell, eyes welled up. "Is he ... is he one of the ...?"

"We're looking for him now, ma'am," I said carefully.

"That means he's ... he's ... dead, doesn't it?" She swallowed heavily and swayed back toward the wall behind her. "Oh ... oh no ..."

I turned my head to look at Augustus and caught a humorless expression in return. "Uh, no, ma'am," I said, stepping up to deliver the hard news, "we think he's the one who caused the explosion."

Suddenly, she didn't look like she was going to faint anymore, and her eyes snapped right to me. "Say *what*?" She'd gone from worried and concerned to more than a little pissed off in the course of one revelation.

"Can we come in?" I asked.

"No, you damned sure may not," she said, letting the screen door snap shut right in her—and our—faces, as though it afforded some measure of protection. "You're accusing my son of being a damned terrorist?"

"We don't think what he did was intentional—" I started.

"You think he's one of you," she said with contempt, "that he's some ... some *weirdo* with powers straight out of a—"

"Hey," Augustus said, nonplussed, "watch who you call a weirdo."

She made a small snorting noise. "Benjamin is twenty-seven years old. If he were a ..." she made a motion with her hand right at me, but not Augustus, "... you know ... I think he'd have shown some signs before now." She looked right at me. "I mean ... don't you people exhibit some sort of super strength—"

"*You people?*" Augustus said. "Really? You're going to go

with that, like it's better than *weirdo?*"

"Didn't mean it that way," she said, waving a hand from up to down, like she could just bat away what she'd said. "You know, metas."

"Ah, typically yes," I said, trying to steer around what was rapidly becoming a contentious conversation.

"Well, that settles it," she said, shaking her head, "Benjamin could barely lift his own suitcase. He wasn't one of your—"

"Careful," Augustus said.

"But, he wasn't!" she said. "He just wasn't."

"Ma'am," I said, "we don't know the full facts of the case, but the photographic evidence was clear. Your son burst into flames, exploded, and then walked out of the airport afterward, got in his own car, and drove off."

"I'll believe it when I see it," she said in a huff.

"I'm sure it'll be on the internet in a day or two," Augustus said. "Everything else is."

"If he wasn't a metahuman before he went on this trip," she said, still snotty, arms crossed in front of her, "then he couldn't have come back as one."

That tickled the old brain, causing me to look at Augustus, who gave me a look in return. You know the kind; wide-eyed, *oh-shit* type stuff.

It would have been hard to miss. Ms. Cunningham certainly didn't. "What?" she asked.

"If you have anything else to share—" I said, starting to wrap things up.

"I don't have anything else to say to you," she said.

"You people, you mean?" Augustus asked. She grunted in frustration and slammed the door in our faces.

"That was not helpful," I said as we started back toward the car.

"The hell it wasn't," Augustus said. "You think Cunningham got a shot of Edward Cavanagh's Magical Meta Tonic somewhere in his travels?"

"Possibly," I said, feeling the thud of the concrete with each heavy step I took. This case was getting weirder by the minute. "But I thought Cavanagh's formula and stuff ended up in government custody."

"Where none of it could possibly ever see the light of day again," Augustus said. "I'm sure they boxed it all right up like in *Raiders*, and it's probably sitting in a warehouse somewhere waiting for me to conveniently knock it over in a sequel." He shook his head. "No, man. Cavanagh was connected everywhere, not just here in the U.S. His companies were international. Who knows where he sent that stuff? He was planning to 'activate' the whole world at some point, after all."

"This is a weird string of coincidences, though," I said. "Cunningham gets on a plane to Minneapolis? And just happens to be a newly transformed meta? Who goes nuclear at the airport? I mean, any link of that chain could have fallen apart. What if Cunningham hadn't lost control in the line?"

"What if he'd lost it on the plane?" Augustus asked as he got in the passenger seat.

"What if he'd never lost it at all?" I asked.

"Fifty-odd people would still be alive," Augustus said, "and Cunningham's cheap-ass shoes wouldn't have been ruined first by dog crap, then by unseasonable thousand-degree temps."

I slipped behind the wheel, let my fingers slide across the faux leather. I loved this car. "I wouldn't tell that joke in public if I were you."

"Too soon?"

"Little bit," I said. "I've had to hold back a few myself. If Cunningham's gotten 'activated,' as you put it, I don't think there was intentional malice behind this incident."

"So you're not calling it an attack?"

"I shoot someone in the head, it's an attack," I said. "Sienna shoots someone in the head, it's Tuesday." He didn't laugh. "You give someone meta powers and put them on a plane to Minneapolis? Kind of a half-assed way to go about it. I mean, if you want to cause chaos, sending Cunningham to a bigger airport would have been a start. JFK, LaGuardia, Atlanta? MSP is small fish—"

"Small pond," Augustus said then, when he caught my eye, looked chastened. "He's the fish. Your analogy was crap. I fixed it."

"Point is," I said, "this is so clumsy it makes a nerdy rom-com trope heroine look as deft as a ballet dancer by comparison. I don't think this was an attack. It's a misfire at best, an accident by any other name." I waved my hand at the house. "I'm forming an opinion of this guy based on the file and his mother, and it reads like this: Benjamin Cunningham wouldn't say shit if his lips were overflowing with the stuff. If he hadn't had these powers, what do you bet he would have just imploded emotionally and sat down for a good cry?"

"I don't know this dude like you apparently do," Augustus said. "Thought your talent was controlling the wind, not reading minds."

"I knew a mind reader for a while," I said, smirking. "Dr. Quinton Zollers. He taught me some things."

"Oh, yeah?" Augustus looked jaded, wasn't biting with much enthusiasm. "Like what?"

I started the car, listened to the Challenger's engine give off a throaty roar. "Like that you should never ascribe to malice what could better be attributed to stupidity."

"That's called Hanlon's Razor," Augustus said with a frown. "Sounds like your friend didn't have an original thought of his own."

I waited, just a beat for it to set in before I delivered the punch line. "Well, that is kind of what a telepath is known for, isn't it?" He didn't find it nearly as funny as I did.

8.

Benjamin

From down the block, Benjamin watched them leave in their yellow Challenger. He could see the other government car, too, the sedan that was staking out the street. It was a weird feeling, seeing elements out of a spy movie plopped down into his own life. Benjamin had lived on this street his entire life. He knew every car, every neighbor, and most of their friends. A black town car would have stood out around here even if he hadn't known the area this well.

Benjamin had parked in this driveway earlier and had sat slumped down, figuring he'd be out of sight. He wanted to go home, wanted to clean up. He'd had to dress from the dirty clothes in his suitcase, and it felt ... filthy. He was wearing a green dress shirt with khakis, and the wrinkles alone were driving him mad. He'd had black smudges from the soot on his face and had stopped in St. Paul to mop them up. His stomach was unsettled. He'd drunk an iced tea in silence, staring at the cream-colored walls of the fast food restaurant. He didn't even remember which restaurant it was now.

Sitting here was not going to be a valid strategy long-term. Sooner or later someone would realize that he was parked in front of the Snyder house while they were up north at their cabin for the week. A law enforcement officer would realize he was in the car, would realize that the car possessed license plates that could be traced back to him. No, sitting here was not a valid option for long.

But Benjamin didn't know what else to do.

What he really wanted to do was go back to work, go home, to wake up tomorrow in Amsterdam to find that this whole day had been one long, nightmarish fever dream that had never actually happened. He'd gladly sit through the nine-hour flight, even the allergies again and all that followed, to take the day back. He could replay the events at the airport in his mind, but only from a distance, as though they were happening to someone else.

Yes, Amsterdam. That was where it had all gone wrong, wasn't it? Everything before that had been fine.

He could remember what it looked like as the blast hit, as the skin melted off the face of the man behind him who'd been so unkind. He watched it happen in his mind, over and over, revolted, afraid, disgusted. What kind of monster could do such a thing to other people?

Benjamin stared at his hands. They shook for no apparent reason, and he clamped them on the steering wheel, watched the plastic leather bend under the strength of his grip in a way he'd never seen happen before.

But this day was not a dream, was it? He'd done ... what he'd done—but it wasn't his fault, was it? This wasn't something he'd known about; he'd never had powers before. Now the government was after him. He'd seen the lead man, remembered his face, even with the beard. He was Sienna Nealon's brother.

Benjamin was stuck in a loop of needing to do something, anything, but feeling absolutely like he couldn't. "I have to leave," he said, "but I can't. If I do, they'll catch me. But if I sit here, they'll catch me." And it had played in his head exactly like that for the last several hours.

"Where else can I even go?" he asked. "Where they won't see me? Where they won't ..." He took a breath. Maybe it all was a dream, after all, and it was culminating in him losing his damned mind. Metahumans may have existed in the world, but he thought of them the same way he thought of Hollywood celebrities—they were out there, but he never saw them, so they might as well not have existed. Seeing Sienna Nealon's brother in real life, in front of his own house …

It finally let the train on the loop jump the track.

"They're coming for me," he said. "Looking for me. I have to leave." He looked up in the mirror, saw fearful eyes. "I don't want to be caught by them." He'd read the articles about what happened to metas—or what was suspected, in any case. No one knew for sure, after all. There were no trials, no word, and those people never saw the light of day again.

Whatever happened to them, it wasn't for *him*, that was certain. After all, he hadn't *meant* to. It just … happened. It was an accident.

"I want my life back," he said, leaning back against the cloth seat in his tiny car. "I just want … my life back. I just want …"

He opened his eyes. He was still in the Snyders' driveway.

Benjamin took one last mournful breath and started his car. Maybe they'd forget. Maybe it'd be all right tomorrow. Maybe it really was just a nightmare. These sorts of things didn't happen to real people. He'd just …

He'd just wake up tomorrow and go on living. Things like this didn't happen to him. Exciting things didn't just happen to him. And he loved that about his life. It was steady. Predictable. Stayed well between the lines.

Yes, perhaps it was a dream. It was certainly too surreal to be reality.

Though that thought wasn't much in the way of comfort, he clung to it with everything he had. Benjamin put the car in reverse and backed out of the driveway. He needed to sleep. To sleep, to wake up refreshed, and possibly somewhere else.

Then, maybe, he could get back to the business of living life. Go to work tomorrow, come home, put everything else behind him.

Yes, that was what he needed to do. With unsteady hands, he turned the wheel at the end of his street and headed off to find somewhere to sleep, perchance to dream … of a better tomorrow, one in which today had never happened.

9.

Sienna

When I made it back to my barstool, there was a sweet drink waiting for me with pineapple and a maraschino cherry speared together in the middle of it. I wanted a sip but I held off, still a little put off by my experience in the bathroom. I'd peeked into the men's room as I came back out of the hallway and found nothing—no sign of a mirror looking through into the women's room or anything creepy like that, just a normal looking bathroom. Or, as normal-looking a bathroom as you can have with urinals. They sure as hell don't look normal to me. Or private.

"Hey," Brent's face looked out from behind the curtain separating the bar from the kitchen, "burger'll be ready in a few."

"Is that so?" I asked coolly.

His forehead creased, but he mostly maintained his smile as he answered. "That is so. What's up with you?"

"Why? Do I look like I've just seen a ghost?" I asked, trying to mask my irritation.

"Not sure I've ever seen anyone who's actually seen a ghost," Brent said, still sticking half out of the curtain like an actor trying to get a look at the crowd before a performance. "You mostly just look cranky to me. Did we run out of toilet paper in the ladies' room again? Because if so, I'm sorry.

Someone keeps coming in and stealing—"

"No, your toilet paper supply appears to be quite robust," I said. If he was guilty of pulling this crappy prank on me, he was playing it cool in an epic way. Dude must have antiperspirant like a desert, because most people tend to quiver a little at the knees when I get mad at them. One time, at the Target returns counter, I sent a teenage clerk running into the back room when I "gently" (and accidentally) dropped a malfunctioning tablet through their wooden countertop. I thought it was a very savvy move on her part, actually.

Strength. I haz it. Control? Eh. Working on it, still.

"So what's up?" Brent asked, emerging from behind the curtain. "In thirty seconds or less, please, unless you like your burger well done. Which is a funny way to say 'burnt to a crisp,' I always thought. I would have gone with, 'poorly done—'"

"Playing pranks on me is not cool," I said. "And by 'not cool,' I'm understating it like 'well done.' I actually mean, 'potentially fatal.'"

"Whoa," Brent said, hands in the air in utter surrender. "I have absolutely no idea what you're talking about. I would not prank you, and not just because of the fatal thing. I have not pranked anyone since primary school, and it was tossing a worm on Berrie Jansen's dress in hopes that she'd notice me." His voice diverged into a strange, quasi-European accent, and he sounded ... stressed.

"Okay," I said, in measured tones, lifting my head to look at myself in the massive mirror that stretched above the bar, "well, I just had a ghost-story type experience in your bathroom."

He frowned. "Like ... full torso apparition? Would it spike the PKE meter?"

I sighed. "Why do I encounter geeks everywhere I go? Yes, Egon. The mirror went dark, a shadowed shape told me I wasn't supposed to be here—"

"That sounds more like a slasher movie." Now he was frowning like he was mulling over what I was saying. Still no sign of deceit or trickery, and I was reasonably good at knowing when people were lying to me.

"Whatever it was," I said, "it was clearly meant to freak me out."

"Yeah, well," he said, "it doesn't seem to have done the job on you. I, on the other hand, might need a change of undershorts after that oblique reference to you killing me." He leaned forward on the bar. "Do you still want your burger and drink?"

I thought about it for a minute. He seemed guileless, but that could have been a disguise. I'd been fooled by clever liars before, but ... dammit, I was hungry, and it wasn't like my cabin was going to be stocked with food. "Yes," I said, "I still want the burger."

"Then let me get that for you before it becomes not just poorly done, but shittily done." He disappeared behind the curtain and a moment later his voice wafted out. "You can come watch me if you want, make sure I'm not ... I dunno, lacing it with hallucinogens or whatever it is you think I might do."

"I'd be more concerned about a hearty spit from you at this point," I said, slipping up and behind the bar in a couple seconds, quietly moving aside the curtain. He glanced over his shoulder from where he stood at a prep station, plating my burger and made a hocking noise in his throat while smiling. I shook my head. "Gross."

"I wouldn't," he said. "Not for accusing me of ... uh ... whatever you accused me of. Rallying ghosts against you or something."

"I'm not accusing you of anything," I said. "I was ... probing."

He held up a plastic-gloved hand. "You might need one of these if you're going probing."

"Try to pretend like you wouldn't enjoy it."

He chuckled as he put a tomato, lettuce and mayo on a bun before slapping the burger on top. "It's like you already know me." He picked up the plate, pulled some fries out of a cage above a still-bubbling deep fryer, and dumped them on my plate before salting them. "Your lunch is served, madam."

"Oh, I'm a madam now?" I asked, making way for him to carry my food out of the curtain. "Explains why you think I might be okay with that sort of probing."

"I like how we've already established this easy rhythm back-and-forth," he said as he sat my plate on the bar next to my drink. "It's comforting, isn't it?"

"After the bathroom incident," I said, "a spiked toilet seat might be considered comforting."

"But seriously," he said, leaning on the bar as I sat down, "this is the kind of relationship a bartender is supposed to establish. Make you want to be here, make you want to feel comfortable—"

"Ghost stories aren't much of a comfort read."

"—to make you feel like you're someplace safe, where—"

"Everybody knows your name?" I asked, taking a bite of a fry.

He smiled wryly. "Hackneyed, but true."

"Everybody already knows my name," I said, "unfortunately. And speaking of hackneyed, aren't you going to ask me how the first couple of bites are tasting? Isn't that in the restaurateur's guild guidelines or bylaws or something?"

"Ah, but you see," he said, throwing a towel back on his shoulder, "I am a bartender."

"And a short order cook," I said, "and a waiter, and a one-man ghost prank—"

"I deny that last bit," he said, frowning, "though now I am going to have to look into the women's room—in a non-pervy way. Never heard that particular complaint before, ghosts and whatnot."

"Yeah, well," I said, finally grabbing the burger off the plate because my hunger could wait no longer, "maybe I'm just crazy. It's not like my brain is bereft of reasons to be nuts. I can think of six perfectly good ones off the top of my head."

"Maybe you're just stressed," he said, "or maybe the women's loo here is haunted. Who knows? Have a drink, kick back, relax, and I'll have a look at the ladies' room while you eat." He tossed the towel back over his shoulder. "Apparently you can add janitor to my list of titles."

"Sanitation engineer nowadays, I think they call it."

"That's garbage man," he said, disappearing down the hall into the shadows. I heard the squeak as he opened the door to the women's room. "My God," he said, loud enough I could hear him.

I paused mid-bite, staring after him. "What? Did you see something?"

"No, I just marvel sometimes at being allowed to go into the ladies' room," he said, turning to grin back at me; I could see his smile in the near dark back there. "Spend your whole life being kept out, like it's got an invisible force field or something ..."

"It's called the force of law," I said, taking another bite of the burger. It was juicy, delicious, and hit the spot. "Or possibly human decency? Social stigma? I don't know." I gave up and took a swig of my drink. It was creamy and sweet, and I couldn't taste the booze.

"I don't see anything in here that would lead me to believe a haunting has taken place," he said, closing the door and walking back toward me. "No ectoplasm on the floors, just good ol' fashioned urine."

"Gross," I said, "and also a lie. I was just in there, I didn't see any urine." I took another swig of my drink, which came in a martini glass, presumably in order to make me feel like a grownup.

"You're really taking that down," Brent said, slipping

back behind the bar. "You want me to start on another?"

"I shouldn't," I said.

"Come on," he said, coaxing, "have a drink. All work and no play, you know what happens."

"You end up shouting, 'Here's Johnny!' while chopping through a door with an axe?" Even the pickles on this burger were so good. Sooooo good. They crunched, were beautifully sour, and went with the mayo, which was like … seasoned or something. It was amazing.

"Something like that," he agreed. "So, that second drink? Yea or nay?"

"I still have to drive to my cabin to check in," I said, pushing the now-empty martini glass away. I devoured the last few bites of my burger in quick order, then ignored the fries. Not that they were bad or anything, but that was a whole lot of carbs.

"Believe it or not, we actually have a taxi service on the island—in case you get too loaded to drive yourself," he said, leaning one arm on the bar. "Just FYI for later, if you're of a mind to get annihilated."

"Usually I'm the one doing the annihilating," I said dryly as I stood up and idly tossed a twenty on the bar before heading for the door.

"Hey," Brent said. "You want change?"

"Keep it," I said, looking over my shoulder. "Maybe I'll be back later, and I won't have to tip again."

"With a generous heart like yours, you might just get patron of the year," he said, smirking. "Except for that whole thing where you made me check the women's room for no apparent reason."

I shook my head at him. It was impossible not to like the guy, he had charm. "Let's hope it was no damned reason. The alternative …" I let my voice trail off as I headed for the ramp.

"The alternative is what?" he asked, and I looked back to see his features pinched with concern.

"Nothing good," I said, shrugging, as I headed down the ramp and back out onto the rainy street. I was soaked before I even made it to the car.

10.

Reed

After interviewing the mother and spending a little time canvassing Benjamin Cunningham's workplace, a small tech firm about ten minutes from his house, I was out of ideas and told Augustus so: "Well, I'm tapped."

Augustus was frowning, hadn't looked happy in a while. "I can't believe I missed class for this."

"Hey, this is a serious crime," I said.

He made a grunting noise. "I'm not saying the crime wasn't serious. I'm just saying I'm not sure it was worth missing class so I could tag along and watch you flirt with an FBI agent then get called 'you people' by an angry mother. And Cunningham's workplace was a total dead end. That man is bland as unsweetened oatmeal. Nobody even knows him other than his boss and his cubicle-mate, and that girl didn't *want* to know him."

That was true. Cunningham shared a cubicle with a woman named Jessica whose whole faced pinched up at the mention of his name. They did not have a happy history, which she did not fail to mention in excruciating detail. It wasn't all that interesting, though; her criticism basically boiled down to the type of petty stuff you'd hear first-time roommates squabbling over.

"What's the move?" Augustus asked.

I looked over at him from behind the wheel. It was just before rush hour, technically, which meant interstate 694 was already packed in the stretch near Fridley that we were driving. "Back to base, I guess."

Augustus looked out over the traffic. "I don't know the city that well yet—"

"They call it 'the cities,'" I corrected gently. "Plural, because the metro is Minneapolis and St. Paul—"

August just rolled his eyes and shook his head, going on like I hadn't said anything, "—but I'm thinking that's going to take a while."

"Safe bet," I said. I longed to hit the accelerator, to let Baby—my affectionate name for my car—run. "On a good day with clear roads, we'd be like forty minutes away. Tonight? Probably two hours."

"Augh," Augustus said, leaning his head back. I could tell he reacted a little bit to the lovely headrest because his expression softened. "What do you do in cases like this?"

"Work it until we find the guy," I said. I could feel the tension in my shoulders. I'd probably need Isabella to work on them later. "This guy's no genius. He'll turn up."

"Yeah, and maybe when he does, he kills a whole bunch more people," Augustus said.

"He's not a killer by nature," I said.

"Just keep in mind you're not only staking your life on that if you run into him," he said, "you're also betting other people's."

"I get that," I said. "But we're not just out here to serve and protect at all costs. This isn't a war. If it was, we'd just use sniper rifles, drill these guys from a distance, and call it a day."

"Might be safer if we did," he said and went back to staring out the window. "You think anything is going to break loose on this tonight?"

"Who knows?" I asked and took the University Avenue exit ramp as soon as I could. "Might as well stop and eat, because with our luck, he'll be sighted just after we make it to the other side of town and we'll have to turn around and fight our way back through this mess." I looked over at him. "You hungry?"

"I could eat," Augustus said.

"There's a huge Asian buffet over here," I said. "Biggest in Minnesota. It's pretty good."

"Yeah, all right," he said as I made the turn. It wasn't a great solution, more of a holding action, a time killer. But I had to do it.

Because for some reason, I had a feeling Benjamin Cunningham wasn't quite done yet for the day.

11.

Sienna

I found the cabin place pretty easily. I was fortunate in that however good Brent had made that particular drink, he hadn't made it strong, because I'm not all that useful when drunk.

The place I was staying was a series of semi-private cabins that were each located on their own wooded sites. The main office was a cabin of its own, complete with log—or faux-log—sides. I looked the place over when I got out of the car, the rain tapping down as I stood there for a moment before I legged it for the front door. The air smelled even fresher than on the boat, the fall rain drenching everything and giving the world around me an earthy aroma.

I walked inside to another ringing bell alerting someone that, hey, there's a customer here. I paused at a front desk and glanced through a door separating it from a room behind it. A television was playing inside, some game show. I looked back into the room just as a young woman came out with black, heavy-framed glasses. "Oh, hello," she said with a tentative smile. "Are you Sienna?"

"Yeah," I said, wondering if she knew my name because of the reservation or whether, once again, my infamy preceded me. "Checking in."

"Wonderful," she said and starting futzing around behind

the desk. "You're here with us for ... two weeks?"

"Yep," I said, leaning on the counter and waiting. Patience is still not my greatest strength. Strength is my greatest strength.

"My name is Apollonia, and I'm the day clerk," she said, looking up at me through those glasses.

"Who's the night clerk?" I asked, being a little bit smartass about it.

"Oh, I'm the night clerk as well," she said seriously. "But we close at five, so don't expect an answer if you call." I tried to find a way to reply to that without being an utter ass and failed, so I just let her keep talking, because apparently she was not done. "You're all set. You're in cabin thirteen." She stared at me. "Will you be ... trashing the room?"

I blinked at her, unsure I'd heard her correctly. "Will I ... what?"

"Are you going to trash the room?" she asked, still absolutely straight-faced. "I mean, you're famous and whatnot, so if you trashed the room it feels like it might be good for business. We could advertise by saying that—"

"I'm not a rock star, kid," I said, because she actually did seem a little like a kid in that moment. "Also, my ability to destroy goes way, way beyond a room—or entire cabin, as I hope the case may be—"

"Well, it's a one-room cabin," she said. "Two, if you count the bathroom—"

"I'm not trashing the place," I said, frowning. "And I doubt the owner would find it much good for business or advertising or whatever."

"I suppose you would know," she said with a shrug of near indifference, which ... actually, she'd been pretty indifferent the whole time, so it wasn't a marked change for her. "Anyhow, the town is back that way," she pointed back the way I came, "along with every restaurant, bar and business on the island."

I stood there and digested that little tidbit, reaching right past the fact that I knew the town was back the way I came because *I'd just freaking been there.* "It's almost like you're telling me not to go the other way or something."

"You can go anywhere you want," she said, "but it's all private residences in the other direction. No businesses or anything. Not really even any decent views unless you want to go trespassing."

I considered making a smartass remark about how I might consider conducting a flyover of the island in the morning for the hell of it, but passed. What was the point? This girl was just doing her job, though kind of poorly. "Okay," I said, just letting it go.

"Here's your key," she said brightly and handed me a key on the end of a comically large key chain with an enamel tchotchke at the end of it shaped like a pine tree. The whole thing looked like an oversized air freshener you might pick up at a car wash for the sake of novelty, or to cover the smell of blood you've accidentally tracked in. (Don't judge me. It's a perfectly normal thing that happens.) She must have caught me staring at it because then she said, "It's so you don't lose the key."

I looked down at my pocket, which was mightily insufficient for fitting this particularly oversized nightmare, then looked back up at Apollonia. "Clearly." I shook my head and walked out, into the rain. "Lose a lot of keys around here?"

"Not yet," she said, "probably because of this." She gestured at the garish decoration.

I didn't even know how to reply to that, so I just nodded then backed away slowly. Once outside, I drove to my cabin. The tchotchke had the number 13 painted on it, so I drove down a dirt path until I saw a cabin with a 13 helpfully displayed in brass numbers on the side of the trim. I parked in the space available and hoisted my suitcase out of the back seat, prepared to run for the door.

I got soaked again anyway because I had to pause to

unlock the front door, and the eaves of the cabin sluiced the water helpfully right onto the front step where I was standing. The rain was really coming down now, and I'd just reconciled myself to the fact that the weather was going to be shitty today because—well, because it could be, I supposed. It was a cold autumn rain, too, with that bitter chill that made me want to jump out of my skin, the kind that made my teeth start chattering instantly. I half wished I hadn't imprisoned my souls in a chloridamide prison out of petty spite and a desire for quiet, because right now going Gavrikov and bursting into flame, while hazardous to my clothing, would have at least cut the chill right down.

Once the door was unlocked I stepped inside, dripping on the linoleum entry, a three-foot by two-foot space directly in front of the door. Thin carpeting covered the rest of the living area, which I could see from where I stood. To my right was a queen-sized bed, and to my immediate left was a small kitchenette. The bathroom was tucked into the corner past the bed with a wooden door for privacy, and to the left of that space, which was cut off from the rest of the cabin's primary room with a wall, was a Jacuzzi tub. Just out there in the middle of the room. While it would have made bathing while sharing a room with a stranger kind of awkward, I didn't really care; I wasn't staying with a stranger.

This place was all mine, and I'd damned well use the Jacuzzi in my living room without a care in the world.

I stood there dripping on my little entry for a few seconds, listening to the howling of the wind and hammering of the rain against the windows, and pondering how quickly I could cross over to the bathroom. I could make it pretty fast, and the carpet would dry. I was drenched, but I wasn't leaking water like a bucket or anything. I put my suitcase down at my side, listening to my soles squeak against the linoleum, and then another noise caught my attention.

It was a low sound, almost a background screech that was gaining intensity, something under the weather's effects on the cabin's exterior. I listened, using my meta senses to reach out, trying to catch what it was. It sounded ... unnatural, like a scratching of a record, faint but growing in volume.

Suddenly it hit me like a bellow directly in my eardrum, like a punch right to the nose, and I fell to my knees from the power, like a message screamed right into my face. When I regained control of myself, my legs stung from the impact on the floor, and one of my hands ached from where I'd caught my weight as I fell. And in my head, that same voice kept ringing, an aftereffect of someone's attempt to get my damned attention.

GET OUT!

As I rubbed my sore spots, I felt my eyes narrow. "I'll get out when I'm good and damned ready," I said and went to get a towel. If I didn't take any crap from my boss, who signed my paychecks, it was for damned sure that no disembodied voice was going to tell me what to do.

In retrospect, though, maybe I should have listened.

12.

Reed

I stared at Augustus across the table as he picked at his plate. He'd picked up some crawfish, some sort of cheesy crab dish, and a whole pile of sautéed mushrooms, and he was tackling them a little at a time. In contrast, I'd avoided most of the fried stuff. I had a plate of sushi coupled with a fair helping of ginger, wasabi and soy sauce in a dipping dish to the side. The wasabi was scorching my nasal passages with each bite, and I loved it.

"You're a good guy, Augustus," I said, breaking the silence we'd shared since we'd both gotten back to the table after hitting the buffet. The restaurant was crowded, filled to the brimming with a highly diverse crowd. I saw blacks, Asians, Hispanics and white folks, and all in huge numbers. The buffet was clearly a popular destination for everyone here in mostly white-bread Minnesota.

"Uh, thanks," he said, scowling a little.

I couldn't quite tell how I'd trod on him there, but clearly he'd not taken that quite the way I intended. "What?" I asked.

"Doesn't matter." He picked up one of those fried donuts that was coated in sugar grains and took a bite. I tried not to flinch thinking of all the calories it must have had. Time was, I would have taken one of those down, too. Since getting together with Isabella, I was on a much healthier eating path.

"Clearly my intended compliment bothered you," I said. "Spill it. How did I offend you by calling you a good guy?"

I watched him watch me as the gears turned in his head while he debated answering the question. After a moment, he put down the doughnut and leaned in to share a piece of his mind with me. "All right, I'll lay it out: you and your sister got problems, but really, you're both alike in a lot of ways. One of them is that you both have this whole … veterancy thing going on."

I blinked. "Is that a word?"

"It should be," Augustus said. "You've been doing this for years. Been here, done this, been there, done that. Seen everything. Or at least way more than me. Which, fair enough. I'm the new guy. I get that. I'm the rook. But you both still treat me like I'm the kid, and I don't know, maybe it's been long enough you don't remember what it's like being treated as the kid—it sucks. I don't want to go clean my room and put away my toys, get hit with smug as hell shit like 'Oh, Augustus, you're a good boy—'"

"I said 'guy—'"

"You meant 'kid,'" he said dourly. "You can't even argue with that."

I looked back at him, and most of the anger had fled his dark eyes. "Okay, I meant 'kid.' That's true. But—you are new—"

"I know that," he said, "but you don't have to be a smugly superior dick about it. I mean you can either be an empowering mentor or be a very experienced and patronizing jackhole, but you can't do both at the same time."

"How am I being a … patronizing jackhole?"

"This is how it goes when your sister and I go on a mission," he said, talking with his hands. "She teaches the whole time. Not great, but she tells me what's going on, how she's run across this type of experience before, whatever. I mean, I have to pry it out of her, but she'll talk for a while until she gets her point across at least, and she's not so busy trying to convince me she's right that she's overcompensating for—"

"I'm not—" I sputtered, not really sure how to respond to that. "Overcompensating? I'm—uh—I mean—"

"Come on," Augustus said, "you haven't been in charge. You haven't been running the show. You've been second fiddle for years, and you're sick of sitting back and thinking about how this thing would run if you were in charge. Well, guess what? You're in charge. Stop talking about how it's going to be and just do your thing. If your way is better than hers, you get to show it. Just *stop* beating me over the head with how much different you are than her. Because I like your sister. She's not stupid, and she's not pointlessly cruel, which you seem to think she is. She doesn't love hurting people, she just doesn't shy away from it." He shrugged. "Do your thing and stop making grand pronouncements. It reeks of a lack of confidence."

I sat there, trying to use my mouth to form words. "I … am confident," I said after a moment, unintentionally confirming the opposite.

"Yeah, okay," Augustus said, and I could tell he was through arguing with me by the way he went back to his doughnut.

I sat there silent, watching him eat, listening to the ambient noise surrounding me from the crowded restaurant. It was a low roar, a hum of families, of children's delighted screams, of parents exhorting them to be quiet, of silverware and plates clattering. Somewhere, far in the distance, I could hear the stony koi pond's waterfalls burbling away. "All right, maybe I'm a little insecure," I finally admitted.

Augustus looked up at me warily, popping in the last bite of doughnut. He spoke with his mouth still partially full. "You don't need to confess your sins to me."

"It's not a sin," I said, feeling the burn of shame. "It's a fact. You're right, I've been second fiddle for a while. Maybe I am talking louder than my actions. I should just do and stop worrying about saying. That's a fair critique. It's just been a while since I've been in charge."

"Mm," Augustus said, spooning mushrooms into his mouth. "You still aren't in charge. Phillips is."

"Well, you know what I mean," I said. "I'm in charge of this op."

Augustus didn't respond to that, but I could tell by the way he turned his eyes away that he was thinking something else. I started to ask him what that might be, but he stood before I could. My eyes locked on his plate, which was still mostly full, and then I looked up as I started to ask him why he was going back when he hadn't finished his last helping. As I opened my mouth to speak, I stopped because he was just standing there, mouth slightly agape. Right then, I realized that the buzz of conversation, of families speaking and dining and living had died off around me. The lonely sound of a plate shattering caused me to turn and look for whatever had rendered Augustus speechless.

I brought my head around to see a man walking up the aisle between the restaurant booths. He was wearing a flannel shirt, the kind of thing you'd either find in a hipster's closet or an L.L. Bean catalog page. He wore it tucked in, with blue jeans, and old, worn-out tennis shoes, like he was a farmer straight out of the Midwest.

Except he wasn't. He really, really wasn't.

It was the scarring that shut everyone up. He looked like he'd been burned over and over again, until his flesh could no longer hold any shape at all, like his skin had been poured over his head in liquid form, sloughing over his features until they settled and cooled on lumpy bone. It was almost like he was wearing creature makeup, some effect from a monster movie that looked disturbingly real. He had no hair on his head, on his eyebrows, or his face, and his furious eyes found me while his lips remained more or less lifeless, pulled back in a rictus that exposed perfectly even teeth barely hidden behind a misshapen mouth.

"What the hell …?" Augustus muttered.

I just stared, feeling the blood drain out of my face. It was him. He'd changed dramatically since the last time I'd seen him, when he disappeared in a blaze as my sister unleashed a white phosphorus grenade that scourged his flesh with unquenchable fire. But it was really him, and I couldn't help but feel a very slight quiver inside as I spoke his name aloud in something lower than a whisper.

"Anselmo."

13.

Sienna

I came back into Shorty's Bar and Restaurant to find that an apparent evening crowd had moved in. I know—I was shocked too, but apparently Bayscape Island was actually big enough to produce a crowd, albeit a small one. There were probably seven people in the place besides Brant, who was holding court at the bar, talking to a dark-haired guy in a police uniform that was somewhere between grey and black. He was holding one of those large-brimmed lawman hats under his arm and leaning against the bar, smile creasing his handsome profile as I walked in. Brant was nodding along with whatever the lawman was saying, and I watched them stop talking as I approached, making my way across the restaurant portion of the establishment.

I ignored the other groups seated at the tables around me and headed for the bar, feeling another rumble in my belly. I'd hung around my cabin for a little while, Jacuzzi'd for a bit, tried to ignore that uneasy feeling that someone was messing with my head. I hadn't heard any more voices, so that was a plus. Part of me was staying just to show the voice I wasn't scared, I think.

I watched the lawman draw his head back from Brant as I walked up, regarding me with a cool glance as I plopped down on one of the barstools. Music was playing in the background, slow and full of feeling. The lawman nodded to me and moved off down the bar as Brant broke off and headed my way. He caught my gaze and smiled. "Back for another round, eh?"

I paused, finally realizing why the music playing sounded so familiar. It was Scott Bradlee and Postmodern Jukebox playing their Haley Reinhart-fronted version of Radiohead's "Creep." It was slow and lovely, full of soul and feeling. I looked into Brant's smiling face as he leaned against the bar and nodded toward the ceiling to indicate the music. "They're playing your song."

Brant just grinned in reply. "You think so?"

"Jury's still out," I said. "Though I did have another, presumably-unrelated-to-you haunting experience at my cabin a little while ago."

One of his eyebrows arched up. "You seem calmer than I'd expect from someone having paranormal experiences."

"First off," I said, "I'm not having a paranormal experience because there is no such thing. Someone is screwing with me, and I'm going to give them enough rope to twist in."

He nodded, cautious. "Nice. And second?"

"It takes a lot to scare me," I said, putting my elbows on the bar.

"Is there a third point?"

"If I get boozy enough, point three may be graphic and oddly specific promises of violence for the parties responsible," I said. "I'm not the forgiving sort."

"I'm getting that," Brant said. "Was there a drink order hidden in there somewhere, or am I wishfully thinking?"

"Well, I certainly didn't come back for the ambience," I said, looking around at the newly semi-crowded room. "Though I like your music choice. I'll have what I had before."

"Non-booze-flavored beverage coming right up," Brant said, nodding as he turned back toward the bar.

I watched him work for a minute before I spoke again. "You're not afraid?" He glanced over his shoulder at me as he poured amber liquid into the mixed drink he was making me. "Of my threatening nature?"

He shrugged. "I'm not responsible, so … no. Though it might be interesting, purely from an intellectual standpoint, to hear these threats that you'll make later." He set the drink in front of me on the bar.

"And you're not afraid of me?" I asked. "You know, as a patron who wandered in this afternoon sounding crazy as hell and talking about hearing voices?"

That brought him up short, and he took a few seconds to craft an answer. "Well, I guess my natural curiosity is overcoming my caution in this case, because … well, you're sort of a celebrity, and we don't get many of those around here. It's like if, you know, one of those drunk and crazy actresses came wandering in and trashed the place. Sure, I'd have to clean it up, but at least I'd have a hell of a story to tell."

I snorted into my drink. "The girl at the rental place asked if I was going to trash my cabin. That's the second time someone's asked me to do that, like destroying the place is good for business in some way."

"I don't think it'd be all that good for business, to be honest," Brant said, "though we are going into the slow season, so maybe it wouldn't matter as much. That said, as fascinating as I find this bit of oddness to break up the monotony of a very slow week, I'm not all that excited about seeing this … uh … whatever you've got going on," he waved a hand at me, "getting much more intense than it already has. You're fun to banter with and all, but I'm not wealthy, and I had to get a high-deductible insurance policy on this place—"

"Understood," I said, nodding my head. "I will avoid trashing your place of business unless our very lives are in danger." Not that it would matter; acts of metas weren't covered by insurance anyway. Needless to say, I kept this helpful information to myself, since it would probably only have served to make him nervous.

His face grew pale. "Uhm ... how likely is *that* to happen?" Nervous-er.

I started to answer him but was interrupted by a gentle tapping on my shoulder. I spun quickly to see Jake flinch back from my sudden movement. He was standing there next to Sarah, who was watching the whole thing with a cool eye, which was probably how she watched everything. "Whoa!" Jake said. "No harm intended." He held his hands out in front of him. "Just wanted to say hi."

"I didn't even hear you come up," I said, the muscles in my back at full tense. My fists were clenched, already prepared for an ambush, and I could hear my heart pounding even over the music, which had moved on to the Postmodern Jukebox version of "Poison" sometime during my conversation with Brant. Good taste, bartender.

"Didn't try to sneak," Jake said, taking a step back to stand next to Sarah. "Sorry. Wasn't intending to surprise you, either." He lowered his hands, and for the first time I noticed the gold watch on his left wrist. It had handsome links.

"I should be apologizing," I said, lowering myself back onto the barstool. "Or I should buy you a drink, or something."

"I like this idea," Brant said from behind me, "because it involves money going into my pocket rather than coming out to make repairs to my oh-so-quaint establishment."

Sarah's cool gaze flicked over me. "Your hand is bleeding again."

"Huh?" I looked down and unclenched my left hand. Sure enough, there was crimson spreading out across the bandage. "Hell. Must have squeezed it tight enough to break the skin when I, uh, overreacted to your husband's approach."

"I often overreact to his approach, with similar results,"

Sarah said, sliding onto the barstool next to me. If I wasn't mistaken, this was probably as close as she got to sympathy, but it was sprinkled with her über-dry wit. "I'll take a martini, Brant, since the young lady's paying."

"I feel like I just got an unpleasant glimpse into your sex life," Brant said, frowning slightly as he stared off into space past Sarah. "I don't think I like it."

Sarah's eyes rolled hard. "You're reading too much into it. Now go fix me a drink."

Jake slid onto the barstool next to mine, sandwiching me neatly between the married couple. I probably would have felt more uncomfortable, but Sarah was already ignoring me in favor of the little bowl of mixed nuts sitting on the counter. "Settling in?" Jake asked, with that broad grin I'd seen him display more than a few times already today.

"More or less," I said, getting back on my barstool with a little effort. Those things were tall, and I am not.

"So which is it?" Sarah asked, not even bothering to turn to face me while she spoke. "More? Or less?"

"Probably less," I said, giving her side-eye. Brant was a few steps away and turned his head to look at me as I spoke, but he offered nothing to my story, which was good. I may not have been the most popularity-obsessed person around, but even I wasn't eager to share a crazy story with near-total strangers. I looked up and caught a glimpse of myself in the mirror that stretched above the bar. I let my sightline drift over to the tall, dark-clad lawman to my right at the end of the bar, and caught a flash of him staring at me before he averted his eyes to go back to his drink, a tall glass of golden beer. "Much less. I don't settle so easy."

Sarah made a full-shoulder shrug even as she stared straight ahead. "At least you've always got a ready quip about it."

"Less useful than you'd think," I said, taking another drink of my beverage. So sweet.

"Have you had a chance to look around the island much

yet?" Jake asked. Brant put a big mug of dark beer in front of him unasked, and I watched Jake take a long pull from it while he waited for my answer.

"I pretty much sat around this afternoon," I said, skipping over the part where most of the actual sitting was done in the Jacuzzi bath, with the jets working my weary-yet-technically flawless muscles. "And when I spoke to the girl at the rental place about exploring the rest of the island, she was pretty discouraging about the whole thing. I got a real, 'whatever you do, don't go to the elephant graveyard' vibe from her, and we all know that's really just an invitation to do the thing you've been told not to."

"Let me guess," Jake said with that grin, "Apollonia?"

"Good guess," I said, gracelessly stealing a peanut from the dish in front of Sarah, drawing a somewhat annoyed look from her. "Though I suppose you don't exactly have a wide selection of suspects to choose from in this case."

"You'd be right about that," Brant said, setting a martini down in front of Sarah as he re-entered the conversation. "But Apollonia, she's a special sort. Ingrained in this place. Been here as long as I have."

"Anyway," I said, "between the grim warning and the weather, I haven't had much inclination to look around. Figured I'd just hang out within easy run of car or roof until things cleared."

"Is this the part where I'm supposed to play the creepy, crackly weather report on the radio?" Brant asked me with a gleam in his eyes.

I raised an eyebrow at him. "Why? Has my life become a horror movie?"

"I hope not," Brant said, "because I'm very much the comic relief that's bound to get offed first." He ran a hand from his waist up to his face, brushing at his facial hair. "I mean, look at me. I'm too pretty to live in any nightmare scenario."

I saw Sarah lean back on her stool to my left so that she

could talk to Jake. "Are they speaking in some sort of code? Am I too old to understand what they're saying?"

"I'm a bit lost myself," Jake said good naturedly. "But I did hear the weather report, and it sounds like a horror all its own." I looked over at him, and his lips pursed in a thin line. "Storm's moving in hard. Expecting more rain before tomorrow—torrential downpours." He brightened. "Fun vacation, huh?"

"Yeah," I said, turning to pick up my drink, "it's a real rain barrel of laughs." I brought my glass up to take a sip and my eyes alighted on the mirror above the bar as a fierce pain shot through my entire body.

Darkness swam in front of my eyes, the shadow swirling in the reflection like a cloud of darkness closing in across a stormy sky. Searing tendrils of raw nerves ran over my scalp, causing me to cry out as I fell back, my gaze still locked on the dark shape in the mirror staring back at me with an implacable, unceasing darkness.

A low, rumbling voice rang in my ears, sending icy fingers of fear rippling across my back and up my neck in the moment before I hit the ground. *"GET ... OUT!"* it said, and then I struck the floor of the bar and everything went dark.

14.

Reed

I rose to my feet and stared at Anselmo Serafini, who was grandly holding his scarred hands up in a gesture that seemed to encompass everything around him. Plates rattled and people gasped at the sight of the man with the sloughed skin. There was a smell of food in the air, sharp and tangy, but it was tinged with a burnt aroma that wafted into my nose and came to rest on my tongue. It was bitter and ashen, and I lost my appetite immediately.

"Reed Treston," Anselmo said, staring at me from behind one of the folds of burnt flesh that partially covered his left eye. "I have waited for this moment for ... oh, so long."

"And here I thought we'd resolved our issues back in January," I said, sliding out into the aisle between tables to face off with him directly. There were twenty civilians or more within the fifteen feet between us, tables filled with families who were watching us but who hadn't scattered out of fear just yet. "You know, when you ... lost your cool."

"Terrible," Augustus said behind me with a groan. "That was one of the ones you should have kept to yourself."

"Save the critique for later," I whispered without looking back at him. "So, Anselmo ... I have to admit, I'm surprised you're not in Italy. Feels like America isn't really your ... uh, speed?" I'd started to say, "I figured the heat here would be too much for you," but Augustus's previous rebuke held me off.

"How could I leave when I have business yet unattended?" Anselmo took a step toward me slowly, almost non-threatening. He looked calm, relaxed, like he was just here to talk. But then again, that was how Anselmo had always looked until he became completely unhinged.

A sensation like spiders crawling up my back made me want to shiver, but I held it in. "You know you're a fugitive from justice, right? I'm obligated to arrest you and return you to jail." That got a few of the civilians moving around me, sliding out of their tables slowly.

Anselmo hammered a wooden segment of counter holding up the servers' computer and printer for bills. I blanched as a rain of splinters flew into the air surrounding him. I heard a few shouts, cries, and saw a woman hold up her forearm, pinpricked with blood in four places. She looked at him fearfully, but Anselmo did not take his eyes off of me. "No one move," he said, but he barely got the words out before screams tore through the restaurant and panic flooded in.

People broke and ran, and only a small part of me was surprised it took that long. Anselmo blinked, casting his gaze around as the panic rose. I watched a Hmong man wearing a polo scoop up two toddlers, one under each arm, and flee, bent low, a raven-haired woman I took to be his significant other close behind him with a baby in her arms. They kept the line of booths between them and Anselmo; very wisely, I thought. I watched a few others following their example.

The family closest to Anselmo was a couple with a girl that was probably ten, and they seemed to have fallen into a state of catatonia, of panic turned to paralysis. The father held his fork six inches from his mouth, though now it was shaking so hard that the chicken he'd had speared on it was splattered on the table, lying in a little pool of its own sauce. His wife and daughter sat across from him with twin looks of horror matching each other almost as closely as their auburn hair.

"You," Anselmo said, addressing the man as the cacophony of the exodus raged around him. "What is your name?"

The man put his shaking fork down with a clatter. "Duane," he said, and his voice matched the fork, the pitch leaping all over the place.

"What is your daughter's name, Duane?" Anselmo asked.

Duane's head swiveled slowly, robotically, as though he were articulated by gears that ratcheted into place one tooth at a time. His head turned two clicks to rest on his daughter, whose mouth hung open just an inch. Her hands were on the table, shaking, no plate before her.

"What is her name, Duane?" Anselmo asked, so calm, so pleasant, like he was standing over a family dinner table making conversation. "Tell me, or I shall snap her neck as though I were cracking one of these crab legs." He reached down and delicately picked one up from Duane's plate and *snap!* broke it, sending tiny shards of carapace into the air.

"C-c-Clarissa," Duane said, not taking his eyes off his daughter.

I started to move but Anselmo held up a hand to stay me. "Do not." Anselmo's eyes gleamed. "Clarice," he said in that thick Italian accent, somehow mangling the name and turning it more lovely all at once. Duane did not correct him. "It is a beautiful name. Did it take you long to have your Clarice?" Anselmo's eyes narrowed, showing me veined scars on his eyelids. "Was she an accident?"

"Not—an accident—no," Duane said, between breaths. He sounded like he was starting to hyperventilate. "And no, not—long."

"She is important to you, yes?" Anselmo asked, taking another step forward. His scarred hand came down slowly, gently, on the back of Clarissa's neck, and I tensed, my fists clenching. He waited for Duane to nod. "You wanted to have a child. It was planned."

"Yes," Duane said, and how he let out a high rasp, nearing complete panic. I couldn't see his face because he was looking at Anselmo, but I could imagine the pain, the fear, that had to be written across it by now.

"I am certain you enjoyed your many, many attempts to have her," Anselmo said. "What would do if someone took away something you wanted?" His fingers kneaded the back of Clarissa's neck soothingly. Clarissa's eyes were riveted downward, at the table, and then they closed as I watched a tear streak down her pale, freckled cheek. "She represents … years of time invested, yes? You have loved her, poured your life and effort into her, cared for her, nurtured her?" Anselmo drew a steady breath and looked right at me. "What would you do if someone put to death all that you had labored so hard for? If someone came along and ripped from your very hand everything you wanted?"

"I—I –" Duane's voice became a keening sound, only an octave lower than a wail, and I judged him seconds from a panic attack.

"Leave her alone, Anselmo," I said, feeling the bitter plunge of guilt right to the ground floor—in this case, my guts. It was an icy sensation, and I wasn't far from panic myself. "Your quarrel is with me and Sienna."

"I have no quarrel with your sister," Anselmo said, massaging the back of Clarissa's neck. "My quarrel with her is done." He lifted his other hand and pointed a finger at me, and there was a pit between his first and second knuckles like a blister had popped and never healed. "My quarrel with you, on the other hand, has yet to come to a similar close."

"What do you want, Anselmo?" I asked. Perspiration welled up on my palms, making my fingers slick as I held my balled-up fists together.

"I want to hurt you, of course," Anselmo said, quiet, not breaking off his gaze from me. "To make you suffer." There was very little menace in the way he said it, so simple a statement of fact. From anyone else it might have meant nothing, a declaration with as little power behind it as carried in a wind-up toy.

From Anselmo, it felt like it had the power of a hurricane. He was loud by nature, boisterous and swaggering, full of life and energy even now, in his questioning of Duane as he used Clarissa as a prop in his little drama. "You know," I said, "Ricardo Montalbán said that a lot better in *Wrath of Khan*. But then, you've always been a second-rate villain."

Anselmo smiled, and if possible, this made him look even worse. He leaned in close to Clarissa, and I watched her shudder as he brought his deformed cheek within inches of hers, never breaking his gaze with me, predator to presumed prey. "I am no villain. I was to be a god." He took his fingers from Clarissa's neck as he straightened up, smile disappearing as rage filled his eyes and coldness knotted his rasping voice. "Do you know what gods do to those who defy them?" He waved a hand magnanimously toward Duane. "You should leave. She does not need to see what is about to happen." There was a brief pause, then Anselmo looked straight at Duane. "Be a man, not a coward. Get your daughter out of here."

That snapped Duane out of his rising panic and he clawed for Clarissa's hand as the girl's mother slid out of the freestanding booth on the aisle opposite the one where Anselmo and I were facing off. She wrapped her arms around Clarissa and pushed her forward as Duane's face, a panicked sheet of white interrupted by a black hole where his mouth hung open while he gasped for breath while running away, followed behind. I'm sure Duane's body was following, but honestly, his face was all that I remember seeing as he retreated.

"Thank you," I said to Anselmo as we stood there.

He cocked his head at me and regarded me with something on the measure of disgust. "For what? You think I would hurt the girl?" He made a sound like a furious bull.

"You are a depraved and sickening creature, and my revenge on you will punish you for all the affronts you have leveled against me, starting with—"

I'm sure Anselmo would have kept talking, but a rock twice the size of his head zoomed out from behind the booth next to him and hit him squarely in the face. It shattered into pieces as it struck, clearly meeting an object stronger than it. Another followed, sending Anselmo rocketing into the booth Clarissa's family had been occupying only moments earlier, shards from the impact showering me as I rushed to cover my face.

"I know y'all forgot I was here," Augustus said from behind me, "but I feel like I should take an active part in this conversation."

"Didn't forget you," I said as I raised my hands, "just didn't know how much use you'd be in the middle of a restaurant without an ounce of dirt in sight."

"Oh, there's plenty of dirt," Augustus said, leaping onto the table behind me. "But I figured against a guy who's pretty much invulnerable, I might borrow a few of these loose rocks from the koi pond out front before I start resorting to the dirty tricks."

"'Dirty tricks'?" I asked. "Funny."

"Huh?" Augustus asked. "Oh. You people and your puns—"

"'You people'?" I threw back at him.

Anselmo came up from behind the table by throwing it at us, and I had to duck to avoid decapitation. The throw was rough, and the wooden support that affixed the table's base to its top hit me with a glancing blow as it flew past. I heard Augustus making an *oof!*-ing sound behind me, and knew he'd not been quite as artful a dodger as I had.

I was barely straightened back up when I saw Anselmo charging toward me. I threw my hands out and summoned the winds at my disposal. Over three years ago when I'd first faced off against Anselmo, he'd been insanely strong and possessed of near-invulnerability. In fact, I'd never actually beaten him, not really. I'd made him run, I'd hurt him in a couple different ways, but I'd never really beaten him. Sienna had beaten him. Just like she had everyone else.

But I'd had three years to practice my skills while Anselmo probably hadn't put an ounce of effort into anything but sitting around, being a giant, throbbing penis. I'll give Sienna credit for this: training was important. Vitally important. And no one had realized this like her. She'd had these giant, industrial fans installed in our facility when it was rebuilt, and I'd spent every day for the last six months building up my strength until I could reverse the currents within them. For the Reed that faced Anselmo Serafini three years ago, this would have impossible, right up there with the idea of flying through the streets of New York City.

Which is why when I hit him with the focused gust of air I summoned up as he leapt at me, it caught him mid jump and hurled him twenty-five feet into the wall behind him.

Beige-white wallpaper broke as Anselmo smashed through it and disappeared into a hole the size of a door. I didn't harbor any belief that this would be the end for him, though, and so I moved swiftly as I could as soon as I saw him vanish into the cloud of dust and darkness.

"Augustus!" I shouted, swiveling to look behind me. Augustus popped up, holding the side of his head. I could see a little blood in his short-cropped hair, dripping down his shoulder and onto the white shirt beneath his suit jacket. "You all right?"

He cringed, rocking his head left to right on his neck as though he were testing it out. "Barely got me. I'm good."

I spun back and saw one of the waiters hiding fearfully almost twenty feet from me, ducked behind one of the wooden pillars that stood at the back of a booth where there was no other to meet it. I could see one of his eyes peeking from behind cover, astonishment and fear mingling on his features as he alternated his glance between me and the giant hole I'd just put in the wall by flinging Anselmo through it.

I advanced on the hole in the wall, hands out defensively, until I could see into the space behind the wall. It was certainly dark, but looked like an empty shopfront, with light streaming in through windows in the distance. I heard the shattering of glass and watched one of them, almost two hundred feet away, break into pieces as the colored paint with the foot-tall "GOING OUT OF BUSINESS" message fell to the ground and broke. "I will see you again soon, Reed," Anselmo called from across the space between us. "Consider well how I might be using the intervening time to prepare my revenge."

With that, Anselmo leapt out the window and disappeared at a run. I watched him go, pretty sure I couldn't catch him and equally certain that chasing after him unprepared would result in very bad things for me more than him.

"He's getting away," Augustus said from just behind me. He made to shove past, but I held him back.

"We're not ready," I said, feeling that queasy, icy sensation in my gut. "And he can outrun us both." I was already reaching for my cell phone and dialing a number I knew by heart. "He's already gone."

"You just going to let him go?" Augustus asked, fingers tense on my shoulder. I got the feeling he still wanted to push past me and go into hot pursuit.

I didn't answer him; I just waited for the voice at the other end of the line as my cell phone trilled in my ear. When Andrew Phillips picked up, I didn't even wait for him to get out more than a syllable before I spoke. "Anselmo Serafini is back in town. We need to add a manhunt for him because, unless I miss my guess ... he's here to cause some havoc."

15.

Sienna

There was cool liquid seeping through my shirt as I awoke, a rude awakening if ever there was one. Faces swam into view above me and I took a sputtering breath, my head hard against the floor. It wasn't the first time I'd woken up on the floor, not by any means, but it was the first time I'd done so on the floor of a bar a long damned way from home.

Jake and Brant were on either side of me, faces heavy with concern. Just above me, upside down but much more neutral about the whole thing, was Sarah, who looked just about the same when she realized I was awake as she had a few minutes earlier sitting at the bar.

"Can you hear me?" Sarah asked, calm and collected, like this was a thing that happened all the time. For all I knew, it did.

"Hear you, see you, smell the martini on your breath," I said, lurching up to sitting position while the three of them gave way for me to do so. "You know what I'd like to hear, though?"

"Postmodern Jukebox do some Sinatra?" Brant asked innocently. "I feel like they'd knock it out of the park, really. Just a fantasy I have."

"That wouldn't be very postmodern," I said, focusing on the bar beyond the three of them. "And no. I mean, yes, it would be amazing, but not right now. I want to hear someone start spilling their guts about what's happening to me here."

Sarah regarded me as coolly as ever, while Brant and Jake exchanged a look. Brant ended up speaking first. "What do you think is happening here?"

"I think someone is messing with my mind," I said, getting to my feet. Cool drops of my drink slid their way down my belly under my shirt. "A telepath."

"Uhh ... can't say I have much experience with telepaths," Jake said, probably trying to sound reassuring. "Are you certain you're not just ... overworked or something? We tend to get a lot of folks that have trouble unwinding when they first get here."

That brought a stock-still quiet, and I looked past them to see that the place had cleared out, that we were the only ones left in Shorty's. "Where's the lawman?"

"You talking about Z?" Brant asked, looking toward the door. "He left a while ago."

"Z?" I asked, looking around the bar. "Please tell me his middle name is also Z, and his last name is Top."

"Hah," Brant said, pointing a finger at me. "Good one. No, his name is Zebulon Darwin, so people call him Z." He looked toward the door nervously. "Uhh, you want me to call him back over? He's probably off for the rest of the night."

"Does that mean if I dial 911, he'll show up sometime tomorrow morning?" I asked, brushing past Jake to head for the door. I went down the ramp and burst out of Shorty's into a torrential downpour. Rain fell from the sky in a steady flow, and my hair was soaked two seconds after I got out there. The little overhang of Shorty's roof did nothing to stop the hard-blown rain from blasting me like it had been turned loose from an elephant shower.

"Aww, you didn't need to go out in this," Brant said from a few steps behind me as I stood on the edge of the sidewalk, staring up and down the street.

"Sienna, it's got to be forty degrees out here," Sarah called from just inside the door. I looked back to see her silhouetted in the entry to the bar and did a double take because she looked oddly familiar. My eyes pierced the veil of light that cast her in shadow, and I realized it was just Sarah, truly her, yelling to overcome the sound of the rain hammering the sidewalk and rooftops around us with deafening sound.

"Hey," Jake said, and he laid a reassuring hand on my elbow. He'd ventured farther out than the other two, with Sarah still lurking in the entryway and Brant only a couple steps out of the bar, blanching at the dousing he was receiving. I felt the rain patter on my head, soak my shirt, my pants, my skin, and I didn't care. "Come back inside," he said.

"I don't like this," I said, staring back down the darkened street. I couldn't even see the clouds above, and an artificial night had set in, because I knew for a fact that if it hadn't been raining, the high-summer sun would still have been shedding its light in the sky.

"It's some pretty crap weather," Jake agreed, not realizing that wasn't what I was talking about. "All the more reason to go back into the bar."

The visibility was so poor I couldn't even see the dock at the end of the street. A curtain of rain cut off my view of the world about thirty feet away. "Not that," I said. "I'm talking about this thing that's being done to me."

"I don't really know anything about what you're going through," Jake said, stepping to where I could see him, standing there in the freezing cold downpour, looking desperately uncomfortable, "but I don't think you're going to solve it by standing out in this mess, catching your death."

I snorted. "Only mothers say 'catch your death.'"

Jake smiled. "You've met my wife. Which of us do you think is the most maternal?" My stony resolve broke under the light laugh I let go at that, and I shivered at the chill.

"Come back inside," Jake said. "We'll talk about it if you want."

I cast my eyes once more around the town, wondering where Z had gone. I could feel the sense of paranoia start to settle in, that desire to run through town and grab hold of everyone, shaking each of them while questioning them about what was happening, as though the physical act of rustling them like a dirty carpet would loose the dirt they were hiding. I questioned whether I was crazy to even still be here, talking to Brant, Jake and Sarah. They could have been involved in this psychological warfare exercise, after all. They could have been the key players for all I knew.

I pulled lightly against Jake's hand on my elbow. He wasn't maintaining much of a hold, so I slipped free without even trying. He didn't attempt to grasp me again, just stood there. "Come inside," he asked once again, gently. My suspicious nature warred with my desire to talk to someone, anyone, to not be … alone, in a cabin, by myself, while this … whatever this was … was going on.

"All right," I said and followed him back toward the bar. It wasn't as though I was in any real peril. Not yet, anyway.

Besides, at least now I knew what I was dealing with. A telepath. And when I got my full strength back with my other souls tomorrow, I was going to track them down and crack their skull open like an egg for messing with me. Then maybe I'd get back to this business of vacation, all fun and fancy free. Or something like that. Because it was still me, after all.

16.

Reed

When Andrew Phillips came driving up in his company car, I'll admit I had to stifle a little bit of a grin. As I've said before, I like the guy, but about nine months earlier Sienna had destroyed the agency director's car while fending off a terrorist attack, and the replacement was, uh, tied up in budgetary issues. Phillips had made his fair share of enemies in his short tenure at the agency, and while I didn't count myself as one of them, Ariadne Fraser, our head of finance, clearly did.

So, for now, Andrew Phillips, on the rare occasions he needed to leave the agency campus for work reasons, had been assigned a Volkswagen Beetle. Not a normal government car by any means, but the motor pool had assured him that it was well-treated and normally used for surveillance work when we needed something nondescript. It was low mileage, probably the lowest mileage vehicle we had in the motor pool, and since we'd had the aforementioned budgetary issues and no one else had surrendered their car, Phillips was kind of stuck. He could have demanded someone give up their SUV or he could have pitched a fit and looked like an ass. He'd chosen the more politically astute move of simply going with the flow and had not complained about it, as I suspect more than one person in his position might have done.

Oh, and this particular car? It was orange. I didn't even know they made them in this shade of orange/brown, which I would characterize as a burnt sienna (no pun intended). Apparently when the agency bought it, we were aiming for the 'hide in plain sight' style of surveillance.

Phillips came squealing to a stop in the middle of the crime scene, lights mounted in his front window flashing. Credit where it was due, he'd driven himself (because a budget for a chauffeur also got, uh … lost) and when he levered his tall frame out of the small car, he stretched. I was sure the drive hadn't been all that pleasant, especially since rush hour was still going on. The Beetle looked way out of place in the middle of all the cop cars and ambulances and fire trucks.

"What's going on, Harry Dresden?" I quipped as Phillips stalked over to me. He had a pretty neutral expression most of the time, calm just this side of thunderclouds drifting over his brow.

Phillips came at me full steam, stopping just short of running into me. I guess he was in a hurry. "What the hell is going on here?" he asked, voice clear but not very pleasant.

"Anselmo Serafini is back in town," I said, though I knew he already had this tidbit of information. "He attacked us while we were eating dinner."

"That doesn't answer my question," Phillips said, leaning forward. "What the hell is happening here?"

"It's a crime scene," I said, after taking everything in. "There were witnesses, some minor injuries—"

"And you started a manhunt for him," Phillips said, and at this I caught a flash of anger in his eyes.

"I'm sorry," I said, "I guess I could have waited for you to give the approval—"

"Do you realize how incompetent this makes us look?" Phillips asked, folding his arms in front of him. The storm clouds were gathering over his head now. "This is the one who got away, and in addition to the incident at the airport earlier, it makes us look like we're complete boobs."

"Serafini is a serious threat," I said, shrugging my shoulders. "I couldn't just ignore the fact that we had a very obvious sighting of him here in our backyard—"

"Have you ever heard of anyone on the FBI's Ten Most Wanted list walking into a bar in Washington, D.C. and smacking around a couple of their agents?" Phillips asked, surveying the scene briefly before letting his gaze fall back on me. "Of course you haven't. Because it doesn't happen. And if it did, the criminal in question damned sure wouldn't have gotten away afterward!" He raised his voice loud enough to include several other people in the immediate vicinity in our conversation. I glanced behind me and saw Augustus looking over at me from where he was talking to one of the local cops. He raised an eyebrow at me and I quickly looked away, back to Phillips, whose face was slightly red.

"Well, if the FBI had as one of their nemeses a guy who could shrug off bullets like some of us ignore parking citations," I said, "maybe that would happen more often. It's not like I could just shoot Serafini and be done with the problem."

I could see Phillips chafing under that argument, like he wanted to burst free and fight it out some more. "Where did he go?"

"I've got J.J. working the traffic and other surveillance cameras in the area," I said, "but it looks like he found a gap in them and waltzed off." That was true, and Anselmo had done it very quickly after making it out of the empty storefront, almost like he was being guided by someone who knew where the cameras were located. "I doubt we're going to find anything."

Phillips watched me carefully. "You think he has help."

I nodded. "I think he's working with the Brain, the one who masterminded the Federal Reserve heist and the subsequent jailbreak. Probably Eric Simmons, too, because we've had zero notice on either of them since they disappeared in January. That just doesn't happen in the modern world. Everyone leaves an electronic trail—whether it's on cameras or some other way. Someone's covering for these guys, helping them escape our notice."

"Making us look like idiots," Phillips said, tearing slightly looser of the restraint he'd shown before. "What's Anselmo's game?"

"Axe to grind with me or us," I said, shaking my head, a little more casual now that Phillips was pointing his irritation elsewhere. I frowned, remembering something he'd said. "He said his quarrel with Sienna was done." I scratched my hairline on my right temple, where a little itch was starting. I hadn't really thought about this after he'd said it, but now that I was, I started to feel a little uneasy.

"Done how?" Phillips asked, still sweeping the scene with his eyes. His faint blondish hair was being turned red and then blue by all the flashing lights.

"I don't know," I said, shaking my head. "I have a hard time imagining he's done anything to her." I started to feel nervous, then dropped it. Sienna could beat the living crap out of Anselmo with one hand tied behind her back. Maybe both.

Phillip's eyes were heavily lidded. He looked tired. "Might want to warn her, in case he's got ill intent."

"I can't imagine Anselmo ever having good intent," I said and started to walk away, fumbling for my phone.

"Get back to the agency when you're done," Phillips said, tossing the order after me. I turned and watched him beeline for the police commander, who was talking with the fire commander on scene. He didn't follow up on it, and part of me wondered why he'd bothered with it at all.

"Whatever," I muttered to myself. I'd head back to the agency, all right, because there wasn't any point in just standing around in the north metro waiting for something to happen. Besides, now that rush hour was over, I could be here in half an hour, tops, if anything went awry during the night.

I looked at the screen on my phone as I walked back toward the car, making a gesture for Augustus to follow me. He disentangled himself from conversation with the cop he'd been talking to and threaded his way through the crowd toward me as I pushed the button to call someone who I hadn't actively called in several months. I listened to as it went straight to voicemail.

I pulled the phone away from my ear and stared at the screen that flashed "Sienna Nealon." She was up north, and that meant shoddy phone reception, right? It was perfectly normal. And she was a big girl, she could take care of herself. A villain like Anselmo had way, way more to fear from her than she did from him.

"What's up?" Augustus asked as he fell in beside me. I headed toward my car, but slowly, hesitant, mulling everything over in my mind.

"Probably nothing," I said and hit redial. The phone rang went straight to voicemail once again. My hand went back to my hairline, to that same itch, and this time I found a little, lonely bead of sweat waiting. I rubbed it back into my hair as I put away my phone, letting it drop into my pocket like a ten ton weight that threatened to drag me down. "Hopefully nothing," I amended, and picked up the pace back to my car. "Hopefully nothing at all."

17.

Sienna

Brant got me another drink, which I took a quick swill of as soon as it was in my hands. I swished the sweet, fruity flavor around in my mouth, let it permeate my taste buds and waft up into my nose where it lingered before I dropped it down my throat into my wildly fluttering stomach below. It did not seem to put that particular part of me at ease with its arrival.

I sat on the stool with Sarah watching me carefully from one side while Jake drank his beer on the other as he studiously tried to avoid looking at me, both of them acting in the oddest sort of concert to ignore me and pay attention to me all at once. They were a strange couple, I thought, but probably well matched.

I took another drink.

"So," Brant said, looking over the now-empty bar before letting his eyes settle on me, "do you want to talk about it?"

"Not much to say." I took a sip this time. My nerves needed soothing. Work, alcohol, work, damn you. "I'm done with passively sitting back and waiting for this jackass to show himself."

Brant paused, and looked uncertain when he spoke again. "How do you know it's a him?"

"When it comes to villainy," I said, "it's usually a him. When the stats start to shift in the other direction, I'll start to assume it's a she when things go wrong for me."

"Oh," Brant said, "well, okay then. So long as you don't think it's me."

"It's someone close by," I said. "They're here on the island if they're monkeying with my head." I took another drink. "And tomorrow, I'm going to find them, and commence to skinning them for the rest of my vacation. In fact, I may need to take some additional time off just to do the job properly."

"You could just take them to a taxidermist back on the mainland," Jake said, smirking slightly. "Probably get the job done quicker. Or slower, since it sounds like you might be aiming for that."

"I don't get it," Sarah said, shrugging, finally pulling her gaze away from me and having a drink of her martini. "You're some sort of über-hero. Aren't you used to people trying things like this with you?"

"No," I said. "I tend to send a very strong message against messing with me. People are mostly smart enough to avoid it, and it's because they know that people who try it always come to a bad end." Say what you want about my YouTube videos; they mostly got people to steer wide away from me.

"Sounds lonely," Jake said, picking up his beer.

"It's not so—" I stopped. I'd started to say it wasn't so bad, but … "It's all right," I said, still not very convincingly. I had …

I blinked. What did I have? My privacy? Hah. I'd been exploited and betrayed on national television for ratings. Tabloids paid for scoops on me, ninety percent of which weren't based even loosely on fact. Friends? Lulz. They were all pretty much gone, except for Ariadne, who I kept at a distance, and Augustus, my new best buddy—who was more of a co-worker. Romance? I'd had a couple of one night stands in the last year or so, but that didn't exactly qualify as romance.

Hell, my last boyfriend didn't even remember that we dated. That one was my fault, but still.

"You all right over there?" Jake asked, and I turned to see him looking at me, concern in his dark eyes.

"I'm fine." I smiled faintly. "At least I've got my health." I could see the shared looks around me, but I just didn't have it in me to argue at the moment.

I picked up the glass and took another drink, hoping that maybe after a few more I'd bury this sense of growing unease, and maybe—just maybe—start to enjoy my time off.

18.

Reed

Augustus and I came out of the top floor elevator in the agency with a destination in mind. We cut through the cubicle farm like men on a mission, like Tommy Lee Jones and Will Smith (but without the sunglasses) and headed straight for the only man that could help us.

Also, I think I'm funnier than Tommy Lee Jones.

"Well, well, well," J.J. said, spinning slowly around in his chair to face us with his fingers steepled, "if it isn't the most improbable pairing I've seen since Wailord and Skitty."

I stopped just inside J.J.'s cubicle. "I need—what the hell did you just say?"

"It's a Pokémon thing," Augustus said. "Don't even ask."

"Right," I said, looking back to J.J. "I need help tracking fugitives."

"I know, I know," J.J. said and spun back to his computer, which had a live surveillance feed from the elevator banks pulled up in the corner. Huh. So that was how he knew to spin around like that and do his little intro. "But I got problems, man. I can't get the cameras of the world to eat out of my palm like they used to, at least not around the area where your friend Mr. Serafini is. There were just a few outages in critical places, enough to mask him from me. I can't see where he came from or where he went."

"How does that even happen?" I asked, taking a few steps forward and leaning over to look at his screen, which was pointless because the only thing I understood on it was the live feed from the camera back at the elevators.

J.J. typed some gibberish into a small black box, then hit enter. I watched it disappear. "I'd tell you I don't know, but we both know I do. Anselmo's got a guide, and she's pretty damned good. She's barely having to do any work to steer him clear of the monitors that are out there, and she's shutting down the few cameras that she needs to in order to help him evade." J.J. shrugged. "I can't even get a good read on where she's coming from yet, because her IP addresses are being masked. I'm getting everything here; she could be in Austin, Texas, Melbourne, Florida, Calabasas, California, Billings, Montana—"

"Okay," I said, trying to cut him off before he listed every municipality in the U.S. "What can you tell me?"

J.J. froze. "Who said I could tell you anything?" He did not look up.

"That's like an admission of guilt," Augustus said. "Why don't you confess now?"

"Well, I didn't do anything wrong," J.J. said quickly, "but I might have pursued some of those IP addresses to see what other traffic was generated from them, and I might maybe have discovered an email address that's coupled with them." He looked a little guilty. "And I might have hacked said email address and looked at what had been sent out—"

"You're allowed to do that," I said a little dryly, "we're the government."

"Well," J.J. said and tapped on his keyboard to bring up something in his browser. "I'll spare you reading all these emails in the 'Sent' box, because I've already parsed them and basically they're variations on a theme—this so-called 'Brain', as we've gotten to know her, has been feeding every major news network and gossip rag in the U.S. stories about Sienna that are … well, they're pretty much calculated to make her

110

look like crap."

"She doesn't need help," I said. I started to fumble for my phone. "Which reminds me, I need you to find Sienna for me."

"That's easy," J.J. said. "But seriously?" He clicked on one of those emails on his screen. "This is a smear campaign. Some of this stuff is taken out of context just to make her look bad, some of it's demonstrably false, and the rest is just … well …"

"True?" I asked, letting out a sigh. I felt suddenly like J.J. had drained the energy out of me.

"You could be a little more supportive of your sister," Augustus said.

"Some of it's true," J.J. said, "but it's slanted like an old church roof."

"Yeah," I said, and stood up, rubbing at my eyes. "Okay. Can you give me a location on Sienna's cell phone?"

"Hmm," J.J. said and messed around with his computer for a minute, opening up a program. "Looks like it's offline at the moment."

"Figures," I said, sighing. "She's gone off the grid."

"Well, wouldn't you?" J.J. asked, spinning his chair around to face me. "After what happened?"

"No," I snapped. "I wouldn't." I ignored the gnawing sense of doubt I felt in the pit of my stomach. She was fine. She'd just turned her cell phone off because she didn't want to even deal with the remote possibility that Andrew Phillips might call her back to work for an emergency. Not that he would. The suspension was pretty damned set in stone.

"I would," J.J. said. "I wouldn't answer anyone's phone calls, not even yours, bro."

"Hell no," Augustus agreed, "I'd thunder my ass out of here like a herd of buffalo."

I shot him a look that said he was not helping.

"All right, well," I said. "Would you mind tracking her down by her hotel reservations and giving her a call?"

J.J. shrugged, spun back, and fiddled for a minute. "She's staying at a cabin place on Bayscape Island. I've got the phone number here, but it says the office is closed outside of certain hours."

"Did you pull that out of her email?" Augustus asked, looking alarmed. "I am not using the company email to make my plans, that is for sure."

J.J. clicked his mouse, and the sound of a phone ringing filled the cubicle. It rang four times before a female voice answered with a recorded message. "You have reached Bayscape Cabin Rentals. Our office is currently closed ..."

"No love there," J.J. said, and clicked to an alternate screen. He shrugged. "I got nothing. How urgent is this? You want me to leave a message?"

"Yeah, tell them to tell her to call us," I said, and started away. "Maybe inform local law enforcement she might be in danger, too? Tell them we've had a credible threat against her. Nothing too urgent, just ... let her know to be on the lookout because Anselmo Serafini threatened her."

"You think the man's bitter because she ruined his rugged good looks?" J.J. asked. His eyes flitted about as he considered that. "Of course he is. Never mind. Rescinding the question."

"Just make sure you get the message sent," I said, and started to leave J.J.'s cubicle behind. I checked my phone as I walked to the elevators, listening to the ding as I pressed the button to find the one I'd ridden up was still here, waiting for me.

"Where are you going?" Augustus asked. He was walking a little slower, his fatigue showing. I understood that; it had been kind of a long day.

"There's a place in Eden Prairie I go to sometimes," I said. "It'll put us closer to the cities in case something breaks with either Cunningham or Serafini, and the bartender there is a friend of mine."

"Nice," Augustus said. "Fifty people die at the airport this afternoon, your personal nemesis comes to town vowing revenge, your sister is one of his targets and she ain't answering her phone, but you want to go to the bar." His hand came up and he smacked himself in the forehead. He was probably going for a theatrical thing, but my guess was he'd forgotten he had meta strength, because he looked like he'd over done it by the way he blinked his eyes. "Well … I was going to say your actions didn't seem all that bright, but since I just humiliated myself that way, I guess I'll reserve judgment."

I chuckled. "You'll get used to the powers. Come on," I put a hand on his shoulder and steered him into the elevator, "there's nothing else we need to be doing at the moment. Let's blow off a little steam while we wait for something to happen."

19.

I strolled into my favorite bar like I owned the place, Augustus following a little more cautiously behind. He looked like a good stiff drink would put him out, so I vowed to make sure he took it easy tonight, because who knew if Benjamin Cunningham was going to make an ass of himself in the middle of the night? I might end up needing Augustus's help, and him being tanked wasn't going to be of much help, that was for sure.

I bellied up to the bar, dodging around the wooden tables and ignoring the bright pink and blue neon that gave the place one of the strangest color palettes I'd ever seen in a bar. It wasn't exactly a working man's joint, that was for sure. Being in Eden Prairie, it tended to cater mostly to the yuppie crowd, young singles and marrieds that were looking for a little action in their evening but didn't want to brave the drive to join the downtown scene in Minneapolis.

I understood that desire. Downtown was a zoo. This was more like a petting zoo. But, uh, with a lot less petting. Then again, I thought as I looked at a young couple lip-locked a few tables away from the bar, maybe not.

"Charles, my good man," I said as I plopped down on a stool directly in front of the big, shiny, oaken bar, "a round for me and my friend."

The bartender, Charles, had a dark beard and dark, long hair wrapped in a ponytail behind his head. He was wearing all black, as was appropriate for a bartender in this place, and he nodded to me with a friendly smile. "Coming right up. What do you want, Reed's friend?" he asked Augustus.

Augustus got up on his stool a little more cautiously. "Diet Coke," he said, and then looked at me. "Reed's friend isn't twenty-one yet."

Charles grimaced. "Got it. No liquor for this man." He looked to me. "Whiskey and Coke for you, and a Coke and Diet for your friend, coming up."

"Gracias, Charles," I said and spun my stool in a slow roll so I could see the rest of the bar real fast. Place was mostly empty, as it tended to be in the evenings on weeknights. Weekends it got a little nuts, but during the week I had a feeling they broke even at best on their burgers and beers. "So ... what you think?" I asked Augustus.

"I think it's been a long day," Augustus said, not spinning to join me. I leaned against the bar while he sat hunched over it like an old-timer protecting his booze. Which he did not have any of. "And I think this is a peculiar way to end it, given we've got two threats rolling around that we haven't tracked down and we still haven't been able to get ahold of your sister."

"Sienna's going to be fine," I said, more sure of it by the minute. "We're talking about a woman who killed like fifty armed mercenaries and several metas when she had no powers at all. I know for a fact she has her gun with her, and she's got all her powers, so I seriously doubt that Anselmo has done anything to her. If he had, he would have been a lot more vocal and obvious about it." I felt my expression turn more serious. "That's not the sort of gloat that Anselmo would pass up on."

"I guess you'd know your arch-nemesis best," Augustus said as Charles came by with his Diet Coke and set it in front of him.

"Anselmo's not my ..." I paused. "Huh. I guess maybe he is my arch nemesis."

"Good to know someone's still got an arch nemesis around here," Augustus said, a little glumly.

"Yours got killed, right?" I asked as Charles put a cool tumbler of Jack and Coke in my waiting hand. I didn't even turn back to the bar to look, just felt it slide right into the open hand I had waiting for it. It looked cool, like it was something that happened all the time. Which it did. Charles and I had a rhythm, we were simpatico.

"Edward Cavanagh?" Augustus asked. "Died in jail. Coroner ruled it a stroke."

"You don't sound convinced."

Augustus took a sip from his drink out of a straw. "Man was healthy as a horse, worked out, just got his meta powers. You're telling me he strokes out at the age of forty-five on the day he goes down for a crime? And just leaves ten thousand questions unanswered?" He shook his head. "Smells wrong."

"Hm," I said, shrugging my shoulders. "Still. You had your nemesis, and you didn't kill him. Points to you for that." I took a swig. "Unlike others 'round here."

"You keep talking that passive-aggressive crap," Augustus said, suddenly heated. "Why don't you just give voice to your sister issues instead of just making snippy little comments all the time?"

"Okay, fine," I said, setting my drink on the bar. The place smelled of booze, and the scent of the musky drink combined with the sweet Coke was a wonderful tonic that oozed into my nasal passages but didn't quite erase the smell of burned flesh that still hung on me from the airport earlier. "At least you didn't kill your villain, unlike my sister, who has killed more people than George R.R. Martin and Joss Whedon combined."

"You're still aching over the death of Wash, huh?" Augustus deadpanned, taking a drink from the straw.

"Always," I said, letting the bitterness fly. "And I'm still bitter over the fact that I've been supporting someone over the last few years that I thought was just trying to do the right thing. She wasn't. She was … enjoying herself the whole time, I think. On some level, she gets off on killing people. It satisfies her soul, if you can call what she has one." I shook my head. "And that's not even the worst of what she's done. Do you know what she did to her last boyfriend?"

Augustus sat his drink on the bar coolly and then turned his barstool around to physically face me, leaning one elbow on the white oak bar top, his whole manner reflecting his utter lack of energy. "How do you envision this playing out?"

"This what?" I asked, suddenly confused. "This manhunt?"

"This conversation," he said. "You brought me here to your little hidey hole, and before that we went out to your restaurant. Did you play it out in your head beforehand? Like we'd just sit here like bros, talking about women and life and eventually get on the topic of your sister, our boss, and you'd just … what?"

My face burned. "You asked, okay? You've been asking all day, in one form or another. Well, here we are, and now I'm spilling. You wanted to know my problems with Sienna? Here they are, simple as can be. Heart of the matter. Now you don't want to hear? Methinks you doth protest too much."

"Fancy way of saying I'm calling it out that I don't want to hear it while I lean in to catch a little more, right?" His face was set in stiff lines like a statue. "Let me help you with this: My name is not Elroy Patashnik, and my hobby is not encouraging white people. That'd be a full-time job around here, and I've got one of those already, plus school. You've got family drama problems that I don't want any part of, something bordering on the level of Hamlet." He gave me a knowing look. "So let's roll with this and stick with the example you've pulled out in your attempt to throw Shakespeare at my unknowing and youthful ass. 'The play's the thing wherein I'll catch the conscience of the king.' You remember that line?"

"Vaguely," I said, face still burning but now for maybe different reasons related to me feeling like I'd gotten called on being a smug, superior-ish ass.

"Hamlet tries to draw out his uncle's guilt," Augustus said, "by staging a play that mirrors the death of his father. Problem is, if your sister's like you say she is, she's got no conscience. Somewhere in your mind, you've equated her with a monster. She doesn't think, she doesn't feel like a normal person, she just killssssssss ..." He made it sound overly evil and dramatic. "Doesn't feel bad about it, doesn't worry that it makes her a more callous or hard person, doesn't worry about it at all, just ... murders away. That about cover your thesis?"

I let my mouth gape open while I tried to produce an answer. It took a few seconds. "Basically, yes."

"Okay, so," Augustus said, leaning toward me now, "here's how I see it. Girl saved the world. We all agree on that, right? In spite of what they say on TV, and although you could maybe argue she killed some folks that could have been dealt with slower and less 'expeditiously,' she saved the world, right?"

"Right," I said, tense. I got a hint of where this was going and I didn't love it. "I'll grant her that."

"So she saves the world," Augustus said, "then she gets dragged through the mud by the media, has that shit interview with Gail Roth, and people start leaving."

"Are you approaching a point or just listing out the chronology of her life?" I asked. "Because I was there for all this. I know what happened."

"I don't think you do," he said. "Because everyone left, didn't they? Except you and Ariadne? Everyone close to her? They either left or died?"

I thought about it. Zack, Breandan and her mother died. Kat, Dr. Zollers, and even Scott left—though there was more to that story, something horrifying that I was almost eager to share. "Yeah, okay. Almost everybody left. Sienna took it all right."

"Oh, no," Augustus said, "you *think* she did. And maybe she did for a while. But see, then, after all that, the one person she thought was always in her corner—well, he turned on her."

"Oh, bullshit," I said, rolling my eyes. I grabbed my glass off the bar and took a deep drink, downing the rest of it. "My sister's a rock, okay? She shows no signs of cracking. This violence she unleashes? That's who she is, at the core. She's a machine."

"It's like you don't know her at all," Augustus said. "Look, I'm not saying she hasn't killed people—"

"Good, because you'd lose that argument in about two seconds flat—"

"—I'm just saying she *feels*," Augustus said. "She feels it like a human being. She doesn't enjoy it like you think she would, like a psychopath would. She's taken this rift with you hard, harder than she lets on. She's taking this shit with Kat and with the press hard, too. She may not be the most social creature, but—"

"She was raised a hermit," I said, shaking my head. "This isolation is her preferred state of being."

"She didn't have a choice how she was raised," he said. "You think she would have chosen that? To be cut off from everybody?"

"Maybe not," I said with a shrug, "but she's choosing it now. She's comfortable with it."

"Girl's got the voice of multiple psychopaths and her first love stuck in her brain," he said, turning back to the bar. "She's never alone. And she's not with good company when she is by herself, you see what I'm saying?" He paused, thinking. "I try not to dwell on this too much, but I thought about something a few weeks ago, when I was home for Taneshia's birthday. When did you and Sienna fall out?"

"January," I said, spinning back around to the bar and

huddling over.

"When's her birthday?"

"March," I said, picking up the glass. The perspiration from the melting ice cubes fell over my fingers. "Why?"

"What'd she do for her birthday?" he asked.

"How the hell should I know?" I asked and then felt like some strongman had brought down a sledgehammer in one of those contests of strength. He landed it right on the inside of my belly, and my ill feelings shot straight up my esophagus so hard I had to swallow immediately before they overwhelmed me and choked me up on the spot. When I spoke again, I couldn't quite eliminate the huskiness from my voice. "I don't know."

"Yeah," he said, "I don't know either, but I'm guessing it was ... quiet."

Those feelings that threatened to overwhelm me, this sick sense of guilt, spread over me. "You're not arguing against her being a monster."

"She's twenty-three years old, man," Augustus said quietly. "She's got a weight like Atlas on her shoulders. She got confined and abused by her mother, she's been pummeled for years by strangers, had to kill people even when she didn't want to, been abandoned by friends, had everyone else she cared about ripped away one by one, and had her last living family member turn his back on her." He blew air out the side of his mouth as he shook his head. "You try making it out of that without letting the darkness touch you all over the place."

"Hey, guys," Charles said, stopping back by. "Get you some refills?"

"Not right now," I said, looking at my nearly-empty glass.

"What are you guys talking about?" Charles asked, peppy, and leaned in. "Your sister being a bitch again?"

I caught the look from Augustus and felt guiltier than ever. Shit. "Not right now, man," I said to Charles. "Can you just give us a few minutes?"

"Sure thing," he said, like it was no big deal. "I'll check back on you in a few minutes." He turned and went off down the bar to his next customers.

"Dude," Augustus said, more disappointed than angry, "you talk smack about your sister to a bartender? That's low."

I felt my cheeks burn scarlet again. "I vented to him, okay? He's my bartender."

"That's still low," Augustus said, and leaned down to finish the last of his drink with a slurp that rattled the ice. "That's a caterpillar with his legs cut off low."

"Maybe you're right," I said and slid the drink back from my fingers. I hadn't shared a civil moment with my sister in months. She'd been isolated, alone. If she wasn't an unfeeling monster, I'd been incredibly unfair to her, possibly driven her even deeper into her harsh shell. "Maybe I've been wrong about her all along."

"Damned right," he said and stood up as I lay cash on the bar to cover our tab. "Because I guarantee you, wherever she is, she ain't doing that shit to you."

20.

Sienna

"My brother is such an asshole," I said as Brant nodded, taking it all in. "Such. An. Asshole. Let me tell you ..."

21.

Benjamin

The day dawned glorious blue, the sky adorned with white, fluffy clouds that rolled slowly across the cerulean backdrop at a slow, steady clip. Benjamin could see them from out of his window as he awoke in his car, sleeping on the top floor of a parking garage, just one level below the roof. He'd chosen it because it was a medical device firm that had a big enough workforce to justify a full parking structure, but not enough of one to justify a night watchman. He'd driven by this place countless times, enough to know it was dead as a doornail at night.

Benjamin took a deep breath as he opened his eyes. The world of yesterday seemed very, very far away, so far away he was sure none of it had even really happened. His life was one of steady, boring predictability, after all, of routine and sequence, of work and home, of organized, tireless patterns that made him an effective employee and son.

Benjamin took another breath, then another. The air felt different. His window was cracked, letting a little morning chill seep in. It was invigorating. His back didn't even protest at the night spent in the car, and he felt ... good. Everything that had happened had clearly been a bad dream brought on by allergies and travel exhaustion. He'd just walked out of the airport overwhelmed by pet dander, clearly. The hours and hours of tears, of sneezing, had conspired to make him sickly. Perhaps he'd even picked up a fever along the way, sending him into a delirium. That had happened once before, a fever so high he'd needed to be admitted to the emergency room. He remembered the feeling of it, that sweating, sickly sensation that reality was operating at a heightened and unreal state.

Yes, he decided, that was what had happened. He'd been lucky to make it here. And so close to work, too. His office was just down the road, after all.

Benjamin took another pleasant breath and stepped out of the car. He walked to his trunk and popped it open, finding exactly what he expected—his suitcase—waiting for him.

It was going to be a much better day, he thought as he selected the first of his alternate changes of clothes from the top of the suitcase. Everything was neatly folded and put away carefully, strapped in so that even rough handling by baggage attendants couldn't have dislodged it easily. The TSA had made a mess of his suitcase once.

Benjamin saw a brief flash of red as he thought about that time, about finding the paper notice as he opened his suitcase to find everything shifted and pushed aside, his neatly folded clothes replete with lines and mess, the perfect creases lost to some ill-mannered lout's fumbling fingers—

Benjamin took another gulp of fresh air and latched on to the blue sky in the distance as he nodded while serenity returned. He picked up his dress shirt, his pants, his spare pair of shoes, his belt and socks, and zippered the suitcase shut behind him. Yes, today would be a better day. The air was clear and fresh, with none of that smoky scent he'd dreamed about during the night.

He almost started to whistle as he got back into his car to change for his day.

22.

Sienna

Blinking the sleep out of my bleary eyes, I awoke to the sound of gentle tapping. I stirred under a mountain of blankets, a sense of cotton stuffed in my mouth. I flicked my tongue around and realized that there actually wasn't any real cotton, but my mouth felt like it was dry as a dusty desert gulch, and my head felt like it had been repeatedly punched from the inside by an Atlas-type as he grew to explode from my skull. It gave me a moment's pause, wondering if maybe there had been some sort of truth to that old myth about Zeus's kids springing forth out of his skull. Then I remembered that he had lived to be a massive dick later on, so probably not.

That tapping came again and I lifted my hammering head to find myself in bed, at my cabin. The noise was coming from the door, light streaming in from the half-dozen windows around the cabin. I threw off my blankets and felt the morning air nip at my skin. It didn't do much for my headache unfortunately, and I drew the covers back around me as I fought my way out of bed and staggered to the door. I unlocked it and tore it open as I clutched the blankets around myself before realizing that I was still wearing my clothes from last night. "What?" I asked with more than a little irritation as I pulled the door out of the way. "Holy shit," I said as I took in the sight before me.

"I know," Brant said, deadpan as he stood on my doorstep, a small wax-paper bag in one hand, steaming cups of coffee borne in one of those recycled cardboard trays in the other, "I'm stunning in the morning, aren't I?"

"Not you, dumbass," I said, stepping past him and dropping my blankets on the linoleum entry as I walked outside. Snowflakes drifted around me, framed by an orange sun forcing its way through thick clouds.

"I bring you coffee and pastries to ease the passage of your hangover," he said, letting that slight accent peek through again, "and I get called a dumbass. Bartenders are so unappreciated."

"It's snowing," I lamented, standing beside him, looking up at the unyielding sky with a certain level of annoyance that registered below that which resulted when someone punched me in the face but above when a reporter said something nasty about me. "In September."

"That does happen here sometimes," Brant said, taking it all in with a steady nod. "But I have coffee and pastry in my attempt to appease the angry goddess, so maybe it'll all turn out all right?"

"Goddess?" I caught the humor in his look. "Well, that's a start. I knew I liked you for a reason. Come right on in." I stepped back inside and gestured toward the small table just to the left of the entry, a plain wooden thing that seated two. "Come, let us break bread together here in my meadhall or whatever."

Brant cackled. "And then, later, maybe we'll tackle this Grendel problem that has the whole town in an uproar."

"What did you bring for pastry?" I asked, suddenly ravenous in spite of the pounding head and dry mouth. "Donuts? Long Johns?"

"It's a kind of Romanian sweet bread, actually," Brant said. "Bakery here on the island does it." I was too hungover to hide my disappointment, but he took it in stride. "Trust me," he said. "Take a bite, you won't regret it."

"Does it have copious amounts of sugar and carbohydrates?" I asked, tearing off a little bit of it. It reminded me of one of those grocery-store pastries that came in a baker's pan and was suitable for probably five or six servings. Unless I got ahold of it, in which case it'd maybe last ten minutes. "Because those are the key ingredients for buying my love, and any food that doesn't have them automatically loses points in my estimation."

"I can guarantee the presence of both those things," Brant said, watching me take a bite. He revealed his nervousness as I chewed. "Verdict?"

"Guilty," I said, "and I sentence this pastry to be devoured whole, immediately." I tore off another strip and crammed it into my mouth, waiting until I got it down before taking a drink of the coffee, which was perfectly sweet and heavily creamy, just the way I like it. "You are a good bartender."

Brant bowed with a flourish. "I do try. And I had feeling you'd be in dire straits since I did have to bring you home in quite the state last night."

I looked around the cabin. "I notice you use the phrase 'home' somewhat loosely."

"Home is where you hang whatever you've got," he said, and then looked to the coat rack, where hung … nothing. "Uhhm … well. I guess it's not really your home, obviously."

"It's not bad, though," I said, shoving my last bite of the Romanian whatever into my mouth. I chewed slowly and when I finished swallowing, I studied Brant a little closer. "So, are you the lonely type looking for a friend, or were you just extremely bored this morning?"

"You probably didn't hear," Brant said a little glumly, "but they shut down the ferry due to the weather. So my business is going to be somewhat … spare this morning. Not that it would have been overflowing with busy-ness anyway. More like a placid-ness, I suppose, during the week …"

"No local customers?" I asked, sticking my fingers in the blinds next to my head and pulling them open enough to confirm that yes, it was still snowing, albeit gently.

"Not many people in this tourist town are going to get out today if there aren't any tourists," Brant said. "Sarah and Jake might be the exceptions, but everyone else will probably shut the doors and hunker down 'til the storm passes. They're predicting high winds and blizzard-like conditions, which, as I'm sure you know, is a real party-starter for most people. Just makes them want to get out and have a picnic."

"Ugh," I said, tipping up the coffee and letting it wash down my throat.

"What?" Brant sounded a little disappointed at my reaction. "I thought you were staying with us for a couple weeks anyway."

"I was planning to," I said, letting the coffee cup radiate its heat into my hand, "but with this telepath thing going on, I don't like to be confined. Freedom of movement is always a nice thing to have. Otherwise I start to feel trapped."

"You could always just fly off now, right?" Brant asked. "What with your powers being back?"

I blinked. I hadn't even thought of that. I reached down deep inside and whispered, *Gavrikov?*

I waited a moment. The seconds passed, and no answer came.

I was still without powers.

23.

"Sonofabitch," I whispered.

"So, that's a no, then?" Brant asked, watching me nervously.

I still had the remnants of the Romanian sweetbread mingled with coffee on my tongue, and the sound of my own blood rushing in my ears was heavy and pounding. I cleared my throat, mostly out of annoyance, as I answered. "It's a no."

"That because of that drug you took or—"

"The telepath might be restraining my power," I said, trying to think this through. I was stuck on this island while this bastard messed with my mind, but I didn't have to like it and I certainly didn't have to take it lying down. I fumbled in my waistband for the familiar lump of my Sig Sauer P227 and exhaled when I found it right where it was supposed to be. I pulled it out as Brant's eyes widened in front of me, and while pointing it in a safe direction ejected the magazine and confirmed there was a bullet in the chamber. I did the same for my secondary weapon, a Smith and Wesson Bodyguard .380 that I kept in an ankle holster, and then put it right back where it belonged.

"I don't think you're allowed to have those on you while drinking," Brant said nervously.

"I don't think it'd be smart for me to go anywhere without them," I said, "and I suspect my drinking is over with until I've got this problem settled."

"Fair enough," Brant said, looking like he wanted to run out the door but doing a remarkable job of resisting said urge. "I'm going to say something ... a little strange right now, so bear with me."

I watched him carefully, waiting to see what he did next. "Go on."

"Come with me if you want to live," he said and extended his hand.

I blinked, then looked left, then right, waiting for either a camera crew to spring out of the bathroom or Arnold Schwarzenegger to come lunging out of the closet to whack him for misappropriating a classic line. "Yeah, no," I said.

"I don't mean it in the, 'Oh, come with me or you're going to die,' sense," he said, still holding out of his hand, "I mean it in the sense that ... I don't think you're really think you're living your life."

I stared at him in disbelief. "I've flown around the United States more times than I can count, traveled internationally to all sorts of different countries—"

"Is that living?" he asked slyly and offered his hand again.

"Some would say so," I said carefully, staring at the proffered hand.

"Would you say so?"

I blinked and felt the twitch of my fingers. "I've kind of got a lot going on at the moment."

"Yes, indeed, what with your racking of guns and preparations to hunt ne'er-do-wells and whatnot," he said. "But if you might spare ... just a little bit of time before you set out on your quest for justice, I think it would be a good idea."

"Really?" I asked. "Because I think it'd be a good idea to find whoever is messing with my head and expose the interior of their skull to the snow so we can measure the depth of the fall, don't you?"

"We've got the weather service for that. And they do a

bang-up job, really." He paused, cringing. "Other than not being able to tell us this mess was coming before it hit."

"I always go after the threat first," I said and started to move past him.

"You do seem like a job-first kind of person," he agreed. "But tell me honestly … how's that working out for you?"

"Just fine," I said tautly as I stepped out the door. The snowflakes were falling a little more rapidly now, and they'd accumulated in very small patches on the already sodden ground. I stepped into a small dusting of white and heard it crunch underfoot. Brant followed me, and I whirled around as he came out and shut the door. "I'm doing important work, you know? It's very taxing, and it requires a lot of time and focus."

"No doubt," he said, standing there on the doorstep to my cabin, looking around at the sky, which was darkening by the moment. "Do you have any friends?"

That one hit me like a bowling ball tossed by a meta. "I have a dog," I said quickly. "That's like woman's best friend, next to my Sig Sauer."

"Huh," he said, not taking his eyes off of me. "You're lonely."

"I'm busy," I said and started to pace away. I walked around the back of the cabin, not really sure where I was going. I didn't have a plan, I didn't have a clue, couldn't really run from what had happened here, and didn't know what to do about it. I didn't even have anyone I could really call, other than Augustus, and I didn't know if it was even time to press a panic button. What had happened so far, really? Voices in my head, that was what—of the unfamiliar variety. And of course, the absence of the voices of the familiar variety. That last part could have been explained away by me taking too big a dose of chloridamide, really.

I came around the back of the cabin and caught sight of the vista spread out before me. It was Lake Superior in all its glory, with the haze of the falling snow coming down on the surprisingly peaceful waters. "Wow," I said, not really intending to give that thought voice.

"Not bad, eh?" Brant asked, catching up to me.

"Not bad," I agreed, stopped in my tracks. The ground sloped gently down about a hundred feet to kiss the waters of the lake, which was lapping at the rocks at its edge the way my dog licked at me. Green grass was mixed with white snow in a strange patchwork, and I stared at it as I took a breath. "I am lonely," I said, watching my breath frost in front of me.

"This important work you're doing," Brant said, taking it all in, the silent sentinel watching the world's quietest moment unfold beside me, "maybe ... you don't have to do it? Maybe ... the cost to you is getting too high?" He looked over at me, but I didn't meet his gaze. "Maybe you don't belong there anymore?

"Maybe," I said, looking out at the grey ceiling that hung over the world as the snows gently fell, pouring white out on everything. "Or maybe I don't belong anywhere."

24.

Benjamin

Benjamin walked through the door with a smile on his face, not a trace of nervousness to be found within him. His back was straight, his head was held high, and the lobby of his workplace seemed filled with new life. It was the same old place, of course, but he hadn't been in here in a week due to his little trip overseas, so it all seemed so fresh and vibrant. There were planters in the giant glass lobby, soaking up the sunlit morning. People were filing through the turnstiles as they scanned their employee IDs and moved in to go about their day. Benjamin pulled his from the lanyard around his neck and scanned it, listened for the beep that signaled him to enter, watched the little screen on the entry turnstile flare a bright, verdant green and smiled at the lady behind the security desk. Her head was down and she didn't notice him, but that was just fine.

It was going to be a good day.

Benjamin stepped into the elevator just before the doors closed on a full compartment, and he didn't even mind the person humming behind him along with the music. He almost felt like humming himself.

He listened and waited through four different dings as the elevator stopped on every floor below his. That was all right, too. "The Girl From Ipanema" was playing softly overhead, and the fluorescent lights hummed pleasantly in the background, audible in the still and quiet between floors as the pulleys outside the box did their good work.

Benjamin took in a deep breath and sighed it out in pleasant release as the elevator dinged that last time, and the doors opened on his floor. It was abuzz with activity, people moving to and fro in the cubicle farm that spread across the floor. Executive offices were situated to his left and right, but Benjamin didn't directly report to anyone high enough up in the company to have ever been in any of those. No, he was a cubicle man, and a very junior one at that, which was fine by him.

Benjamin got into his cubicle and sighed another breath of relief as he slid his chair up to his computer and started to log in. He cast a look back at the computer behind him, the chair pulled out all askew, the workspace messy with sheaves of rumpled papers. His was in perfect order, left that way before he had gone on his trip. In truth, though, he cleaned up every night, but even his messiest day wasn't anything like what his cubicle mate regularly left out.

Her name was Jessica, and they'd been unwilling cubicle partners for almost a year now. It was not a happy arrangement by any means. She was petty, mean, cold, and selfish. They seldom spoke, and that was all for the better. Once upon a time he'd tried, very hard, to make inroads with her, but then she'd stolen his tape dispenser without so much as asking, while he was sitting right there in front of her, watching in shocked silence. She hadn't brought it back even an hour later when his thudding heart had subsided enough for him to politely ask for its return.

He regarded Jessica's chair with a little disdain and turned away. No, even she couldn't ruin this day for him. It was good to be back.

He typed his password into the network when prompted for his login. He waited, still humming "The Girl From Ipanema" as he sat, still and upright, in his chair. A frown creased his face as the message came back:

Login failed. Please contact a network administrator.

"Hmm," Benjamin said to himself, and simply tried again. He waited, certain that this time would be different, but the same message was spit back at him a moment later, all in red text.

failed

you

failure

Benjamin shook it off, ignoring the sudden, mild stab of pain behind his eye. Something like this always happened on the first day back from vacation, after all. Best to roll with it.

He stood and made his way out of his cubicle toward the desk of the tech support woman who serviced their floor. She was in the corner and he could see her talking on the phone. She was one of the few who merely had a desk, with no cubicle to shield her. What was her name? Alanna? Yes, that was it. He felt sorry for Alanna. He'd heard the rationale for not giving her cubicle walls was to make whoever was in her position more approachable. They were there to help, after all, but Benjamin would have died of embarrassment to feel so exposed, so out there in the middle of the floor.

As he approached Alanna's desk, he caught sight of Alanna herself. She was talking on the phone, pushing her dark, curly hair back over her ear as she spoke into the receiver. "Yes," she said. "No, I think what your problem is—" She stopped as her eyes alighted on him. They widened just a hint, and she swallowed visibly. "I'll have to call you back," she said, and hung up the phone, spinning out of her chair and leaving her desk behind in something just below a bare panic. He watched her rush off and disappear behind a row of cubicles to her left.

Benjamin just stood there, speechless, for a long moment after Alanna's rapid departure. It was almost as though she'd seen something—

a monster

him

horror

—and simply run off. Benjamin took a slow breath, watched the yellow sun glint off the windows at the curve of the building just beyond Alanna's desk, and resolved himself to leave a message on her voicemail so that she could deal with his problem in an orderly fashion when she returned. It had been rude of him to try and jump to the head of the queue, after all. She was a busy person, had a whole floor of people constantly tugging at her sleeves for attention, and for him to presume he was somehow entitled to help immediately simply because he was here earlier than most, well, that was simply the height of—

entitled

i do deserve it

dammit

—presumption, really.

That sting of pain behind Benjamin's eye had started to become something more. It was throbbing now, and he turned to go back to his desk with a little hitch in his step. He looked down at the floor, the shining grey tiles muting the color palette of the sun's glory that had been blindingly in his eyes only a moment earlier. Perhaps some Tylenol would take the edge off, make it easier for him to think again. After all, these were simply minor problems—

all of you are my problems

hate you so much

why do you TORMENT ME so?

—that could be dealt with in time.

When he reached his cubicle again, he paused at the entry, momentarily taken aback. His pulse quickened, the throbbing behind his eye intensified, and he was filled with the desire to—

kill

burn

torch

flame

murder the b—

—go visit the washroom and compose himself before he sat down. But he did not, instead skirting around Jessica's chair, which was pulled out, the woman herself hunched over her computer and already typing something. Probably a sordid missive to her current lover, which, from what Benjamin could determine via not-quite-hushed-enough phone calls, was a different man than her husband.

"Hello," he said politely, trying to bury the hatchet as best he could. What better time to try, after all, than when he was refreshed from his trip?

Jessica straightened in alarm, almost as though someone had pressed a Taser directly to the base of her spine where that awful—what did they call them? Tramp stamps?—where that awful tattoo rested, nestled in the waistband of her pants. He didn't mean to look, but her shirts frequently parted from her pants, and there it was, a giant, pale bit of negative space that was darkened with some sort of Asian symbol. It practically dared his eyes to not look at it.

Jessica slowly spun around in her chair with an expression not unlike the one that Alanna had worn only moments earlier. "What are you doing here?" she asked snottily.

"Working," he said, as politely as possible. He navigated around her and sat in his chair, facing his computer. "And I—"

Benjamin did not hear her approach, nor did he see her hit him in the back of the head with her desk lamp. But he damnably sure felt it, that crack across the back of his skull, that pain that flamed over his scalp, that sent a flashing spectrum of colors pulsating in front of his eyes—orange, yellow, red, pink—all in speedy sequence, melding together and pulling apart, until he couldn't tell the difference between them.

Benjamin's chair flew out from underneath him and he hit his jaw on the cubicle desk as he fell, landing in a heap, chair back catching him in the ribs before it departed him entirely. It hurt, it all hurt, and when he looked up, he saw Jessica there brandishing the desk lamp, raising it above her head again with a look of utter—

anger

pain

rage

you dirty whore

His hand flew up automatically to shield himself from her wrath, and he watched the fire leap from his fingers—

red, orange, yellow, pink

oh, the pretty colors

see how she BURNS

Jessica's turquoise blouse and navy blue capris burst into flames, and her rose pink skin followed shortly thereafter. She dropped the lamp, and the bulb shattered as it fell, spreading white powder out in a puff through the air. Benjamin watched, dimly worrying about the mercury contained within. Someone should clean that up, he thought.

The screams were terrible, horrific, reminding him of all those awful movies he never cared to watch—

take that, you bitch

—and the smell was worse somehow, worse than anything, like something rancid had been put on the grill—

looks like it's pig for dinner tonight!

—and he just sat there, feeling the trickle of blood run down his skull as he watched her burn, burn—

BURN

"Oh, God," Benjamin whispered as what he was seeing crashed through the wall between his eyes and his mind, screaming and panicking like the woman on fire in front of him. He scooted toward the cubicle exit as she danced around like a flaming ballerina. Benjamin crab-walked his way out of the cube and stopped as Jessica's spinning circuit carried her into the cubicle desk and she slammed into it and fell to the ground, writhing furiously as her screams filled the air until they were drowned out by another, louder screaming—

serves her right
got what she deserved

—of the fire alarm, klaxon wailing like a police siren, deafening Benjamin. He sat there and watched her burn, horrified, wondering how such a thing could have happened—

what do you mean, how did it happen?
you made it happen, you idiot

—and the horror of it all drove him at last to his feet, his breaths coming short and sharp as the first drops of the fire sprinklers started to rain down on him, the torrential downpour beginning in earnest.

Smoke steamed from Jessica's blackened flesh, dark as night itself, twisted and melted—

yeah yeah yeah
take that, you

—and Brian heard another scream, deeper, issuing forth from his own mouth, and cut off by a voice that was so loud—

so grating
so impolite
like her

—that came from behind him and forced him to turn.

There, standing in the downpour of the sprinklers, were two men in dark suits. One was black, one was white, and the white man stood in front, staring at Benjamin. The man's hair was long and slicked back by the sprinkler's artificial rain, but his voice was commanding, and Benjamin found himself listening to—

the bastard
gonna burn him, too

—the man as he spoke. "Benjamin," he said, "my name is Reed Treston. I'm here to help you."

Benjamin just stared blankly, nothing coming to mind—

i'm gonna burn you alive, pig
just like I did to this bitch

25.

Sienna

"Do you ever think about the future?" Brant asked me as we stood there on the shores of Lake Superior, watching the snowfall intensify and the grey skies knit in even closer, like blankets pulled over the top of the world. Cold air flooded my sinuses, a brisk shot of life that felt like it was infused right into my brain.

"I try not to," I said, walking up to the shore's edge. Over the bevy of head-sized rocks that met the shoreline, I saw a small beach made of stones. They were bigger than pebbles, a good size for throwing, or skipping. I stooped over and grabbed one, a flat one that fit oh-so-easily into the palm of my hand, clutched it between my thumb and my forefinger, and chucked it out across the lake. It skipped ten times before it flew out of sight.

"Oh my," Brant said, coming up to join me. He selected a rock of his own and gave it a throw, sideways. It only skipped four times before it sank in a sea of ripples. "Why not?"

I picked up another rock, trying to decide if I should bother with skipping it, since I'd already proven it was a fruitless game. Maybe if the cloud cover wasn't so heavy, I could actually see how far I could land it. Instead I just threw the rock as hard as I could, and watched it zip out of sight in a second.

"Wow," Brant said. "That flew fast. Like, faster than—"

"A speeding bullet?" I smirked.

Brant frowned. "I was going to say, 'Walt Flanagan's dog.'" He looked at me seriously. "Why don't you like to think about the future? Most people tend to enjoy dreaming of a better tomorrow."

I stared out over the lake in all its limited, semi-majestic glory. "My father flew over Lake Superior at one point, did you know that?"

"Uhm, no," Brant said, "How would I have known that?"

"An old ... friend of mine sent me an email," I said, hesitating to call Janus a friend. "Sent me a file that this other organization had on my father, after the war was done. He was on a ship called the *Edmund Fitzgerald*—"

Brant raised an eyebrow as he interrupted. "You serious? Was he in the song, too?"

"I doubt it. He was on it when it broke up, and he used his powers to whisk a girl named Adelaide to safety on the shore. Took every bit of power he had to do it, but he made it safely." I looked out onto the cloudy waters, thinking it wasn't so very different from an ocean, really. "I wonder if he flew by here?"

"It sank over near the upper peninsula of Michigan if I remember correctly," Brant said, pointing to our right, "so ... probably not, unless he decided to take a very indirect route to shore."

"I think about that sometimes," I said. "About how he did that. He was a windkeeper, and they can't really fly very well. My brother—"

"The asshole?"

"That very one," I said dryly, "he can fly a little, but he does better in a place like New York City, where he's got some natural drafts to work with. But my dad, he did it for ... miles." I looked up at the clouds and wondered how high they were. Probably not as high as my dad had been flying that day. "When Reed heard that story, he was shocked. I think he looked up the distance to shore and just about crapped himself. It was … inconceivable to him." I glared at Brant. "Don't make a *Princess Bride* joke."

"That word is ruined forever," he said. "Which is a shame, because it's a good word." He eased a little closer to me. "Why did you bring up the topic of your father when I asked about your future? I mean … no disrespect intended, but he's dead, isn't he?"

"He is dead," I said.

"Seems like that would be something of the past, then," Brant said. "Why don't you like to think about your future?"

"My dad died before I was born," I said, then paused. "My mom died … during the war. We weren't that close."

"Difficult childhood or something?" he asked, and I turned my head to look at him. I'd read the scandal rags reportage of my upbringing. It had broken recently, complete with photos of the box that still remained in my basement because I didn't know what else to do with it. Some asshole had broken in and sold the photos, and of course the press gobbled them up, penning a thousand wanking think pieces about how damaged I was.

"Classy way to say it," I said. "My mother … never left a mark on me, but she left her mark, if you know what I mean. She also died early."

"Both of your parents died early," Brant said, nodding. "I'm starting to understand this reluctance to talk about the future now."

"What is this?" I asked. "Are you angling for your junior psychologist merit badge or something?" I watched for his reaction.

"Just asking," he said, shrugging expansively with his broad shoulders. "Like I said … I thought maybe you could use a friend. Or at least a bartender."

"Yeah, well …" I tried to decide what to say next. My thoughts were surprisingly clear on this matter, but I wasn't sure I wanted to spill them to a near stranger.

Then I realized ... what did it matter? Nobody could think any worse of me than they already did, even if Brant ran to the internet and posted our entire conversation.

"My grandmother lived over five thousand years," I said, continuing with my thought.

"Whaaaat?" Brant asked.

"Yeah," I said, waiting for the startled look on his face to subside. "So ... here's how I see my future every time I think it out." I tried to hold myself steady. "I'm either going to die violently while I'm still young ... or I'm going to get to watch everybody I love and care about—a rapidly thinning list, I might add—die around me. Which has already happened too many times." I met his eyes. I knew mine were sad, laden with a level of concern that most people never even had to think about. "See why I don't like to think about the future?"

26.

Reed

Augustus and I had been enjoying an uncomfortable breakfast in Roseville, following my instinct that maybe Cunningham would try something today, when we'd gotten the call that he had, in fact, tried something, and that the something he'd tried was apparently showing up to work like yesterday hadn't even happened. We rode in silence to the scene, and just as we popped out of the elevator on his floor, we found the man in question committing an act of interpersonal arson on one of his co-workers, who was screaming and dancing like a stuntwoman from a movie before she finally dropped to the ground as the sprinklers came on.

It was a downpour, like a rainstorm going on indoors when I shouted out to Benjamin Cunningham that we were here to talk to him. I could feel Augustus on edge behind me, waiting to rumble. I was skeptical about how much rumbling he'd be able to do with the nearest dirt about seven floors down and outside, but he was chafing to act, I could tell that much. I couldn't really blame him; we'd walked in on an incriminating scene. It wasn't like she'd chosen that moment to spontaneously combust, after all.

"Benjamin," I said quietly, straining to be heard over the sprinklers dousing us with cold, kind of smelly water, "we need to talk."

"We need to help this dude into a cell," Augustus said behind me.

I cringed, hoping that the sprinklers drowned out his pronouncement, figuring it wouldn't do much to help Cunningham's state of mind. "Benjamin ..." I said.

Cunningham was shorter than I figured he'd be, with slumped shoulders and a distinct scorch pattern on the sleeve of his shirt. It might have started out grey, but with the soaking of the water it looked almost black at this point, and his hair had lost any distinctiveness to its shape, turning into a wet, plastered bowl that covered his forehead and ears. "I don't ... this isn't my fault," he said, gesturing to the burnt and blackened form on the ground next to him.

"Okay," I said, holding out my hands in front of me like I meant peace. For most people, that might have been a gesture of peace. In my case, I was ready to blast his ass through a cubicle wall at a moment's notice. "Why don't we talk about it?"

His head shook in a terrible tic as he looked over at the body again, then away abruptly. His eyelids fluttered. "I ... I didn't do that."

"Okay," I said, opting not to point out the mounting evidence that he, in fact, had done that. "Well, why don't we go outside or ... somewhere quieter ... and just talk it over?"

"I have to work," Cunningham said, and his head shook again. "I have ... work to do. This is my job."

"If you're planning to work in this," Augustus said, not really helping the situation, "you might want to get a poncho."

"That's the fire alarm, Benjamin," I said. "They're evacuating the building."

"Yes, I know that," Cunningham snapped at me. "I'm not stupid." His stunned persona vanished and was replaced by something that hissed when he spoke.

I looked back at Augustus and he looked back at me. I

was no psychologist, but that was not normal. "Okay, well ... don't you think we should evacuate?"

"I've got work to do," Cunningham said, jumping right back into that particular groove again. It was like talking to someone whose mind had completely slipped. I was instantly reminded of the circular conversations I had with my grandmother as she succumbed to dementia, like a *Choose Your Own Adventure* novel that you couldn't get out of regardless of which conversational choice you made.

"Benjamin, no one is working right now," I said, trying a different tack. "They're all gone."

"She's not gone," Cunningham said, gesturing to the piece of blackened human toast that used to work with him.

"Oh, she's gone," Augustus said, "and so are you, dude. You are *gone*."

Cunningham's blank eyes went past me to Augustus. "I don't understand," he said, and I believed him wholeheartedly.

"What my colleague means to say," I took over, before my junior partner spoke enough truth to get us both broiled alive, "is that we're worried about you. You're not well, Benjamin."

"I feel ... fine," he said, and I caught the hint of stress between the second and third words. It was subtle, but spoke a pretty big volume or two.

"Do you?" I asked.

"Yes," he snapped, and I observed the patience lost again. This time a sheen of steam hissed off his shoulders and head as the sprinklers continued to douse us all, like the water had reached boiling point in an instant.

"All right," I said, "but we should get you checked out by a doctor anyway."

"A doctor?" he asked, squinting at me. "Why?"

I tried a different tack. "You picked up something—a sickness—in Amsterdam."

"I was only in Amsterdam for a few hours," he said,

shaking his head in that twitchy way again. "Couldn't possibly have picked anything up while I was there."

"Where were you before Amsterdam?" Augustus asked.

"Before?" Cunningham's face scrunched up as he considered the question. "Why, I was staying in Bredoccia. Why?"

I'd heard of Bredoccia, the capital city of a country in Eastern Europe called Revelen. They'd had some sort of ad campaign recently to advertise how good they were for business and tourism, just like every other third-world hellhole on the planet. Like Iowa. They had tons of billboards around the Twin Cities a few years ago talking about how wonderful they were, suggesting people move there or visit. As if a cornfield were a great tourist destination or something. Maybe if they invested in a hill, people would come visit them.

Benjamin blinked his eyes, again and again, and finally I saw him catch a glimpse of his burned sleeve. "Oh, God. What happened here?" Cunningham thrust his arm out, look of disgust burning in his eyes and horror etching his mouth into a downward line broken by the gap of his parted lips. "No. No. I ... no, it couldn't ... only a monster would—"

"There are no monsters here," I said, trying to soothe the savage, flaming beast before he could flare up again. "Just people. And accidents happen, Benjamin. They happen, okay?"

"This was no accident," Cunningham said, turning his head and taking in the burnt corpse behind him. "It couldn't be an accident. People don't just catch on fire." His hand shook, and steam began to pour off of it.

"Oh, hell," Augustus said behind me, and I watched his hands rise into the air as—presumably—he started to bring some dirt our way. He never got a chance to finish his attempt, though.

I heard footsteps in the sprinkler wash behind us only a second before I heard Augustus's sharp, shocked cry and watched him fly, twisting, through the air to my right. He hit a cubicle wall and it shattered around him like a bowling ball rolling through pins. He disappeared under a folded, broken segment of the furniture, and I whipped my head around in time to see a very familiar face leering at me from entirely too close.

"Here we stand again," Anselmo said, a broad grin breaking his scorched face, identical in so many details to the body just over Cunningham's shoulder, "eye to eye, man to man, once more ..."

27.

Sienna

I'm not much for publicly attended pity parties, so when Brant asked me to go with him to the bar to "hang out or help out, whichever you prefer," I begged off. I'd just told him more about me than I'd shared with anyone in recent memory (not that anyone but Ariadne had asked of late) and I felt ... exposed. And that didn't even factor in the recent ghostly attacks on my mind that the telepath had been staging.

So instead of going back to the bar and drowning my sorrows in the time-honored tradition of my people—by which I mean working human beings—I decided instead to sit in my cabin and stare at the walls while the snow fell outside.

So far, it was really boring.

And the flakes just kept coming, too. I had my window shades up, and I could see the ground getting covered over a little at a time, gradually accumulating. The flakes were getting more sizable, too, it seemed, and coming down at more of an angle. I could hear the wind against the side of the cabin when it blew particularly hard, and it started me thinking about the tale of the three pigs. Should have gone for a brick cabin instead of a stick one, I guess.

I sat in my wooden chair and sulked, thinking over what

I'd said to Brant—and what I hadn't. I'd bled my bitterness all over him, but he'd asked for it. At least I hadn't just stumbled into the bar and vomited my emotional nausea everywhere.

Uh, unless I'd done that last night while drinking. It could have happened.

I realized about the time that the snow had completely blotted out the last of the green that my car wasn't parked out front of the cabin anymore. I panicked for a few seconds until I remembered that Brant had had to drive me home last night due to drunkenness, and cursed my poor decision making—or maybe my desire to just forget for a little while. If I had Gavrikov's flight abilities at my disposal, this wouldn't have been an issue. As it was, town was a good five to ten minutes' drive away, and that meant I'd have to either walk or run, or reconcile myself to being stuck … in a cabin with no food … until the snow cleared.

I've been called many things, but a little shrinking daffodil who didn't eat? Never been accused of that. Had jerks in the press say quite the opposite, in fact. I hadn't killed any of them … yet … but they were on my radar.

I decided to just stick with what I was already wearing, since it was dirty from the day before, and pulled on the light jacket I had in my suitcase. It wasn't exactly a winter coat, but it was the best I had available. It was a fall coat, and here winter was showing up months early, the rude bastard. Reminded me of another jerk named Winter I'd dealt with in the past who'd showed little consideration.

I put that nasty trip down memory lane out of my head and walked toward the door, the steady clicking of my thin, steel-toed boots against the linoleum. I paused, listening, as the echo of my footsteps … kept going?

I turned around, looking around the dimly-lit cabin as the light from the windows began to fade. It went quickly, like someone had drawn the shades, and suddenly I found myself steeped in darkness just inches from the front door. I sighed and fumbled for the light switch, but I couldn't find it anywhere on the door frame on either side of the door. The light from the windows was down to nil, and I narrowed my eyes in hopes that it would widen my pupils and allow me to see better. Futile hope, but that was all I had at that moment in the dark.

Then I heard the sound of footsteps again. I couldn't tell if they were coming from over by the little kitchenette, or the bathroom, or even somewhere beyond the back wall. They were crisp, slow, measured, like someone was strolling with soft shoes on a hard surface, the rubber soles kissing the ground as they peeled off with each step.

"What the hell," I muttered under my breath as I renewed my search, sliding my hand along the wall for a foot to the left of the door. I thought about cracking the door, but given that the light outside had just died—which happened sometimes in howling snowstorms—I doubted it would do much other than sweep a ton of wet snow into my cabin.

My fingers ran across the ridges of the wooden wall paneling. It was smooth, save for the normal knots and pits in sanded, varnished lumber. I gave up after searching three feet out from the door in a two foot radius near my hand level. There was no light switch on this side, I'd have bet my life on it.

I shuffled over to the other side of the door, pausing to listen again. That sound came again, that noise like footsteps. But it couldn't have been footsteps; this cabin was small. Like, one room. I would have smelled someone if they'd been in here with me, would have heard them breathe. Maybe the noise was coming from the roof. It certainly wasn't coming from behind the back wall, because the sound was all wrong for footsteps on snow, and there was nothing but snow out there.

I ran my palm across the wood on the left side of the door, more urgently now. I found the same imperfections in the wood as I found on the other side, and in my haste, I sped up my search. I jabbed my hand up and down, and felt something bite right in the middle of my palm, drawing a sharp sting right in the center. I yanked my hand back and clapped it over my mouth in surprised. As I extended my tongue, I tasted blood.

Great. Either my hand hadn't healed properly, or I'd just reopened yesterday's wound. Of course, I was reopening all sorts of wounds today, but so far they'd only been metaphorical.

This one was more than metaphorical. Blood dripped down my hand in lines that I could taste and smell. It was a grim feeling, standing in the dark, holding my cut and bloody hand up to my face. It never took this long for one of my wounds to heal, not even when I was a plain old vanilla meta, bereft of Wolfe's healing abilities.

"Messing with my head," I said to the darkness, "messing with my abilities. Let me tell you something—that's not going to end well for you. Mark my words."

The darkness in front of my eyes shifted, like smoke blown from a strong wind. It was one of the spookier things I've seen; pure eeriness brought to life, like something straight out of a ghost story. I saw it move, coalesce into blurred features, like the face leaning out of the mirror, but it held only a little better clarity. A low rumble shook the cabin as power channeled in from some unknown source.

"*Get ... out ...*" the voice said, and the windows rattled at the force of the suggestion.

Maybe I was supposed to feel scared at that suggestion, but I let more than a little of my irritation slip out as I opened the door and a blast of frigid wind hit me full in the face. "Way ahead of you there, dickfish." And I stepped out into the storm and slammed the door shut behind me.

28.

Reed

"You're not much of a man," I said to Anselmo through the artificial rain that poured down between us, and watched as my attempted goat-getting did, indeed, get his goat, as well as the rest of his petting zoo. Anger flashed through those partially obscured eyes, the scarred flesh hanging around his eyes darkening as he flushed to the shade of a tanned piece of leather.

"And you are far too close to being a woman to deserve the one you have," Anselmo said, surprising me by holding back from swinging at me. "The good doctor is plainly settling for a lesser stag." The ridge where his eyebrows had been in less-burned times raised as he stumbled on a thought. "Perhaps you need a good cuckolding—"

I shot a double gust of wind at him using both hands that tore him free of the ground and sent him sailing backward six feet in a wash of spray. Anselmo rolled through the puddling water as he landed, his off-the-rack suit not quite conforming to his figure. The douche was wearing a dress shirt, which came untucked when he rose, but he showed a surprising lack of concern for the fact I'd just physically hurled him through the air. I hadn't been able to overmatch him with that particular strength when last we'd fought, but to see his reaction, you'd think I hadn't done anything at all.

"You are a tiresome thing," Anselmo said as the sprinklers tapered off above us, the fire system deciding that maybe its job was done. "Full of sound and fury, sig—"

I channeled a hell of a blast right at him, and this one sent him back ten feet, right into a cubicle. He hit the wall with a crack, breaking the board and ricocheting off. He came down in a crouch and sprung upright to standing like it was nothing. He looked down at his sleeve, which was torn, plucking a splinter while wearing a look of—I assume, tough to tell with all the scarring—mild annoyance at the damage to his garment. "You fight like a little girl, slapping about at your opponent, afraid to get close, to share the look in the eyes as you attempt to best one another. I will show you what it is like to fight a man, to be beaten by a man, to have what you care about most taken by a true man—"

I shot another gust at him, but he dodged with blurry speed, ducking behind a cubicle. My gust hit it and the top wall folded, but the bottom of the structure remained snug to the floor. It was a good twenty feet from me, if not more, and my range for directed gusts fell off fast when someone was that far away. I could hear his faux-leather shoes scuffing as he bent low and circled toward me. "I can hear you crawling around like a rat, Anselmo," I said. "I can hear y—"

The heat was the first sign I was in trouble. The second was the scorching fire that went crawling up my sleeve a moment later. I recoiled in shock, spinning around to see Benjamin Cunningham standing a few feet from me with a furious look in his eyes, like he had a fire of his own dancing within them.

"Don't you ignore me," he said, voice thick and husky as I batted at the flames creeping up my sleeve, burning my skin. "Don't you—know who I am—see what I can do—kill you all—" His voice pitched and changed in the middle of what seemed like a sentence, like he was stringing thoughts together in mad sequence, performing word surgery that left gaping, obvious stitches in the middle.

Plus, he lit me on fire. I started to get the feeling Cunningham had left part of his mind behind when he came back from vacation.

I resisted my first instinct, which was to stop, drop and roll. I'd been thinking about something like this happening since I'd heard about Cunningham. During our feverish training after Sienna's London revival, we'd practiced for any number of contingencies, including occasions when Sienna turned loose her various powers on me to 'prepare' me for those sort of attacks. I think she actually enjoyed it, seeing me dance around while she shot bursts of flame to either side of me, and occasionally on me, but it might also have been that she enjoyed watching me dance around like the floor was on fire and my ass was next.

Either way, it had prepared me for this moment, and to deal with it in a somewhat orderly fashion, no ass-is-on-fire-type dancing required.

Cunningham advanced on me, fury in his eyes, and when he got close enough to reach out for me, close enough for me to see the killing rage in between the lines of purest anger etched in his crow's feet, I did the thing that Sienna's constant flamethrowing had taught me to do, the single greatest defense to fire attacks that a keeper of the winds could possibly manage.

I took all the air in a five foot radius around me and I drove it back, creating a forced bubble free of all oxygen.

It didn't last very long—probably three seconds—but it snuffed out the fire that Benjamin Cunningham had lit on my jacket, and it drove away all the air that he was planning to breathe and to use to burn me to death.

It also prompted his crazy, killer eyes to open wider than Arnold Schwarzenegger's when he got sucked out onto the surface of Mars in *Total Recall*, which was kinda cool, too.

I, of course, being the originator of the plan, was totally ready for the lack of oxygen. I'd exhaled everything I had to prepare for the vacuum effect. Cunningham had the wind forcibly ripped from his lips and lungs, and it left him with a shocked look. He fell to his knees as the bubble around us collapsed and the oxygen rushed back in, and I wasn't too high-and-mighty to do a Sienna and kick him right in the gut as he went down. I'm not an über-succubus, but I can hit a dude when I want to, and in that moment, I damned sure wanted to. I wanted to hit Benjamin Cunningham hard enough to knock his punk ass out of the fight so I could deal with the Italian Stallion of Invincible Doom (I'm floating it as Anselmo's nickname. Whaddya think? Too much? You're right, too much.) without getting sucker punched. Or sucker fired. Sucker flambéed? Whatever.

Cunningham left the ground, turned a flip in mid air, and landed gut first on a cubicle wall before bouncing inside the damned thing. I lost sight of him as he fell, but the noise of the air rushing—once again—out of his body as he took the divider in the solar plexus was unmistakable. And very satisfying.

I spun around as Anselmo came right for me, the sound of his footsteps thundering across the carpet behind me as certain as the sound of doom's approach. I'll admit, he scared me. Scared the hell out of me. He packed a nasty punch and was well nigh invincible when it came to taking a punch. I could throw him around all day and he'd just keep springing up after each attack, fresh as a daisy and ready to do some plucking of his own.

I poured all my fear, all my adrenaline, all my instinct and training into the burst of wind I hit him with. It came at him like a transit bus on the freeway, and I watched his face take it like a bulldog in a windstorm. His scarred jowls blew back, the hanging flesh over his eyes blew out, exposing the whites as well as tiny little pupils. I'd caught him with one foot off the ground as he was running at me, and I was coming up like a batter hitting the ball with a rising swing.

Home run.

Anselmo left the ground once more with a look of utter

shock, but instead of just going five or ten feet, I watched him fly all thirty feet between us and the glass window. He shattered it as his body passed through, and the last sight I caught of him at that moment was a look of utter shock comparable to that of Wile E. Coyote as gravity took over and carried him seven floors to the ground below.

"Cunningham?" I called out, turning to look to the cubicle where he had fallen. "Augustus?" I glanced at where he'd fallen, and found my partner holding his back in pain. I hoofed it for him first.

"I'm all right," he said, holding himself still. He started to move, then cringed. "Might have broken my back, though. Can't feel my feet."

"Dammit," I said and stood. "I've got to—"

"Cunningham, yeah," Augustus said. "And Anselmo's gonna be pissed once he scrapes himself up off the concrete below."

"Maybe he landed with a tree up his ass," I said, "keep him busy for a while."

"Hope he enjoys it," Augustus said with a grimace. "Ow."

"You're gonna be okay," I said, patting him on the shoulder as I rose. "This will heal, trust me."

"Good to know," Augustus said, "because I'm still holding out hopes for a pro football career ahead of me at some point, y'know. Probably beat the piss out of everybody in rushing yards." His voice cracked with nerves. I'd be scared too if I'd felt paralysis setting in.

I carefully walked through the wreckage of cubicles, easing toward the one where Cunningham had landed. "Cunningham?" I called, announcing myself because I knew he could hear my footsteps anyway. "I'm not here to hurt you, but you've got to realize that something's wrong by now. You're hurting people, man. You've slipped the moorings of your mind. Something's wrong. Let's get you some help—"

I jumped out in front of the entry to the cubicle that I'd

hurled Cunningham into, hoping to find a man in pain. Or, even better, passed out.

Instead, I was greeted with an empty cubicle, with nothing but the sign of his impact where his weight had cracked the top of the cubicle wall to mark his passage. I looked left, I looked right, and then I jumped up on the desk so I could see farther. No sound reached my ears save for that of Augustus's pained grunts.

Cunningham was gone.

29.

Benjamin

Benjamin descended the stairs in his sopping clothes, one shoe lost somewhere in the fracas above. He still wasn't sure quite what he'd seen. Jessica, somehow lit aflame. Reed Treston had said ... said so many things, really. Yellow light shone brightly from the bulbs on the staircase, and Benjamin simply ran. There was no other course for it, after all. Things were happening all around him, mad and terrible things, things that he wanted nothing to do with. The only logical solution was to run, to get away, to remove himself as far as possible from the situation and even the city.

Up north. Yes. That was the place to go.

There was a cabin he'd rented before, two hours north near the Pequot Lakes chain. It had been his very first vacation that he'd paid for after getting his job. A full week spent in a cabin, by himself, reading and looking at the lake he'd been encamped on by sunrise, day, and sunset in turn. It had been marvelous, serene, blue skies reflected on shimmering, glassy waters.

None of this present madness of airport lines exploding, or people suddenly bursting into flames. No, this was the pressure of the city, surely. This sort of thing didn't happen up north, where the crazed pace of city life gave way to the ease of country living on the lakeshore. Benjamin's heart thundered in his ears, his head throbbed in pain behind his eyes. No, he couldn't stay here. There was a monster on the loose, he'd seen it twice now, though he'd wanted to believe it neither time. He had to escape, had to—

Benjamin hit the emergency exit door and knocked it off its hinges in his panic to escape. He stared at it blankly, not sure how that had happened. Probably damaged when everyone else had fled, and his passage had been the last straw, as it were. He stared at the blue door for a moment then shook it out of his mind and charted his path against the background of the green planters and trees that dotted the parking lot. He had to get out of here.

People were huddled in clusters around the building, milling, questioning, talking among themselves. Benjamin ignored them all, dodged around their little conversational circles and close-knit groups. His car was over there, and all he needed to do was get to it—

As he passed a bush, strong hands grabbed him and dragged him inside. Branches and twigs tore at his sleeves, but the arms that held him were strong. He started to protest, to let out a little squeal, but a lumpy hand made its way into his mouth, wet and tasting slightly burnt with the scent of a hard-blown wind over it. Benjamin tried to make a noise, but the arms anchored him in place, putting him in a hold as secure as any wrestler could have managed. Hot breath fell on his ear, whispering.

"I won't hurt you," the voice said, raspy but spoken with an unmistakable European accent. Benjamin was eminently familiar with those by now. "Don't scream." The man ripped his fist free of Benjamin's mouth.

Benjamin let out a whimper, his hands still tightly bound. "Wh-what do you want?"

"To help you," the voice said, soothing.

"You can't help me," Benjamin said, "I have to get out of here. There's a monster—"

"Yes, of course there is," the voice said, reassuring,

straight into his ear with a warmth that Benjamin found oddly … comfortable. "There is a monster."

"I need to get away from it," Benjamin said, never more sure of anything in his life. "I have to—"

"No, no, no," the voice said, tsk-ing him. "A man does not run from his problems."

"But—"

"No buts," the voice said. "Benjamin?"

"Y-yes?" Benjamin asked, surprised to hear his own name.

"My name is Anselmo Serafini," the man said, breathing so lightly on his neck that it almost tickled. "And I can teach you all about dealing with monsters. About being a man. Do you want to learn?"

His words sounded so warm and inviting, even though being stuck in a hedge row, encircled by strong arms was such a … well, it was odd.

"I …" Benjamin licked his lips as Anselmo's grip on him loosened. Benjamin almost wished it hadn't; he felt strangely uncomfortable being loose, like the next good jarring he received would send him crashing to the floor like a saucer off a table, shattered. "I'm afraid. I don't want to be afraid."

"I will teach you," Anselmo said softly into his ear. "Do you wish to learn?"

"Yes," Benjamin said, feeling a sudden relief from the fear that had clutched him tight in its hand. Anselmo was here, and whoever he was, Benjamin believed that touch, believed that voice, believed … him. "Yes. Teach me, please. Don't let me be afraid … anymore."

30.

Sienna

I stormed my way through the growing snowfall, kicking it out of the way in fits of pique as I wrapped my arms tightly around me. This was a hell of a vacation so far, experiencing the symptoms of a haunting while someone played mind games with me. The chill seeped in through my fall jacket, which was wholly inadequate to the task of protecting me from freezing winds and medium snowfall, which this was turning into. I had resolved to beat the Minneapolis weather man with a blunt instrument of some kind when I got back to town, because he had not even mentioned this as a possibility when I had tuned in to learn how to pack for my trip. AccuWeather, my flight-capable ass.

Gusts of wind slapped me in the cheeks in less than a playful manner, causing me to flush with irritation. My eyes were burning as I lowered my head against the wind, passing Apollonia's cabin and noting the "Closed" sign out front. I thought about knocking and asking for a ride, but I didn't see a car anywhere nearby, just a bike chained up out front, as though someone was going to come along and steal it.

I quick-stepped my way out to the road and looked left, then right. I was at least still faster than a normal person, so I could jog my way into town fairly quickly if I were of a mind to. The wind reared up again, blowing and swirling around me and forcing me to lean into it, so I quickly decided that sacrificing sure footing in order to run was a bad idea, especially now that I was as subject to gravity as everyone else. How annoying. I'm not sure how you people do it, honestly.

I turned toward town and started to walk fast. The cold air lashed at my face and found the thinness of my jacket, probably laughing its evil, frigid little head off at how ill-prepared for its relentless press I was. "I should move to Texas," I muttered. "Or Florida."

A car's lights appeared in the distance, churning slowly toward me. I moved to the side of the road, hitting a very slight rut and turning my ankle a little in the process. Just enough to sting. I cursed, then adjusted myself as I stood there in the subtle ditch that the snow had covered over. The car rolled past at about five miles an hour, giving me plenty of time to stare at the gawking, red face of a man who clearly didn't expect to see anyone out in this mess. He kept going, though, not so much as bothering to stop and ask me if I needed a ride. Which was fine, because I didn't need his stupid help anyway, the jerk.

I leaned back into the wind as it shifted direction to oppose me. It was like this whole island was hating on me, which was a familiar sensation by this point. Why should this place be any different than the rest of the world, after all? But much like them, I was determined to soldier on purely out of ornery spite.

The snow deepened as I went, going from barely an inch of accumulation in drifts to two inches, and it happened fast. I looked up at the darkened skies above me; grey light was barely visible shining down, and I could see a lamp lit somewhere far in the distance. The snows were thickening, increasing in size of flakes and volume.

If I had my fire powers right now, I would have turned this whole island to melted slush, dammit.

Melted flakes dripped down my jacket, seeping into the

worn brown leather. I swiped ineffectually at my shoulders with fingers that were beginning to lose feeling. Which was weird, because it had only been snowing for a little while. How could the temperature have dropped steeply enough for me to already start to lose feeling in my fingers? Probably the wind.

Or some dickhead playing a trick on my mind.

"Oh, you're hilarious," I said under my breath. Every time I inhaled, my nose was assaulted with frigid chill, far harsher than what Brant and I had experienced on our walk earlier. That had been a little brisk, like one would expect late fall to be. This ... this was getting to be January-type crap. Way out of season.

I pulled my left hand up and looked at my palm. The blood was still running there, seemingly unaffected by the cold that was freezing everything else. It wasn't gushing or anything, just streaming lightly.

Part of me wanted to ask what else could go wrong, but I wasn't stupid enough to fall prey to that temptation. I knew for a fact that if I did, I'd find out in mere moments, and it would be something that sucked, a lot.

The world closed in around me, the visibility clamping in tight as a particularly harsh gust kicked up snow from the ground. The drifts were getting higher still, and I was beginning to wonder if this was that much-vaunted "lake effect" snow I'd always heard about. If so, I really pitied the people who lived on this natural wonder. My next vacation was going to be in the middle of civilization, dammit, where I could order a pizza at any time. Maybe someplace where they didn't know me, like Barcelona. No one would think to look for me in Barcelona. I could dress like a tourist and people would ignore my pale, pasty ass. Not that I would show my ass, at least not in a literal sense.

My eyes started to tear up, and it wasn't from the emotion of planning my next vacation. They were burning like hell from the ever-intensifying winds. Was it possible to have a freezing hurricane on an island in the middle of Lake Superior? Because that was what this felt like. Either that, or my brother had decided to give up his day job and start importing cold from the north pole just to torment me into feeling guilty about the long list of wrongs that he perceived I gave no damns about.

I rubbed my freezing hands against the slick sleeves of my jacket, inadvertently rubbing blood on the left one, like I was preparing myself for sacrifice or something. I sighed when I saw it, sending another cloud of warm breath steaming out into a damnably cold world.

I started to stomp my feet as I walked, drawing my eyelids closer together and peering out through narrowed slits. It was getting harder to see, even absent my current squint, and it was then that I realized—

Oh, shit.

I looked down and there was not one trace of the road remaining. The trees that had lined either side were gone, the visibility so poor that I couldn't see more than twenty feet in any direction. The only good news was that I hadn't wandered off in the middle of a forest … had I?

I had the presence of mind to keep my body pointed in the same direction, which I both hoped and presumed was right, and took an opportunity to look left and right as best I could, trying to see any sign that I was on the right path.

There was none.

I was lost, completely and utterly.

31.

The paramedics helped me by delivering Augustus directly to the infirmary on the agency's campus, and I followed behind their ambulance with its wailing sirens, never once having to press Baby's accelerator too hard to manage it. I kept my lights flashing the whole time so that anyone I passed knew that I wasn't just ambulance chasing or coasting behind like some asshole.

I'd stayed long enough at the scene of Cunningham's outburst and Anselmo's appearance to rule out the possibility that they were there. So, the good news was that no one else got hurt in that one, other than the co-worker that Cunningham had burned to death in a fit of … well, I don't know what kind of fit it was. It was spaztacular, though.

The bad news was that J.J. had already mustered up a lone camera image showing Cunningham and Anselmo fleeing the scene together before he lost their trail … again. That was what we in the industry called a bad day. Actually, pretty much anyone with half a brain would call that a bad day.

As we pulled into campus driveway, the ambulance finally killed the sirens and I took the lead. I drove my Challenger right up to the rear entrance to headquarters where I caught a glimpse of a beautiful, dark-haired woman standing there waiting, white coat fluttering in the wind.

Any look of concern she might have had evaporated the moment the ambulance doors opened, but she couldn't hide it from me. Isabella was an enigma to a lot of people, but I knew her better than anyone. She was a tempest, a beautiful and furious storm that destroyed all but the unprepared.

Me, though? I had experience with high winds.

"Careful," she said, probably unnecessarily, to the paramedics as they brought Augustus out of the ambulance on a gurney. His neck was immobilized with one of those white cervical collars, and he was strapped down. The legs of the gurney deployed as they brought it down to the sidewalk.

"We've got this," I told them as I stepped up to the side to wheel Augustus into the building. Isabella took up position on the other side, directly opposite me, face inscrutable. The sun was shining overhead, and a gentle breeze rustled over us, disturbing the thin sheet that covered Augustus's body. I could tell the paramedic had cut his clothes off already. He didn't look too upset, though, so I assumed he was already over it.

As we approached the back entrance to headquarters, Isabella smacked the automatic open button for the double doors with a little more violence than she needed to. I could tell by the way she did it that I was probably going to be getting an earful of something in the next few minutes, and it wasn't going to be anything good, like sweet nothings. She waited until we were all the way into the medical unit before she cut loose. "Did I hear you right before? It was Anselmo?"

"It was Anselmo," I said as we slid the gurney in place under the big light in the center of the medical unit. I lifted Augustus's backboard and him in one good heave ("Whoa!" he said) and settled him down on the table. "He's been dogging my steps the last couple days. J.J. says he's getting help from the brains behind the January attack."

"I don't like this," Isabella said, shaking her head as she leaned over to examine Augustus. "Your sister should be here to deal with him."

"Phillips suspended her for a reason—" I started.

"A good one, no doubt," Isabella said.

"A stupid one," Augustus said at the same time. Their eyes met and then they both looked away from each other abruptly, both more than a little sullen.

"I doubt he's going to allow her back for anything short of the apocalypse," I said, finishing my thought.

"So you are forced to deal with an invincible man all on your own?" she asked. "That is insane."

"Hey, he wasn't on his own," Augustus said in protest.

"But he is now," Isabella said, standing up straight, her lab coat rustling as she did. "You are out of action for a week to heal. You will probably be mostly healed by end of day tomorrow, but if you agitate your injury it could be longer. Healing spinal injuries as a meta is tricky business; misalignments add considerable time to the process."

"Great," Augustus grumbled. "Can I at least go to class during recovery?"

Isabella gave him a severe look. "In three days, perhaps."

"Well, that's the weekend," Augustus said, and if he could have, I think he would have thrown up his arms in exasperation. "Doesn't do much good."

"Find that cute girl on Monday," I said, "get her notes."

"I'm missing more than one class," Augustus said irritably.

"There are a lot of cute girls on that campus," I said, smiling. I caught a very closed-off look from Isabella and stopped immediately. You know that look. The one that throws into question whether you'll ever get laid again. "I assume. I wouldn't actually know myself, having never been to that campus, or ever really laid eyes on a cute girl other than this one doctor I know who—"

"Stop groveling," Isabella said.

"Yeah, it's really pitiful, watching you do that," Augustus said. "I think I'm going to be sick."

"Hush, you," Isabella said.

"Why?" Augustus asked seriously. "Is it bad for my back?"

"Merely your health," she said, "if you continue to interrupt the conversation of the grown-ups."

"Burn," I said, watching his face fall. "Anyway, I don't think Sienna's coming back for this." A little rumbled persisted in my belly. "I haven't heard from her yet, in any case." I picked up my phone and dialed a number.

"You are calling her now?" Isabella asked, watching me all the while.

"Not exactly," I said as the line picked up. "J.J.!"

"Yo yo yo," J.J. said. "Reed, my man … you know how to bring forth the chaos, bro. You're the Loki around here."

"I think he's mischief, not chaos," I said.

"Didn't Sienna kill him?" J.J. asked, musing aloud.

"Probably," I said, "her body count is both prodigious and far-reaching." I caught a glare from Augustus at that and mouthed an *I'm sorry* in mildest contrition. "Dude, have you gotten any word on her whereabouts yet?"

"Ummm," J.J. said, "not really. I left messages—like I'm a secretary or something—but I haven't heard anything back from the cabin rental office or the island's law enforcement yet. It's like they keep bankers' hours, if bankers didn't come in until noon." He lowered his voice. "Also, Phillips is helicopter parenting me at the moment."

"What?" I asked.

"He's like … hovering, man," J.J. said. "All over the top floor, constantly this morning, asking for updates."

"Updates on what?" I asked, frowning unintentionally at Isabella, who gave me a quizzical look in reply.

"Oh, I don't know," J.J. said, voice growing in vehemence as he went, "maybe that giant cluster-flummox you had up in Anoka County this morning."

"I didn't—that wasn't —" I paused. "Wait, that was in Anoka County?"

"Dude, you have stepped in the poop landmine once again, you have stuck your head into the bear's mouth, choose your metaphor for the crap you have unleashed upon us, the poor servants of this agency," J.J. said. "Whichever you pick, know that it has rolled downhill unto us, the lowly, and that we—"

"Are really delivering this in an overwrought kind of way," I said, taking the steam right out of him. "What's Phillips up your tailpipe about?"

"How about the newly formed alliance of Mr. Flames and Mr. Invincible?" J.J. asked. "And the fact that we can't get a decent idea of where they're heading at any given moment in time? And that I'm being perpetually hampered in all my efforts to follow them because someone with a big brain is totally blocking me with her—"

"What about Harper?" I asked. "Doesn't she have a drone in the air?"

"She does!" J.J. said with mock enthusiasm. "And you know what she's been able to do with it? Nothing. And I know this because Phillips is bouncing back and forth between her station and mine like a ping pong ball that … uhhhh …" His tonality changed abruptly. "Yeah, we should totally get together to play Pong later." He covered the receiver of the phone, muffling himself slightly. "It's Reed."

I heard the phone yanked out of his hand. "This is Phillips," came the boss's voice, utterly bereft of good humor.

"No, this is Reed," I said, smarting off completely inappropriately. I never would have done that a couple days ago. What the hell was happening to me?

"Not the morning for it," Phillips said, heading me off. "What the hell were you thinking?"

I didn't intend to play coy, but it came out that way. "You're going to have to be more specific if you're going to come at me like that—again, I might add."

"You let them get away," Phillips said. His voice was still

flat. "Both of them. Together."

"'Let' is a strong word in this case," I said. "My partner had a broken back, and I was up against one guy that's as near as to invincible as you'll find this side of an armored cavalry regiment and another who's running a little hot and crazy right now. I didn't *let* them get away; I chose not to abandon my partner or the innocent people at the scene by trying to run blind and pell-mell after them, completely unprepared."

"Why didn't you shoot Cunningham?" Phillips asked. "That'd be one half of the problem solved right there."

I cringed. That probably would have been smart. Sienna had certainly encouraged me to get better with my pistol, and I was. But I still didn't like to draw the thing. It wasn't ever top of mind for me like it was for her. Like an old pervert, she whipped it out on every occasion, whether it was appropriate or not. "Maybe," I conceded.

"Maybe?" Phillips came at me with a little more emphasis this time. "If that guy kills anyone else, I want you to remember this moment, because that death is on your head." And then he hung up on me.

"Crapola," I said, pulling the phone back from my ear.

"Boss enjoying a piece of your flank steak right now?" Augustus asked, with a strangely satisfied look. "Because that conversation—you know, the side I heard of it—sounded kinda familiar."

"Bag it," I said. "He was right. I should have shot Cunningham." I sighed. "I'm just not used to ..."

"Yeah, yeah," Augustus said. "Things are going to be different under your leadership, I remember."

I tried to put up a stone mask to hide my irritation, but I knew Isabella saw through it. "It will be okay," she said.

I looked right into her deep brown eyes. "Really?"

She waffled, and it was obvious she was lying to make me feel better. "Perhaps."

"And perhaps not," I said, spinning away from the two of

them. "Dammit. Now I've got to go after two extremely dangerous metas without the benefit of help."

"Phillips cannot possibly expect you to do this thing," Isabella said, stepping around the gurney to land a hand on my shoulder. The latex gloves she wore squeaked as she squeezed my tense, sore deltoid. "Not against the two of them, not by yourself."

"I've never seen Phillips like this before," I said. "So irate. So unreasonable."

"At least not with you," Augustus said, a little snappily. I could tell he was enjoying this.

"It's got to be pressure from above," I went on. "Every time he landed on Sienna like this, it was always heat from Washington that prompted it."

"Or, conversely," Augustus said, "maybe the dude is just a dick."

"Even if that were true," Isabella said, and I couldn't tell whether she was suggesting it was Augustus, me, or both of us that was right, "it doesn't change the fact that you have a daunting and highly dangerous task before you. He can't expect you to do it all on your own."

"He can expect quite a lot," I said, and I turned back to see Augustus nodding along. "But you're right; I can't do it alone."

Isabella nodded slowly. "Very sensible. You should stay here until your sister—"

"No," I said, shaking my head. "That'll be two weeks, and this city can't wait that long for help. People are dying."

"But you just said—" she started.

"I said I can't do it alone." I let a very small smile creep out, enough to reassure her. "And that means ... I'm going to need some help from an old friend ..."

32.

Sienna

Caught out in the middle of rapidly worsening snowstorm without a fit coat, my left hand dripping blood and my skin gradually freezing, my eyes squinted almost shut because of the ferocity of the wind, dealing with occasional—or maybe even perpetual—mental attacks from a telepath intending to scare me ... no, this was not how I wanted to spend my vacation.

I hated to sound like C3PO, but I was really beginning to wonder if maybe it was my lot in life to be constantly forsaken. Had I really been so very bad in the karma department that it had to rain—or snow, as the case may be—crap on me all day long? I mean, really? Did Hitler have to deal with this shit? Did Stalin? Did Kat? No, she was sunning herself on camera in SoCal for mad money while I froze to death slowly in the lakeshore district of Siberia.

This was not shaping up to be my year, which was par for the crappy, snowed-over course.

"So this is what Westeros has to look forward to," I said, pushing forward in the same direction I'd been going before I paused to take stock of the situation. I had no idea if it was the right one, but honestly, standing around and hoping help came just wasn't in my DNA.

A wind eddied around me, blowing a swirl of snow in a

miniature tornado that passed in a second. It was visually interesting, at least insofar as white on a white background could be. "Shoulda gone to Hawaii," I said to no one in particular. Talking to myself made me feel marginally better, like I wasn't desperately alone in the middle of a crapstorm. "No one regrets going to Hawaii. Except maybe the Japanese that one time."

I saw a very faint outline of something in the distance. It was in the air, vaguely circular, and reminded me a little of a time when I'd seen Aleksandr Gavrikov lift off into the sky in preparation to destroy a town. It was just a halo of light visible through the growing gloom and wind-whipped snows. I squinted, trying to determine what it was, but I gave up as it disappeared in a gust of flurries.

Still, it gave me an idea of direction. It had appeared slightly to the left of the direction I'd been heading, maybe forty-five degrees off my course, so I adjusted and headed for it. After all, at least it was something. Before, I'd just been heading toward nothing.

I walked a few aggressive steps, a little faster than the pace I'd been going before. After a few moments, I saw it again, that halo of light in the midst of the dim and snow. It gradually grew brighter as I drew closer, until, finally, about fifteen feet away, I realized what it was.

A streetlight.

Halle-fricking-lujah.

I'd stumbled, mostly blind, into the far edge of town. I fought the wind and the snows that were now threatening to reach above my ankles to get to the base of the light. It was a post stretching ten feet into the sky and curving over to shine its light down. It was quaint, kind of colonial in a way, probably fit in well with the island's charm or something. I didn't care about any of that, though. For me, it was the sign of civilization that told me that the country road that led off to my cabins was coming to an end, that the town proper was just ahead.

I stood under its faded light and peered into the distance.

There it was, another halo, about forty-five degrees to my right. It must have been across the street. I stared harder and saw the faintest outline of a building catching the light just beyond it. Yep, town.

I trudged ahead, using the new lamp as a marker. Shorty's was close by, I was sure of that, and I was already on the right side of the road. No need to stumble blind again, crossing the road just to seek the lamp light like a moth with a fire. I walked as quickly as I could down what I figured had to be the sidewalk, the blistering wind feeling like it was freezing my eyeballs right in my skull. Tempted as I was to close them for sweet relief, I had a vision of them frosting over, keeping me from opening them again, so I refrained.

I made my way ahead, step by step, until I saw a wall on my left side. I peered into it, trying to discern what I was looking at.

The clinic. I could see the sign in the window, snow already accumulating at the black L-joint of the window's frame. Just behind it, a sign with a clock face that read, "Will be back at ..." The clock hands were set for midnight. I guess Sarah was done for the day.

It wasn't far now. Putting my shivering left hand against the wall, I moved ahead. I could barely see ten feet in front of me, so I let my frozen fingers guide me, my walk hampered by the depth of the snow now and my aching ankle. I plunged forward, catching my injured left hand on the door to Shorty's sooner than I expected. I cried out, then swiped at it again, ripping it open. At least the door *was* open, I reflected. With my luck, it could have been closed, leaving me to freeze to death outside.

Without ceremony or shame, I threw myself into the warm air at the bottom of the ramp at the entry, landing my cold and sopping wet back against the wall at the bottom of the ramp. I'd made it, and as I watched the ice and snow swirl around outside the glass door, I knew for sure that I wasn't going to be going anywhere for a good long while.

33.

Reed

The sandy-haired blond man got out of his Torch Red Mustang with a familiar swagger. Shutting the door behind him, his fingers drifted along the paint job, leaving a little glistening shine behind wherever he touched. He was parked in the curve of the headquarters driveway and stood there in the late summer sunlight like he owned the place and everything in it, wearing a black suit jacket that looked like he might have had it perfectly tailored to him just that morning. He'd skipped the tie, though, and had a silver-grey shirt that had just the slightest sheen to the fibers. His black shoes glinted in the sunlight, reflective in their high level of polish. He grinned at me in a friendly, familiar way as he ambled over, taking his time and ultimately sticking his hand out in greeting as he approached.

"Scotty," I said as I took his hand and pulled him up for a bro hug/shoulder bump, "thanks for coming, man."

"Not a problem," Scott Byerly said, still grinning to beat the band. He nodded at Baby in a show of respect. "I see you finally traded up to something that befits a young man on the move."

I glanced back at my darling car. "Well, you know, when you're dating a woman like Isabella ..."

"Hot cars, hot women," Scott said, nodding along in

understanding. "You're living the life, my friend."

"Coming from you, that means a lot," I said, taking in his Mustang with a motion of my hand. Scott came from money. "Because you are a man who knows how to pick out a car."

"You are a hell of a flatterer," he said. "Mastery of wind extends right up to your verbal ability." His expression turned serious. "So … you end up taking the express ferry up shit creek before losing engine power or what?"

"To put it mildly," I said, leading the way toward Baby. "This guy I dealt with over in Italy, Anselmo, you remember him?"

"I remember him disappearing under a flaming curtain of white phosphorus when Sienna popped that grenade in his mouth," Scott said. "I got the impression from both of you that he probably got off light with that punishment."

"He's a bad man," I said. "Long story short, he's back, and he's inserted himself into this manhunt for the airport bomber. It's become a supervillain team-up."

Scott let out a low whistle. "You don't have small problems, do you?"

"They let Li and the FBI handle those," I said. "Small problems for the small penised. And what with Sienna out of town and our new hire injured in a tangle with Anselmo this morning … I'm kinda on my own here. Was hoping for a watery hand to cool the situation off."

Scott shrugged his shoulders like it was NBD. That means no big deal, for those of you who don't live your lives online. "I'm at your disposal, man. What do you want to do?"

"I'm glad you asked," I said, opening my driver's side door and getting in. I pressed the hands-free call button and waited for the beep. "Call J.J. on cell." Scott got in while the car did its thing, and pretty soon we were treated to the sound of my phone ringing.

"Reed," J.J. said, almost in a whisper, as I started the Challenger.

"J.J.," I said, "find me someone to punch in the face."

"Funny you should ask," J.J. said, voice no longer hushed, "because Director Phillips is orbiting my way again just now. So why don't you come on over?"

"Yeah, not doing that," I said. "Find me a different face to punch."

"Too bad," J.J. said with only a hint of acrimony, "you were starting to sound like Sienna for a minute there."

I sat there in the driver's seat, stunned, my mouth slightly agape. That was something Sienna would have said, down to the tone.

But I wasn't like her. Dammit, I wasn't. I hadn't even drawn my gun this morning when—

I blinked, the harsh sunlight aligning perfectly with my windshield to throw glare in my eyes. I pulled my sunglasses out of the cup holder and put them on while I let the dead air hang as I contemplated a reply that wouldn't make me sound like an overly aggressive psychopath (something like, "No, I'm fucking not!" was right out). "J.J.," I said finally, aiming for higher ground, "we've got a real problem to solve here. I could use some help."

"And if I had any help to give you," he said, clearly nonplussed, "I would. But unfortunately—" He paused, and sounded muffled. "Yes sir, I'm working on that right now, but the traffic cameras in that area—look, this isn't my specialty, that's more Rocha's—"

"Well, he's not here," I heard Andrew Phillips thunder in the background. "I have the Secretary of Homeland Security and the White House Chief of Staff up my ass about this, so get it done, or I'll be transferring my governmental enema to your rectum, are we clear?"

"Yep," J.J. said levelly, "you'll be giving me a bureaucratic enema if I don't do work that's plainly out of my job description. I bet that's going to be so much fun. It'll probably smell like Hai Karate and failure, given—"

"Stop being a smartass and work the problem," Phillips

said, but his voice was already fading.

"Reed, I've got to go," J.J. said and for the first time, he hung up on me without another word.

I looked over at Scott, who was nodding his head with a slightly amused expression wrinkling the corners of his mouth. "Sounds like the new boss is a real joy to deal with."

"He's under pressure," I said, absentmindedly defending him.

"He's not exactly being David Bowie and Queen about it," Scott said.

"No, it's not nearly that musical," I said, racking my brain. "We've got no leads, a cold trail …"

"Hrm," Scott said. "Whenever I was in these situations, having to do this kind of agent-type stuff, I'd always ask myself, 'What would Sienna do?'"

"And then you'd go kill ten people and call it a day?" I snarked, running fingers through my hair in utter frustration.

"Heh," Scott said. "If all your leads are played out, maybe we should re-examine the ones that came up dry the first time?"

That triggered a faint hope in me. "We talked to this guy's mom yesterday, but she was pretty unhelpful, all pissy to me and Augustus." I frowned. "And I think she might kinda be a racist. Maybe she'd respond better to your charm than mine."

"Yeah," Scott said, nodding along, "maybe she's more interested in the 'rugged, good-looking' type than pretty boys." He flashed a grin at me. "I could take a try at talking to her, I guess."

"All right, then," I said, and shifted the car into gear, pressing the accelerator hard enough that it jerked us both back in our seats. I was prepared for it; he wasn't, but he laughed anyway. "Let's go gigolo you out to an angry, frightened mother and see if it gets her to roll over on her baby."

34.

Sienna

I didn't wait long in the entry to Shorty's before someone came over to check on me. It was Brant, who popped his short-haired head over the railing and looked down at me from above, all quizzical and surprised that someone was darkening his door in weather such as this, I was sure. "What the hell are you doing here?" he asked, brow knitted in surprise at my appearance. "And looking like the abominable snow woman, no less."

"You've got my car," I said. "It was not exactly a summer hike to get here, either, let me assure you."

"Your appearance proves that," he said, waving me up. "Either it's snowing to beat the band outside, or you were standing under the Stay Puft Marshmallow Man when he got flash fried."

"What is with all this *Ghostbusters* talk?" I asked. "Is it because of what's going on? Also, I could go for some marshmallows right now." I shook out of my coat. Little chunks of ice that I hadn't even known were there came off in sheets as I did it. I left a pile on the floor suitable enough to mix a whole pitcher of frozen margaritas. "Or anything, really."

"Well, good news for you, then, because I have food and abundant time to cook it," Brant said, disappearing behind the railing. "Apparently, flash blizzards are somewhat bad for business. Who would have thunk it?"

"Oh?" I brushed more of the ice off my coat, but by now it was sloughing off in liquid form. I stomped my boots while I did it, dislodging even more of the white stuff I'd waded through to get here. "Gee, am I your only customer today?"

"No," he called back, already almost to the bar, "you're the second."

"Who was the first?" I asked as I came up the ramp, finally sure that I'd gotten about as much of the snow off of me as I was going to. I paused at the top of the ramp as I caught sight of a familiar ponytail of dark hair attached to a feminine figure seated at the bar. "Oh. Her."

"Yes, her," Sarah said, not bothering to turn around on her barstool to look at me when she spoke. "It was either hunker down over here when the storm came blowing in, or sit in the clinic staring at the walls without so much as a TV to break the monotony." She finally turned her head enough to glance at me. "I know it's hard to believe I chose the non-solitude option, but here we are. It was probably the promise of food that swayed my vote, honestly. I forget to pack my lunch one day ..."

"And this, of all days," I said, hanging my coat on one of the pegs mounted on the nearest booth. Given the weather conditions, I was unlikely to forget it when I left. I realized now that Brant was nowhere in sight. "How about that humidity, huh? Absolutely muggy."

"It's thick," Sarah said, turning back to the bar. She had a martini in front of her again, and she took a drink as I sat down in the stool two down from her, leaving one empty between us so as not to crowd either of us. She eyed me, and I wondered if I hadn't left enough of a gap. "How are you doing?" she asked, with about as much enthusiasm as if she'd been compelled to ask by some outside force.

"Ripped open my hand again," I said, expecting her to display ... I dunno, surprise? Amazement? Sheer professional interest?

She gave me none of those. "Oh, yeah?" She looked over at my outstretched hand for a moment. "You should probably run some water over that."

I blinked at her careless reply. "Maybe you are like my doctor after all."

There was a flash of annoyance in her eyes before she replied, utterly dismissive. "Well, I'm not your mother." She took a minute to settle down, then, with her hackles a little less raised, asked, "Do you want some stitches?"

I felt a sting that was unrelated to my hand. "No."

"What are you two lovely ladies talking about out here?" Brant asked as he emerged from behind the curtain to the kitchen.

"You," Sarah said pointedly. "Go back in the kitchen, we're establishing a comprehensive list of your faults and need a few more years to compile it properly."

"Ouch," Brant said, holding his hand over his heart like he'd been wounded. "Listen, Sarah, I know you're worried about Jake, but that's no reason to take it out on the rest of us."

Her eyes smoldered so hot I thought they were going to burn the air around her as she turned a fiery glare on him. I was no shrinking violet, but I would not have enjoyed being on the receiving end of that one, not remotely. "So," I said, trying to defuse the tension for once in my life, "how long is this going to last? Any bets?"

"Satellite TV went out this morning," Brant said glumly. "Short answer—no one knows."

"Yay," I said with a modicum of sarcasm. "This is getting better and better all the time."

"Had any more of your telepath attacks?" Brant asked, fingering the curtain separating us from the kitchen like he wanted to retreat.

"Yeah, I had one just as I was leaving the cabin," I said, drawing a look of surprise from Sarah. "Same old boring story, though—'Get out,' all spooky and rumbly. Very high on drama, low on anything actually scary."

"What does it take to actually scare you?" Sarah asked. I could tell by the way she asked that she was serious.

It was my turn to shrug. "I've gone nose to nose with some of the most powerful people in the world. What does it take to scare me? A lot, I guess. More than dark faces in the mirror and a deep voice from the shadows."

"I bet," she said, looking at me like she was thinking deeply about it. "Would losing the people you care about move the dial for you?"

"There aren't many of those left," I said breezily. There really weren't. Ariadne, Augustus, and … maybe Reed, depending on how much of an ass he was being at any given point.

"Hmm," Sarah said, turning back to the bar. "What about you, Brant? What scares you?"

"The English," Brant said without missing a beat. "You just never know when they're going to invade your homeland."

I blinked at him. "Yes. I suppose that has been a persistent fear around here since that whole business in 1812." I looked at Sarah. "What about you? What scares you?"

She pursed her thin lips and took a long drink of her martini. "Anything happening to my kid, I guess."

I'd forgotten that Jake said something about having kids on the ride over on the ferry. "How many do you have?"

She shot me a quicksilver look, eyes flashing with something like anger. "Just the one. The highly ungrateful one."

"Okay, then," I said, backing off from whatever nerve I'd touched. I could have sworn Jake had used the plural when talking about his kids; but I supposed maybe he had more than she did. I sniffed the air. Something was cooking, and it smelled good. "Hey, Brant, are you making …?"

"I put on some breakfast for you," he said with a smirk. "Unless you'd like to take your keys and drive back to your lonely cabin where you can sit in the dark and talk to ghosts or telepaths or your mirror or what have you."

I sighed. "I think I'm going to be here for a while." I took another look back to the windows outside, barely visible over the railing that looked over the ramp. I couldn't even see the street beyond. There was nothing but white outside. "No TV, huh? Anyone got a deck of cards?"

35.

Benjamin

Benjamin was huddled against the passenger window of the car, forehead against the glass, sweating even though the air conditioner was set at what he considered a reasonable temperature. His palms were wet and his mind was spinning, stuck in a rut of a very different kind than he had been over the last few days.

Now it was no longer about denying the monster, or denying that things had happened. No, now he'd shifted. These terrible things happening, there was no way to close his eyes to them any longer, nor ignore that—that voice that broke in every now and again, harsh and low. The police were after him; those metahuman cops were on his trail as well, no denying that.

No, now his mind was stuck in an entirely different place, a perfect spin of chaos punctuated by two poles: "I can't have done this" and "But I must have done it."

And at somewhere on the other two points that made up that particular compass came the alternating thoughts of, "Well, if I did it, it must have been an accident," and the absolutely mad, "They clearly all damned well deserved it."

The last one scared Benjamin immensely. It was hot, raw, red, violent, and caused his breath to smoke out of his nose when he reached that point in the train of thought. He had just about come around to it again, too, when he felt a hand land on his shoulder, jarring him out of this particular feedback loop.

"It will be okay," Anselmo said again in that heavily accented voice. "As I told you before, you need no longer be afraid."

"But they're coming for me." Benjamin's voice sounded small even to his ears, a whimper in a hurricane.

"But they will not get you," Anselmo said. "You have seen what my friends can do, what I can do. We have shepherded you safely from right under their noses. You watched me hurt one of them when they came to take you, did you not?" Anselmo's fingers kneaded the knots in Benjamin's shoulders. It was ... rather nice. "I will not allow them to harm you. Trust me."

In spite of the scars, in spite of the fearsome visage, Benjamin believed that Anselmo believed that. The man had a certain conviction that Benjamin found intensely refreshing. It was a confidence of a sort that Benjamin had never once felt in his entire life, and the scarred man projected it effortlessly. "Okay," Benjamin said, rather limply. He felt as though all the emotion had drained out of him, as though he were grey, near death from emotional bleedout.

The jangle of a default ringtone sounded in the car, and Anselmo fumbled to raise the phone that he'd had in the cup holder to his ear. "*Pronto,*" he said. His eyes flashed in surprise as a female voice burbled on the other side of the connection. "Hmmm. That is predictable."

"What?" Benjamin asked before he could stop himself.

"Mr. Treston has found himself a new partner, and they are heading in a direction that suggests they will visit your mother's house," Anselmo said. "It is of no consequence, of course—"

All that grey, mental pallor fled in a hot instant for Benjamin. He flashed through to yellow and then red in short order, saw what seemed like flames dance from his eyes as that voice broke loose—

at my house
aGaIN?
how dare they—

A strong backhand lashed Benjamin in the jaw, smacking his head against the window hard enough to jar him, but not break him. He squealed in surprise, hand flying instinctively to where he'd been struck, and turned his eyes in surprise to Anselmo, who was staring at him with the phone clutched to his neck. The Italian brought the car to a screeching stop and stared at him, hard eyes peering out of a scorched face. "Do not do that."

"Do what?" Benjamin cried out, holding his jaw.

"Do not whimper and cry like a girl in that voice," Anselmo said. "The first lesson of being a man is that you must act like a real, true man, not these wimpy girls and—what do you call them now? Metrosexuals? *Pfah!* They have to wax their genitalia until they find the pubic hair that bleeds, their manhood is so small! The girls of olden days in my country had bigger balls than these pansies that walk the street in their skinny jeans." Anselmo spit. "You are not to be one of them, not any longer."

"Oh-okay," Benjamin said, nodding along helplessly.

Anselmo glared hard at him. "Do not sit there, nodding your head like one of the sheep in girls' clothing. Does this anger you, this thing that they do? Going to see your mamma?"

"Y-yes," Benjamin said, nodding along, dragging up a little emphasis from deep within. "It … it positively enrages me."

"Then do something about it," Anselmo said and slapped him again, lighter this time. "Direct your rage to revenge, in the way of a man. Do not sit here and steam idly, like an iron. I will let you know if my pants develop wrinkles and I need that from you." He touched Benjamin on the chest, delicately. "You have fire within. I know you have let it out, but it has been the petulant screams of a small girl, pushed on the playground by a boy she craves. A man does not do this craven thing. A man goes in the direction of what he wants. He does not hide his intentions like a woman hides her genitals. He proudly displays what he has to offer and goes at what he wants directly." He made a motion, a gesture of grabbing himself. "Do you see what I mean?"

"Uhh ... I think so?" Benjamin asked, staring at him.

"Not now, Cassidy," Anselmo said into the phone, with more than a shade of irritation, "men are speaking. You will wait." And he hung up the phone, tossed it into the cup holder, and grasped Benjamin's face with both of his hands, cradling it. "Listen to me, son. You have been babied your whole life, yes?"

"I ... no," Benjamin said, mildly offended. "I've—"

Anselmo thumped his ear with a simple flick. It hurt enough to draw a grunt of pain from Benjamin. "Do not argue. You live with your mother still? And you are grown man, yes? And it is not because she needs your care?"

"... no," Benjamin grunted. The last flick had hurt badly enough that he wanted to cry.

"Then this is the day that you grow up," Anselmo said and brushed his hair back from his eyes. "This will be the day that you find your—" He pointed to Benjamin's groin. "Those. *Sí?*"

"Well, at the risk of sounding utterly ludicrous ..." Benjamin said as Anselmo let him go and turned back to the wheel. "How do I do that?"

"It is very simple," Anselmo said, putting the car back into motion. His scarred hands grasped hard on the wheel, and Benjamin saw the sign as he headed west on Interstate 394 toward the western metro. "You find what your opponent cares for most ... and you rip it screaming from his grasp."

36.

Sienna

I had this feeling in my gut like the sun was sinking low in the sky way too early, as if sundown for me meant a swift end to the day. It shouldn't have mattered, should it? It wasn't like colonial times, when I'd have to light a lantern in order to proceed with my life, but seeing the white outside gradually turn darker over the course of twenty minutes was … disconcerting, especially when my own sense of time made me think it was far, far earlier than it appeared to be judging by the light.

"What time is it?" I asked, sitting on my barstool, my breakfast/lunch done.

Brant pulled his wrist up and looked at the leather-bound monstrosity with the big clock face on it. "Seven o'clock."

"That can't be right," I said and turned back to look outside. "Where'd the day go?"

"Buried under the snow, probably," Sarah said. She hadn't really spoken since our last exchange, and I didn't think that was necessarily a bad thing.

"Huh," I said as the door behind us opened again, "that went fast."

"Tends to happen when you're sleeping it off 'til noon and then fight your way through ghosts and a snowstorm," Brant cracked.

"Gah," a young man's voice came from the door, "it's dropping like feathers in a pillow fight out there." The clomp of heavy boots resounded through Shorty's and I saw the hat before I saw the rest of the guy that came in. It was the lawman's hat, that big-brimmed, quasi-cowboy thing, with a snow-covered star sitting right on the top of it. What his name? Zebulon?

"Z!" Brant shouted out to him as he entered. "What's going on?" His voice sounded funny again, like he was letting his words lilt.

"Well," Z said, his steps driving snow off his boots and onto the floor, "it's pretty much turning into a whiteout. Other than that? Nothing. Been quiet all day around the office."

"Hard to perpetrate a crime when you're stuck inside your own house, I guess," Brant said, drawing a beer for the lawman as he sauntered up to the bar, skipping the stool next to me and taking the next one over. I approved; it was exactly what I'd done with Sarah, and it maintained a healthy margin between us. I call it 'minimum safe distance.'

"Yet somehow the Wickmans manage to pull it off every month," Z said, taking the beer and sipping from it. I hadn't gotten a real good look at him yesterday, but I was seeing him pretty clear now. He was probably in his late twenties, handsome features, and I could see under the hat that he had brownish-blond hair. "I get called out to their place so much I feel like they ought to set up a special parking space for me on their driveway. That Stephan, he's got a temper. And Colleen, I just don't know about her."

"And here I thought Cherry was your most frequent offender," Sarah said darkly.

"She's right up there," Z agreed, setting his beer back down.

"Sarah's sister," Brant stage-whispered to me.

"Your sister is here, too?" I asked as politely as I could.

"It's not like she's got anywhere else to go," Sarah said

and took a slug of her martini. I took that as a sign to leave further inquiries on this topic the hell alone, even though she'd brought it up.

"So," I said, looking over at Z, trying to catch his eye, "any word on when the weather will let up?"

He didn't answer me, sitting there, hunched over his beer and popping the shell on the peanuts on the bar. His clean, neatly manicured fingers were clearly struggling with popping the shell efficiently. He was breaking one on its end and taking forever to do it. "Hello?" I asked, but he didn't look up. "Fine, be that way," I said at last.

"Maybe he can't hear you," Sarah said.

"Or maybe he's being a giant dick," I said. "An enormous, turgid—"

"Watch your mouth," Sarah said, and it held not a bit of suggestion.

I started to bite back, to verbally slap her upside the head in lieu of doing it for realsies, but I was in a bar, confined by the weather, and I could see Brant eyeing me nervously. So instead I bit my tongue. Hard. Literally. And I bled a little.

"You need another drink?" Brant asked.

"I'm sticking with water," I said. Booze would just give me the excuse I didn't need to fly off the handle, and make me vulnerable in a way I didn't need to be right now.

"Coming up." And he refilled my glass and set it right in front of me before walking off down the bar.

"You don't belong here." The voice rumbled, rattling my water and shaking some out onto the bar before I could even pick it up.

I stood up in a flash, on my feet and off the stool, eyes fixed on the water glass for just a second before I remembered that water glasses didn't talk, and that the voice must have originated somewhere else. "You sonofa—"

"Language," Sarah said again, nonplussed. She did not bother to turn and look at me as she addressed my profanity.

"Fuck off," I said. "Like you said before, you're not my

mother."

Her head snapped around and I caught a glimmer of blue-green eyes under dark hair that told me just how annoyed she was. "You've got no respect for the rules."

"Well, at least you sound like her," I said, and swiveled my attention to Z. "Hey. When is the weather letting up, have you heard?" I took a step toward him. "Yo, Zebulon, I'm asking you a question." He still didn't look back, and my politeness all ran out.

I'd been sitting here on this island, dealing with all manner of crap from all manner of directions on my vacation—telepath attacks, weather incidents, and now this—and by this I meant shitty behavior from Sarah (which was kind of expected based on what I'd seen of her personality) and the frigid shoulder from the local law (which was not).

"Hey," I said and reached out a hand to clap him on the shoulder. When I touched his heavy coat, it was like getting jolted by a small dose of electricity, like static being turned loose on my fingers, and I pulled away in an instant.

He must have felt it, too, because he finally deigned to notice my presence. "Hey," he said, annoyed.

"Yes, 'hey,'" I said. "I've been trying to get your attention for like, ten minutes."

"Well, you've got it now," he said, spinning around and standing up. He was taller than me, but then, most guys were. "And you're about to regret it."

"So you're one of those local fascist pig officers that they make a cliché of in the movies, huh?" I took a step back and kept my hands at my sides, nonthreatening. I didn't really want trouble, but this guy had an attitude problem, and while I wasn't going to make the first move, if he wanted to take my gentle, apparently static-laden touch as assault and battery, I was damned sure going to give him both of those things, for real.

"You're out of control," he said, announcing his role as

my substitute villain of the week.

"Not out of control," I said, "just out of patience."

He came at me less clumsily than I thought he would have, but he still did that awkward, reaching thing that told me he was thinking he'd just grab hold and subdue me or something. I slapped his hand away, hard, but not enough to break anything. The look on his face told me I'd stung him, though, and the anger flashed across his face as he came at me again.

Only this time, he was much faster.

Like … meta fast.

If I'd had Wolfe's strength and speed, or even if I'd been aware that it was coming, I probably could have dodged it. As it was, getting jabbed in the jaw by a meta while in a bar in the way damned north of Wisconsin was not the sort of thing I expected, ever. But it happened, and I heard the joint crack in my jaw as I staggered back.

"Yoo … muv … er … f … ferr …" I drooled, doing my best to recover from what had been a staggering blow out of the blue clear sky. Or the hazy, grey sky, as the case was. He came at me again, and I let him have a jab of my own that knocked him back into the bar. Even without Wolfe, I knew how to throw a damned punch.

I also knew how to follow up on an opponent that was staggered, and my last thoughts of vacation flew right out the window as I jumped all over that bastard and started pounding the snot out of him with all the pent-up fury I'd been accumulating this last couple days.

"Unf!" I landed one to his midsection, "Urgh!" I unloaded on his right kidney. I had him against the ropes— the bar, in this case—and I peppered him with ten good punches in five seconds. He crumpled at the midsection, trying to keep me from turning his stomach into a hammered haggis, but as soon as he did it I blasted him in the jaw with everything I had and he smacked his head against the bar. "Taaak … thaa …" I drooled, my jaw still aching. It might even have been broken, for all I knew.

Stars flashed as I saw the sucker punch too late to do anything about it. It hit me like my suspension, right out of the blind side, and knocked me straight out of the fight. I hit the floor jaw first, and that took the last of the wind out of my sails. My eyes rolled, fighting to focus on the person standing above me as my brain begged me to let go and shuffle off into the waiting darkness.

It was Sarah, and she had a look on her face that told me she didn't regret knocking the hell out of me in the least.

I let go, and let unconsciousness end this craptacular day on a low note.

37.

Benjamin

The guard had died in flames, and Benjamin had watched, horrified, as Anselmo had pointed Benjamin's hand to do the deed. Benjamin watched in sick fascination as it happened again, right before his eyes, fire consuming a human being and turning their pink skin a scorched black.

"Watch," Anselmo said, a hand on the back of Benjamin's head, anchoring it in place. He didn't close his eyes, even though he wanted to. He watched, just as Anselmo told him to, watched out the car window as the man burned to death in the little guard shack. The guard didn't push the alarm button, didn't call out for any help that could hear him, he simply ... danced, then fell, then writhed ... then died. Screaming all the while.

When it was done, Benjamin couldn't tear his eyes away from the blackened corpse, even after Anselmo took his hands off his head. The Italian stepped out of the car and pressed a button in the guard shack. Small fires burned on the carpet, on the desk where a sheaf of papers held together by a clipboard had caught, but Anselmo ignored them and flipped a switch, raising the blockade out of the road. Then he got back in the car and shifted it into gear, setting them in motion again.

"That was ... so ..." Benjamin said, trying to shake off

the horror.

"Satisfying, yes?" Anselmo said, and then looked at him. "The word you are looking for is … 'satisfying.' Repeat it to yourself until you believe it."

Benjamin's mouth felt so dry. "Does that … does that work?"

"When I was a boy," Anselmo said, steering them down the tree-lined road, "my father took me hunting for the first time when I was very young, probably four or so. I was a child in my thinking, much like you are now." There was a cruelty in the way he said it that bothered Benjamin only slightly less than what he'd just witnessed. "We were looking for birds, and my father, he made me pull the trigger when we found our quarry. I caught a bird with a very off-center shotgun blast." He made an exploding gesture with his hands as he took them off the wheel. "Destroyed the wing, but left the bird alive and suffering."

"How terrible," Benjamin said, whispering.

"So then he retrieved the bird, which was trying to hop around," Anselmo said coolly, "and he brought it over to me. 'This,' he says, 'is a chance to take a step toward being a man.' And he offered it to me, head first, while he held the body. The meaning was obvious, even to a child of my age." Anselmo looked over at him. "So I snapped the neck."

"Oh, God," Benjamin said, unable to keep it in.

"That was a step toward manhood," Anselmo said. "It was building a callous upon my flesh in the way a working man develops them, yes?" He looked his burned face toward Benjamin and nodded. "Your problem is, you have no callouses. Your little heart is weak, and the slightest adversity sets it aflutter, thump thump—" he smacked Benjamin in the chest, "—with fear. You are incapable of dealing with these feelings, these setbacks. Your mother has raised you to be a plump offering to people who have the will to take what they want. In prison, you would be everyone's bitch."

Benjamin made a guttural sound of horror at the mere

thought. "I ... I ..."

"Do not fear," Anselmo said, waving him off. "We will take care of this. The work of twenty-plus years' failure to raise you, I will fix in mere hours. We will build some callouses together, yes?" At this, he grasped Benjamin's hand and held it up. It was ... soft. Pink. And it shook.

"Callouses," Benjamin said, staring at his own pristine flesh, then back at the man, the scarred, lumpy man to his left. "I ... I ... yes." He nodded. "Yes, I ... need that."

"Yes, you do," Anselmo said, and he steered the car right as the road curved to lead into a massive series of structures. A tree-lined campus, like a corporate headquarters or a college. The main building was just ahead, and Benjamin could see a beautiful red car parked out front. There were no people in sight, and the afternoon sun was creeping low into the sky. "Now ... let us go around the back of this place, this *agency* ... and see a doctor about your condition."

38.

Reed

"Well, that didn't go so well," Scott said as he got back into the car, looking more than a little put out. I'd let him out a block from Benjamin Cunningham's house, figuring it'd be better if his mother didn't see me anywhere close to Scott, so as not to poison her first impression.

"Oh, no?" I asked, shifting in my seat.

"I think it's safe to say she sniffed me out," Scott said. "Either that, or she's really just a rude person in general."

"I could believe either," I said, putting the car into gear and pressing the accelerator. I started drumming idly on the steering wheel as I went, trying to figure out a next move. "I only talked to Cunningham for about ten seconds, but I think that man is probably suffering from an overbearing mother."

"I haven't met him," Scott said, "but I wouldn't have any trouble believing that." He rested his elbow on the window and put his hand, balled up into a fist, against the glass. "So … what now?"

"I always hated the passive part of this," I said, turning at the corner to take us back to the freeway, instinctively. "This was the thing back in the day, at the Directorate, or the agency, later. Felt like we were always waiting for things to happen."

"Tough to get too aggressive with the bad guys," Scott

said. "Sounds like you think things have gone in that direction lately, though."

I forgot that I wasn't dealing with Augustus anymore, someone who was tired of me picking at these scabs between me and Sienna. "Yes," I said with more than a little relish. "I mean, during the war it was one thing. We were dealing with stakes like—"

"The end of the world as we know it?"

"Yes," I agreed, "exactly. Sovereign wanted to wipe out our entire people, and that was without doubt. Sienna saw the vision, we watched him and Century tear through the metas in that extermination, I mean ... it was righteous, you know? Fighting against the twilight of our kind."

"You're still fighting," Scott said with half a shrug.

"We're fighting mostly against wanks like Anselmo," I said. "Actually, like less than Anselmo in most cases. Anselmo actually had this crackpot plan to make Italy his personal kingdom. Most of the people we're using the surveillance state on are pikers like that Simmons guy. He wanted to rob the Federal Reserve Bank, so we watched his every move for a few days, busted him after his robbery, and then Sienna beat the holy hell out of him on film. Pretty far cry from the end of the world, that guy."

"I dunno," Scott said. "I think you know I was the first to speak up in criticism of some of the things we were doing back then, but ... seems like the game hasn't changed all that much."

"Duuuuuude," I said, shaking my head, "if there was one person I figured would understand ..."

"I understand," Scott said, a little huffy, "but I think you're splitting hairs. You were totally fine with shooting Sovereign in the back of the head without a trial, remember?"

I flushed. "He was uncontainable."

"What do you want to do with this ... what's his name again? Cunningham?"

"He needs to go to jail, or at least be ... contained," I

said. "The Directorate had the tech to contain Gavrikov, remember?"

"He killed fifty people," Scott said. "And Dr. Sessions is dead, man, and I'm guessing that all the scientific expertise that might let you keep that guy under wraps went with him. He's a danger."

"I think it was an accident, what he did at the airport," I said.

"What about when he turned his co-worker into barbecue this morning?" Scott asked. "Still an accident?"

"Maybe," I said. I'd seen the video footage J.J. had appended to the file when I checked in online while waiting for Isabella to treat Augustus. It certainly didn't look good. "I don't know. I just … it feels like Sienna started crossing lines at some point," I said, bringing the conversation back to where I wanted it. "Or maybe I just woke up to the fact that … she doesn't care, man. We watched her grow up to become the most powerful person in the world, and she just … kills whenever she feels the need."

"My God," Scott said, deadpan, "does she kill the rude? Like Hannibal? Eat them?"

"Not funny," I said. "She's just gotten to the point where … I don't know, it stopped for a while after Sovereign. I legitimately thought that maybe he was the last person she'd ever kill. But then she went to London, and left an ungodly mess there, and since she's been back … I mean, in January alone, with those terrorists that stormed the campus—"

"I have nearly infinite water at my command and I can't even muster tears for those guys," Scott said. "They were trying to kill her, Reed."

"Yeah," I said, "and she killed 'em right back."

"She had no powers at the time. What did you expect? Should she have used riot shotguns laden with beanbags? Because I'm pretty sure she didn't have anything like that."

"Her killing people is like shooting an unarmed man," I said, finally coming up with an analogy I thought fit.

"Because an unarmed man can't hurt you?" Scott asked.

"Because it's a clear disparity of power."

Scott blinked at me. "Okay. Let's go with that for a second. You realize a human with a gun theoretically is more powerful than me, right?"

"Yes."

"Can I kill a man with a gun?" he asked.

I let out a low sigh. "I've seen you do it, back at Terramara—"

"Okay," Scott said, "can an unarmed man kill an armed man?"

"Well, Sienna certainly did, though she was an unarmed woman at the time—"

"So, let me get this straight," Scott said, "you get mad at her when she's superpowered and kills weaker people, you still get mad when she's unarmed, with no powers, and killing armed people who are out to kill her ... I gotta be honest, it sounds a little like you kind of just want her to lay down and die."

"Don't be a douche, okay?" I was heated by this point. "I don't want her to lay down and die. But you see all the articles and news pieces and crap, right?"

"The ones condemning her for every crime known to man? That'd be hard to miss, even for someone who doesn't read the news, like me."

"She brings it on herself," I said, putting aside that little revelation that J.J. had brought to my attention earlier regarding the origin of the press heat coming her way. I'd read some of the worst stuff about her, and I couldn't disagree with the assertions they made about how quick she was on the trigger.

"Look," Scott said, like he was giving up the fight, "I don't know your sister like you do—"

Nor half as well as you used to, I wanted to tell him.

"—but it seems to me, as an observer from way back, that you've gotten the front row seat to the next level of her personality getting hardened," he said. "Because I saw her after the whole Zack thing, when she was going after M-Squad with a holy hell vengeance, and it was ... intense. I don't see that here, that desire to do cold-blooded murder and unleash havoc."

"Which is what worries me," I said. "And is entirely the point. She agonized over Wolfe when she killed him. Wolfe. A serial killer. And when she had to kill Gavrikov to keep him from turning Minneapolis into a smoking crater like he did to Glencoe, she lost sleep over that, too. She wouldn't kill after that, remember? She wouldn't. Flatly refused when Old Man Winter kept pushing her and pushing her, until finally, the old bastard did—well, what he did. And after that, the kid gloves were off. It was a carnival of bloodletting. Which, in time of war, I turned a blind eye to. But now the war's over, and she's still killing like it's on."

"War isn't quite like it used to be," Scott said. "I mean, I was reading a thing a while back talking about how war is not a thing of nations anymore, it's a thing that one person can bring to the table. Think about it; this Cunningham? He's got more power than any pre-World War One army at his disposal if he's anything like Gavrikov. He could stand in the middle of a battlefield and kill thousands of people—or millions, if he decided to unleash in a city."

"So, we're always at war?" I asked. It was not an answer that satisfied me.

"You don't just kill at war," Scott said. "I mean, I killed a Century meta in Vegas because he was trying to kill me. By your logic, maybe I should have just hit him with ever escalating force until he stopped, maybe starting with a flick on the arm, I dunno—"

I thumped my head against the back of my headrest. "Why does no one get where I'm coming from on this?"

"Because I think you're torturing the hell out of your logic to get here," Scott said, rapping his knuckles against the window. "And if you're that worried about Sienna's soul, or human decency, or whatever, why haven't you talked to her about it instead of … whatever you're doing?"

"I tried," I said. "I tried on the night of the attack in January."

"And?"

"She made excuses," I said. "Blew off my concerns like they were nothing to her. Said she was … I dunno, that she did what she had to do."

"And you don't think she had to kill those people, on that night?"

"I don't think she needed to kill all of them, no—"

"Dude," Scott said. "I have to ask you—are you under the impression we live in a world without violence or something? Because we don't. There are mean people out there. You've met some of them. Feels like your friend Anselmo is one of them."

"And he deserves to be tried," I said, exasperated, "and locked up for a very long time, maybe the rest of his life—"

"You think he's going to go for that?" Scott asked. He blinked. "Man. I can't believe I'm the one making this argument. What the hell happened to me?"

"I honestly can't fully explain it," I said truthfully, "but it sounds like you pretty much crawled into my sister's head and live there."

"Because your sister knows bad people," Scott said, "and she damned well should. Wolfe and Bjorn are among the worst on the planet, and they're in her head."

"And I think they're making their influence felt," I said, as the cold snap of revelation hit me in the back of the head like a rubber band. I paused and let it sink in. "She didn't used to be like this."

"She made some hard—some terrible choices," Scott said quietly. "But she also saved the world. I don't work with her every day, but I don't think the news gets it right at all. And I doubt she's just going out and killing indiscriminately."

"Not—I didn't mean—ugh …" I let my head sink. "I'm

not saying she's a psycho killer that's about to start cooking her enemies and serving them like—"

"Wolfe?"

"Hannibal," I said. "Wolfe ate his prey raw, by all accounts."

"Ew."

"I'm saying that she's lost sight of what's okay in a fight," I said. "That she's too quick on the trigger. That she'd just as soon put down a Benjamin Cunningham as try to save him. And that's not right."

"Huh," Scott said, pulling his lips together. "I guess you and I learned a different lesson when fighting for your life. Because I always figured if someone was trying to kill me—and I think that's what Sienna is dealing with most of the time—it's perfectly acceptable to kill them right back. No pulled punches. No—aim for the leg or whatever, which is a stupid idea that can kill them anyway. Just ... getting the job done."

"But is it *right*?" I asked, letting the doubt show through as I asked. "She's the most powerful person in the world, deigning to stoop low among us fleas. She could stomp us all flat, like Sovereign wanted to. You're telling me she doesn't have the obligation to be different, to do things different?"

"She's not invincible, Reed," Scott said, looking at me with ... pity? "One good shot, she's as dead as any of the rest of us. I think that's something that people forget. Humans are frail creatures, and it doesn't take all that much to kill any of us, meta or otherwise. I knew a guy ... he got an argument with a teenager over something stupid, and the guy just slugged him in the back of the head when his back was turned. Caused a brain hemorrhage that killed him." He snapped his fingers. "Just like that. And that could have been Sienna, honestly. Just the right timing, the right punch, the right place, and his life was over." He looked over at me, and I tried not to look back, tried to concentrate on the road, on the freeway in front of me. It was clear, but I still needed to concentrate. "Reed, people are trying to kill her, and she could die any time. What would you have her do?"

I stared straight ahead, but I felt that burning in my throat again. "I don't know," I finally said. It wasn't something Augustus could have ever even forced me to admit, but Scott had ripped it out of me, damn him. I took a deep breath and sighed it all out. "I honestly have no idea."

39.

Benjamin

They entered the building through the back entry, without regard for whether anyone saw them. Benjamin found it thrilling and frightening all in one, his heart pounding in his chest and blood rushing through his veins in a way he couldn't recall feeling before he'd come back to Minneapolis changed. He realized that before he'd met Anselmo, before the airport, before the monster, his whole life had been some bloodless exercise in survival, and that only now—now that he was being guided by someone as powerful as Anselmo— was he finally living, taking the deep breaths of life.

Also, he had to pee and wondered when he'd get the chance to go.

"This is the way," Anselmo said under his breath, steering Benjamin down a stark hallway, bereft of color. "This is the way that Cassidy suggested."

They paused before the obvious double doors, glass with the cross insignia upon them. They whooshed open as Anselmo stepped in range of them, and Benjamin followed, his shadow, trying to learn everything that Anselmo had to teach him, even down to trying to walk taller and prouder, like his mentor did. It was not effortless; that much was certain. He sucked in a breath and followed into the medical unit to see two people talking in the middle of the room to his left. One was the African-American meta cop that he'd seen Anselmo hit earlier, at his work.

The other was a woman. Tall, voluptuous, with a white lab coat and dark hair that was mussed in all the right ways. Benjamin found himself licking his lips nervously merely at the sight of her. He watched the two of them for only a stark moment and he already felt like he was invading someone's privacy, like he ought to be elsewhere, not watching this, watching *her*, unasked.

Before he could fold back into himself, Anselmo spoke, captivating his attention once more. "Doctor," he said, bold and loud, "I find I have gone without worthwhile female company for entirely too long. Perhaps you might find it in your tender mercy to aid my plight?"

There was no mistaking the woman's response. Her face went from somewhat neutral to surprise to sheerest loathing in the space of seconds. The tautness of her jawline, the puckering of her lips in disgust, the jerk of her head in revulsion at the sight of Anselmo—they would have been obvious to anyone. Once more, Benjamin felt the shame he had cradled to his bosom in secret blossoming out, threatening to steal all his courage and make him run from the room in tears.

"Anselmo," the doctor said, clearly clamping down on all those emotions she'd let play across her face moments before. "It is such a strange thing to see you here, so far from Firenze or Roma. You seem … different, since last we met. Perhaps a touch out of place."

"I belong everywhere I go," Anselmo said, striding deeper into the room as though he owned it.

"Especially that jail cell you were in for a couple years," the black man said from his place on the gurney. "That was a real good fit for you."

Anselmo chuckled softly, but his laugh sounded rough and raspy, much like every noise he made. "I find it appalling that Mr. Treston did not find time to make the introductions between us. You are Augustus, yes?"

"He knows my name," Augustus said, "I think I'm flattered. Especially since you decided to break my back without even saying hello this morning."

"My quarrel is not with you," Anselmo said, waving a hand at the man on the bed. "It is with Treston. We have a long history, he and I, one that needs to come to an end. Soon."

"He is not here, Anselmo," the doctor said.

"Oh, I know this," Anselmo said. "He has gone to visit the childhood home of my new friend here." He waved broadly to encompass Benjamin, who suddenly founding himself wishing he could simply melt away. "Have you met Benjamin Cunningham?"

"Only a couple seconds before your fist made my acquaintance," Augustus said. He was lying still on the bed, as though he couldn't move, covered to his armpits by a sheet, and with a cervical collar on his neck. Good grief, was he actually paralyzed? Benjamin saw his fingers twitch, answering that question: apparently not.

"Regrettable," Anselmo said, "but necessary. I needed to have a conversation—and a confrontation—with Treston. Those who get between us will inevitably be harmed."

"Am I between the two of you?" the doctor asked coldly.

"My dear," Anselmo said, and his blackened lips parted to show his teeth, "you and I should be alone, always, with no other man anywhere near us whilst we—"

The doors behind Benjamin whooshed open and before he could turn to see what they brought, a shadow flew over his head and dropped squarely on Anselmo, like a pillar of darkness ripped straight from a storm cloud. It took a moment for Benjamin to realize by the flashes of green here and there that it was dirt, pure and black, ripped from the earth with its roots and in sufficient volume to fill a dump truck.

The dirt moved as though it had a life of its own,

descending on Anselmo in a great flow. Benjamin watched, shocked, seeing the darkness turned brown and black by the overhead lighting as it swallowed Anselmo whole. It moved like a worm, undulating, a six-foot tall worm that stood on its ends and—

A hand punched out the side of the dirt as Benjamin cried out in shock and took a step back. Another hand came out the other side with a hard punch that sent specks of detritus and wet earth across the clean, blue floor of the medical unit. It took Anselmo almost a full minute of warring with the black soil before he finally broke free with a flexing of his muscles in pure strength, shattering the last of it across the floor as though it were shards of glass.

He stood there, adjusting himself, brushing his suit off, dusting the remainder from the folds of his scarred skin, and then, finally, he looked up to Benjamin and tossed him something approaching a wink.

Cool. Calm. Uncaring.

What a man.

"Now," Anselmo said, "where were we?"

40.

Sienna

Colin Hay's "Waiting For My Real Life To Begin" was playing softly in the background when I awoke to bars in front of my face, and the smug, handsome face of Zebulon Darwin was right there in front of me, squatting so he could look me in the eye as I stirred back to wakefulness.

"Morning, Sleeping Beauty," he said.

"I'll say this for you sucker-punching islander hillbillies," I said, pushing up to all fours. Apparently he'd deposited me unceremoniously on my face in the cell, "at least you've got good taste in music. I've got this one on my own playlist." I got up and stretched, listening to my back pop softly as I realigned my spine. "Also, even though you just called me a beauty, you're still an ass."

"And you are awfully big for your britches," he said, rising to his feet and towering over me, the sturdy metal bars between us. The sound of the wind came howling from somewhere outside the stone walls of the jail. I was in a room that was all cells, about six of them, with the only visible exit behind Mr. Z, who was clearly the sheriff from *Wayward Pines*. The book, not the show. I haven't seen the show.

"Is that a remark on the shape of my ass?" I asked, ready to rip the bars off the cage I was in so I could stuff them up his nose. "Because you don't have to be a hater just because you're not all about that bass—"

"Just stop," he said, looking suddenly disgusted. "How did I know you were going to be one of those people that just goes on and on, energized by the sound of her own voice and infinitely amused by her own self-indulgent quips?"

"Because you've seen me on TV …?"

He rolled his eyes. "I'm charging you with disturbing the peace—"

"Yeah, well I'd charge you with being a total prick—"

"—and assaulting an officer of the law—"

"—which I also am, and you punched me first, knuckle-dragger—"

"WILL YOU JUST QUIT IT?!" He waved his arms in the air like he'd lost his shit, teeth bared and gritted.

"Probably not," I muttered under my breath. "I never did know when to quit."

"You're in jail, idiot," he said, "quit now. It's a dignified time to do so. It's actually past it, but you're only damaging your case by continuing to be so damned insolent."

"Is insolence a crime now?" I asked. "Is that something I'm going to get charged with, too?"

"I'm not going to sit here and listen to this," he said, turning away from me and heading for the door.

"Are you sure?" I asked. "I get funnier with time. Or maybe people just lose the will to fight my particular brand of humor and give up all hope of—" He slammed the door behind him. "Finally. Thought he'd never leave."

I put my hands on the bars and started to pull. As far as idiots went, I had the lawman pegged for a big one. He'd stuck a meta in what was pretty clearly a human jail, which—since I presumed he was a meta himself—was something he damned well should have known better than to do.

Then I tugged on the bars for five minutes without any success and started to wonder if maybe the idiot in our relationship was the person standing inside my cell, breathing hard from the exertion of trying to bend bars that had zero give.

"Sonofa," I muttered. "FML."

"Doesn't that mean—" A voice came from behind me, causing me to jump into the air a good foot or three.

"Gyaaaaaaaaaaaaaah!" I shouted, shaking my hands in front of me out of sheer surprise. I came down and whirled so fast I slammed my back into the bars. There was nothing but shadows behind me, and I blinked, wondering what the hell was going on. Was this the voice? The ghost? Had they been warning me all along to "Get out!" because, in fact, this place was an evil trap put together by my enemies—

Before I could follow that thought to its crazy paranoid conclusion, my eyes locked on the windowsill about seven feet up the wall to my left. It was open a little, and the voice was coming from there. I stepped closer, tentative, and spoke toward it. "Who is that?"

A hand snaked into the cell, but all I could see was a watch on the wrist. It looked familiar. "Jake," I said.

"None other," he said from outside. "I, uh ... heard you had a rough time tonight?"

"Did you?" I asked snottily. "Did your wife tell you that she knocked me out with a cheap shot?"

"She did mention that," Jake said, and he almost sounded sorry. "Said you looked like you were about to kill Z."

"I wasn't going to kill him," I said, sullen. "I wasn't even going to beat him stupid. Because he already is stupid."

"You got into a bar fight," Jake said, surprisingly free of judgment.

"Something weird is going on in this town," I said. "And Z? He's no ordinary guy." I cracked my jaw and massaged the side of it. "Also, your wife? Hits like ... harder than most of the villains I've tangled with. Yeeouch."

"There's a reason I don't cross her," Jake said, withdrawing his hand. I could still hear the howling of the wind outside the window, and the draft coming from that inch or two of opening was wicked cold.

"Are you standing out in a mini-blizzard?" I asked, easing closer to the window.

"It's a little snowy still, yeah," Jake said. "Hasn't really let up. The good news is that I was able to pack some of the snow together to stand on. It's really accumulating out here."

"Marvelous," I said, "maybe by the time it all thaws out, I'll be done serving my sentence." I stared at the window. "Unless you came to bust me out."

"Nothing so bold as that, I'm afraid," Jake said. "I don't think you deserved this, though."

"Well, thanks for the moral support," I sighed. "But I don't think that's going to do me much good."

There was a pained silence. "I've got to go," Jake said.

"Thanks for stopping by," I said in resignation.

"You going to be all right?"

I took a moment to unpack the curious mix of feelings swirling around me. The answer came naturally. "I saved the world when I was eighteen and for the last few months I've been dealing with the fact that everyone in the world hates me. I think I can spend some time in jail without coming to pieces. It's not exactly my first time being a prisoner."

"Okay," Jake said, and he sounded a little sad about it. He reached his hand in again and waved, the light catching his watch, a golden one that still looked vaguely familiar. "Take care of yourself, Sienna." He hesitated. "It'll all be all right." I waited to see if he said anything else, but he didn't. I heard the sound of snow crunching as he walked away.

I placed my back against the stone wall of the jail and tried to decide what to do. I had none of my other souls or their powers, which would have gotten me out of here in an instant, and I had no idea when—or if—they'd be back. There was a telepath mucking with my life, and something strange was going on with this town and its lawman. He might even have been the one responsible.

My head sagged, heavy with the weight of utter despair.

"I'll be fine," I said, more to reassure myself than because there was anyone around to hear it. "I will."

But I didn't believe it for a minute.

41.

Benjamin

"You were about to chill out," the lady doctor said in response to Anselmo's question, and then she took a long, metal cylinder that was smoking out of its end and threw its contents squarely into Anselmo's face.

Benjamin just stood there, stunned, as it all seemed to play out in slow motion. The stuff she threw looked like liquid as it left the steaming cylinder, which was almost the size of the helium tanks he'd seen used to fill balloons.

This one, though, had a hazardous materials warning plastered on its side.

oh

dear

The liquid hit Anselmo as he was turning to look at the doctor. He did not dodge it, did not see it coming in time. He was still partially covered in the last of the dirt, which clung to his ridged and marred skin. The liquid splashed him in the face like she'd thrown a bucket of water. Anselmo flinched, closing his eyes as it hit.

For a moment, he seemed like he'd be fine, like everything was totally normal and he'd just had a good bucket thrown over him in a water fight, that was all.

The first hints of ice crawled across his skin a moment later as the doctor followed her attack by spitting on him in pure fury. White frost dripped slowly down Anselmo's face as if he were freezing from the inside out. His eyes crusted over, partially opened, and his hands crusted into place with harsh crystals over them even as his body staggered, his mouth frozen open without a scream emerging. His lips were stuck in that horrible rictus, like—

The doctor carried through with her metal cylinder and hit Anselmo squarely in the cheek. Benjamin watched in fascination and horror as the man's face—

shattered
broke
glass out of a window
light catching it in a million sparkly shiny pieces
diamonds in the light
casting rainbows

Anselmo spun to the ground and landed on his hands. That glasslike sound of shattering filled the air again and this time a scream filled the air, a horrible, awful, tormented scream of utter pain burst—

out of his
his
ohmygod
he doesn't have a
where is his

—from the remains of Anselmo's face.

Benjamin barely kept back a scream of his own, the light in the room going yellow as he watched in complete horror what was going on in front of him, powerless to—

to stop
this will stop
they're just like the rest
i'll stop it
BURN THEM

A rush of black soil, reconstituted from where it had been broken aside, swept Anselmo forward like a tidal wave. The Italian hit Benjamin squarely in the legs and took him along, the dirt reaching out and laying its filthiness—

ew

ugh

ahhhh

dirt

—all over him. They flooded out the door and hit the opposite wall hard, Benjamin's breath leaving him in the rush.

Benjamin curled up, gathering his knees to him, and rocked there, on his side, letting the world go away for a moment. This was just so—so—so violent. He reached up and brushed his hands against his face, finding wet dirt mingled with tears.

Anselmo was

he had to be

no one could survive

A hand, covered in blood, seized hold of his arm. Benjamin screamed, uncontrollably, until the hand slapped again across his face. "Controllll yourselfff ..." Anselmo said, looking up at him. His face was—

oh

my

The hand slapped him again. "Be a mannnnn," Anselmo said, and bloody spittle fell out the side of his cheek as he slurred, his tongue fully exposed all the way down to his gullet. "Annnnd ... get meee out of ... heeeere ..."

42.

Sienna

I was lying on my back, staring at the boring ceiling when the door opened and admitted a single person. I had to admit, I was figuring on Z. After all, sooner or later he'd have to come back to feed me. Until then, I was just biding my time, trying to figure out if the wiser option was escape or waiting. Escape, currently impossible anyway, held the peril of likely further legal troubles, while waiting left me open to the sinister schemes of whoever was messing with me.

Had everything in this town gone completely, utterly crazy? Was there a weather meta messing with me along with the telepath? That was possible. Add a few surly, difficult townspeople—a couple of whom could actually double as those metas—and boom, we have the nutty conundrum I was buried in.

If nothing else, it had the virtue of being unique in the annals of Sienna. No one had ever set up a crazy weather pattern to trap me in a town of slow-boiling rage inducement before. Of course, if I got my powers back and discovered that was what was really happening, it was 50/50 and dropping fast whether I'd be feeling merciful enough to spare lives. Because this had been one of the most emotionally upheaving experiences of my life.

"Thought maybe you'd be sleeping," Sarah said as she

eased into the room. She had that quiet reserve about her that made me surprised she spoke first.

"Did enough of that already, thanks to you," I said, staring out at her. I was sullen, and I'm not ashamed to admit it.

"You attacked a police officer," she said.

"There were extenuating circumstances," I said. "Like ... static electricity." When I said it like that, I realized no court was going to buy it. Shit.

"You just can't keep yourself under control, can you?" She started to pace outside the cell. It took everything I had not to mirror her on my side of the bars.

"What are you?" I asked. "The town's resident Sienna Nealon expert?"

"Someone has to be," she said, shaking her head. "I know you. I know your type."

"Know a lot of succubi, do you?" I asked.

"Oh, come off it," she said, halting her pace so she could spin and face me. "You think you're the only bad girl with a temper out there? Most of the time, people like you end up on YouTube videos as part of a white trash roundup, the type of fights that degenerate into hair pulling."

"I would have resorted to hair pulling with you," I said, "if I'd known you were going to come at me when my back was turned, I would have—" I caught myself in the middle of another furious, pointless rant and just stopped.

"And that's why you're on that side of the bars," she said.

"I've been in worse," I sniped back.

"Want to stick me with a sob story?" Sarah crossed her arms. "Tell me your tragic experience in life?"

"Who cares?" I pushed the back of my head harder into the thin pillow. "I mean, really. You people are going to do what you're going to do. Which begs the question, what do you do for justice up here? Do I get a trial, or is it straight to the stake when it warms up enough for the torches to burn?"

"Very dramatic," she said, "like your problems aren't

mostly of your own making."

"I got in a bar fight," I said. "As if that's never happened in northern Wisconsin before."

"Even now, you don't see it, do you?" I caught a glimpse of those blue-green eyes in the half-light of the single bulb above me. "Even now, you're running away from responsibility for your actions."

"Do I get a reduction of sentence if I continue to listen to your lecture? Because maybe I'd prefer to go in the opposite direction and go straight for the death penalty instead."

She regarded me with a careful look. "Once upon a time, you told your brother, 'I don't live with humanity.'"

I sat bolt upright in my bed, spun my head to look at her so fast I thought I might break my own neck. "How did you know that?"

She didn't answer, just shook her head. "Do you know why you don't live with humanity?"

"You're the telepath," I breathed, my eyes locked on her. I came up to the bars that separated us and grabbed hold of them, felt the cold steel in between my fingers.

"Do you know why?" she asked again.

"Because I'm metahuman," I said, locking my eyes on hers. The urge to snap, to try and reach through the bars and seize her was strong. What would I do once I got her? Ohhh, I don't know. But it would have probably been primal for me and painful for her, trying to squeeze her into the cell to join me.

"Yes," she said, still looking straight at me. "Metahuman. As in beyond human, past what they are. Most people think of it in terms being better, but you can be beyond in other directions, too—like down." Her voice turned harsh. "You're subhuman. Worse than anyone." She lowered her voice to a whisper. "You're a murderer."

I recoiled from the bars as I watched a sliver of a smile cross her lips. "And," she said, with sudden relish, as if she were telling me a fantastic secret of life, "you're going to die here."

43.

Reed

I brought my car to a screeching halt and flew out of it in a mad rush toward the infirmary entrance to headquarters for the second time today. I put the wind squarely at my back, adding a little extra oomph to each step, and ignored Scott's footsteps as they fell further and further behind me. I was on a mission. I was walking with fury. With a purpose.

And when that purpose collided with Anselmo Serafini, one of us was going to walk away bloody.

I noticed an enormous hole in the lawn just outside the medical entry, a clot of soil the size of a couch ripped out of the earth. Grass was left hanging over the sides of that sad and lonely hole in the landscaping, and seeing it only increased the fervency of my pace.

I shot through the doors without pause, practically ripped them off the hinges as I did so. I darted past agents with assault rifles and submachine guns to come to the medical unit's open doors. Dirt was everywhere, scattered around like someone had spilled a giant bag of potting soil. It was black and rich, and I imagined it had come out of that gaping hole in the ground I'd passed on the way in.

I shoved past some administrative wank with a clipboard, not caring if I'd just stepped on toes today attached to a butt I'd have to kiss tomorrow. I ignored the cry of protest that followed and made my way inside to find …

Isabella, safe and sound, talking to Kurt Hannegan.

I caught her eye as I entered, but she stayed cool even after seeing me. She was like that—old school, not into the PDA. I restrained myself, knowing she'd pretty well kill me if I ran up and kissed her right now. Later, though … later …

"Doctor," I said, easing up to her.

She met my gaze with cool relief, like she was exhaling now that I was here. Or at least, that's how I imagined it. "Mr. Treston." Just the way she said it, all Italian and sexy … it gave me a little relief.

"How'd you stop Anselmo?" I asked as Scott crowded in next to me, nodding at Hannegan like they were old friends.

"Liquid nitrogen," she said, pointing to a metal cylinder that was sitting on its side on the ground.

"What the hell were you doing with liquid nitrogen here?" I asked, a little boggled.

"It's used for cryogenic treatment of warts," she said. "It burns them off. As it turns out, it also worked on Anselmo's new and not-much-improved face."

"Ouch," Scott said with a grimace. "The guy was scarred before, right?" His grimace got worse. "Can't imagine what he looks like now."

"Where is he?" I heard a cool voice behind me and turned to see Andrew Phillips shouldering his way into the room in much the same way I just had. When he locked eyes with me, he headed straight for me like a missile. "Oh, *now* you're back," he said, sparing none of the sarcasm.

"Yes," I said, "now I'm back. Back from investigating and manhunting, which is what I'm supposed to be doing."

"You missed your man while engaging in your hunt." Phillips broke his way into our little circle. "Both of them, actually."

"Make sure you note that on my performance review," I said, channeling the spirit of my sister. Did he not think I'd noticed Anselmo and Cunningham had just tried to kill my girlfriend? I may not have known they were going to come at us like this, but I wasn't completely stupid.

"Yeah, that's getting worse by the moment," Phillips said. "What's your plan now?"

"Well," I said, holding back a little sarcasm. "I don't have one. So you can tell me what you want me to do."

"I want you to catch this guy," Phillips said, and he stuck a finger right in my face. "That's what I've wanted all along. It's what the president wants; for you to stop making us look completely incompetent to the voting public."

"Really?" I asked, drawing it out with low disbelief. "I didn't see you predicting Anselmo was going to attack our headquarters. No one predicted it, actually."

"It doesn't matter what you can predict," Phillips said, "it matters how it looks. Word's out. Did you see the press?"

"I saw two guys with cell phone cameras at the gate," I said. "I wouldn't call that the press. I mean, that's not even as many as were at the scene when—"

"They're coming," Phillips said, cutting off my little reminiscence before it hit him in an emotionally painful memory. "Local news will be pulling up momentarily, if they're not here already. We just got a black eye in full public view."

"If you think you can hunt these guys better than I can," I said, taking a step back from Phillips, "be my guest."

"What I want you to do," Phillips said, closing up the distance between us to get in my face, "is what you promised to do for the last few months: take over for your sister and deliver the same results in the field with less violence and fewer public relations disasters. It's all you've talked about, and so far you've delivered public spectacle after public spectacle. Fighting in a Chinese restaurant? Demolishing a tech company? The damned airport exploding?"

"I wasn't even on the case when the last one happened," I said.

"Doesn't matter," Phillips said. "We're not two rational

adults hashing this out, and that's what you don't seem to understand from your sister's experience. I'm not the one judging you—either of you. You're being judged by a much harsher boss—the public. It's not even the media that's your enemy; they're just the lens you're being viewed through. Your problem is that there are three hundred and thirty million people in this country watching you from a distance and making their judgments as to your motives, your intent, your competence. They're not forgiving people—"

"To say nothing of the rest of the world," Isabella said.

"They don't vote, so they don't matter," Phillips said, not even looking at her as he spoke. "I'm not your enemy. I'm your accountability. If it was just you and me, I wouldn't care that you've had some false starts, or that Anselmo is being tricky and getting help from someone who's manipulating technology in order to hide him. But I'm not in charge of public opinion, I'm in charge of getting the results we need so that Gerard Harmon can get re-elected without the metahuman problem exploding like the Minneapolis airport." Rage infused his diatribe, and his face was red throughout it. "You told me you could make it happen, this vision of yours of doing things different."

My face burned. I was getting my ass torn off in ragged strips in front of my girlfriend. "I can—"

"Don't tell me," Phillips said, holding up a single finger. "Show me. And better yet ... show them." He waved in a half-circle, presumably indicating the world around us—or at least the U.S. voters' portion of it—and then went right for the door.

"Man," Scott said as Phillips went out of earshot, "first, I'm glad he didn't ask about me, and second ... I am so not sorry I quit."

44.

Sienna

Sarah left after that last little goad, making me wondering what the point was, other than to make me feel like shit scraped off a boot. On the other hand, maybe that was good enough for her. I did have a certain mild dread by now, knowing I was in up to my chin with the water rising fast. It may not have been the first time I had been in a jail cell—by my count it was at least my third—but it was certainly the most isolated I'd felt. I mean, bars I couldn't move? On an island in the middle of Lake Superior? This was isolated. And I was supposed to be here two more weeks, weeks in which none of my extremely limited circle of friends were going to come looking for me.

Not a great predicament.

I started to wonder about Jake as I sat there, back against the concrete wall. I'd already tested the concrete and found it really hard on the ol' knuckles. My left hand was bleeding again, both from the squeeze of balling my hand into a fist and also from said knuckles after a half dozen punches had failed to so much as crease the block. Made me wonder if they'd seeded the concrete with iron or what. Not exactly an exciting place to be, realizing that even your basic powers were useless.

It led me to take stock of where I was, to really think

through what I had. I searched all my pockets and found nothing, not even my cell phone with its minimal contact list.

Plus, I was hungry. How fun was that?

Worst. Vacation. Ever.

Errr ... actually, had I ever really taken a vacation before?

I blew air through my lips in boredom, staring at the light fixture just outside the cell. Even if they'd had one inside the cell, what could I really do with it? Absorb enough juice to electrocute myself and turn off the lights in the jailhouse? Stall my heart enough to make them come investigate, at which time I could ambush and pummel them to death, start enacting a bloody vengeance?

Why did it always come back to bloody vengeance with me?

I stared at the washed-out grey concrete floor and saw my hand dripping blood on it in dark drops. Maybe it was because I was constantly spilling my own blood. Like I had some sort of mythical need to replace it by drawing out that of others. It was all very psychological, and made me wonder what my old therapist, Quinton Zollers, would have said about it.

Of all the people who had left me over the last few years, I think I missed Dr. Zollers the most. Probably because he was the one who understood me best. Without him ... I think I was working on autopilot. I couldn't tell if I'd changed or not. Reed swore up and down I had, just before he stopped talking to me, but I wasn't so sure. I was probably a little too close to the source material, and it's hard to see the picture from inside the frame. Ariadne wasn't much help either, because I didn't let her be. I always kept her at arm's length, because ...

Guilt, probably. I did kill her girlfriend, after all.

I looked back at the steadily growing blood puddle that my hand was forming and wondered how much of it I could afford to lose. In theory, a wound like this wouldn't let even a low-level meta bleed to death. Our healing ability was fast, and for a higher-powered meta like me, a succubus, I had regrown a hand overnight before even without top-level Wolfe powers. Nothing but the destruction of my brain or maybe a direct hit to the heart that ripped it completely asunder would kill me. I mean, there were probably other ways. I'd given it some thought—destruction of the lungs beyond my ability to heal them, complete and total decapitation—

Yeah. I'm morbid in my spare time, what little I have.

It had been a long time since I'd been reduced to being a base succubus. I tried to focus, to think, to work on that mental inventory. I had clothes enough to hang somebody (not myself, though, because that was the easy way out) or garrote them. I had enough strength to beat most people and metas to death. I could touch them and steal their souls, given enough time, but then I'd be left with them in my head whenever this chloridamide or telepathic interference finally cut out.

You know what the most commonly asked question is, when people hear about my powers? "Why don't you just absorb every bad meta you run across and add their powers to your own?" Probably assuming I'd become invincible or something.

Sad to say, it doesn't work like that. In order actually use the powers, you need the consent of the people you absorb, one way or another. This is the reason why most incubi and succubi had been walking around for thousands of years without being able to channel the powers of the metas they'd absorbed. It was able to remain a secret for millennia because getting someone you've killed to offer their power to you willingly? Not the easiest thing to do. If you've ever pissed someone off, then you know getting them to cooperate with you afterward is kind of a difficult proposition.

Surprisingly, killing people makes them really mad. Mad enough to not want to work with you. Most incubi and succubi had a solution for that—they could mentally wall off their wards, keep them imprisoned in their minds and basically never think about them again. Which is a neat trick, but it doesn't exactly prompt cooperation from strong-willed metas.

The only other incubus and succubus I'd met who could do what I do, using the powers within ... I don't know how they did it. I mean, I had a suspicion that Sovereign had somehow coerced his souls in a line, but I didn't know exactly how. And Adelaide? That was not a question she'd answered for me, either. She'd had some form of cooperation from the metas in her mind, which suggested to me that when Omega had fed her, they might have had some willing volunteers in the mix.

Whatever the case, Sarah was blocking my souls, so that was a dead end. On to the next thing.

I could steal people's memories or even selectively alter their minds, which took less time than a full-blown soul steal. Just taking memories didn't require cooperation to view, either. I also had the ability to reach people in their dreams—

Ohhhhhh.

Wow.

Sometimes I feel dumb.

I didn't enjoy using the "dreamwalk" ability that I had. In fact, I hadn't used it in ... years. It had been kind of a special thing that Zack—my first boyfriend—and I used to do. Since that relationship ended in tragedy, I hadn't really wanted to play with it much. But overall, it was a pretty simple thing to use. All I had to do was think of a person before I fell asleep, and I could draw them into my dream.

Perfect for summoning help right to your prison.

I eyed the cot in the corner of the cell. It didn't exactly look like the sort of thing you'd find at a five-star hotel, but I wasn't picky. The problem was, I also wasn't tired. Damn me and my sleeping until noon. Probably shouldn't have taken that sucker-punch nap, either. It was surprisingly refreshing. "Shit," I said to no one in particular.

The lock to the jailhouse door clicked, and I turned my head in surprise. It took a moment, but then the door opened, and standing there was Brant in all his bartender glory, carrying a tray bearing food. "My food's not shit," he said, looking a little faux-hurt.

"Agreed," I said, watching him warily. "Are you who the jail contracts to provide meals to the prisoners?"

"It's a charitable thing," he said, stepping up to the bars with a little wink, almost conspiratorial. "How are you holding up?" He offered the tray through the slit in the bars that was there for prisoner feeding.

I looked at the burger on the tray with a little skepticism. "You're really allowed to bring me this?"

"Sure," he said. "Why not?"

I was starving. I wolfed down the burger in about twelve bites, then drank hungrily from the metal sink in the corner. "Sorry for the lack of beverage," he said apologetically. "That I wasn't allowed to bring in. Not that I had much non-alcoholic selection in any case."

"That's all right," I said. "Food will do. I can just take my water straight from the tap. It isn't too gross."

"Very noble of you," he said seriously, "to lower yourself in that way."

"Ha ha." I sighed. "So. Sorry about the bar thing."

He waved it off. "It was predictable."

"It was predictable I'd get into a fight in your establishment?" I asked. "Ouch."

"You came in threatening from minute one," he said. "Threatened me more than a few times, I might add. It's almost as if you're ... the dangerous sort."

"Well, I can't argue with that," I said, coming up to the bars and wrapping my hands around them. "It is why they've got me caged, after all."

"Looks good on you," he said, and I had a hard time telling whether that was an actual compliment or not.

"Thanks, I think?"

He shrugged. "So … I wouldn't worry too much. You're not going to be here long."

"Speedy trial?" I asked, feeling a faint rumbling in my stomach.

"Oh, no," he said, shaking his head. "There's not going to be a trial."

That froze me in place. "Wow. So they're not even going through the pretense?"

"Pretense of what?" he asked with a short laugh. "Do you think you deserve a trial?"

I watched him through narrowed eyes. "Maybe you could explain what you mean by that. Do you mean I'm going to be released because what I've done doesn't warrant a trial, or did you mean—"

"You're subhuman," he said, looking at me almost pityingly. "Do you really think someone as low as you, who doesn't live with humanity—you think you deserve a trial?"

I stared at him, mouth slightly agape. "So you're with them."

"Yes, I'm with humanity," he agreed smoothly. "Do any of the prisoners you keep get trials, out of curiosity?"

My fingers tightened on the bars. He was keeping his distance from me, quite smartly. "I can promise you that none of *you* will."

He made a face. "Ooh, threatening. A bit old hat by now, don't you think?"

"You were playing nice last time. This time I know you're my enemy. That changes it from a threat to a promise."

"You can't do any worse to me than you've already done," he said, and went on before I could get him to elaborate. "Did you enjoy the burger?"

"Yeah, it was a real piece of culinary artwork, right up there with all those flower drawings Monet did," I said snarkily. "Why—" My stomach rumbled again, more insistently this time, and a realization dawned on me. "Did you … poison me?"

"Nothing too serious," he said with a slight grin, "but I wouldn't wander too far from that toilet for the next little bit. Not that you can get very far from it, but ... you'll probably need a bucket as well." He leaned his face just a little closer to the bars, and the grin went wide. "See ... we need to talk to you, first."

"We're talking right now," I said. "If you want to have a more intimate conversation, feel free to step inside the cage."

"Not just me," he said. "*We*. We need to have a conversation. Need to talk to you. To get you to understand—"

"Because that'll really make me regret however I've pissed you off," I said. "All I need to do is understand, and I'm sure I'll be magically sorry for whatever wrong I've done you."

"Oh, I don't care if you're sorry or not," he said and started toward the door, giving it a firm slap with the palm of his hand that resonated through the building. "I just want you to understand before the living hell starts ... so you know what you've done to earn the most painful death I could possibly imagine." He pointed back toward the toilet. "Enjoy your next few hours as you purge yourself of some of your resistance—and your sins. I think you'll find you're a little more ... shall we say ... malleable? Once you're done. Once you're weaker." That grin was harsh, wide, haunting, and somehow terribly familiar. "I think it'll be a new sensation for you, feeling weak. And we'll just keep making you weaker and weaker, adding an ounce of pain at a time, until you break ... and then, maybe, if we're feeling merciful, sometime in the future ... we'll finally let you die."

45.

Reed

"What in the hell are you thinking?" Isabella asked me when we were finally alone. The sun was sinking below the horizon, and we were in my quarters in the dormitory, a silent dinner passed between the two of us. Scott was down the hall in spare quarters, waiting, Augustus was recovering in the infirmary. We were waiting.

And being yelled at, in my case.

"I'm thinking … I'm glad you're all right," I said, watching her slit her eyes so small I'd have been lucky to slip a dime between the lids without FDR crying out in pain.

"What are you thinking about Anselmo?" she asked, way beyond her typical level of huffy. Isabella gets worked up easily, which is both good and bad. She's got passion, and it can be a lot of fun sometimes. It can also be a lot of apologies at other times.

"I'm thinking he's an asshole, and I should catch him," I said, not really sure what she was getting at. "J.J.'s looking, and I'm not leaving campus again until we've got a legitimate line on—"

"What in the hell are you thinking?" she asked again, with more emphasis this time.

I just paused. "I'm … why don't you just tell me how you want me to answer this?" I asked, thinking I was cleverly sidestepping the fight I sensed coming.

She made a noise of frustration, guttural, deep, and totally Italian, all while waving her hands in the air and looking to the sky as if someone was going to answer from there. She spit out a long string of words in her native language, the only word of which I recognized was *Dio*. "You fought Anselmo this morning, yes?" she finally directed at me.

"Yes," I said, cautious, sensing my doom impending.

"Why did you not kill him?" she asked, and her voice had gone quiet, her face now weary bordering on sad.

"We've talked about this over and over," I said, trying to conceal my shock. "About how I wanted to be different from her, about how I could do things my way and—"

"All that is out the window now," she said, shaking her head emphatically. "Do you know what he came here to do?"

I pursed my lips. "Nothing good."

"No, nothing good," she agreed. "He hates you. How you've unmanned him."

"Well, he should hate Sienna even more," I said, "seeing how I suspect that the scourging fire she unleashed on him probably did actually unman him." I paused. "He doesn't seem too exercised over her, though. He even said …" I let my voice drift off. "He said something about how she wasn't a problem anymore."

"And this does not concern you?" She looked at me with wild eyes.

"I know you're not her biggest fan—"

"That doesn't mean I wish to see her dead," Isabella said. "We might end up sisters-in-law some day, which means in the Italian way that I must loathe her—check, this is already covered—and speak ill of her behind her back—also check—but that I must defend her to the death if anyone else says anything poor of her, because we are family."

I stared at her in mild surprise but tried to keep my thoughts inscrutable. "Wait, did you just suggest we might get married?"

"Urgh!" She ran her fingers up her throat and out at me in a gesture that I understood the gist of without understanding the specifics. "You are so frustrating! Anselmo came here for me, and you stand around still thinking that there is any way on the earth that you could make him yield to you. I froze his face and broke it off, yet still he lives. Still he walks. He is likely furious with me at this point, and when next we meet, I expect he will kill me in a disturbing way." She said it all surprisingly coldly, like it didn't bother her. "How does that fit into your vision of a less violent capture? How does that work with your ideas of gentle policing?"

I stared at her, my chest tight with angst. "What do you expect me to do?"

"I hate to say it the way that Phillips did," she said, but more gently than he ever would have, even when he was acting like my friend, "but Anselmo is not a man who will stop unless you kill him. He certainly means to kill you—and your sister, if he has not already."

"He can't have killed Sienna." I shook my head, hard. "Can't. He's not strong enough, not smart enough—" I froze. He didn't have to be smart enough.

He had the Brain working for him.

I dialed my phone swiftly, listened to it ring with J.J.'s name on the faceplate. When he answered, I started talking before he got out a "Hello" or a "Reed the Greed!" or whatever he'd say in greeting. "Did you get hold of anyone who's seen or heard from Sienna?"

"Hi to you too," J.J. said, "and no. The police guy or whatever up on Bayscape Island said they haven't seen hide nor hair of her, and the place she's staying still hasn't called us back after ... like eight messages? Maybe nine. I can check." He paused. "Yeah, nine. It's like they're not even running a business up there—"

"Okay, got it," I said, nerves eating at me. "Let me know the minute you hear something." I hung up on him.

Isabella stared at me, and I could see by her eyes she

knew what he'd said. "It will be okay."

I balled up a fist, walked three steps to the wall, and busted right through, giving me a clear view into my bedroom. I pulled my fist out, glanced at the bleeding knuckles, and then put my hand through again, shredding drywall and splintering a stud. "Son—of—a— !" I hit it again, and again.

"Reed!" Isabella said. Her hand landed on my shoulder, squeezing with gentle pressure that commanded me to stop immediately. "Destroying your quarters will not bring her back safely."

"What if nothing brings her back safely, Isabella?" I couldn't control the way I looked at her, with haunted eyes that probably gave her a direct glimpse into the utter horror roiling around in my soul. I'd ignored Sienna for months, and now here I was, in her shoes, with impossible choices.

"You will find a way," she said, "I am confident in you."

"I don't share your confidence," I said, voice hoarse and scratchy. "Because they could have gotten her anywhere between here and Bayscape ... and with Anselmo on the loose, I can't even go looking for her without giving that maniac and Cunningham free reign on the whole Twin Cities—and you."

46.

Benjamin

They were staying in what amounted to an enormous hole in the ground, a dusty crater that was teeming with weeds, devoid of anything else for as far as Benjamin's eyes could see, which, on this moonlit night, was quite a distance.

The chirp of crickets was in the air, and silvery clouds rolled across the sky, avoiding the giant disk in the middle of it all as though on purpose. That was both good and bad; Cunningham could have done with a little less of a view, really. He knew where they were, and it made him shudder more than a little. He'd never been to Glencoe, Minnesota, before in his life, and this didn't seem like the time to visit this graveyard. But, then, this hadn't been his idea, no, nor Anselmo's either.

No, this had been the brainchild of the voice on the phone, the woman with the rasping voice who had spoken in his ear when Anselmo shoved it up next to his face and told him to do as she bade him. And he had, finding them a new car, stealing it as she'd walked him through how to do it. He'd never stolen anything in his life, but now he'd stolen a car. Then he drove them here and carried Anselmo, whose face was still missing, eyes sightless, bones and muscle and cartilage exposed, all the way to the middle of this near-lifeless crater, where they sat in a field of weeds, assured that no one could or would watch them.

"Do you know how many people died here?" Anselmo asked. The Italian was sitting with his back to Benjamin, moonlight washing down on the scarred back of his bald head, leeching the dark color from it and making it appear that his complexion was whitish-silver.

"Thousands," Benjamin said. "The whole town exploded. Some sort of … incident. Gas leak? I can't recall."

"It was a metahuman," Anselmo said, "named Aleksandr Gavrikov."

That perked up Benjamin's ears. "He … scorched this place? With fire?"

"Yes," Anselmo said. Benjamin hadn't seen it, but he thought the Italian had probably regained his mouth by now, since he was no longer making the noise indicating he was drooling, lipless, all over his whole face. "He was like you."

"Like me …?" Benjamin felt a tingle within. "I … didn't know anyone was like me."

"Do not get me wrong," Anselmo said, "he was a man, and made his own decisions, a skill you have yet to learn." He drove the knife squarely into Benjamin's heart. "But you will learn." That lessened the sharp, stabbing pain just a little.

"What … what are we going to do here?" Benjamin asked after a few minutes passed. He watched the silver light play over his fingers, and just to try, attempted to draw flame from them. His fingers flared to life, causing him to cry out and jump to his feet.

"We are going sit for a few more minutes while my eyelids grow back," Anselmo said, with a strange sense of satisfaction.

"Uh … very well, then," Benjamin said, and sat back down. He looked down at a seed pod, a dandelion. Thankfully, he was not allergic to those. He extended a finger toward it, and imagined himself burning just the little white strings of seed. A small fire, no more than a cigarette lighter would produce, sprang forth from the tip of his index finger and consumed the seed pod whole, making a tiny light in the night for the three seconds it took to burn it into nothingness. "Ah!" he cried out in pleasure.

"Yes, yes, very good," Anselmo said, now facing him. Benjamin started to say something in surprise, but halted before he even opened his mouth as he caught sight of Anselmo's face in the moonlight.

It was ...

It was ...

Flawless.

"You're ... you look so different," Benjamin said, cocking his head to stare.

"Yes," Anselmo said, smiling with full lips and skin that looked as new as a baby's. It only extended between his forehead and cheekbones, however, providing a bizarre spectacle—scarred skin around the sides of his head and newly grown, pink flesh in the space that the doctor had broken off with her freezing liquid. "I am ... renewed."

"But how?" Benjamin asked, coming to his feet and easing closer. "How did you ...?"

"Reed Treston's sister scarred me with a grenade of fire," Anselmo said, mimicking an explosion with his hands. "It burned my skin, over and over, not allowing it to heal properly before burning it again. I had assumed I was ... permanently disfigured in ... all ways." Anselmo's head sagged downward. "But the doctor ... she has done me an unintentional favor. It turns out that beneath this scar tissue, if it is removed ... my true face can re-emerge."

"But ... how could you possibly remove it all?" Benjamin asked. "Go back to her and ask for more of that freezing solution?"

"No," Anselmo said, and his lips were tight with discomfort. "I am afraid that will not work. I would be vulnerable while she did it, and thus at her mercy, and I cannot be at anyone's mercy. No," he said, and stood, rising to place a hand upon Benjamin's shoulder, "the answer is right here."

That answer came to Benjamin in short order, and he blanched. Visibly. Obviously. When he spoke, his voice went high. "Me? You want me to—?"

"I want you to make me whole again," Anselmo said. "I have told you I will help make a man of you, and I will do this thing. We have already begun. I undertook this without selfish motives. I simply thought that you would be a useful ally in the battle against our common foe. But now I see something that you can do for me as well, a favor that would repay this thing that I do for you."

"But ... but ..." Benjamin said, trying to come up with a perfectly reasonable reason why he shouldn't have to do this thing. "I'm not a doctor. You could die."

"Since this happened to me," Anselmo said, squeezing Benjamin's shoulder, "I have not lived. It has been a half-life, a shadow life, one in which the women who were with me when I recovered—the cows—could not even look upon me as a man. And I could not look upon them as a man would, either, because of the nature of my disfigurement." He looked deep into Benjamin's eyes, and there was already a fire there. "You, though—you can restore to me what I am giving to you. As I make you a man, you, too, can make me whole again. And, then, together ... we will finish this, and you will be free of worry, of fear, of always looking over your shoulder and concerning yourself what others think of you."

Benjamin swallowed hard. "Truly?"

Anselmo looked him hard in the eye. "Truly. Now ... help me." He offered his hand, holding it out before him in a manner that told Benjamin that he did not intend it for being shaken.

Benjamin stared at the scarred, pitted, puckered flesh, knotted and ridged over the back of Anselmo's hand. "All of it?" he asked, not looking up in Anselmo's eyes, for fear of what he might see.

"To the bone," Anselmo said and drew a deep breath.

"Which is what we will do to our enemies, yours and mine, when this is over."

Benjamin swallowed hard and nodded, raising his hand. It couldn't be that hard, could it? He imagined the fire licking out of his fingers, and it was there, a torch in the night. He looked once at Anselmo, who nodded, and brought his own flaming hand down on Anselmo's scarred one, and the screaming began—both his and Anselmo's.

The sounds, the horror, the fire lit the night, and drowned Benjamin in the sensations of another's pain. It was a screaming that filled his ears, filled his head, and made him want to shut his eyes and run away more than once.

but that's not
what a man
DOES

And so he looked on, quieting that screaming voice in his own head, letting it wash over him and ignoring it, and proceeded with his task, burning away every inch of scarred flesh he could find, searing all the way to the bone, a little at a time, watching the blood fall boiling to the ground, until the task was finally done, and he was sure that he was deaf from screaming and numb from the horror of what he'd seen.

47.

Sienna

It didn't take long for Brant's gift to start working, flooding my nose and taste buds with the awful smells of my body at war with itself. I didn't know if it was hours or minutes that passed, but they seemed to move both at the speed of light and desperately slow, as my bowels went into upheaval and my stomach churned as though it was being threshed by a particularly violent shark. Maybe a whole school of them.

I made it to the toilet before hell began, but it was ultimately irrelevant, because I was vomiting uncontrollably within minutes of the start of the show, and there was no holding back the storm that was raging in my body. I was sweating and feverish, the open window to the frosty storm outside completely ineffective at keeping me cool. I shivered and burned, my hair matted down in front by profuse sweat as my digestive tract fought against me with a violence it normally reserved for meatloaf.

However long it took, my guts purged in both directions until there was nothing left. I managed to clean myself up, sweating and feeling sick all the while, my shirt sticking to my chest and back, my jeans absorbing my diffusion of liquid slightly better. The smell remained, though, and it was awful, a scent of sickness that was thick as smog in the air.

When the worst of it passed, I couldn't even raise myself

up enough to walk to the bed. I tried to crawl, but gave up because it was so. Damned. Far. My arms were weaker than I'd ever felt them, my legs shuddering like a newborn calf who was trying to stand for the first time. If Brant had come into my cell right then and gotten down on his knees to put his neck into my hands, I don't think I could have physically managed to strangle him. I mean, I would have tried like hell, but he probably would have ended up laughing at the neck massage.

I curled into a ball and cursed a lot of names, but mostly my own. I should have left town at the first warning of "GET OUT," but I hadn't. I'd been arrogant and overconfident, thinking that just because I was a total badass who consistently cut through my enemies that somehow I was invincible. I wasn't, and I knew it deep inside. I'd had it driven home to me more times than I could count, even as recently as last April in London with Phillip Delsim, and in January when the damned Brain had temporarily chemically castrated me of my powers.

Maybe Reed was right. Maybe I'd gotten so damned full of myself that I'd started to think I was a goddess, and that my judgment was paramount. That I could kill at will, for the wrong reasons, and who cared, because of my power.

I thought a lot of thoughts while curled up on that hard, cold stone floor. My body may have felt paralyzed with weakness, but my mind was sprinting in circles, moving like a greased wheel down a smooth hill.

Also, I think my ability to make analogies and metaphors might have been compromised by my sick feeling.

I felt another round of fever shakes coming on and I let it rack me, shuddering as though it would bring me the warmth I desired. I hoped that the lack of a blanket and the air from the window would keep me cool enough to avoid horrendous brain damage. I wasn't sure how it would affect me, but I needed my wits about me if I was going to escape and murder every one of these assholes.

Errr, excuse me. If I was going to escape and find some way to bring these jerks to some form of justice. Which may have included me ripping their spines from their still-living bodies. Or not. Maybe it would just involve jail time.

I felt utterly debased and humiliated as I lay there, my stomach railing at me for a crime I hadn't even committed against it. I wanted to tell it that if I'd known the hamburger was poisoned, I wouldn't have eaten it, but when I said that, it called me a crone in response.

Yes, my stomach called me a crone. And that was when things started to get really weird.

The light above grew in blinding intensity until everything around me was nothing more than a white light, and suddenly I could see a face in there somewhere, a face that was more than familiar, a face that was old, was creased with the lines of that age, was the living embodiment of that furious storm outside my window—

"Oh, God," I said in a whisper, on the floor of the Bayscape jail one minute and in an office hundreds of miles away the next, an office that I knew for a fact didn't even exist any longer.

The stone desk was the giveaway. It looked like an enormous slab of rock that was stood up on two pillars that held it in place, the surface just smooth enough to write on. The view behind the man with the wrinkled face was a window that looked out on snowy grounds, rolling green flatlands that had been completely overtaken by the seasonal drifts of—

"Winter," I said, standing before him with something just short of horror.

"Hello, Sienna," Erich Winter said, rising from his chair to look me right in the eye. His voice was deep and smooth, with a Germanic accent. "It is so pleasant to see you again."

48.

Reed

I was between the metaphorical rock and the hard place, and both my choices sucked. I talked with Isabella for hours, and we went round and round between the answers, boiling them down to two choices.

Hang around here and wait for Anselmo in order to stop him from killing again or go north in hopes that I could maybe, just maybe, find out where Sienna had gone missing.

Like I said, both choices sucked.

"If I go north, I may find nothing," I said. "I might end up driving hours and hours to get there and never see a single sign that Sienna had ever been there. And then Anselmo strikes here, kills people—and boom. I'm shit out of luck. Or has the Brain track me on the road and bushwhack me up north somewhere—like Sienna." We already knew that Anselmo and Cunningham had ditched the car they'd made their attack on the agency with. We'd found it in a nearby carpool park-and-ride where we had agents standing by to catch the third-shift workers when they got off in a few hours, hoping to identify what kind of car had been stolen in exchange for it. That'd at least give us something for Harper and J.J. to look for through their digital eyes in the skies.

"Or you could find her quickly," Isabella said. "Perhaps she simply decided to go elsewhere. It could be as you have said, Anselmo merely referenced her obliquely. Anselmo is not a subtle man. He would have taunted you more if she were dead or dying."

"He wants her to suffer," I said. "He wants us all to suffer. And we have no idea what the Brain is like. She could be unleashing hell on Sienna right now for all we know."

"What are you going to do?" Isabella asked, after pausing a moment to allow the thoughts to percolate.

Dammit, this was where the choice really started to suck. Because I knew what Sienna would say to do.

The job. She'd led by example in this regard. Say whatever else you wanted about her, she'd blown up her own relationships for the job, pushed everyone else away to be the shield she thought she should be. Whatever her motives, she did the job like no one else, and she let nothing interfere with it.

"I have to stay," I said. "With Anselmo and Cunningham out there working together, I need to be near the cities. They could try almost anything." And really, while I suspected Anselmo was going to confine his crazycakes revenge schemes to me and my most dear, Cunningham had proven himself a wild card on multiple occasions now. If he'd been accidentally drawn into this by a failure to control himself in the Minneapolis airport, since then he'd shown that he was moving toward intentional killing by both choice and his associations. Even if I sliced it in the most favorable way possible and gave him the benefit of many doubts, he'd somehow killed his co-worker and come along with Anselmo on the man's attempt to kill Isabella.

My understanding had reached its limit with him. He was dangerous, and it was clear that for whatever reason he had put himself in cahoots with a man who had proven himself power-mad and perhaps even more explosive than Cunningham himself.

I couldn't leave Minneapolis and St. Paul nearly defenseless against that.

"What are you going to do about Sienna?" she asked, with a little more emotion than I would have expected, even after her talk about them being a kind of family.

"I'm going to do what I can," I said, trying to figure out what that was. "I'll send agents up there to try and track her down. They won't be of much use here, and maybe I can get them working out from underneath Phillips's nose." I knew for a fact he wasn't going to give two shits about Sienna being missing. He wouldn't even give one shit if it was plugging him up for days and getting rid of it meant he'd be comfortable at last. "Hopefully Hannegan can find some sign of her." And hopefully wouldn't get killed by whatever was responsible for her disappearance. I looked straight at her. "When's the soonest you can get Augustus back in the fight?"

"Tomorrow perhaps," she said, shaking her head. "He could probably walk now, but he is weak. I fear a reinjury would set back his progress significantly, or may lead to spinal scar tissue of the sort Anselmo carries on his body. It could paralyze him for life."

"We'll play it safe, then," I said. "We'll hold off for now, hoping that Anselmo moves soon." I felt my mouth grow dry as I circled closer to the grim pronouncement of the decision I was making in my soul—one I didn't think I'd have to make. "I'll deal with him first, and then—"

"How will you deal with him?" Isabella asked, but forcefully this time. Her hand found my arm, snaking around it and squeezing me tight. "You can't fight him like you did before."

"I know," I said, swallowing hard. "I know. And I won't. Because this time ... I'll do it."

"Do what?" she asked. She knew. She knew what I was saying, but she pushed me anyway, because if I couldn't say it, I probably couldn't bring myself to do it.

"I'm going to kill him," I whispered. And so help me, I was going to do it.

49.

Sienna

Fever dreams are absolute hell, and even knowing somewhere inside that I was dreaming, Erich Winter didn't help. I could feel the spin of unreality around me, of a world moving too quick by half to be real, of my forehead burning and my eyes pressed closed, the color of things not quite right. It wasn't reality; it was surreality, and the vision of the man who had most hurt me in my life standing in front of me just added the extra dash of crazy it took me to buy into it for the moment.

"This isn't real." My words slurred, like I was drunk.

"What is real?" Winter said in that low voice. I hadn't heard him speak in years, and I hadn't missed it. "Is life real? Matter, real? Liquid, solid, gas? Are any of them really real?"

"You're leaning pretty hard on the 'gas' part of it right now, arentcha?" I asked, being just as much of a smarty to him dead as I would have been in life. But with less face punching. I never really did get to face-punch him to my heart's content. "As in filling the air with your useless gas."

"There was a time when you listened to every word I said," he turned, exposing his back so invitingly to me, "searching for the truth and meaning as though all of it were a revelation handed down from above."

"You pining for the good old days when I respected

you?" I stood my ground but my knees felt weak. "Maybe you shouldn't have killed—"

"I did not kill anyone." Winter turned, piercing blue eyes as shocking in their cerulean as if they'd been CGI'd into a White Walker's eye. "You did."

"Oh, screw you," I said in disgust. "I'm arguing with a specter. A dead man who doesn't seem to know he's dead."

"Of course I am dead," he said. "You killed me as well."

"If only," I said with false regret. "Sovereign pulled your card. I didn't much regret him turning you into a human flambé, though. The smell was a bit much—"

"You are responsible," he said, as forbidding in death as he ever had been in life.

"Uh huh," I said. "I'm totally responsible for you holding my boyfriend against my skin until he died, and I'm also responsible for you getting flash fried by a supervillain. Okay. Sure. Let's go with that."

"Don't you know?" I turned my head at the sound of the voice behind me. "You're responsible for everything."

"Sarah," I said, watching the dark-haired woman walk into sight behind me. It was surreal seeing her here in the ruins of the old directorate, which looked way different from the agency in all the tiny details. "Of course you'd show up to taunt me now, when I'm hallucinating."

"You're almost of sound mind," Sarah said, easing into the room. I couldn't tell whether I was imagining her or if she was effing with my mind from within the room, honestly. My stomach was quivering, though, and the nausea had followed me.

"You're messing with my head and accusing me of diminished capacity," I said. "Nice. There's an irony there."

"And you're all about the irony, aren't you?" Brant asked, appearing behind me. I jumped and backed away from him, but I was unintentionally caught between the three of them in a sort of rough triangle. The way he spoke, that strange accent I'd been hearing was creeping back into his words.

"I do find it fun to play with," I said, trying to figure out how to put my back against a wall.

"No one else finds it fun when you do it," Sarah said, standing there with arms folded. "We're all tired of it."

"And you've only known me a few days," I said, "imagine how people who have known me longer feel about it."

"They can't stand you," she said, dark eyes boring in on mine. "No one can. It's why you're alone now." It did hurt, even though I knew she meant it to, because it had the ring of truth to it. "And let's face it, no one sticks around you very long because of it."

"You drive away everyone you don't kill," Brant agreed, doing that voice thing again. It was driving me nuts, like an itch in the back of my head that I couldn't reach to scratch.

"But you kill most," Winter said.

"Man," I said, "this is fun. I should do this more often. Come to confession with the dead," I nodded to Winter, "and those I'm soon to kill. Good times."

"You have no idea." Another voice entered the picture, causing me to whip my head around yet again. This time it was Z, and I was prepared for him. Because of course they'd add another log to this particular fire, now that it was already burning hot and painful.

"Oh, boy, it's Zebulon," I said. "Yay for Zebulon, and that awful name. How much did your parents hate you?"

"My parents loved me," he said, completing the little circle around me. Now I was surrounded literally as well as figuratively, in this dream as well as this town. "You'd have known that if you'd ever met them."

"If I'd ever met them?" I blinked at him. His hat was gone, his blondish hair styled in a very ... very familiar way. "Sorry, I don't guess I care to meet the parents of strangers. My stomach was gnawing at me again, but this time it was different. This time, it wasn't the nausea, it was a sense that something else was wrong. A sense that I was about to have the rug jerked out from beneath me again.

I hated this feeling of exposure, this circle of heaping judgment being thrown at me. I wanted to protect myself, to find a wall to put my back against.

Sarah noticed my discomfort first. "You want to run, don't you?" She seemed to derive a grim satisfaction from it, lips twisted in bitter triumph. I'd seen that look before.

"Not so much run," I said, "as put my back to the sea and take you all on until you're dead."

"She's got a real fire in her," Brant said. He ran his fingers over his upper lip, playing with his mustache.

"You have no idea," I said, thinking how much fun it'd be to have Gavrikov to unleash right at this moment.

"Must be nice," Z said, dragging my head around to look at him again, "to live without the guilt of those you've left dead in your path."

"Well," I said, readying myself in case Winter decided to say something suitably prickish next, "it's hard to feel guilty when you've killed so many classy people. Like, for example, the entirety of Century, a band who was trying to take over the world." I had a feeling I knew, now, where they were coming from, and it was time to start drawing them out with smartassed jabs. If I could figure out their angle, I could maybe goad them into making a mistake. After all, taunting and witticisms were a power that they couldn't take away from me.

"How noble," Sarah said. "But you know they're not the only people you've killed."

"You're right," I said continuing my fishing expedition, "there was also Omega, a criminal organization of metas that wanted to squeeze the world for all it was worth. I might have killed a few of them as well. Were any of them your mommies and daddies?" I made my faux sad-face for them. "Because if so ... I'm not sorry."

"Your victims are legion," Winter said.

"The trail of human death you've left behind you is staggering," Z said.

"The cost in lives abundant," Brant said, and now I knew that I was delusional if they were all talking as one voice in one steady sequence.

"And you—" Sarah started, but I headed her off by throwing myself at her with all the strength I had left.

I passed right through her like she was a cloud. I hit the ground and rolled, coming up on my feet and feeling the weakness of my body as my intestines quivered at the movement, threatening upheaval once more.

Sarah's form was blurry, insubstantial, the colors of her body and clothing dissipated like a cloud blown by a strong wind. I watched as she pulled herself back together, the black leather jacket first, the dark hair gaining focus and coherence as she reconstituted. Her face remained blurred, though, even after her body had reformed, and she stared at me through the only feature that was sharp—those blue-green eyes, filled with a fury that was obvious even without a mouth to compliment it.

"You little fool," she said, "as if you could kill me."

"I hope you don't think I'll stop trying just because you vanished on me once," I said. "Because I tend to get a lot of people who tell me that I can't kill them, and I just keep proving them wrong."

"You can't kill me," she said, shaking her head.

"And so says half the other people I've killed." I made a fake yawn. "I'm way past tired of it."

"You can't kill me, either," Brant said, drawing my gaze back him. I blinked when I saw him; his face had gone blurry like Sarah's.

"Nor me," Z said, and I looked, knowing what I'd find: the same thing, his face was featureless, like it was vibrating so fast I couldn't discern any of the detail.

"Really?" I tried to sound unimpressed, but the truth was … this was new. I mean, I was still going to find a way to kill them, but it was at least kinda different. "Why is that?"

"Because," Sarah said, "you cannot kill—"

"—what—" Brant continued.

"—is already dead," Z said, and his face was suddenly clear as if someone had wiped the glass in front of it clean.

I felt my knees lose the last of their strength, and I caved to them, barely noticing the pain.

My heartbeat thundered in my ears, the drum sound of doom, fear, horror.

Z …

I whipped my eyes around to Brant and saw him clearly, now, with the clarity that had been missing before.

Brant …

I spun my head to look at Sarah, already knowing what I'd find, and horrified when she was there, looking down on me, just the same as she had countless times in my life, with that look of utter contempt and coldness.

Brant was Breandan Duffy, my friend.

Z … was Zack Davis, my first love.

And Sarah was Sierra Nealon … my mother.

"You can't kill what is already dead, daughter mine," Sierra said, pitiless, looking down on me like the scum I always suspected she thought I was, "and you killed every single one of us long, long ago."

50.

I was on my knees in stark horror, surrounded by people I'd loved and failed, people I'd killed and seen die, who'd died because of me or for me, and I felt sick in a way that my body did not currently possess the ability to express.

"Ohmyshit," I whispered, staring from Zack to Breandan to Sierra to Winter.

"Your shit?" my mother asked. "I think you're losing it."

"Lost it already," I muttered, looking up sullenly at Breandan, "thanks to you."

"I do what I can," he said in that lilting Irish accent of his. It had been trying to burst through in the way Brant spoke all along, and I'd never caught it.

"I did what I could, too," I said, looking straight at him. "I tried to save your life."

"Oh, yeah," he nodded, "and hers too, I'm sure." I looked where he pointed and saw Apollonia, the clerk from my cabin rental place, appear out of the shadows. Her face distorted like theirs had, and I blinked in surprise. It was Athena, a girl I'd tried to save from London before the extinction. "But she died just the same as I did, when your enemies came charging in with guns a blazin'. Even you, with a few guns of your own to blaze, couldn't protect us." He stepped closer to me and knelt down to look me in the eyes. His were bereft of the warmth they'd possessed in life. "You got us killed. As good as murdered us yourself."

"I didn't kill you," I whispered.

"But you did," Sierra said, stepping in and kneeling like Breandan had. "You killed him, and you killed me."

"You died to save me," I said. "You gave your life for me—"

"Maybe I wouldn't have," she said, "if I'd known what a miserable, worthless failure you'd turn out to be."

"Then you'd just have died when Sovereign came for you," I served back at her. Hey, she was my mom, and vision or not, I had more experience being a smartass to her than anyone else.

"You always did enjoy a good argument," Zack said, kneeling down with the other two. Winter hovered in the background, a pillar next to their shorter figures. "But try and argue that you didn't kill me."

"Maybe literally," I said, looking right at him. "But you know I wouldn't have made that choice."

"Choices?" Zack smiled. "Your choices led to death even when you didn't want them to. That either makes you incompetent or a hell of a butcher."

"Jury's out," I said, muttering. "Apparently not literally, though, because I appear to have been judged already here."

"We know the truth of your guilt," Breandan said and stood. He towered above me as he had in life.

"We don't need a trial," my mother said, standing, judging me from above—also, like she had in life.

"Zack," I said, looking right at him, "if it's really you … you know I didn't kill you."

A shadow fell over his eyes before he answered. "But I'm dead, aren't I? Just as cold and dead as if you'd put your hands on me yourself, with your own will."

Before I could muster an answer to that, Breandan closed in on me, looking at me with those piercing, dead eyes. "You're a murderer. Killer. Destroyer. Everything you touch dies, and I'm not speaking figuratively. You carry death in your very skin, even when you're not spreading it with guns and fire. You're an aberration. An abomination. And you don't belong anywhere." He grinned, and his smile was frozen in a too-wide rictus, like he'd been hit with Joker gas. "Why, you told me so yourself."

"Everyone hates you," Sierra said, seizing me by the face. Her hands were so strong, and I was so weak, I felt powerless to resist. "And why shouldn't they? You are death. Death incarnate."

The world around me started to shake, and I couldn't tell whether it was some symptom of the fear or the sickness, clawing at me to get out, to make itself manifest in the world, until the voice rang out through the surreal, sunlit office.

"RESIST."

The hands clutching at me were like withered claws digging into my skin, ripping at my flesh by slowly sinking through it. It was painful, and my eyes were wide and grew wider at the sound of the voice. I looked around, trying to figure out if my visions could hear what was being said, but they gave no reaction.

"... and you'll continue to bring death to everyone," Sierra said, "and you'll die alone in thousands of years, in the middle of a dead planet, all by yourself like Sovereign would have—"

"Get ... help!" the voice rumbled again, deep and familiar, heavy like a weight on the ceiling of the world, trying to break through the facade of the sky.

"What help?" I cried out, and my mother clutched me harder.

"There is no help for you," she said, "you've killed everyone."

"Everyone," Breandan and Zack chorused, with a measure of baritone Winter thrown in.

I blinked back the tears. "Not everyone. Not Scott—"

"Oh, him?" My mother turned her head to look at something, and I followed with my eyes. In the corner of the office, sitting placidly in a chair, was Scott Byerly.

"Scott!" I called out, rushing headlong into the hope the voice gave me. If he was here, maybe he could help; he certainly wasn't dead. "Scott!" I called again.

He did not move, he did not speak, did not turn his head at my call. Instead, he stared straight ahead, eyes blank as though death had claimed him alive, and his body had yet to react to it.

"Scott!" I called again. "Please. Please … help me."

There was a hint of movement in his neck, and my heart leapt within me. He was turning his head to look, to look at me—

And then I saw the first crack run through his neck like cement breaking under pressure.

The next one appeared in his head, running down from his hairline, spider webs lacing over his ruddy skin from out of his sandy blond hair. My relief turned to ash as I watched him crack and crumble like a broken vase fallen to the hard ground. He dissolved into pieces in the chair, taking my faint hope and dashing it, along with his body.

"He's nothing but a hollow shell," Breandan crowed, "like someone scooped him out and left him empty inside. So fragile, he breaks with nothing but the slightest pressure applied." His eyes seized mine again. "Maybe you didn't kill him, but he's not whole. He's missing things, and sooner or later, your mark of death'll hit home, and he'll die as sure as if you'd had your way with him without a condom."

"You're death, sweet daughter," my mother said, eyes boring into mine like she was performing some sort of mental brain surgery on me just by looking into my soul. "You've known it all along, and you've done everything you could to carry that philosophy out into the world, from Wolfe to M-Squad to Crow Vincent to however many nameless flunkies you've slaughtered over the years. You've killed enough hired guns to put a fifty percent premium on the worldwide mercenary market."

"You're making that up," I said.

"Don't you read the intelligence briefings?" my mother asked with sadistic glee. "Or is that another of your failings, along with the touch of death?"

"I haven't killed everyone—" I said.

"Everyone." Winter led the chorus this time, and I looked back at the tall man, saw the snows rising outside the office window like an ice age had settled in.

"Not … Reed," I said, and thoughts of my brother flooded in. I pictured him through the pain, the thought of him smiling. It had been so long since I'd genuinely seen him smile at me. Now he was stiff upper lip Reed, so serious all the time, so judgmental.

I didn't even care. Maybe he was right. Maybe I was wrong. Maybe I've let myself get too quick to anger, too quick to kill. Maybe I was …

… was …

… maybe I was a cold-hearted murderer.

… was death.

Reed was right. They all were. And part of me wanted to tell him so right then, to look in his eyes and tell him he was right so that maybe I could at least see him smile one last time before—

"Sienna?" My brother's voice filled my ears as the world distorted around me.

"What are you doing here?" Sierra asked, her voice a high-pitched shriek.

I opened my eyes to see Reed standing there, in his suit, beard in full bushy bloom and his hair back in a ponytail. "Reed," I breathed, a silent whisper of thanks. "You were right … about me," I choked out, barely able to form the words.

He looked around, his eyes widening. "Sienna, where are we? Where are you?"

"Bayscape Island," I said. "It's …" I glanced at my mother, whose hands were still anchored on my cheeks. I could feel the blood dripping down my face. "… I'm here."

"You shouldn't be here," Breandan hissed at Reed.

"*I* shouldn't be here?" Reed asked, more than a little offended. "You're fricking dead, man, I think you should be in the great beyond, not hanging out on Lake Superior's scenic coastal islands."

"I killed him," I said to Reed, because he needed to know he was right and I was wrong, "I killed him. I've killed everyone."

"Sienna, what the hell is going on here?" Reed asked, and he moved forward to push my mother aside. She hit the ground with a scream and rolled back to her feet, hissing at him like a snake all the while. He shoved Breandan and Zack away as well, prompting similar responses. "Get off her, you wraiths!" He shook me, and looked into my eyes. "Sienna, I don't think you're on Bayscape. Is this a dreamwalk?"

I blinked, looking around. Everything was surreal, otherworldly. I had passed out, hadn't I? Was I hallucinating? "I ... maybe?"

"Sienna, I need you to tell me where you are," Reed said. "I need to find you in order to help you."

"I was on Bayscape," I said. "I was there on the island, and there were these people, but they were really ..." I gestured out to Breandan, to my mother, to ... Zack. "They were ... them."

"You met your mother, your ex-lover, and your dead Irish friend on Bayscape Island?" he asked. I wasn't far enough gone to miss the skepticism.

"Well, when you put it like that ..." I said, feeling weak again, like the blood was draining out of my hand. I held it up, and yep, it was still bleeding. "This won't heal. I can't reach my souls."

"You have no soul of your own," my mother hissed, "so you have to take those of others—"

"You're a fucking ray of sunshine, aren't you?" Reed said, and my mother recoiled. "Sienna, tell me exactly what happened from the moment you left the agency."

"I drove ..." I said, "... up to Bayscape. Took the ferry. Met Jake." He looked at me like he wanted to ask who Jake was, but he held it in as I went on. "Met Sarah ... Sierra," I gestured to dear old mom, "Brant ... Breandan, and Zebulon ..."

"Dumb name," Reed said.

"Screw you," Zack said. "I never liked you anyway."

"Well, you were never good enough for her anyway, dick," Reed replied without missing a beat. "Also, your mini-fauxhawk was always stupid."

"This from a man who's one plaid shirt away from being a lumbersexual," Zack shot back.

"I met them all," I said, ignoring all the asides flying around. "And then the weather ... the blizzard started." I giggled, and looked at Erich Winter. "Winter is coming ... he's here!"

"Blizzard?" Reed asked. "What blizzard?"

"It swept over the island," I said, my voice taking on a singsong quality, "shut down the ferry. Trapped us all there. I got caught out and couldn't find my way," I said. "Then they threw me in jail and started tearing me apart inch by inch—"

"Sienna, it's September," Reed said. "There are no blizzards in September. It's fall."

"It's Minnesnowta," I said.

"Wisconsin, actually," Reed said, "but it's not Hoth, is my point. There's no snow on the ground right now."

I blinked at him. "No, there is. I saw it." My head tilted, and I looked at Winter. "I saw the snow, saw the blizzard. Saw it with my own eyes and—"

Something shifted in the world, and I felt that gut-wrenching sense of things shrinking around me, like the sun had gone down long ago and I was trapped in the woods, all alone, in the middle of the night.

I stared at the place where Reed had stood only a moment earlier. "Reed?" I asked, and my voice cracked.

"He's gone," my mother said, inches from my face. I

could smell her breath, her sweat, and it reminded me of the times beyond counting that she'd dragged me physically, screaming all the way, into the dark and heaved me into a metal box. "Now ... you're all ours again." Her voice brightened, but it did nothing to assuage the choking, gripping fear that was suffocating me in its hand. "You should feel right at home, because this ... is where you belong."

51.

Reed

I awoke in a sweat. I hadn't even thought I'd get to sleep, let alone thought I'd be dreaming lucid, surreal dreams about Sienna being tortured by the people closest to her who had died. My skin was covered in a sheen of perspiration, and my smooth cotton sheets clung to my body as I sat up, gulping in breaths like I'd just emerged from a dive into the darkest depths of the ocean and hadn't had a bit of oxygen in months.

My fingers came up and found the wetness on my brow, the soaked edge of my hair, which I'd loosed for sleep. It was drenched an inch out from the scalp thanks to my nightmare, and my breaths were still coming in hard gasps, like I was seconds away from being submerged back into the icy cold water again to struggle under the surface of the nightmare.

"What is it?" Isabella asked, awake. She clicked on the lamp next to our bed and sat up, her red slip falling loose on her shoulders.

"I just ..." I said, still not in control of my breathing. "Had a ... dream? Nightmare?" I brushed the hair back out of my eyes. "I don't even know."

"What was it?" she asked, eyes bleary but concerned.

"I dreamed of Sienna," I said, my chest still heaving up and down. "I dreamed she was in trouble, that she was being

… attacked by nightmares."

"Sounds terrible," she said, her long fingers delicately wiping sweat from my brow. I stared down at my smooth chest and it gleamed in the lamplight. "But it fits very well into what is going on in your life at the moment. It wouldn't take a psychologist to connect the dots on this, I think."

"Right," I nodded, my breaths finally slowing down. "Natural. I'm afraid for Sienna, so I pictured her in the most frightening environment possible. Yeah. Totally makes sense." I ran a hand back through my cold, wet hair. Something tugged at me like I tugged at my hair. "It felt so … real."

"Do you think she is trapped in nightmares?" Isabella asked. "Somewhere, suspended in darkness?"

"It'd be a horrible thing," I said. "She was … powerless. It's like those visions of those people were preying on her guilt—"

"I thought you said she didn't have any of that," she asked.

My face settled in a hard mask. "Really? Right now?"

"Sorry," she said, genuinely contrite. "Do you think she reached out to you with the dreamwalk, then?"

"Maybe," I said. "I asked her where she was." I sat up straighter. "I felt like I had my wits about me. It wasn't really that dreamlike, on my end. I felt in control of myself, and I didn't do anything weird. The world was weird around me, but that's … that's maybe because of Sienna." I lapsed into thought. "She said she was on Bayscape, but there was a blizzard."

Isabella frowned. "God, already? I hate this state."

"There's not a—" I paused, and reached over to my nightstand and fumbled for my phone. I picked it up and dialed J.J., and he picked up on the fifth ring.

"Hello?" he asked in a sleepy voice.

"J.J.," I said, "Did we ever get anything else back from the cabin rental place where Sienna was staying?"

"No," he murmured, sounding like he was rolling into his pillow, "we did not."

"Do you know what the weather is on Bayscape right now?" I asked.

"What?" J.J.'s voice rose. "Why? You want to vacay, too? Will you promise not to call me from there?"

"J.J.," I said, "I need to know what the weather is on Bayscape Island right now."

"FFS, man, there's an app for that," he said, completely disgruntled. I heard him shifting on the other end. "Okay, Bayscape Island weather, since you're an incompetent who doesn't know how to Internet like an adult. Currently, it's 65 degrees and the moon is shining down on fluffy clouds. Good enough? Can I sleep now?"

"No," I said, "I need you to call the rental car agencies and find out who Sienna rented her car from and see if they have GPS in it."

There was a pause. "That ... is actually a really good idea. But Phillips will kill me if I pull resources off the hunt for Anselmo and Cunningham."

"What are you doing right now?" I asked.

"I *was* sleeping," he said pointedly. "Now? Not so much anything but hoping faintly that someday I'll be able to close my eyes and return to peaceful slumber—"

"Great, so I'm not taking you away from the manhunt," I said. "Get on that, will you? It's important. It might give us a clue where they got her."

"'They'?" J.J. asked, and he didn't sound sleepy anymore. "Are you seeing a conspiracy theory here, my friend?"

"I'm a seeing a league of villains," I said, "forming with the intent to take out some revenge on Sienna."

There was a dead silent pause. "For realsies? Man, we are stepping further onto the comic book page every day 'round here—"

"J.J.," I said, "I think she's being kept in nightmares, tortured. I need to know where we lost her so I can pick up her trail."

To his credit, he said, "On it," and hung up.

I clicked on my lamp and hung my feet over the edge of the bed, felt my toes touching the soft carpeting. "What now?" Isabella asked from behind me, and I felt her silken touch on my shoulder.

"I need Augustus," I said. "I need more force at my disposal."

"I will see what I can do," she said, getting up with a squeak of mattress springs. I heard her putting on her robe, the soft cotton dragging the floor while she raised it up on her shoulders from where she'd left it puddled on the ground last night. "But do not expect miracles."

"I don't know what to expect," I said as she walked out the door into the living room. I heard her turn on the coffee maker, listened to the soft hum of it heating up. My eyes found the gaping hole I'd made in the wall in my fury last night, and I resisted the urge to add another.

Was Sienna really in danger? Had I really seen her? A chill ran across my scalp like someone had massaged cold fingers over it, leaving goose bumps behind.

"Where is she?" I muttered to myself, letting my brain stir into thought. "Bayscape? Really Bayscape, just unconscious and imagining a blizzard? Or did they get her before that? Some rest area?" I paused. "Why didn't she fly?"

"Luggage," Isabella said as she passed through the bedroom into the bathroom and shut the door behind her.

"Oh," I said. "Right." My skin tingled, my flesh cold. I pulled the covers tighter.

Maybe they hadn't gotten her. Maybe I had just had a nightmare, all my own. But it had seemed so ... photo-real in places. I'd been in a dreamwalk before, and this hadn't quite felt like that. Sienna was in charge of her dreamwalks, was able to set the location, control the decoration, even the clothing of the participants. Here, she felt wildly out of control, like she was just being dragged along by those things.

Those … wraiths. It was as good a word as any.

Manifestations. The word popped into my head unbidden, faint, like a whisper from across the room.

I stood, spinning to see if someone had snuck in behind me. Isabella's side of the bed was empty, the sheets awry where she'd gotten out, her lamp still lit. My scalp still tingled, and my spine was ramrod straight from my reaction to that chilling sensation.

My breathing was fast again, but this time I had it under control quicker. The tinted windows offered a view of the campus, but at this time of night the only thing I could see was lamps lit across the grass-covered grounds, fireflies in the night that never moved. There were a few lights on in the headquarters, I saw as I looked out the window. The response team, no doubt, still working the manhunt.

Somewhere between here, home, and Bayscape Island, someone associated with Eric Simmons, Anselmo, and the Brain had grabbed Sienna. Somehow. Somehow they'd gotten her, had subdued her, and were torturing her with nightmares. That was my theory.

My admittedly crazy theory.

Somewhere between here and there …

My scalp tingled again, and another lone word popped up like an apple coming to the top of the barrel, breaking the surface, mid-thought with buoyant violence. Somewhere between—

HERE

—and there.

"Oh." I blinked my eyes twice. "Between—"

HERE

"—and there," I finished, already in motion.

I ripped open the front door without unlocking it and sped down the hall, the soft carpeting absorbing the impact of my run. I stopped in front of Sienna's door and hammered at it, slapping the palm of my hand against the wood. Lines began to appear, splits in the solid construction, and one final kick broke it down, ripping it free of the hard lock that was keeping it closed.

"Reed?" Scott's voice reached me from over my shoulder, full of sleep, but I ignored him.

"What's going on out here?" Ariadne called from down the hall.

I surged into Sienna's quarters, almost running over the mewling dog (imaginatively named "Dog"—my sister is such an unwitting hipster), who managed a feeble bark and then ran back around the corner like Lassie on the way to Timmy in the well.

"What's the dog doing here?" Ariadne called from somewhere behind me. "He's supposed to be kenneled-"

I strode through the darkened apartment already fairly sure of what I'd find. The apartment was quiet, the living room peaceful, but the sounds of music playing faintly reached me from just behind the closed bedroom door. I made for it like I was unleashed from the chain, grabbing the handle even as Dog scrambled aside to make way for my violently unpredictable charge.

I rolled the handle in my hand and shoved against the door. It opened, then stopped with a thump. "No," I whispered, and shoved again, gentler this time. Something was blocking the door, something that was at least a little heavy. A smell hung in the air, like the dog hadn't been outside in a long while.

I pushed until I made a big enough crack in the door to slip through, and I did so as I heard footfalls behind me. "Reed, what are you doing?" Scott said from the entryway. "What's he doing?" I heard him ask someone else with him, probably Ariadne.

I knew exactly what I was doing.

I pushed my body through the narrow opening into Sienna's bedroom and turned as I stumbled in, eyes trying to pierce the darkness. I fumbled for the light, trying to find it on the wall, missing a couple times before I hit it, bathing the room in light. The dog mewled again outside like he'd been whipped, just as my eyes fell on the object behind the door.

"No no no no no," I said, falling to my knees. Her skin was cold, flesh paler than the death she was being convinced she was, even at this moment. Her eyes were closed, and her hair hung limp as I lifted her back up off the ground to cradle her in my arms. "No, Sienna, no …"

My sister did not respond, she just hung there in my arms, a prisoner in her own tortured mind.

52.

Benjamin

Benjamin sat curled with his knees against his chest, rocking on his haunches, muttering in low tones to himself as the night stretched over the crater. "Never should have … can't believe I …" His balance kept him from tipping over one way or the other, but his sanity felt like it had finally slipped completely out of reach.

The voice that he heard in times of stress, the one that brought with it its own range of color and horror, no longer seemed to be a monstrous form outside himself. Now it seemed like the other half of his whole, a part of him that he truly despised, that he wished he could have left somewhere behind him.

But, no, he hadn't left it behind at all. He'd seen it awaken when he'd been overseas, hadn't he? He'd seen it the first time outside that café in Bredoccia, in Revelen, on the day he was leaving, when the men in leather jackets had come at him and he'd watched fire dance out of his fingers and burn them alive.

He'd seen bright orange that day, a mix of yellow and red that made him fearful, made him want to be home. He hadn't wanted to come on the vacation in any case, but he'd done so when the deal had been so good, figuring he'd see some sights, take in some exotic places.

It hadn't gone the way he had planned. She'd seemed so nice, that Frea. He couldn't believe she'd gone back to the hotel with him. It had been far, far more than what he'd expected. He could still faintly remember the sting of her last kiss on his back, when he was in an almost dreamlike state. She'd slipped out without a word of goodbye, knowing that he was leaving the next day.

Was all this down to her? Had she—

No. No, surely not. She'd been kind where few had, done something for him that no one else had ever done. Benjamin clutched his hand tight, pulling it close to him.

No, that wasn't where things had jumped the track. Had it been the airport? That had certainly been ... monstrous. He could see it all in his waking dreams now, when he closed his eyes. The laughter of the others, the tears that had streaked cold and wet down his cheeks, the painful itching in his throat.

The red that streaked his vision, the sight of fire burning through people and faces—

deserved it

—that was ... just horrible.

But not as horrible as this. Benjamin turned his head to look at Anselmo, who lay flat on the ground. His skin was back, returned from where Benjamin had seared it off a few inches at a time. The man had passed out partway through, but his urgent screams had driven Benjamin forward like a horse-drawn carriage that had lost its driver. He followed the road, the commands given before Anselmo departed him, and it looked like his work had paid off. Despite the lack of hair, Anselmo looked like a man again, all traces of the marred flash gone, replaced by new, hairless, smooth skin.

And all it had cost Benjamin was a vision of a man being burnt to the point of flaying, flesh sloughing off as it melted and charred like marshmallow on a s'more.

Benjamin shuddered at the thought, wondering if he'd ever get the vision out of his mind. He'd watched faces burn off before, but it had seemed distant enough to give him a certain peace. He wasn't in control, after all, not him. Not meek, mild, Benjamin, who took what came along and accepted it without question, even when it wasn't what he wanted. That was his lot in life, after all, and he was resigned to it.

"Oh, good," Anselmo said, sitting upright.

"Gyahhhhh!" Benjamin shrieked, pure, uncontrolled panic causing him to let out some of the pent-up emotions that he'd just been working through. "You nearly scared me out of my skin," he said, once he'd gotten control of himself.

"At least I did not burn you out of it," Anselmo said, amused. He glanced down at his arm and saw the new flesh there, and a wide grin broke out on his face. "Did it work?"

"You look normal," Benjamin said, glancing quickly away from Anselmo's unclothed crotch. He'd thought about re-dressing the man after the healing had completed, but decided against it, instead leaving his naked ass against the weedy dirt.

"Mmm," Anselmo said, letting out a sensual moan, "it feels good to be back. To have ... all of me back."

"Yep," Benjamin said, not looking at him. He heard Anselmo rise and dress in near-silence, the sound of him rubbing himself to check the skin obvious even to his unpracticed ear. He heard sand being slapped off skin as well, and a muttered curse. Then another noise, something more guttural and satisfied, and he dared not turn around.

"I think we should go and visit our enemies once more," Anselmo said.

"Don't you think they'll be ready for us this time?" Benjamin asked, a painful tug of fear ringing through him.

"You can breathe the fire of a nuclear bomb anytime you choose," Anselmo said as the sound of a zipper being tugged up filled the air behind Benjamin. "Tell me how they would prepare for that?"

"You want me to ..." Benjamin swung an arm around to

indicate the crater around them, "do this?"

"No, no," Anselmo said, appearing at Benjamin's shoulder. He was shirtless, and the man's skin looked just a little red, like he'd been mildly sunburned. "Well ... perhaps, if the occasion calls for it."

Benjamin felt himself swallow heavily. "I don't ... I mean, I don't think I want to do what happened in the airport ... again. Can't we just ... confine our vendetta or whatever it is to the people who deserve it?"

"You speak the word *vendetta* but you know not what it means," Anselmo said, slipping on his button-up shirt. "A true vendetta requires a commitment beyond that which you Americans casually intend, throwing it in to suggest two co-workers prancing about in a war of slap-fighting and practical jokes. A vendetta is a blood feud, and requires blood to sustain it. Our enemies have drawn our blood, and we have not answered in kind yet."

Anselmo grabbed Benjamin by his shirt and hauled him to his feet. "But I mean to have blood. I mean to have it. Now. I will be revenged upon them ... and you will help." The wide smile on the Italian's face somehow reminded Benjamin of how he'd looked a few hours earlier, a grinning skull, bereft of flesh, a death's head that smiled its horror in a way that made him nauseous and sick at the thought of what was inevitably going to happen next.

53.

Sienna

"You are descended from Hades," my mother said. "You are descended from death, true death, and you are his heir."

I took it all in. "Don't you mean heiress?"

"Don't interrupt," she said. We were in our house, and the world was dark outside the windows, like a perpetual night had fallen.

"But death interrupts," I said, words bubbling out of my mouth. "He gets you when you're in the middle of a dream, takes you when you're spelling a word out in black ink on crisp paper, will drag you screaming out of your hospital bed or carry you from around the primeval fire while you're roasting your day's kill for dinner." I stared at her dark eyes, partially hidden in shadow, and the smell of my brother's cologne, so out of place, washed over me. "Death interrupts when it pleases."

"You are rude," she said, lips pursing together into a blade-thin line.

"I am death," I said simply.

She stood, and I realized now that we were in our basement, and the sunken egress windows seemed to stream pure darkness around me, like beams of light tinged with tar and corrupted for the purposes of night. "I think you need to spend some more time in the box."

"You can't confine death," I said. "Can't hold back the tide." My voice was monotone, lifeless, droning. I felt so very little, like the darkness had come in around my heart and squeezed me tight, pushing out the air and all my feelings with it.

"Did you ever think that maybe I didn't lock you up to protect you?" she asked, circling me like a shark, like a wolf, like a Wolfe, preparing to spring and shred me like she was death and not me. "Did you ever think that maybe I locked you up to protect the world from you, you human cancer? You Midas of pain. You hateful girl."

"It's not as though she's done a bang-up job of protecting anyone," Breandan said, sliding out of the shadows to stroll in front of me, an angry red dot streaming blood from his forehead on down.

"I can see your brains," I said. "You must be smart."

"Look at me," Athena said, drifting out behind me, animated like she was being pulled along on a cart, legs unmoving. Her olive skin was bled of all color and her neck hung to the side, limp. "Look at what you did to me."

"And me," Breandan said, poking a finger into the hole in his forehead.

"I died for you," my mother said, drifting in front of me.

"You died for death," I said, strangely amused at that thought. "Dead for death, bled for death—"

"Suffered for death," she said, eyes blazing in that cold blue-green, given an otherworldly light. "Suffered for *you*."

"They'll all suffer for you," Breandan said. "Suffer for knowing you, for being around you. Because you—"

"Because I am death," I said, the cold reality drummed into my head. The world faded dark around me, and I was alone in it, resigned.

I am death.

And soon, I would be dead.

And in spite of a strange cry in the back of my head, that news made me oddly peaceful.

54.

Reed

"She's cold," I said as Isabella stooped over Sienna's bed to examine her. It was true; my sister's skin was ice-cold as if she'd been outside all night and all the warmth had leached from her. She'd never been the warmest person (metaphorically or literally), but now she was chilled to the bone.

"Her respiration is slow," Isabella said, using her fingers to separate Sienna's eyelids. "Pupils unresponsive to the light." Isabella pitched to her right, catching herself on the bed. "Also, I cannot touch her again until I get some gloves." She lifted a hand to her forehead and took a step back from the bedside. "Her power is still working."

"Dammit," I said, and cast a look nervously over my shoulder. Ariadne was watching in a gown of her own, somewhat more conservative than the one Isabella wore to bed. Scott was gone, sent to run and fetch a gurney from the medical unit for us to use in transporting her.

"How long has she been here like this?" Ariadne asked.

The room stunk, and my sister's clothes were sticking to her. "A couple days, at least," I said, and gestured to a bag I'd knocked off the bed. "Looks like she was packing when she just keeled over."

"There has to be a medical reason for this," Isabella said,

leaning against the nightstand, looking positively exhausted. It was the middle of the night, after all. "Perhaps narcotic."

"It could be a telepathic-induced coma or something," Ariadne suggested.

"It could be that she just laid down to die of annoyance," I said, with more than a fair amount of annoyance of my own, "but it's unlikely and we're not going to find any answer without tests, right?" I waited until Isabella nodded her head. "Speculation is pointless. I mean, I suspect that Anselmo, Simmons, and the Brain are the ones responsible for this, but I can't say for certain until I rip the truth out of their still-breathing lungs—"

"This sounds familiar," Ariadne said, "but not like you."

"I'm going through some changes," I said. "It's a time of intense stress."

I heard the elevator ding down the hall and around the corner, and then Scott came rattling along with a gurney seconds later. "My access card still works for the elevator and this hallway," he said as he rolled the gurney into the room. "Weird, huh? I would have thought they'd have removed that after I left the agency."

"Well, you still needed it to see Sienna," Ariadne said, staring at him as he worked his way around the other side of the bed and started untucking the sheets under my sister.

"I still needed it to see Sienna what?" he asked, not really paying attention to Ariadne as he prepared to lift my sister.

"Doesn't matter now," I said, cutting off that particular line of inquiry as I caught Ariadne's perplexed look out of the corner of my eye. "We need to focus on saving her life, on getting her back out of … wherever they're imprisoning her."

"In her own mind, it looks like," Isabella said. "But how do we do this? I can run tests to find some medical answers for what is happening to her, but it will take time to prepare a toxicology report." Her eyes narrowed and her brow knitted together as Scott and I lifted Sienna out of the bed and onto the gurney with the sheet supporting her weight.

"And there's no guarantee what's happened to her is even chemical," Ariadne said. "How would they have gotten chemicals to her?" She shook her head. "This reeks of metahuman abilities, of a telepath."

"Fine," I said, "let's assume it was a telepath." I steadied Sienna on the cart, carefully pushing her arms up on the gurney, crossing her hands on her chest so they didn't hit doorways as we steered her out of here. "What the hell do we even do? It's not like we're prepared for this. We'd need professional help of the variety the agency doesn't employ anymore. We'd need—"

"An expert," came the voice from the doorway, drawing four sets of wide eyes to the figure standing there. He had mocha skin, hair that was dark, but showing signs of grey in the years since last I'd seen him. His voice was the same, deep and rich, but he looked tired, like he'd been awake for entirely too long without any respite. "Luckily for you," Dr. Quinton Zollers said, giving us a weary smile, "there just happens to be one close at hand."

55.

Sienna

The light outside the windows was beautiful, azure skies visible through the tinted glass. Green grass stretched out underneath perfectly sculpted clouds, and off in the distance, I could see headquarters. Its glass windows were dark and nothing moved within them, a sign that finally, perhaps, the campus was at peace.

It felt like a lazy Sunday in the spring. A slight breeze stirred my clothes. The windows were open, and white sheers that I didn't even know I had hung from the windows, billowing as the wind swept gently through. I watched them swirl around me, painting my living room in shades of white like I was in the middle of the clouds. Then they receded as the wind died.

The smell of good food was in the air, wafting through my nose and drifting onto the back of my tongue, making my mouth water. I was hungry, and I had that instinctive feeling that I'd be eating soon. It was almost like I could feel my full belly in advance, knew I'd be satiated soon enough. There was a satisfaction that warmed my limbs, that stretched from the tips of my toes and tickled my mind.

I smiled in a way I hadn't smiled in a long time and turned to look at my living room.

"Happy birthday, baby," my mother said, kissing me on

the forehead.

I blinked in surprise. "Is it my birthday already?"

"Of course," Breandan said, and suddenly there was a crowd in my quarters. They filled the rooms with activity, with a healthy buzz of warmth and happy conversations. I could hear the pleasant laughter, the talking—

"—she's cold—"

I blinked, some of the chatter cutting through into my warm, pleasant party like an icy knife ripping harshly through those wafting sheers. I felt a chill of discomfort and waited for it to pass.

"So, Miss Nealon," Zack said, slipping up next to me and stealing a kiss, his hand on the small of my back, "what does it feel like to be a hero?"

I'd heard that somewhere before. Hadn't someone asked me that once? "Feels like I'm hungry," I said.

"Food's coming in a few minutes," Breandan said. "I put on a great spread."

"I didn't even know you could cook," I said.

"There's a lot you didn't know about me," he said with a wink. "So ... is this the best birthday ever?"

The warm sepia tones of the world around me seemed so inviting, and that faint feeling of joy just settled on my bones. "Worlds better than the last one," I said with conviction. Etta James crooned "Sunday Kind of Love" in the background somewhere, and I took a contented breath.

"What happened last birthday?" my mother asked, a look of concern on her face.

I saw the world change, the light darken, the room shift to a gloomy place, bereft of people. "Nothing," I said truthfully.

"That's a shame," Zack said, his arm around my shoulders practically weightless. I turned to look up at him, but his eyes were sunken and hollow, black pupils growing to encompass his entire eye. "You should never have to be alone on your birthday."

I pulled away from him suddenly, unable to muster so much as a yelp of shock at what I was seeing. I looked around as the light faded from the windows, as the sheers whipped as though they were in a hurricane, gale-force winds ripping them off their hangers and swirling them around the darkened room. Zack, Breandan and my mother remained there, but the rest of the party guests faded, their skin turning to dust and dissolving in the wind until they came to rest in a still calm, the room silent once more.

Silent as death.

"This is a harbinger of things to come," Breandan said, the skin sloughing off his jaw. "We're just the first to die around you." He turned to bone and then dust before my eyes, joining the desert on my floor.

"We're only the start," Zack said, his skin crawling with bugs as it putrefied before my eyes. He, too, collapsed in on himself, became dust, indistinguishable from the rest of the drifts on the ground.

"Everyone you ever meet will follow," my mother said through cracked and rotting lips. "You think spending your last birthday alone was bad? Imagine how you'll feel in a thousand years, two thousand years, five … when everyone and everything you've ever known is nothing but ash and dust, and you know that everyone you'll meet from now until the day you die will follow.

With that, she shriveled and joined them on the floor, and the wind kicked up and blew the remains of everyone I'd ever known and failed out of my life, out of my home, out of my sight.

56.

Reed

"I can't tell you how damned good it is to see you, Doc," I said to Quinton Zollers as we wheeled Sienna into the infirmary, the lights springing on automatically at our motion.

"Whuzzz … going on here?" Augustus asked, sleepily, blinking his eyes as we came in.

"Explain later," Ariadne said, still hugging her nightgown close to her.

"Sienna's in some sort of coma," Scott offered.

"Or now, briefly," Ariadne said, sounding a little resigned.

"Move her onto the bed," Isabella said, motioning us toward a hospital bed in the corner. She went ahead of us and lowered the rail at the side. "I need to get her cleaned up."

"She does smell a little ripe," Scott said, wrinkling his nose.

"How do you think you'd smell after being insensate in your room for a few days?" I asked, snapping as I lost my temper. "Because I'm guessing you'd be a little rank, too."

"I need to get a catheter in," Isabella said as we lifted her onto the bed. "Quinton? Can you be my nurse?"

"Been a while since I've done anything like this," Zollers said, "but I suppose."

"The rest of you, away," Isabella said, shooing us. "Don't

make me get a broom."

"Uh, okay," Ariadne said and took a step back, closer to where Augustus lay on his bed in the middle of the room. He was watching us all with eyes open in surprise.

"You're not dreaming," I told him, "but she is."

"Uhm … if you say so," Augustus said. "How do you know she's dreaming?"

"Because she dragged me into it," I said. "And dreaming might be a strong word for it. Nightmares might be a more apt descriptor."

"'Might be'?" he asked as Sienna convulsed in the corner, hitting the railing of her bed so hard with a stray hand that it bent the metal. "Damn!"

"I see we have at least one new face," Zollers murmured as he covered Sienna over with a sheet.

"Sa—" Augustus began.

"—me one you've always had, yes," Zollers finished for him, "you're very amusing."

"The hell?" Augustus asked.

"It's Dr. Zollers," I said, "the telepath I told you about, remember?"

"You didn't tell me he was a brother," Augustus said.

"Is that … was that something I should have mentioned?" I asked. "Because I'm not really sure how to work that into casual conversation without making it seem awkward and forced. 'Oh, yeah, Zollers and I were good friends, and he's an African-American dude, like you!' Like I'm fishing for street cred cookies, y'know?"

Augustus looked unamused. "Yeah, you probably shouldn't say it like that."

"Her mind is whirling," Zollers said, speaking as he worked to clean her up. "It's bad."

"How'd you know to come here?" I asked.

"I sensed trouble," Zollers said, looking up for a moment to make eye contact with me. He had the warmest eyes I've ever seen, still, even now, looking tired.

"Can you do that?" Ariadne asked. "I mean … from where you were?"

"Where he was?" Scott asked, looking perplexed. "What's that supposed to mean?"

"It means Ariadne's been keeping tabs on me," Zollers said with mild amusement. Ariadne flushed scarlet, roughly the same shade as her hair. "It's all right, I don't mind. I was spending some time in India when I sensed Sienna was in mental distress."

"You picked her up from across the world?" I asked in sheer disbelief. "How? Aren't telepaths limited in their range?"

"When you've spent as much time in someone's head as I've spent in your sister's," Zollers said, "it attunes you to that particular mind, like wearing a path in rough and brambly woods. So yes, I could sense her mind at certain times of great distress from all the way across the world. Most of the time I'd sense physical danger, alertness, basically that was … Sienna being Sienna, getting in trouble. Things would return to calm, her sense of heightened agitation would fade back to the normal levels of angst."

"I like how you call it 'angst' even though she's a grown-ass woman," Augustus said.

"It's an apt word," Zollers said with a shrug. "Emotional distress would also fit. She's been in a state of that on and off for the last few months, but it wasn't urgent, at least not until a few days ago."

"So, you detected it when she first got sent into these nightmares?" I asked.

"Actually, no," he said, shaking his head, "they didn't start out as nightmares. It started out as her on a peaceful island—and that's how I knew something was wrong."

"Beg pardon?" Scott asked.

"Her normal levels of distress faded," Zollers said, "they were muted, like she was unconscious, but for far too long. So I walked down my path into her mind, and found her …

'asleep,' as it were. Trapped in her mind, unable to wake. So I tried to 'shake' her awake. Push into her dream, stun her mind into realizing where she was so that she would snap out of it. When it failed, repeatedly, I knew there was something deeply wrong. So I hopped a plane, in hopes that getting closer would allow me to reach into her mind and jolt her out." He shook his head. "But I can't slip into her dream, even this close. She's so ensconced in the delusion her mind is creating around her that she's losing connection with the real world."

"How did this happen?" Isabella asked, a needle in her hand, a droplet of clear liquid catching the light at the tip.

"I don't know," Zollers said, "but she's stuck in her own head as surely as you or I could get locked in a room. Or a—"

"Metal box?" I offered helpfully. And sarcastically. "How do we get her out?"

"When she reached out for you," he said, pausing in his work, "it was a good sign. A sign that she was cogent enough to recognize the nightmares for what they are to some extent. But since then, there's been a significant degradation of her thought patterns. She's no longer coherent. This little delusion of hers started out as a cleverly constructed fantasy that her mind put on, a continuation of her real life as she embarked on this vacation she had planned. But it's jumped the track; she's shifting back and forth between various scenarios at a rapid pace, all of them centering on unresolved conflicts and emotions—"

"So she's dealing with her guilt?" Augustus asked, sending me a pointed, sideways look.

"Yes, guilt is the prevailing emotion in this case," Zollers said. "Guilt, regret, fear. They're all there, the negative emotional spectrum is lit up in her head right now like the Empire State Building at night."

"What does that mean, long term?" I asked.

"Negative emotions are necessary for life," Zollers said. "Sadness, guilt, fear, they protect us and allow us to process life experiences and put them in emotional context. But the chemistry of the brain is not suited to handle intense bombardment for extended periods of time."

"Is she going to burn out?" I asked.

"I wouldn't worry about that." Zollers shook his head. "What I'd worry about, as her nightmares become more intense and hostile—"

Sienna jerked in her sleep, and a thin lash of fire flew out of her hand, ascending to the ceiling, where it lit a burn mark in the white tile and then vanished in a puff of smoke.

"Is that," Zollers finished.

"What the hell, Gavrikov?" I asked, stalking up to the invisible line that Isabella had drawn when she'd told us to back off.

"This is the bad news," Zollers said. "The souls she's captured are screaming inside her." His eyes were bright, attentive, and worried, hidden behind the wrinkles and bags made worse by his lack of recent sleep, I guessed. "They are unable to reach her or hear anything going on out in the real world because she's not getting much of anything from the real world. She's locked in, and they're cut off without her. But," he said, voice grave, "they're still taking commands, and their panic is growing wilder and wilder as time rolls on. My guess is that it's only a matter of time before one—or more of them—does something a hell of a lot more dangerous than setting the ceiling on fire."

57.

Sienna

"Sienna, how does it feel to be hated by everyone?" The voice was sharp and clear, ringing out on a late summer's day as I stepped out of the door of an eatery in South Minneapolis, a few blocks from my house. I glanced over my shoulder to see a man coming down the sidewalk at an eager jog, cell phone extended in front of him with the camera lens catching the glint of the sun.

I ignored him and turned away, even though my car was in the direction he was coming from. I could circle the block, get to my car, and be gone before he could catch me at that slow-ass jog. The sun's rays shone down on me, warming my skin.

"Sienna, what does it feel like?" he asked again, like I hadn't heard and ignored him the first time. His voice bubbled with excitement, the thrill of the hunter boxing in his prey, I suppose. "A Pew research poll puts your job disapproval rating at 65%. Why hasn't President Harmon fired you yet?"

"I didn't know they polled on my job performance," I said, blinking in surprise and speaking out of turn.

"Sienna, you're supposed to appear before a congressional hearing on metahumans next month," he said, sensing weakness now that he'd gotten me to at least mutter a response. I increased my pace, leaving him behind. "What do you think they're going to say about the escape incident? The Atlanta catastrophe? Any comment?"

"No comment," I said, leaving him in the dust as I made for the corner of the brick building. I was still walking, determined not to let this guy think he was making me flee. I'd fought some of the toughest people on the planet; running from some amateur journo-douche with a cell phone wasn't gonna be a thing that happened.

The second guy sprang out from his ambush just as I was about to turn the corner. I would have reacted perhaps less violently, but I had my head turned to look back at the guy I was trying to leave in the dust, and when I turned back, there he was: another dick with a camera. "Sienna, what do you think your mother and father would say if they could see how hated you are now?"

I don't know whether my response was prompted by my surprise at turning around and seeing another cell phone in my face, or if it was the tenor of the question that provoked me, but I slugged that guy right in the face and he hit the ground, nose already streaming blood. As his cell phone came clattering down behind him, I stomped it as I broke into a sprint around the corner, leaving the other paparazzo in the dust. He didn't even stop to tend to his compatriot, just stood there filming me until I turned the corner out of sight.

Fortunately, I didn't break into sobs until I was safely in my car, driving away.

"This is pathetic," my mother said from the seat beside me as the world darkened around me. "That's what I would say about where you've taken your life."

I just kept sobbing, curling up as the car drove on toward an even darker future than I had ever imagined. It wasn't as though things had any hope of getting better, after all. For as long as I could remember, they only ever did the same thing: got worse and worse.

"All this has happened because you're fighting against the truth that you are death," my mother said. "And the sooner you accept that and get on with the business of embracing your end, the sooner you'll find ... peace."

I lay my head down, and once again the thought of that—peace—made its way in, and I felt just a moment of bliss in an ocean of sadness. Then I let the grief and pain carry me away, and my body bucked as I cried uncontrollably.

58.

Reed

"Hell, she's flaring," Scott shouted, and she damned sure did. A six-foot gout of flame shot out of my sister's hand and streaked into the empty space occupied only a second earlier by Dr. Zollers. Scott clamped a hand down on hers and steam hissed as he shot water, dousing her fire.

"Gavrikov and the others are panicking," Zollers said from his new position at the foot of the bed. "They're shouting as loud as they can at her, but they're as confused as she is. They think she's in genuine danger, that all these things are truly happening and that she's unable to contact them for help. They're being almost as emotionally battered watching her as she is in the thick of it."

"So they don't see the truth any more than she does," Scott said. "Everybody in her head is flying blind."

"Just like us out here," I said.

"She's ramping up again," Zollers said, squinting, "Gavrikov is reacting to something she's seeing in her head, emotions are all over the place."

"Not good," Scott said, and I watched his hands shimmer as he drew moisture out of the air. "Ariadne, can you turn on a sink for me? It's easier if I don't have to decrease the humidity of the room."

"I can help," Augustus said from his place on the bed.

288

"Add a little a dirt, do a mudpack, maybe if you want to work together."

"Keeps us from burning to death and gives her more youthful skin at the same time," Scott said. "I like it. There's something for everybody."

"Uh oh," Zollers said, frozen in place. "This next one … it's going to be bad."

"Augustus—" I said, interrupted by the wave of fire that crawled over Sienna's skin, replacing it with flames as she crackled to life, burning—

The hiss of steam was loud, like a speaker crackling in my ear when Scott unleashed his power. Over my shoulder I heard the door to the medical unit whoosh open, the smell of fresh dirt filling the air as clods of black earth flew over my head, not so much as dusting me as they went past. They disappeared into the cloud of steam as I held my hands up in front of my face. The air was hot and steamy, like I'd walked into a sauna, and it was baking my palms and forearms.

The heat radiated out, and Zollers stumbled out of the steam wash, the hiss still filling the air as he caught hold of a nearby hospital bed and steadied himself. "Isabella!" I called, and she came out of the steam wash a moment later with her face red, mildly burnt from the release of heat in the water vapor. She held a hand to her cheek and her eyes were tightly shut. I grabbed hold of her and drew her over to me, pulling her from the densest concentration of steam.

"Okay, got it!" Scott shouted, and the air finally started to clear. I saw him, redder than usual, at the center of it all as the air circulation in the medical unit started to clear the atmosphere. I gave it a helping hand, stirring the air currents toward the vents. Scott's curly hair was surprisingly limp with dampness, and he wore a grimace of pain coupled with exhaustion. He was leaning against the wall, head back. "That … was not good."

"It'll get worse," Zollers warned, still leaning against the bed to my right.

"But of course," Ariadne said from far behind me, near the door. "We couldn't have a chance of it getting better, would we?"

"Perhaps there is a solution," Isabella said, pulling her hand free of me. Her cheek was already starting to blister. "If she is deep in sleep, perhaps I can wake her up with a shot of adrenaline."

"You should stab it right into her heart," Augustus said dryly, "like they do in the movies."

"I will have to," Isabella agreed, moving to the drug cabinet next to her office. "Exactly like that."

"Well, damn," Augustus said, the wind right out of his sails. "I was just joking. You know, trying to lighten the mood."

"We're standing next to a human nuclear bomb that's on runaway reaction," Scott said, "if this mood gets any lighter, we may all float away as individual atoms."

"What if it just makes her condition worse?" Zollers asked. "What if it just causes her mind to race even faster, panic even harder?"

"Kaboom," Scott said. "Anyone remember Glencoe? Fair thee well, see you people in the upper atmo as our component parts."

"You're awfully calm about that," Augustus said, eyebrow cocked.

"Isn't death part of your job?" Scott asked.

"Uh, living is part of my job, too," Augustus said. "Kinda hard to do it if I'm dead."

"This is bad," Ariadne said. "Maybe we should push the panic button."

"Hey, I'm way ahead of you on that," Augustus said. "So glad the doctor hooked me up to a painkiller drip now. I think I pressed it like twelve times."

"It's a wonder you're still conscious," Isabella said, working her way back to Sienna's bedside. The rails were melted, the sheets scorched where they weren't damp with water. "How is she?"

"She's in a trough," Zollers said. "Gavrikov and the others are becalmed, but these delusions of hers are getting progressively worse." He frowned. "It's taking all my concentration just to keep track of what's going on, and I'm not even getting the full picture, just the emotional view. It's like watching a movie through a piece of paper."

"What do we do?" I asked, swiveling to look at Ariadne, the closest thing to an authority figure we had here.

She looked stricken. "You're more in charge of these kinds of things than I am."

I started to open my mouth, then realized I had no idea what to say. I was in charge? In charge of a rapidly spiraling disaster of doom in which my sister was descending into nightmares that might cause her to burn everyone around her to cinders?

Oh, my.

"You wanted to show everyone how different things would be when you were in charge," Augustus said, picking that perfect moment to chip my self-confidence into the corner pocket. "Here's your chance! Try not to get us killed."

"I think we should try the adrenaline," I said, nodding at Isabella, who had the syringe in her hand, filled to the brimming. She nodded at me once and headed toward Sienna. "Ariadne, you should get out of here."

"I'm not leaving," she said, setting her jaw. "She needs us all."

"Yeah, but she kinda needs water and mud and psychic intervention more than conversation, you know?" Augustus said. When every eye fell on him, he seemed to retreat a little. "I'm just putting it out there. Might be safer elsewhere is all."

"If it ends like Glencoe," I said darkly, "there might not be anywhere close by that you could consider safe. In fact, you might just rate this as a catastrophe on the scale of—"

Before I could finish the doors slid open and a voice that usually sounded oh-so-calm broke into a shout that was almost like thunder out of the heavens. "*WHAT ... THE ... HELL* ... is going on in here?"

"Director," Ariadne said, all the blood drained from her face. She was almost as white as Sienna.

Standing in the doorway, his face red for an entirely different reason, was Andrew Phillips.

"Let me finish that for you, Reed," Augustus said, "a catastrophe on the scale of ... *THIS*. *This* right here. Because I think we can all agree that this shit just got sooooooo much worse."

59.

Sienna

"Maybe you don't belong here."

Andrew Phillips's voice rang out over his office, over the view of the green and verdant campus, but it sounded like death to me, like fall leaves should have been fluttering out of the trees, like icy snows should have dumped from grey skies, like life should have paused, fled, and left me in a dark and empty place.

"Excuse me?" As far as witty responses went, it wasn't my best.

"You hit a paparazz—" He paused, mid-turn. He'd been pacing in front of his window, gesticulating with his arms in a way that I hadn't really seen him do before. Maybe he was worked up for once, but his voice remained cool. "Is it paparazzo or -i?"

"What's the difference?" I asked.

"I honestly don't know," he said. "And it doesn't matter. The point is, the news is everywhere. Another hit for us in the favorables. The pictures have been screen-grabbed and turned into memes—again." He sighed and looked faintly disgusted. "Congrats on your internet superstardom. You're heading toward more hits than Grumpy Cat."

"The guy jumped out at me, okay?" I folded my arms. "Jackie says this isn't insurmountable—"

"Jackie's job is infinitely harder because you keep giving the press terrible things to say about you," Phillips said, in a low growl. "She's got the grace to try and deal with it. I don't know how she does. If it were me in her job, I'd be telling you something different right now, like where to go and what to do with yourself when you get there." He drew up to his full height, which was considerable. "But I'm not going to tell you where to go, or what to do when you get there. I'm just going to tell you that right now, you can't be here."

My eyes fluttered as I processed that. "Wait ... are you firing me?"

"You're suspended," Phillips said. "Two weeks, no pay."

"Can you even do that?" I asked. "I mean, I'm a civil servant—"

"You assaulted a civilian while off duty," he said, "hell, yes, I can suspend you for that. This isn't watching porn at your desk. The government does have rules against hitting people who ... well, who legally don't deserve it."

I grudgingly reached for the olive branch he offered in there. "I like how you added the word 'legally' in there."

"In spite of whatever you think, Sienna," Phillips said, and his face flashed in an otherworldly way, looking gaunt and spectral, just for a second, "I'm not your enemy. Not personally. My job coming here was to get this agency out of the spotlight and reduce the number of PR catastrophes that the White House has to answer for. It's two months to the election and you're not making my—or the re-election campaign's—job any easier. It's like you're trying to hand the presidency to Robb Foreman."

"I'm not," I said, lowering my gaze to the edge of his desk, a wooden model that used to be mine. Not that I'd be terribly upset if Robb Foreman were president; he'd be a fair sight better than Gerard "Gerry" Harmon, the twat. I knew who I was voting for on the first Thursday in November, that much was certain.

Though I had my doubts, if things kept going the way

they were going, that Robb Foreman would be able to keep me on even if he won.

The light flashed in the room, and I saw an old stone table in place of the wooden one for a moment before it snapped back to real. "It's wonderful how I can achieve a fantastic apprehension rate in my job," I said, "prevent six major metahuman incidents this year, yet still get sacrificed on the altar of politics and media."

"Don't play martyr on me," Phillips said stiffly. He said everything stiffly. "Any cop in the U.S. would be getting their ass handed to them right now for hitting a journo off the clock. They'd probably be looking at a lot more than a suspension. This is not acceptable behavior in a civilized society."

"You know he wanted to get hit, right?"

"Yeah, I'm sure his life's ambition was fulfilled the day you broke his jaw," Phillips said.

"Well, everyone knows his name now," I said. "You can't deny it got him some fame."

"Maybe, but his fifteen minutes is going to be up soon," Phillips said, "I only wish yours was."

The way he said it was like a spear delivered right to the center of my chest. "I wish it was, too."

I looked out the window behind him, and the green lawn flashed white, snow mounds piled high in drifts, like rolling hills sprung out of the flat earth. It was that way for a few seconds, then it went back to the lawn. I shook the afterimage out of my head.

"Two weeks," Phillips said, drawing me back into our conversation.

"What am I supposed to do with that?" I asked, dragging my ass out of the chair.

"I don't care," Phillips said. "Think long and hard about whether you really want to stay here, because your days at this agency are drawing to a close if you keep acting the way you're acting."

"The way I'm acting?" I resisted the urge to throw the chair at him. "I can barely leave the campus anymore, because the press follows me every chance they get."

"Maybe you should fly away next time," he said.

"I don't run," I said, my temper rising. I could feel the heat in my face.

Phillips' face turned cold—very cold. His broad cheeks narrowed and thinned before my eyes, revealing a thin face that was heavily lined. The green behind him disappeared, and the desk turned to a stone table, the office décor morphing into something eerily familiar.

Erich Winter's office.

"Maybe you simply do not belong here," Winter said, his breath frosting in the air.

"This is the only job I've ever had," I said, saying the exact words to him that I'd said to Phillips at this point in the conversation.

"Then maybe you don't belong anywhere," he said, and the chill in the room rose, driving the heat from my cheeks. The glass frosted over, a sheet of ice forming on its surface.

I ignored the barbed comment. "What are you going to do without me if a meta threat shows up?"

"I know this will come as a great surprise to you," Winter said as the roof opened up and snow began to pour in, heavy white flakes covering the ground a foot in a few seconds, "but somehow we will manage without you."

"With who? Reed?" I scoffed, but a nervous, sick feeling permeated the depths of my belly. "He's not ready. He doesn't have the nerve to do what needs to be done."

"Perhaps what we need is less of your particular variety of nerve," Winter said as the room continued to fill with snow. It was past my knees now, the chill seeping through my legs and into my bones. "Perhaps a steadier hand would serve us better."

"You don't know what's out there," I said, shaking my head. My cheeks were red from the arctic wind that was roaring through the office now. "You won't be able to manage without me."

"That's your ego talking," Winter said. "The world endured a very long time before Sienna Nealon was born. Societal collapse will hardly follow if you were to simply ... disappear." I heard the ghost of Phillips voice append, "for a while," to the end of that statement, like a whisper somewhere beyond the howling winds.

"I don't mean to go quietly into the night," I said. The snows were up to my chest, crushing me. I felt trapped, afraid, but let none of it come out in my voice.

"You are nothing but a footnote in history," Winter said, and this was all him, his voice strong. "You will die nearly unremembered, at the feet of the mob that once embraced you as its hero. How quickly they forget, how slowly they forgive, and how complete is the scouring of the bones of their victims." He stepped through the snow like it was nothing, towered over me as the cold reached my chin and mouth and flooded in before I could make reply. "You don't belong anywhere. As you said, you live apart from humanity, and humanity will not mourn you when you die ... alone."

With that the snows surrounding my limbs, flooding into my mouth, shot through with a hard blue frost that turned everything liquid to solid ice. I choked soundlessly, my throat constricted and filled by the frost that was going to swallow me whole.

60.

Reed

"What the hell is going on here?" Phillips asked again. His face was redder the second time around, and he completely ignored Augustus's painkiller-induced levity, which was a shame, because if ever there was a moment that needed levity, this was it.

"Sienna is in a coma," Isabella said, forming the explanation before I could come up with it.

"Then why is Harper picking up heat flares from the medical unit, that look like Cunningham is in here?" Phillips asked, stepping a little further into the room. I could see black-suited security men behind him, armed well past the teeth. They were armed at least to the foreheads, with rifles and submachine guns and maybe bazookas, I dunno.

"She's under psychic attack," Zollers said, his soothing voice carrying a little extra gusto. "She's lashing out blindly with her powers."

"Who are you?" Phillips asked, but not in as nasty a way as he could have.

"Dr. Quinton Zollers. I'm a consultant."

"Right," Phillips said, nodding. "Okay. Consulting for who? Because we're not paying you. Let's just get that out there right now."

"Right to the purse strings," Ariadne said with a sigh.

"He's consulting to try and save this place from becoming ground zero in a nuclear detonation," I said, wading into the fray. "Because Sienna could make Cunningham's work at the airport look like a four-year-old's sparkler on the Fourth of July."

"She was supposed to be out of here," Phillips said.

"Someone had other plans," I said.

Phillips's eyes narrowed. "Was this coma induced?"

I swiveled my head to Isabella, who shrugged faintly. "Probably," she said. "This sort of thing does not happen naturally in metas, and she's got something in her blood that's causing a reaction."

"So she's poisoned," Phillips said, mulling it over. "She can't stay here."

That casual drop-in left me stunned, and it took me a few seconds to recover. "What? You can't move her now!"

"Why not?" Phillips asked. "Presumably you did, unless she was hiding in the closet when I came through earlier."

"She needs care," I said. "She needs—"

"She needs to not blow up in the middle of civilization," Phillips said, "and preferably not in the middle of the response unit that's currently hunting two dangerous fugitives in the area."

"If you move her," Zollers said, "we won't be able to contain her."

Phillips's face twitched, just a little. "Can you contain her here?"

"Maybe not," Zollers said, and oh, how I wish he had lied. You'd think he'd be good at it, what with being a former spy and telepath and all that.

"Get her out of here," Phillips snapped and pointed at the door. "Get her in a car and drive west, the hell away from here—"

"She's spiking!" Zollers shouted, and the medical unit became a chaotic free-for-all in an instant.

Sienna's skin glowed blue, hotter than I'd seen her go

before. Scott was already moving, directing water from a free-flowing sink in the corner into a floating ovoid shape, just hovering it over her. The dirt that Augustus had piled on as mud earlier was spread out on the bed and floor around Sienna, and I watched as it coalesced below her, flowing like water to cover her chest and legs, completely blocking out the flames. Scott's water dropped, seeping into the soil shell that Augustus had created. Steam began to hiss, the soil began to glow—

"This one's bad," Zollers said, voice back to calm, but I could barely hear him over the hiss of the steam. The temporary entombment around my sister began to glow a harsh orange, cracks appearing in steadily widening fissures around it. Scott kept pouring water over it, and soon that entire corner of the room was obscured. Isabella scrambled away again, coat flapping behind her, her silken gown showing beneath it as she stooped in her barefooted run.

"You should have told me what was happening immediately," Phillips said over my shoulder, voice laden with fury.

"You know why I didn't?" I shot back, not taking my eyes off the steam-filled corner where my sister was baking. "This. This right here. Here we are, in the middle of a crisis, and you want to cast her out to explode on her own—"

"Where she won't hurt anyone, yes," Phillips said.

"She's going to blow up as we're transporting her off campus, dumbass!" I shouted at him. "Unless we're working to contain this, she's going to go off like a bomb and we'll all die, and then she'll just keep going off until she's dead and the countryside around her is completely nuked. Maybe over and over for days, who knows?" My jaw hardened, my eyes cornered him and wouldn't let him loose. "We're trying to stop that from happening, and you're trying to screw it up. Stop doing that!"

"I'm trying to keep this from getting worse," he said. "You should have moved her the second this started. Your head is so far up your own ass that you can't see clearly. You should have someone who wasn't emotionally involved in this crisis giving the orders, telling you what to do—"

"Maybe I've had enough of you telling me what to do," I said, and felt wind flare from the tips of my fingers. "Especially when it's clear you don't give a fig if she lives or dies."

"Security," Phillips said, menacing. "We need to move Ms. Nealon out of—"

"Belay that!" I shot back.

"You will follow my orders," Phillips said over his shoulder, not bothering to look back at the black-clad men behind him.

"You'll get us all killed," I shouted, not daring to look away from my death glare at Phillips.

Phillips's eyes narrowed, and the steam drifted in front of his face, making it look like he was breathing smoke out of his nose and ears. "You—"

A flare of fire interrupted him, pulsating orange and red and nearly blinding me, but this time, it didn't come from Sienna.

It came from the hallway outside the medical unit, and it consumed the entire security team in its angry heat. The men in black danced and writhed, fire rolling up their bodies as it covered them in its hot embrace, sending black clouds billowing up to the ceiling. The clatter of their weapons falling out of their hands was nearly drowned out by their screams, and one by one the men followed, lumps of organic matter slowly cooking, the smell of burning meat overcoming the steam.

Out of the smoke, two figures emerged. I blinked as they drifted out of the leading edge, features fuzzy but becoming clear in seconds. The one in the back I knew as Cunningham immediately; his hangdog look and slumped shoulders obvious even before he cleared the black clouds.

The other, it took me a moment to identify. When last I'd

seen him, he was scarred from head to toe. Now, his skin was new, flushed with pride, or pleasure or maybe even the simple effort of holding his breath as he trod through our burning security men. Either way, there was no hiding the satisfaction on Anselmo Serafini's newly-formed face as he stepped out of the smoke to face me. "And now we meet again, Mr. Treston," he said, "for the last time."

And I knew, one way or another, that he was right.

61.

Sienna

The ice was suffocating, choking, killing me slowly. It covered every limb, to the tips of my fingers and toes, and washed me with a numb burning that felt like slow fire was licking at my nerve endings. I could feel it in a way I shouldn't have been able to if it really had been fire. It was in my nostrils and sinuses, numbing my brain and burning it, all in one. I was immobile, railing against the strength of the hard ice that secured me in place, pain lancing through me from bottom to top, and I had no recourse but to stand there and feel it, feel every bit of it.

I stood there for a minute, for an hour, for an age. I flexed my fingers ineffectually, I tried to curl up without success, I screamed and cried to the heavens for help.

Shapes and shadows moved outside my frigid prison. I saw them distorted, as if through a glass, a spider web of imperfections in the ice giving the shapes a funhouse mirror look.

I saw an eye—blue, but not the blue of Winter and bereft of the green that flecked my mother's. I saw dark hair, a young face that was too distorted to be handsome. I heard a voice, muffled, unfamiliar. "Uhhh … did I catch you at a bad time?"

For obvious reasons, I did not answer.

I saw him move, saw him work, saw him try to free me, but to no effect. "I, uh … guess I'll come back some other time. Sorry."

I screamed and I screamed at him, but he didn't hear a word of it.

I waited another age. Day and night moved steadily overhead, the sun and moon visible in my burning, painful prison.

I wanted to go home.

… but I didn't have one.

I wanted to see my friends.

… but I didn't have any.

The ice hardened and set, the sun disappeared, and the moon as well. The darkness closed in on me like four iron walls had been dropped in around me.

I was alone.

Again.

Cut off from the world.

Again.

In the box.

Again.

Forever.

I am death, I said to myself. *And the world would be a much happier place without me.*

I closed my eyes.

The sound of a faint tapping reached my ears, a subtle vibration in the ice that sounded like someone putting their fingernail against wood, over and over again. It was slow, steady, and gradually maddening.

It grew louder, then louder still, and I opened my eyes, which had never really been shut. A faint light had appeared in the distance, glowing like a penlight in a dark room, but far away, across a moonless night at sea.

Leave me be, I said, *for I am death, and you don't want any of this.*

"Nice," a familiar voice said, reverberating through the

ice. "But I'm pretty sure death talks a little more formal. Probably doesn't say, 'you don't want any of this.' I'm guessing he would have gone with, 'You will receive naught but the taste of ash and grave from me!' With an exclamation point, for emphasis, see."

I tried to frown, but my face was frozen. *Who are you?*

"It's me," he said, and I knew it was a he. The light was larger now, like a headlamp in the fog at midnight.

Me who?

"You'll see," he said, and the tapping was now a pecking, the sound of frost being chipped away. The light was an open door to my room, his silhouette like that of a parent checking on their child in the darkness of slumber.

Whatever, I said.

"Death definitely wouldn't say 'whatever.' Death is not a teenage girl."

She could be. Don't lay your gender stereotype baggage on me. Death could be a kickass teenage girl, all sullen and emo—

"Death would not say 'emo' and would probably find that description insulting."

Oh, leave me be, will you?

"No," he said, "I will not." The light was blinding now, his silhouette and shadow the only thing keeping me from being completely overwhelmed.

I waited, afraid to ask the question I wanted to know the answer to more than anything. *Why not?*

"Because I haven't given up on you yet," he said, his voice warm, kind, and inviting. "Because I would *never* give up on you."

You should, I said. *You should give up now. You should leave me in here to—*

"To what?" he asked. "To wallow in your guilt until you putrefy and truly become this 'death' that they keep pushing you to be? Sorry. I get the guilt thing, but it doesn't work with me."

I killed people. There are reasons I feel guilty.

"There's a time and a place to deal with that guilt, and this ain't it."

It's a perfect place to do so.

"You're just saying that because being trapped in the dark is a familiar place for you to feel this way." He was so close now, inches away.

I'm saying it because it's true.

"You wouldn't say that if they hadn't been bulldogging you. If they hadn't been ganging up on you, running you into the ground—"

You can just go, I said, suddenly afraid that he was going to free me. Really free me.

Because then … where would I go?

What would I do?

Nobody wants me, I said. *Best to just leave me in here.*

"I want you out," he said.

But—

"Come out, Sienna."

And with a last tap, the prison ice shattered like glass and left me standing in the middle of a snowy field, alone with my rescuer. I stared into his face, blinking away my pain and surprise as the aching chill that had seeped into my bones faded.

"Jake?" I asked, not really believing what I was seeing. "Jake Terrance?"

He nodded, and smiled. "Hello, Sienna."

I shook my head, tears forming in the corners of my eyes. "No. You're one of them. You just … came to bring me back."

"I'm not one of them," he said, and took a step forward, strong hands grasping me around the arms. "I'm not. They're guilt … shades of guilt, trying to make you feel terrible because you blame yourself for their deaths. I'm not here for that."

I wanted to shrug out of his grasp, to run away, but didn't. Instead I just stayed there, cautious, feeling like he was about to drop the other shoe, to tell me what axe he had to grind with me. "Why are you here?"

He smiled, and it was so warm and real that I forgot the cold for almost a minute. "To let you know you're not alone."

"I don't even know you," I said, and the tears came back to the corners of my eyes.

"Of course you do," he said, and he pulled me close. He was so warm, his chest against mine, his arms tight around me. They wrapped me close to him, and it was like he had given me a hug for the ages. "I'm the one person whose death you *can't* feel guilty about."

I swallowed hard, trying to eat my emotions before they came rushing out. "But ... you are dead?"

"Yes," he said, a little sadly. "I died before you were born." He pulled back so I could look him in the face, and it started to shift, just the way that Breandan's had, my mother's had, the way ... Zack's had. His features resolved into a face that I'd only seen in pictures, and suddenly I knew why Jake Terrance's watch had kept catching my eye.

It was because once upon a time, I'd had one exactly like it. Reed had given it to me, as a hand-me-down from—

"Dad," I whispered and fell into his arms. His hug was impossible, anguishing, something I'd dreamed of but I always knew I could never have.

And I couldn't hold back the tears any longer.

62.

Benjamin

What the hell is going on here? Benjamin wondered as they stepped out of the smoke into the steamy infirmary. It felt like water was misting onto him, warm water condensing out of the air and running down his skin like sweat on a hot day.

The scene before him as the smoke cleared was a bizarre tableau, like something out of a surreal painting. There were people everywhere, and few enough of them were ones he actually knew. The director of the agency—Phillips? Was that it? Benjamin recognized him well enough from TV, backing away toward Reed Treston, surprisingly cool for a man who was only a few feet from Anselmo. Benjamin might have been more panicked—no, he would have been, no 'might' about it. The black man who'd helped try to subdue him at the office building was there as well, still in a bed and not getting up, though he was watching Benjamin with wide eyes. Another black man was a little further back, partially obscured by the thick cloud of steam that made it look as though a fog machine were going in the back corner of the room. The lady doctor stood just outside the white clouds, her lab coat undone and a—was that a—

she's not wearing much underneath that

—a bit of lingerie?

"Oh, my," Benjamin murmured to himself, feeling

flushed at the bizarre spectacle before him, like he'd walked in on a very private moment. He lowered his eyes by instinct, embarrassed.

"Here we find each other once more," Anselmo said, going on, "I am almost as I was when we first met. Surely this displeases you, as you wished to leave me scarred and humiliated—"

"Outside of confined to a prison," Reed said with a snap, "I didn't much care how I left you."

"Oh, but you care," Anselmo said, wagging a finger. "We have met one another, we have fought one another, and we continue to circle in each other's orbits."

"I get the feeling one of us is about to achieve breakaway speed," Reed said.

"Yes," Anselmo said, "I am going to leave you behind forever."

"Maybe you should—" Benjamin said, trying to get out a word of warning for Anselmo.

"Hush," Anselmo said, holding up a single hand, finger extended, pointing to him. "The men are talking."

Reed Treston struck in exactly that moment; while Anselmo's attention was distracted for but a second, Treston's hands came up and shot toward Anselmo like Treston was going to strike him with both palms from ten feet away. A rush of wind shot forth like a hurricane had been loosed in the room, and Anselmo shot back as if a mechanical donkey had kicked him in the chest. He flew into the dark, smoky hallway, and Benjamin barely dodged his flying body, throwing himself to the floor just in time.

"Cunningham," Treston said as Benjamin pulled his head up, "I don't have time for whatever you've got going on at the moment."

"I—I—I—I—" Benjamin stammered, his arms shaking under the weight of his upper body. It wasn't that he was heavy, it was that the moment was just so … heady. Here he was, in the belly of the beast again, but this time Anselmo wasn't even here—

"You think your pitiful winds can stop me?" Anselmo shouted from the hallway behind him. There was an alarm echoing in Benjamin's ears, and the hiss of water from the sprinklers was followed by the cold sensation of stinking, stagnant water rushing down on him.

"Anselmo!" Treston shouted back. "I don't have time for your bullshit right now!"

"Oh," Anselmo said, striding out of the sprinklers, his suit soaking and clinging to him, "does that mean you've discovered the dagger at the throat of your precious sister? Did you find her carcass?"

"Wait, what?" Benjamin asked, blinking, still on the ground.

"She's still alive, Anselmo," Treston said, glaring back at the Italian with a fire of his own. "You can't even do a simple assassination right."

Anselmo's eyes smoldered as he stared at Treston. "She will die. It was promised. And it will be painful, a slow spiral into madness before her heart stops beating."

"She's going to blow up first," Treston said with a smug, satisfied grin. "She's got a bit of a bomb problem." He waved at Benjamin. "Not quite like him. Bigger, of course."

"Excuse me?" Benjamin asked, truly lost. "There's … someone else … like me …?"

"There is no one as foolish or silly as you," Anselmo snapped back at him. "Stop acting like a child in a mad scramble for your parents' approval. Your mother does not love you because you are a spineless, pathetic, gelatinous mass of a human being. I have met teenage girls with more resolve than you possess. And they shriek less when in pain as well."

"That's …" Benjamin could not tell whether his eyes were blurry from tears or from the sprinklers.

"You're such a prick, Anselmo," Treston said.

"And now, no thanks to you," Anselmo said, "I have one

again."

There was a moment's pause as that sunk in. "I did not need to know that," Treston said. "Hell, no one needed to know that. Ever."

"Oh my," Benjamin said, numbly coming to the realization with a low giggle that seemed desperately out of place, "that's what you were about all along. They took away your manhood with the burns—"

Anselmo twisted his neck to look back at Benjamin, his face purple and dark. "You shut your mouth. I was more of a man without it than you are with whatever you possess." He gestured furiously at Benjamin, who was still on the ground. "Look at you! You remain on your knees, like some pitiful slave, or a scullery maid scrubbing the floors. You are a pitiful wretch, and the only way you can ever feel any power for yourself is when you kill people."

"Pot to kettle," Treston said.

"I was to be a god-king," Anselmo said, whirling back to face Treston. "And you ripped that out of my grasp, took my kingdom, tore it all away from me, you and your friends and your filthy sister. And then, after suffering imprisonment for years, I finally have you in my grip, and you take from me my very manhood."

"You should define yourself less by your dick," Treston said. "On the other hand, this is somehow very fitting."

"There are no more words left to be said between us." Anselmo spoke in a tight voice bereft of the rasp he'd had when he was scarred.

"Does this mean you're finally going to shut up?" Treston asked, and cracked his knuckles. "Because I really want to break that newly-fixed nose of yours."

"You will try to keep me from the ground," Anselmo said, "and you will fail. I will overwhelm your pathetic winds and gain hold of your throat. I will squeeze the very life out of you, watch with joy as your eyes roll back in your head, and then I will kill every one of your comrades by beating them to death with my own fists. And when I get to your sister, know that she will die, suffering, with my fingers crushing her skull to a paste of the sort you would find when the vintner mashes the grapes."

Treston just lashed out again with a windburst, this one tearing Anselmo from the ground and sending him backflipping out of the room.

"Just shut up," Treston said and turned his attention to Benjamin. "Cunningham, I could use your help."

"She's flaring again!" the lady doctor called in her thick, accented English.

"W … what?" Benjamin asked, feeling foolish and cold and soaked and quite out of place. The world was blue all around him, blue from the water washing down around him in a flood, and he tried to find his composure. "I … with what?" he asked rather lamely, not sure if he should resist or run or simply take orders and hope for the best.

"Are you out of your mind?" Phillips asked, seizing Treston's forearm in his grip.

"I'm out of my league," Treston said, jerking his hand free. "I'm overmatched here. Anselmo's probably already up, and we're about to lose this place unless we can contain Sienna's fire." He looked right at Benjamin, and Benjamin felt his heart wither inside. "Without your help, we are all going to die."

Benjamin felt that withered heart seem to catch a drip of water, a drip of hope. "M … my help?"

"You can draw away the fire," Treston said, offering a hand. "Your power, it's not just about destruction. It's about control."

"I … I …" Benjamin blinked, "I have … no control. Never have."

"Did you burn his skin off?" Treston said, and pointed toward Anselmo, who was stalking out of the hallway again, pure fury contorting his features.

"Yes," Benjamin said, "but—"

"That's control," Treston said, and offered him a hand. "Please. We need your help."

Benjamin blinked and took the hand, unthinking. "Uh ... all right." Treston's strong grip yanked him to his feet. "But I—"

"You are all of you fools!" Anselmo screamed, and leapt right at them. "And I will kill you, you little—"

Treston leapt forth and connected with a solid punch to Anselmo's jaw that knocked the Italian back a step. "Go!" Reed shouted. "Help them!" He didn't wave toward the gradually growing frenzy in the corner.

He didn't have to.

For once, Benjamin Cunningham knew exactly what he had to do.

All his nervousness melted away in the heat of the moment's intensity, and he dashed toward the corner, toward the girl whose skin was already turning into flames, and prepared to do the thing that he felt he'd been born to do.

63.

Sienna

The icy wind rolled in around us, and my father's embrace was not enough to protect me from the rising cold. I shivered in his arms and pulled away to see his face, still kind, but laced with concern. "They're coming," he said, "coming for you. For us."

"I know," I said, "I can feel it."

"They want you to suffer, Sienna," he said, "to feel agony beyond measuring, to despair into nothingness. And they won't stop. They'll keep coming."

"I got that feeling, yeah," I said. "But they're not real?"

"They're real enough," he said. "They're all your guilt, your fears, your doubts, poured into the form of people you feel you think you failed." His face hardened. "Or in that frost giant's case, your self-loathing given form, I think."

"Figures," I said, "because I did loathe him." I stared at my father, trying to memorize his features, seeing him for the first time as he would have looked in life. He still seemed strangely like a photograph to me, even though he was lively enough. "What about you?"

He smiled. "You're a fighter, Sienna. There's always going to be a part of you that fights, even when things are as dark as they've ever looked."

"And that's you?" I asked as the icy wind whipped

around me.

"Somewhere between the realm of ultimate wish fulfillment and protective father figure, that's where I come from," he said, turning away to survey the darkness that surrounded us.

"You're awfully self-aware," I said. "And kinda ironic."

"Gee, I wonder where that comes from."

Any response I might have made to that was cut short by a blast of arctic wind that ripped through me like a blade, driving me back toward the darkness behind me. I felt encircled, trapped, like if I were pushed into the dark, I'd be done.

"That's a good instinct," my father said, "trust it." He extended his hand and shot a vortex of air in the direction of the wind that was pushing me, canceling it out and returning it to its unseen sender.

"Do not go into the darkness," I said. "Got it. Any other rules? Like—"

"Don't eat yellow snow?" I couldn't see his face, but I heard the smile in his voice. "I could probably come up with a few pieces of fatherly advice, if pressed."

"Lay it on me, Pops," I said, cracking my knuckles as I placed my back against my father's. I could hear the movement in the darkness and knew that these fears—these doubts—these ... whatever they were—they were circling closer, like carrion birds to the kill. "Because who knows ... this might just be our last chance."

64.

Reed

I blasted Anselmo down the hall and away from the medical unit. His fingers stretched out and left scratch marks in the side of the hall as he flew, straining to halt his runaway momentum. I kept catching him unprepared, because his being a self-righteous windbag meant he kept wasting his breath trying to explain how much I sucked, how unworthy we all were, how we had wronged the amazing him, blah blah blah.

I needed to get him away from Sienna, away from Cunningham, away from the medical unit, so they had time to contain the situation. For the first time in a while, I was actually glad I hadn't caved and shot Cunningham in the face. Not that it had ever been my first instinct, but if Sienna had been in charge, it would have happened right off, probably.

Maybe.

Aw, hell, maybe not. I got it now; it wasn't like she looked for reasons to kill people. The countless prisoners under HQ were obvious proof that she didn't. If she'd just murdered anyone who resisted, that place would be empty, because almost without exception, they fought her tooth and nail—and a little more tooth in the case of Bronson McCartney, an animalist shape-changer. It's a shame there was no vid of that on YouTube, because Sienna wrestling a massive Kodiak bear? Just as epic as it sounds.

Anselmo landed on his feet, coming back up as I prepped my next wind blast. I shot and he dodged down the hall toward the exit, narrowly avoiding my attack as he disappeared from sight. "You can run but you can't hide, Anselmo," I said, then thought it over.

"All evidence to the contrary," he called from around the corner. "I have run and hidden from you on multiple occasions thus far."

"Men don't run," I said, goading him.

That drew a sharp response. "What would you know about being a man?"

"More than you, considering I'm blowing you all around this hallway and you haven't so much as laid a finger on me so far," I said with undisguised glee. "How was that fall out of the office building?"

"Bracing," he said. "A true rush. It made me feel alive—"

"The wind against your skin," I said and slid out into the hall. He was almost at the end of it, by the exit doors. "The feel of fresh air ripping you from your feet and sending you over the edge?"

"If all you have is the ability to blow people around like a flag on a windy day," Anselmo said, looking slightly trapped, "I suppose it must make you feel less impotent than you actually are."

I blew him through the doors with a focused wind tunnel. They hit the maximum extension of the hinges and then slammed shut behind him. "It may be all I've got, but it's not so bad," I said to the empty hallway. I charged forward and shoulder-checked my way through the doors to find Anselmo gone.

Well, hell—

His punch decked me, sending me sideways with a hell of a pain in my jaw. I landed on my side on the pavement, then rolled, once, before I went tumbling off the edge and down—

Uh oh.

I fell into the pit made by Augustus's incessant harvesting of the soil just outside the door. Unfortunately for me, he'd dug a pretty big hole by this point, big enough to swallow a tractor or a backhoe. Maybe two of them.

I hit on my shoulder and neck, snapping my head to the side as I landed like a thrown spear. My legs followed on with the landing a moment later, and rocks or a root poked me in the spine. I lay there, trying to gather my wits about me, staring into the navy blue sky above, faint lights in the distance shedding enough illumination for me to see the shadow as it appeared above me.

Anselmo leapt into the hole, landing catlike at my side. His hand found my throat before I could react, and he pulled me into the air, my throat closing as he made to crush my windpipe. My head swirled, and he slammed me into the earthen wall of the pit, dislodging dirt that fell down my collar and tickled my back.

"And here we are," Anselmo said, and the darkness of the pit swallowed everything but the faint gleam of light on his teeth, leaving him as shrouded as if he were still scarred, "face to face for the last time." He squeezed my throat so hard that I couldn't take a breath, the life fleeing my head as I began to wonder if he would make it explode right off my neck. "At the end at last, Mr. Treston ... any final words before we come to our close?"

65.

Benjamin

Benjamin was at a loss, drawing the heat from Sienna Nealon as quickly as he could pull it away from her. The woman's skin was on fire, the bed's exposed metal frame warping under the intensity of the conflagration. Whatever bedding had been on it when she'd started to burn, it was long since consumed. She swelled with a burst, and he drew it out, and then she waned, almost looking like she was going to snuff out, to return to skin, but that was just a tease. She began to burn brightly again.

"I don't know how long I can hold this," Benjamin said, licking his lips, looking at the blond man across from him for something, anything. Approval, maybe. He got no response, so he shifted his attention to the lady doctor, accidentally looking her straight in the lingerie-clad bosoms. He jerked his gaze away like he was burned and it landed on the kind, brown eyes of the man next to him.

The man smiled at him, and Benjamin felt a surge of hope. "You're doing just fine, Benjamin," he said, and it was like someone had put a load of tinder on the guttering flames of his heart, an encouragement that gave him the strength to go on.

"Well, all right, then," Benjamin said, nodding, as Sienna Nealon began to flare up once more. He stuck his hands out and drew the fire to him for all he was worth.

66.

Sienna

I laid into the jaw of Zack Davis, listened to it shatter as he burst into dust, and knew he'd be back. No matter how many times I hit him, no matter how many times I was forced to beat him into oblivion, this version of him kept coming back.

The same went for my mother, for Breandan. They'd shatter like glass, like dust, and I'd send them off into the darkness, where they'd be reconstituted and come back at me like Ultron drones, infinite and really, really annoying.

"Good times, huh?" my dad called out, sending some shadowy figure that looked a little like Athena off into that dark perimeter that surrounded us.

"It's a real family affair," I said, punching my "mother" in the face. "I actually pictured our family life in my head, like, a thousand times when I was a kid."

"Oh?" my father asked, turning his jet of wind loose on my faux mother, sending her spiraling into the dark with a look of utter rage on her face. "What was that like?"

I thought about it for a beat. "It was kinda like this, oddly enough."

He laughed, and the winter storm blew through again, swirling snowflakes as it brought the cold up a notch. "Your self-loathing is coming."

"Gah," I said, "why do I have to be such a clearly self-actualized person, creating my own guilt constructs and everything?"

"Probably because you have enough mommy and daddy issues to make the Menendez brothers look well-adjusted," he said.

"Also, even my constructs are smartasses," I muttered. "And really good at it." Something occurred to me. "Wait. If this is in my head … how the hell do I get out?"

"I don't think you're in charge of that," he said, whipping a wind of his own through our little spot of light. It did nothing against the cold. "But I don't think retreating into yourself and giving up would be a good thing, you know, psychologically."

"Yeah," I said, "it'd probably result in me waking up a drooling vegetable, right?"

"Another safe bet," he said.

"Like villains who monologue and reality TV stars who overshare on social media, right?"

"You know how the world works," he said sagely. "Here he comes."

When Winter finally showed, I wasn't expecting him in the form he took. I'd seen him like this once before, but it had been a very long time. Also, that time, he was smaller.

He came stomping out of the darkness, clad in a suit of frosted ice armor that stretched over his whole body. Ten feet tall and surrounded with a sheet of protection, he swept a hand down like ice was some malleable thing, like flesh.

And he grabbed my father.

"Sienna!" Dad called.

"What have we here?" Winter asked, his voice a low rumble. "An interloper. An intruder in the cold. Someone providing aid to a lonely soul who does not deserve it." Tiny pieces of ice flecked and crumbled from his massive fist. "We cannot have this."

"Sienna," my father said, voice firm and quiet, his eyes on mine. "Don't give u—"

With a snap, Winter closed his massive hand on my father, and his eyes went as dead as any photograph I'd ever seen of him: cold and lifeless, staring into space, and I shrieked in furious reply to a soul that I hoped was still listening, was still somewhere within, for a help I could only hope was coming.

"Gavrikov ... let's burn this bastard to a screaming death."

67.

"Last words? You're an asshole," I said to Anselmo, and I started a wind half an inch beneath the earthen side of the pit to the right and left of my head. A *whoosh!* shot past my ears as dirt flew through the air like Augustus himself had thrown it, straight into Anselmo's waiting eyes.

I followed it with a short punch right in the throat, then again, not enough to do any damage to his invincible skin, but enough to ripple into the not-so-invulnerable parts beneath it. He grunted and dropped me, and I flung myself into the air with the aid of a well-aimed gust, coming to a rolling, rough landing on the concrete sidewalk above.

My skull ached like someone had pounded on it like a drum, which—hey, someone had. My arm was a little numb from the landing, from the hits I'd taken thus far, and my throat was destined to have some finger-shaped bruises on it, I suspected. I coughed as I crawled to my feet in time to see Anselmo leap out of the pit, his eyes tearing.

"Are you weeping silently for your lost and found manhood, Anselmo?" I asked, twisting the knife, "or is it something deeper? Something more … sensitive?"

He caught that I was insinuating he was being feminine, which I knew he hated more than anything. "What, I wonder, will it take to make you weep, Treston?"

"Remember that cologne you used to wear?" I asked. "That used to bring tears to my eyes."

"You cannot handle the smell of a greater stag," Anselmo said.

"That kinda makes you a big, horny bastard, doesn't it?"

He smiled. "I have miscalculated."

"Got that right," I said, preparing another burst of wind. "Shouldn't have come here, Anselmo. Especially not right now."

He shook his head, tears still streaming down his face from where dirt had gotten into his eyes. "No, no. I failed to consider my plan before coming at you. It was foolish not to go after the ones you cared about first."

I felt my stomach drop. "Like I'd let you—"

He was off in an instant, slamming through the doors and back into the headquarters. I gave up at least a five-second head start to him by the time I realized what was happening and sprinted after him with all I had, afraid of what I'd find when I got back to the infirmary.

68.

Benjamin

"Trouble coming," the man at his left, the encouraging one, said. The way he spoke was so smooth, so kind, that Benjamin was instantly captivated by it. He wanted to follow this man, to follow Reed Treston. The way they talked, the way they acted ... it was worlds different than Anselmo. So ... encouraging.

Anselmo. The name sent shivers of a disgusted sort down Benjamin's back, crawling along his skin like spiders. How could he have been drawn in by the man? Certainly, he'd felt angry. Attacked. Marginalized. But how could he have brought himself to do what Anselmo told him to? It was madness, like listening to that little rage-filled voice that tore out of his skull sometimes, like taking advice from an idiot.

all fools

Shut up, already, Benjamin said to himself. *I need to focus.*

"Heat's rising," said the blond man across the bed from him. "You got this, or do you need a little water on the situation?"

"Got quite enough water, thank you," Benjamin said politely. The sprinklers were still drowning him, still pouring down. They should have cooled the situation off, but all they were doing was steaming up the room, causing him to have to siphon the heat out of the air before it burned anyone. He kept his hands above Sienna Nealon as though he were some sort of spirit healer, trying to drag the dark humors from her body.

"Oh, shit," Director Phillips said from over Benjamin's shoulder, but he had not the time nor the inclination to look, not with the flames rising off Ms. Nealon again. He focused, kept his eyes on his job, mind on the task at hand, eliminated the distractions—

look up look up look up

"Shut up," Benjamin muttered, and then he heard the cry, and his concentration broke.

Anselmo was there, and he had the lady doctor by the throat, on her knees, looking down at her. "You understand, doctor, I would prefer to keep you forever, as my concubine, to show you what a true man is like, but unfortunately," his face darkened, "Mr. Treston needs to learn the error of his ways."

if ever someone deserved a jet of flame right to the eyes
it's that guy

"Glad we finally agree about something." Benjamin muttered. He rechanneled the heat coming off Sienna Nealon, redirected it to his left, and it was a lark as far as these things went. Considerably easier than just absorbing it into himself, which, he felt certain, was probably not good in the long term. The fire shot out in a long pillar, so hot it practically ignored the water falling all around, and caught Anselmo Serafini squarely in the face.

The reaction was immediate and obvious. Anselmo scrambled, clawing at his face, dropping the doctor, who scrambled away on her hands and knees. Anselmo's cries of pain filled the air as he stumbled back, the roar of the flames undiminished as Benjamin kept pouring it on, following the Italian with unerring accuracy until the surge of flame from Sienna Nealon stopped.

"Whoa, damn," the man in the hospital bed said. "Better start calling him the Red Skull." He paused, and when no one said anything, he added, "All right, fine, I'll quit."

"Anselmo!" Treston said as he burst into the room. His eyes scanned the infirmary wildly, until they finally came to rest on Serafini, who was bent over, still holding his face.

Anselmo's hands moved aside, and the sound of gagging laughter, not dissimilar to retching, filled the room. It was liquidy and raspy, like someone with a terrible cold hacking up phlegm. "Fooooolshhhhh."

"What?" Reed Treston asked, adopting a defensive posture. He circled Anselmo warily, moving gradually toward the corner where Benjamin stood with the others around Sienna Nealon's bed. The room smelled of char and burn, and not only from what had happened in the hallway. The water still poured down, though in lesser volume, from above, though now it smelled much fresher than when it had started.

"Burrrrrrning fooool," Anselmo said, lifting his face, now devoid of flesh and nearly of any muscle. There was a thin layer of skin around his eyes, blackened slightly, in the shape of his hand. Benjamin figured he must have gotten a hand up in front of the attack, that was all—

Anselmo leapt at Benjamin without warning, knocking Reed Treston aside like a toy as he came. Benjamin felt the surge of heat coming from Ms. Nealon, but couldn't do anything about it. Anselmo's hands closed around his neck and he felt a hard snap.

Then the world dropped around him, he heard a heavy thud, and all the color bled out of the walls, out of the faces … and everything faded to—

black

69.

Reed

I watched Anselmo kill Benjamin Cunningham, and there wasn't anything I could do to stop him. I was too far away, bowled over by Anselmo's attack as he leapt at the man.

A few panicked thoughts raced through my head once I'd seen what he did. First of all, I reckoned one of my problems was solved. Unfortunately, it was the least worrisome of my three major problems, and one that might have been resolved anyway, so ... that was not so helpful. Also, it was kind of assisting me with one of the biggest problems (i.e. exploding sister) and so it was actually kind of a big minus.

The second thing I thought was that if not for Cunningham, Anselmo would have killed Isabella just to spite me. Just to hurt me.

Just to make me feel the pain.

And that was the moment when I decided I'd finally had enough.

Oh, I'd vowed it before, I know, but there was some part of me that was always holding back, always hoping for another way. Call it the Batman syndrome, that desire to never stoop all the way to the level of a guy like Anselmo. I wanted to live out my moral code, my idea that killing wasn't good, wasn't necessary, that in time of peace like we were living in now, that maybe I wouldn't ever have to kill again.

Watching Anselmo break Benjamin Cunningham's neck convinced me that I was being a delusional fool, and I had been all along.

Because Anselmo Serafini was going to be at war with me until one of us died.

He stood over my sister, letting Cunningham's broken body slide out of his grasp like he was discarding a card in a game. I saw the flare of Sienna's fire starting to act up again, watched Scott Byerly trying to channel all the water in the room her way. Zollers was similarly occupied, eyes closed, focusing his will on something. Dirt flew through the air and past Anselmo, sealing Sienna into another earthen tomb. This time, though, the fiery fissures appeared immediately.

I caught a glimpse of Isabella, getting back to her feet after Anselmo's attack, and a very simple thought ran across my mind, one that finally moved my ass back into action:

Never again.

I leapt at Anselmo, my fingers tightening into a fist. I hammered him in the face as I landed, and his grinning skull took it without any sign of pain. Not that he could give a sign of pain, what with his face being dissolved.

"You cannotttttt—" he started to hiss.

I shoved a hand into his face and poked him right in the eyes with two fingers. While he reeled from that, I dropped my hand mere inches and held it there, steady, right in front of his mouth.

And called forth my power.

I ripped the air from his lungs with all the force at my command. I commanded the air to flee, to create a vacuum in the square foot of space he occupied, holding the atmosphere behind him at bay, keeping it from rushing in to fill the void.

Blood squirted out of his unpressurized and faceless head, a wash of red liquid as his veins exploded. He couldn't even scream, because I'd torn the breath out of his body. He made a wet gagging, retching noise, and I saw part of his lungs surge up into the back of his exposed throat.

I let the air rush back in once I knew his airway was plugged and destroyed, and he clawed at his bony face with helpless hands. He stared at me with bloodshot, bulging eyes, silently screaming at me to help him, help him survive, help him draw another breath, help him any way I could.

"Go to hell, Anselmo," I said, and I kicked him backward onto my sister's bed as her fire burst through the earthen encasement, looking for something, anything, to consume.

I watched Anselmo Serafini burn to death in silence, drawing ragged breaths, and I actually felt bad about it.

For Sienna, not Anselmo. I bet Italian is a real bitch to get out of your hair.

70.

Sienna

"Gavrikov?" I called, waiting.

Nothing came.

Old Man Winter glared at me with glassy, frost covered eyes, hidden behind his heavy ice armor. He cast aside my father's corpse and I watched it disappear into the darkness that surrounded me. "All alone now, girl. As it was meant to be."

"You know what was meant to be?" I asked, cold as the air he'd surrounded me with. He cocked his head, and I leapt at him, throwing whatever strength I had left into the jump. I landed at his shoulder and held on, fingers breaking loose ice as I clawed to get a grip. He squirmed, but it didn't knock me loose, and when I was just steady enough, I brought my fist back for some of that face-punching I like to think of as my signature move. "You're meant to be dead, you damned ghoul."

I hit him square in the kisser and the ice shattered, rippling outward in a shockwave pattern that sent shards of ice spraying in all directions. I rode the destruction of his armor right to the ground, and stood there over him, looking into the cold, blue eyes of Erich Winter, his face emaciated, his skull almost showing through the skin.

"Yes," he said, voice a rattle, as he shriveled up to bone,

"become what you were meant to be ... become ... death."

"I'm not death," I said, kneeling beside him and looking him straight in the eyes. "I'm just real good friends with it. I'm like Abed to Death's Troy. Or maybe vice versa. Which of us do you think is more misunderstood?"

He blinked, my *Community* reference clearly lost on his ignorant and unsophisticated ass, and I punched his head into glassy dust. The last of the light glimmered over it, like sands in the sun. I stood and took a breath. "Try and kick my ass in my own head? This is *my* house. What a bunch of—"

Movement stirred in the remains of Winter, something slithering beneath the surface. I froze, watching, and it exploded out at me, punching straight into my heart—

71.

Reed

"Get his rotten corpse off of her!" Isabella cried as the flames subsided, Sienna's skin appearing under the wash of falling water and the black of charred body.

"I'm running out of strength here," Scott called, sounding as weary as he looked. The man was drenched, obviously, like we all were, but on him it looked like it was in danger of washing him away, he was so weak.

"We might have a chance now," Zollers said. "There's an ebb. She's conquered some of her fears and Gavrikov is holding off—temporarily." He looked right at Isabella. "If you're going to try something, this is the moment." He swept aside the scorched remains of Anselmo, which flaked into dust and ash, scattering as they hit the ground, dispersing into the half-inch of water standing on the floor.

"I want you to put a bullet in her head," Andrew Phillips said, causing me to jerk around to look at him. He had a black-clad man standing next to him, and he was pointing straight at Sienna. "Do it. All of our lives are at stake."

"No!" I shot toward them, already raising a hand. I flung Phillips and his flunky out the door of the infirmary and into the hallway without an ounce of regret. I didn't even wait until they landed before I threw my body against the door as if I could somehow block it from sliding open. Ariadne lurched out of the darkness by Isabella's office and slapped the lock button on the door panel with a honking beep.

"Hold on!" Isabella said, and I looked back in time to see her jab a hell of a needle right into Sienna's chest. Not gonna lie—I cringed.

There was a moment of silence as the spattering rain continued to fall on us from the sprinklers above, drowning us even as the passage of time dragged.

A hand slammed hard against the door of the medical unit. "Open this door!" Phillips called.

"If I just physically assaulted you to get you out of here, do you really think I'm going to just open it up because you ask not-so-nicely?" I shook my head at the idiocy as Ariadne looked me in the eye. I could see the fear there, the worry that we were stepping out on a limb here, one that was cracking underneath us as we—

"She's spiking!" Zollers called, derailing my train of thought. "She's—!"

72.

Sienna

It was so cold, so cold, so very, very cold.

And hurt so very, very—you get the point—much.

He stabbed me right in the frigging heart, and I went to punch the hell out of him, lurching forward, but gravity changed at that exact moment I flung myself forward.

Water rained down on me from above, hard and chilly, and I gagged as I came upright from laying flat, a complete reversal of the standing position I'd been in a moment earlier.

I blinked, trying to get the water out of my eyes, but the world around me was soggy, almost unfamiliar, the lights dimmed by the tide of cold water raining down on me.

Was this ... was it the infirmary?

Dr. Perugini was pressed against the wall to my right, next to Scott Byerly, both of them looking more than a little red in the face. I would have chalked it up to a sunburn in Scott's case, but Perugini actually had blisters on her cheeks.

"Oh, damn," Augustus Coleman said, yanking my head toward him like it was on a string. He was ahead and to my left, on a hospital bed with IVs hanging off him. He had one of those white spine collars on him, and if I'd been feeling better, I might have asked him if it kept him from licking his stitches.

I saw my brother just past him, at the door, leaning

against it like he was exhausted, like he was going to try and keep it closed with his own body or something. He stared at me through the falling rain in numb shock, Ariadne looking sodden next to him in a nightgown that was ready to fall off from being overly saturated with water.

"Here," came a voice from my left, so familiar, and a sheet fell over my body just as I realized I was naked. Naked as the day I was born. The sheet was soaked, sodden, but it was folded double and covered me from my chest down to my legs. I clung to it, grabbing at it with weak and chilled fingers, trying to keep myself covered. A dark, ashy substance looked like war paint on my pale skin, at least what I could see of it.

The sheet settled, my eyes followed over to the origin of the familiar voice, and my heart fluttered.

Dr. Quinton Zollers.

My hands shook as I reached out for him, letting my fingers hover as I stretched out to see if he was real, was really there. The world I'd just been in, been trapped in, been fighting for my life in, was already falling away like every dream I'd ever been in, but parts of it remained, and remained close at hand.

The pain.

The guilt.

The ... loneliness.

Dr. Zollers took my hand in his, and even though I saw the surgical gloves layered double, I didn't care. I pulled his hand to my cheek and kept it there as the water poured down both from above and from my eyes.

"P ..." I started. "P ... please ... don't leave me ..." And he folded me close to his drenched and sodden clothes as I shook in his arms and added my own tears to the wetness on his shoulder.

73.

Reed

I watched Sienna cry on Zollers's shoulder and it was like a gut punch to me. No one said anything. No one dared to, no one wanted to. It didn't take a genius to connect the dots here, after all. Ariadne looked over at me, and I burned in shame.

Sienna was closer to a man who'd left years ago than she was to any of us. The old me would have blamed that on her, but the new me? I could see more than a little of my own fault for the situation.

Ariadne moved to the corner to join them as the sprinklers finally started to slacken off. Her hair was almost crimson, dark streaks through it as she slid next to Sienna, running her fingers through my sister's wet, raven hair.

A harsh banging came again at the door behind me, and I slapped the lock and stepped through swiftly, forcing Phillips and his black-clad yes man to take a step back or have me run through them.

Wisely, they stepped back, though I saw the other guy's pistol clenched tight at low rest.

"Crisis averted," I said. "Sienna's awake, and in control again."

There wasn't an ounce of emotion in Phillips's eyes or in his reply. "Are you sure?"

"I'm sure," I said, folding my arms in front of me. "Why? You worried you won't get a chance to order someone to put a bullet in her skull?"

He shifted a little, not showing the slightest sign of unease at my dig. "She'll probably give us cause to do so again in the not-too-distant future."

My face flushed with loathing. "The problem is solved. Cunningham and Serafini are dead, Sienna's awake. Go schedule your press conference."

"How did Serafini die? And Cunningham?" Phillips asked. I started to snap a reply at his ghoulishness, but he cut me off. "For the press, not me. I don't really care."

"Serafini killed Cunningham," I said, and opened the door to the medical unit by stepping back in front of it. "And then Serafini got burned to ash by Sienna," I lied. Okay, not lied, but left some stuff out.

Phillips stared at me like he was trying to ferret out the truth just from looking at my face. "All right, then," he said, and turned on his heel and started away.

"Aren't you even going to say you're sorry?" I called after him. His security flunky followed a few steps behind.

"I'm not sorry," Phillips said, not turning around, "and if you had your wits about you, you would have shot her in the head yourself to save this place from getting blown up." He disappeared around the corner and his Guy Friday followed.

He didn't leave me with any doubt he was telling the truth—about all of it.

74.

Sienna

I stepped back into my empty quarters through a shattered door to find Dog waiting, wagging his tail at me as if it was going to shoot off like it was launched by a rocket. I petted him absently on the head as I stepped around the wreckage of my door. I wondered idly why he hadn't wandered off down the hall, then realized there really wasn't anything for him to do out there.

"I still think you should spend the night in the infirmary," Ariadne said, trailing behind me by a few steps. I heard the change in her voice as she exerted herself to navigate my broken door.

"Yeah, I'd love to spend the night sleeping on one of the sopping mattresses there," I said sarcastically. "Sounds like a great way to spend my non-vacation vacation."

"I like how you're not calling it a suspension," Ariadne said as she came into my living room. I was already halfway to the bedroom.

When I got there, the smell was like a punch to the face. Not one of my punches to the face, of course, because those will level you, but like a smaller, weaker person's punch to the face. With stink. "Gyah," I said.

"Yeah," Ariadne said, lurking just outside. "We found you in there, behind the door. You'd been in there for days, and—"

"I get the picture," I said. "No bathroom trips, et cetera." For my money, Bayscape Island ought to have been a much smellier place in my delusion. I walked over to my MP3 player and hit the power button, killing my playlist halfway through Postmodern Jukebox's version of "Wrecking Ball." My theme song, it is.

"How'd they get you?" Ariadne asked, framed in my doorway.

"I went to the mall that morning to get some vacation clothes," I said. "There was a note on my car when I came back, and I picked it up. It smelled kinda funny, but I didn't think anything of it." I held up my left hand. "In my dream, I kept imagining my left hand bleeding. Think it was a coincidence that I picked the flier up with that hand?"

"Weird. Did you keep it?" she asked, coming out of the frame. "I mean, that could be an important clue. We could get it analyzed."

"I didn't toss it in the parking lot, if that's what you're asking," I said, as huffy as I had the energy for. "I may be a killer and a horrible person, but a litterbug I'm not."

"Well, there's hope for you yet, then."

"It's probably in the kitchen somewhere," I said, waving behind her. I wondered how I was going to get the smell out of my bedroom. It just hung in here.

A knocking came at—well, at where my door used to be. "Come in," I called back to the entry.

Ariadne disappeared into the kitchen and I stuck my head out the bedroom door just as Dr. Zollers came around the corner into the living room. Reed trailed behind him by a few steps, almost shyly. "Gentlemen," I said, nodding to Zollers.

"Lady," Zollers said, nodding back to me. "Just wanted to stop in and see how you were doing."

"You're not … leaving, are you?" I asked, my body strangely frozen at the mere thought.

Zollers shook his head. "I can stay for a little while, I

suppose. It's not as though I have any pressing business elsewhere, I just … want to stay out of the government's clutches as much as possible, you understand."

"I understand," I said and drifted back into the living room like I was magnetically drawn toward him. "Can I ask you a question about what happened to me?"

"Let me just answer it for you," he said, smiling enigmatically. "It's like you thought. Your brain was shutting down, and as it did so, you were treated to a spiraling series of nightmares that you shaped yourself from your worst fears."

"Knew I shouldn't have watched *Cabin in the Woods* last week," I said, trying oh-so-hard to flippantly dismiss the experience. The faces of Breandan, Zack, and my mother felt like they were lurking just out of my sight, ready to spring on me in my sleep. I turned my head in time to see a leaf drift by outside the sliding glass doors, and I had a sudden, vivid memory of Winter and his winds.

"What I want to know," Ariadne said, "is why your souls were lashing out? Why was Gavrikov doing what he was doing? Did he just think he was protecting you in the nightmare?"

"He couldn't hear her," Zollers said.

"Because of the coma?" she asked.

"Because of the chloridamide," I said. "I think, anyway. I took a big dose a couple days ago, before I was leaving."

Ariadne stared at me, flummoxed. "Why?"

"Because they're arguing," I said tautly, ignoring the cause of the argument, keeping it to myself. "And I didn't want to hear it on my drive."

"I thought," Reed said, finally breaking his silence, "chloridamide only worked for like … twelve hours at a time?"

"Whatever they gave her," Zollers said, "I suspect it reacted in a synergistic manner with the chloridamide, magnifying the duration of some of its effects and dulling others. For example, normally they can't control any part of her body when she's taking the drug. In this case, Gavrikov was able to do a hell of a lot, even blind as he was." His eyes settled on me. "I'm not sure I'd recommend taking chloridamide any more, since it would appear that there are people out there trying to poison you."

"Any idea who those people are?" Ariadne asked him.

"I have no clue," Zollers said, shaking his head. "If they were close by, I might be able to offer some insight, but no one here on the campus seems to mean actual harm to Sienna now that she's settled down."

"It was the Brain," Reed said quietly. "Simmons. Anselmo."

I processed that in an instant. Villains from the past, back to aggravate me. Then I blinked, thinking back to what Zollers had said a moment earlier. "But before I...cooled down," I said, "someone here meant me harm?"

Reed exchanged a look with Zollers, then answered me. "Phillips ordered you shot when it looked like you were going to blow up."

I blinked, absorbing that information. "Makes sense. I would have done the same."

Reed blanched almost imperceptibly then looked at Ariadne and started to speak. He never got a word out, cut off by Zollers before he could even begin. "Ariadne," Zollers said, "why don't we go ahead and leave these two alone? I suspect they've got some talking to do."

"What?" Ariadne's eyes widened. "Someone should stay with her—"

"And I'm sure she'll give us a shout if she needs anything," Zollers said, gently putting an arm around Ariadne's shoulder and steering her toward the door. "How have you been?"

"I—I'm ... all right, I suppose," Ariadne said as she disappeared around the corner with Zollers. He gave Reed a wink as he left us alone.

"Smooth operator, that one," Reed said, stepping deeper into my trashed quarters. His hands hung at his sides, like he was having trouble deciding what to do with them.

"Knowing what people want to hear probably helps you know what to say to them," I agreed. "Did you see Scott off all right?"

"He's hanging around for the night," Reed said, shrugging. "I got him into the quarters across the hall. He was pretty exhausted from moving all that water around. Same with Augustus, churning all that dirt."

I felt my muscles tense. "Is he going to be all right?"

"Broken back," Reed said, "but he's recovering nicely. Isabella says he should be on his feet in a couple days. He pretty much passed out on his back after tonight, though, soggy bed and all."

"What happened to him?" I asked. "That Cunningham guy I had to step over in the infirmary?"

"No," Reed's face got pinched. "No, Cunningham turned out all right. He helped save the day. It was Anselmo did the number on Augustus. On Cunningham, too, actually."

"Anselmo Serafini? That prick?" I clenched my teeth. "I should have killed him in Italy."

"Well, you got him this time," he said. "Or, I guess I should say 'we' got him, since I ripped his lungs out before I tossed him on the funeral pyre that was you."

I blinked, then looked down at the ash that was smeared along my neckline below the t-shirt I had appropriated from Perugini's office. "Is this …?"

"A little overdone, but yes," he said, nodding.

"Ewwwww!" I brushed at my chest, like I could get the smudge of black off my skin, pausing as I realized something else. "And he's in my *hair!*

Reed laughed. "Sorry. But hey … at least we're rid of the version of him that talks back. All you need is a shower or twelve and you'll be done with him for good."

"Oh, you're funny," I said, still scrabbling to try and get

the smudge off my cleavage. I finally gave up. "I hate that he'd actually love that he ended up here."

"I wouldn't worry about it," Reed said, and I could tell he was setting up for a punch line, "it's what he would have wanted. In a way, leaving him there kind of makes you a real metahumanitarian."

"Ugh, awful," I said, shaking my head. I let the humor pass, watched my brother's smile fade. "I thought you didn't believe in killing our criminals."

He opened his mouth and let it hang like that for a moment before answering. "I ... well ..."

"I'm sorry," I said, waving him off, "I shouldn't have brought that up."

"No, it's fine," he said. "I wanted to say—"

"I had kind of a revelation while I was under—" I started.

We both paused in that awkward way, like neither of us wanted to step on the other's line. "You go first," I said.

"No, you," he said.

"All right," I said, swallowing my pride. "You were right. I kill too quick. It's become a sort of ... first resort for me, since London. It's a bad habit to be in—"

"I was talking out my ass, Sienna," he said, shaking his head. "I was the one who was wrong. I've never seen you kill someone who didn't have it coming." He paused, thinking it over for a beat. "You know, since M-Squad. Or Omega's Primus. And even some of those are kindasorta arguable—"

I blinked in surprise. Where the hell was this coming from? "Uh, no. They really weren't. That was ... it was a hint of me at my least controllable."

He pulled back, looked like he'd been slapped a little. "I was just ... I think I've been too hard on you."

"Maybe I haven't been hard *enough* on me," I countered. "You once told me I was a sheepdog here to protect humanity. That I wasn't a mad dog in danger of breaking my chain. But something happened since that day to convince you otherwise, and looking back on what's happened in the last year or so, I've killed a lot of people—"

"I'm not going to explain those away one by one," Reed said, shaking his head, "but I think if you went through your head and really examined them, every last one of them was trying to kill you. Every last one of them had ill intent toward you or another person. Every one of them was conducting their own little war against Sienna Nealon or someone else. You didn't go kill nannies and babysitters on the street, Sienna. These people knew they were in a fight with you. And that's the last place anyone ought to be if they want to live. By now, that's just understood."

"Tell that to the paparazzi," I muttered, and I knew he caught it. "You've got something else on your mind."

He didn't argue, but he looked tentative. "I know that to you, I always seemed like the guy who had his shit together. Even when I was a kid, and Dad ... left me for the last time ... I was like a block of stone, holding it all in. I didn't let him see how desperate I was underneath it all, how much I was barely treading water, how much I wanted to break down. For the last few months ... I've been doing the exact same thing to you. Letting you think I was just some impervious wall that didn't care at all about you, that ignored you. The truth was ... I was just trying to ... I don't know. Harden my heart. Hold you at arm's length because I disagreed with you, with what you were doing. But all the while, I've been isolating you, and that was ... just damned cruel." His face crumpled. "Sienna, I'm sorry. You're the only family I've got left, and I'm sorry I let my pigheadedness get in the way of thinking it through sooner and telling you how much you mean to me ... sis."

I blinked tears out of my eyes for the umpteenth time in the last few days. Seriously, this was going into the Sienna Book of World Records. I don't do the crying thing very much, after all. "You want a hug?" I asked, trying to keep a stiff upper lip.

He grinned. "Hell, no. You've got some Anselmo on you,

after all."

I laughed, and he hugged me tight.

And when it did it, it felt just like my dad.

Just like *our* dad.

He broke after a minute with a laugh. "You hungry?"

"I am so starving," I said, and my stomach rumbled. "Apparently I haven't eaten in the last couple days, and if I don't ingest some fat soon, the tabloids are going to start reporting on my shocking weight loss plan that has my complete lack of friends worried about my health. On the plus side, maybe the internet will stop saying my ass is fat."

"The internet is stupid," Reed said, shaking his head. He put a hand around my shoulders and started steering me toward the door. "And I think you know, after tonight, that you've still got friends ... though it seems like you might have tried your hardest to push a few of them away."

I am death, the voice whispered in my head.

"I didn't want anyone to get hurt," I said. I glanced back and saw Dog wagging his tail. "Stay," I told him, and he parked it right inside the threshold. "Good Dog."

"Cafeteria's shut down for the night," Reed said as we hit the stairs. I wondered if he had an aversion to elevators, but I was letting him lead. "I know a breakfast place nearby that makes killer waffles."

"Yesssss," I said. "Waffles. I will eat all the waffles."

"Maybe not all of them," he teased. "Remember the internet, after all."

"Those people can cram a waffle press up their asses, wide open, sideways," I said as we rounded the bend in the staircase. "It is nice to see people back, though."

"You mean Zollers?" he asked.

"And Scott," I said. He gave me a look that I couldn't decipher. "What?"

He shook his head. "Nothing. It does feel good to have them here again, doesn't it? Makes it feel a little more like ... home."

Something tugged at the corner of my lips. "Home?" I turned the word over in my mouth. "Home. Hmm. Maybe I do belong here."

He frowned. "What made you think you didn't? Phillips?"

I tried to decide if I should tell him or not. "It was something that … my nightmares kept hitting me with, over and over. Playing on a conversation I had with Phillips when he suspended me—that maybe I didn't belong here. That maybe … I didn't belong anywhere. Because of who I am, you know. It was …" I shuddered. "I don't know if I can explain it, but … it was really unsettling. Probably made feel worse than … maybe than I've ever felt."

"This Phillips thing is going to come to a head," Reed said after a long pause, just as we were reaching the exit into the dormitory lobby. "You may find that you don't end up belonging here." I stared out into the night beyond the glass-fronted lobby, the first strains of dawn lighting the horizon. "But you'll find a place, I promise."

I felt my guts rumble, from hunger and fear. "You think so?"

"You've faced death in so many forms and from so many scary people," Reed said, blowing it off, "you're telling me you're scared to go job hunting? Or looking for a new place to live?" He kicked at the ground as we came out of the lobby, the squeak of the doors closing behind us.

"People hate me," I said. "And you should know, because until now, it seemed like you understood how they felt." He grimaced. "But seriously … where would I go? Where *could* I go that they'd want me?"

"Reality TV?" Reed asked, smirking. "Cable news? Politics? Hell, you'd fit right in with any of those."

"Ass," I muttered as we walked under a near-dark sky, his warmth keeping the autumn chill at bay. "Are we going to the garage?"

"Nah," he said, "I left Baby parked outside the medical unit." He pointed straight ahead, and I saw his new car up against a curb across the parking lot ahead of us.

"'Baby'?" I asked, swiveling my head to look at him. "Really?"

He shrugged. "Your dog is named 'Dog.' Get off my back."

I gave that a moment's consideration. "Fair point," I conceded.

We crossed the parking lot, the night air strangely refreshing. As I stepped onto the curb, I could see the dark hole in the ground next to the door to the infirmary. I stared into it for a moment, almost like I could see some evil waiting within.

Then again, I'd just proven I had one hell of an imagination these last few days.

"You all right?" Reed asked, hanging out with his driver's door open, talking to me over the roof of his sporty little contraption. (I don't know cars. But it was sporty.)

"I'll be all right," I said, his face reminding me again of Dad. I eased down into the seat and slammed the door behind me. The leather was damned comfy, I'd give him that.

"I sure hope so," he said, shutting his door. He favored me with a smile that was warm, genuine, and reminded me again of our father. "I'd like you to be around for a good, long time."

I thought about the words I'd said to the faux-Breandan just a few days—or maybe a lifetime—ago, about me either living nearly forever, or watching all the people I loved and cared about die before my very eyes. My breath hung in my throat for a moment, and then I forced a smile, forced myself to start breathing again. "I'd like that, too," I said and meant it.

"Good," Reed said, and nodded as he started to push the ignition button. "Glad we're in agreement, since this is the first time in a while that we've—"

My brother's last words were lost as his face disappeared into fire as the car exploded around us.

Epilogue

Cassidy

Cassidy watched on the monitor as the car flared into a burst of fire, a blinding beacon of light that set her monitor to near-white for a few seconds. The warm, salty water of the isolation tank lapped at her skin, and she allowed herself a little smile. "Gotcha," she whispered, as she watched the flames through the camera's lens, dancing soundlessly into the night.

Sienna Nealon returns in

VENGEFUL

Out of the Box
Book Six

Coming December 1, 2015!

Note from the Author

Yeah, I know. I call this the "Book 5" curse, where I always seem to end book five of each of my series in a horrific place. I thought I might actually cure that this time around, but NAHHHHH. Because I'm me. Might as well embrace it, I figure. The good news (yes, there is some) is that you only have to wait three months or less (depending on when you're reading this) to find out what happens next, and this little storyline (which I call the "Vengeful" arc) that kicked off in Ruthless, the one involving Cassidy, the Clarys and Simmons, it's coming to a crashing end next book. There will be a showdown, and hopefully it will be appropriately epic for your tastes. Oh, and I suppose we'll find out if Reed lives or dies, too, in case you were wondering about that. (I wasn't, but hey, maybe you are.)

If by strange chance you want to know when future books become available, take sixty seconds and sign up for my NEW RELEASE EMAIL ALERTS by visiting my website at www.robertjcrane.com. Don't let the caps lock scare you; I don't sell your information and I only send out emails when I have a new book out. The reason you should sign up for this is because I don't like to set release dates (it's this whole thing, you can find an answer on my website in the FAQ section), and even if you're following me on Facebook (robertJcrane (Author)) or Twitter (@robertJcrane), it's easy to miss my book announcements because…well, because social media is an imprecise thing.

Come join the discussion on my website: http://www.robertjcrane.com !

Cheers (or apologies; whichever, really),
Robert J. Crane

ACKNOWLEDGMENTS

Once again the editorial duties were performed in admirable fashion by the great Sarah Barbour, and clean-up was batted by Jeffrey Bryan while final proofreading was done by Jo Evans.

My cover, as always, was designed by Karri Klawiter.

Alexa Medhus did the first read on this one, and swore like a sailor at me when she got to the end. It was hilarious, I assure you. Thanks, Alexa!

As always, thanks to my parents, my kids and my wife, for helping me keep things together.

And to the fans, too, unless you're cursing at me right now. I'll thank you once you stop.

About the Author

Robert J. Crane is kind of an a-hole. Still, if you want to contact him:

Website: http://www.robertJcrane.com
Facebook: robertJcrane (Author)
Twitter: @robertJcrane
Email: cyrusdavidon@gmail.com

Other Works by Robert J. Crane

The Sanctuary Series
Epic Fantasy

Defender: The Sanctuary Series, Volume One
Avenger: The Sanctuary Series, Volume Two
Champion: The Sanctuary Series, Volume Three
Crusader: The Sanctuary Series, Volume Four
Sanctuary Tales, Volume One - A Short Story Collection
Thy Father's Shadow: The Sanctuary Series, Volume 4.5
Master: The Sanctuary Series, Volume Five
Fated in Darkness: The Sanctuary Series, Volume 5.5*
    (Coming in 2015!)
Warlord: The Sanctuary Series, Volume Six* (Coming in late
    2015!)

The Girl in the Box
and
Out of the Box
Contemporary Urban Fantasy

Alone: The Girl in the Box, Book 1
Untouched: The Girl in the Box, Book 2
Soulless: The Girl in the Box, Book 3
Family: The Girl in the Box, Book 4
Omega: The Girl in the Box, Book 5
Broken: The Girl in the Box, Book 6
Enemies: The Girl in the Box, Book 7
Legacy: The Girl in the Box, Book 8
Destiny: The Girl in the Box, Book 9
Power: The Girl in the Box, Book 10

Limitless: Out of the Box, Book 1
In the Wind: Out of the Box, Book 2
Ruthless: Out of the Box, Book 3
Grounded: Out of the Box, Book 4
Tormented: Out of the Box, Book 5
Vengeful: Out of the Box, Book 6* (Coming December 1 2015!)
Sea Change: Out of the Box, Book 7* (Coming March 2016!)

Southern Watch
Contemporary Urban Fantasy

Called: Southern Watch, Book 1
Depths: Southern Watch, Book 2
Corrupted: Southern Watch, Book 3
Unearthed: Southern Watch, Book 4
Legion: Southern Watch, Book 5* (Coming in
        Late 2015/Early 2016!)

* Forthcoming and subject to change

CPSIA information can be obtained
at www.ICGtesting.com
Printed in the USA
LVOW10s0913250617
539310LV00012B/304/P